The Moon on a Stick

Amy's reflection in the mirror was like Medusa on a bad snake day. She glanced away quickly and tried to work out what day of the week it was.

Her hand reached out instinctively for the tissue box, but then it struck her that she wasn't crying . . . Somewhere along the line, the tears had dried up, but she couldn't remember when . . .

If a broken heart could be classified as a sickness, she'd been at death's door.

About the author

Valerie-Anne Baglietto was born in Gibraltar in 1971. Her grandfather and great-grandfather were both writers, so Valerie-Anne keeps the tradition in the family and writes under her maiden name. Although she always wanted to be a novelist, she also worked in London as a graphic designer. In 2000 she won the Romantic Novelists' Association New Writers' Award for her first novel *The Wrong Sort of Girl*. She lives in North Wales with her husband and young family.

VALERIE-ANNE BAGLIETTO

The Moon on a Stick

HODDER

First published in Great Britain in 2005 by Hodder and Stoughton
A division of Hodder Headline

A Hodder paperback

1

A CIP catalogue record for this title is available from the British Library

ISBN 0 340 82419 0

Typeset in Plantin by Hewer Text Ltd, Edinburgh
Printed and bound by Mackays of Chatham Ltd, Chatham, Kent

Hodder Headline's policy is to use papers that are natural, renewable
and recyclable products and made from wood grown in sustainable
forests. The logging and manufacturing processes are expected to
conform to the environmental regulations of the country of origin.

Hodder and Stoughton Ltd
A division of Hodder Headline
338 Euston Road
London NW1 3BH

For my children once again . . . C, B and ?
And for grandmothers everywhere, especially theirs . . .

ACKNOWLEDGEMENTS

As always, thank you to Dinah Wiener and Carolyn Caughey, for their invaluable wit and wisdom, and to everyone at Hodder. To my children's day nursery, also, for taking such good care of the most precious people in the world to me, and inspiring me to create a heroine like Amy. And of course, my parents, who also look after my two boys, and have such fun doing it, even on the most tiring days.

As usual, too, the RNA deserves a special mention, and especially my local chapter, SEFYDLIAD Y DDRAIG GYMRAEG. (If that's spelled wrong, sorry, it's entirely my fault!)

And finally . . . my husband. Without whom there would be no precious tiny people, and no heartburn or swollen ankles or morning sickness or subsequent dirty nappies . . . How can I ever repay you, my love?

PART ONE

'Star light, star bright,
First star I see tonight,
I wish I may,
I wish I might,
Have the wish I wish tonight.'
Traditional nursery rhyme

I

Smiling grimly, Amy fished the raisin out of the plughole. Mikey's doing, she guessed. There was a trail of dried, shrivelled, little grapes along the wood laminate floor, redolent of the forest in *Hansel and Gretel*. Amy retrieved them as she went down the corridor, halting predictably at the nursery door.

'I thought I told you to brush your teeth?' Her voice was affectionate but firm, reminding him who was the boss around here. Or at least, who ought to be.

Mikey was sitting cross-legged on the end of his small, low bed. He was scouring between his toes for stray fluff from his socks – a favourite pastime lately.

'I ate raisins,' he said, glancing up briefly with a disconcerting lack of respect.

Amy sometimes wished she could blow a whistle like Captain von Trapp, and her three – mercifully not seven – children would scramble to attention, lining up in front of her, awaiting her instructions. But even then she knew that her two eldest boys would just commandeer the whistle for themselves; and her youngest was only four months old, so he couldn't be expected to scramble anywhere. Wriggling his way up the changing mat was the extent of his mobility so far.

Mikey stopped examining his toes, and as if to show Amy some proof to corroborate his statement, held up the little Sun-Maid raisin box, tipping it upside down.

'You could only have actually eaten one or two,' said Amy

with a disapproving 'hmm'. 'The floor had the rest. Who gave them to you anyway?'

'Daddy.'

Daddy should know better, she thought. Then realised with a sigh that he couldn't, because he was hardly there. A fact the boys were rapidly learning to take advantage of. She was just amazed that Nick knew where the kids' treats were kept. Although, on second thoughts, Mikey had probably just pointed to the relevant cupboard.

'Come on then, let's brush your teeth properly.' It was supposed to be 'supervised' brushing, after all. And Amy usually did oversee the procedure with the two-thirds of her brood who had teeth, but sometimes, like today, she was needed in too many places at once. She could never understand why her responsibilities seemed to quadruple when Nick was at home when, in theory, they ought to halve.

There, propped on the basin just as she'd left it, was the stumpy toothbrush with pea-sized amount of paste on the chewed bristles.

'Mummy, brush your teeth, too,' ordered Mikey.

Without a fuss, Amy complied. Her dentist ought to approve of the fact that sometimes she brushed her teeth several times a day, depending on whether she was in or out of synch with the kids. This morning, she was especially careful not to get toothpaste on her pale pink jacket. In many ways it had been a bad idea to get herself ready early, but if she left it for the last minute as usual, she knew she would make them all late. Nick hated to be kept waiting.

She'd set her alarm for seven, just in case the baby didn't wake up for his early morning feed (as opposed to his earlier morning feed at four). And typically today, he'd slept peacefully in his cot until almost eight. Still, it had given her time to shower, blow-dry her hair in the lounge so she didn't wake the rest of the household, tentatively apply some make-up, and still have breakfast on the table ready and waiting for everyone.

Of course, Amy realised as she brushed her teeth, she could have left the suit till the last minute. It would only have taken seconds to shrug off her dressing gown and slip into the new outfit she'd splashed out on in Browns of Chester. She would bet on it needing a bloody good dry-clean by tonight, of course, because pristine clothes and young children didn't mix, even if they weren't the ones wearing them. But she prayed nothing would happen before she even left the flat. This month's Visa bill hadn't arrived yet, so Nick had no idea how much it had cost.

'Amy!' That was Nick now, calling from the kitchen.

'Spit,' Amy instructed Mikey, who promptly missed the basin and hit the tiled floor instead. She frowned, broke off some toilet roll and wiped up the mess before hurrying off down the corridor.

Nick was jiggling the baby about. Both father and child looked fractious. 'Amy, I can't quieten him down. Do you think he's hungry again?'

'He can't be, it's only been ten minutes.' She sighed resignedly. 'Give him here.' As she took the baby from Nick, Lucas let out a loud burp. Almost instantly, she felt an ominous warmth trickle wetly down the front of her suit . . .

Nick grimaced, and handed her a tea towel. 'That was a bad one.' He paused a moment to regard her more closely. 'Is that suit new?'

Amy wanted to cry. For a few seconds, she thought it was solely due to the creamy goo clinging to her wide, intricately beaded lapel. Then she realised it was compounded by the fact that Nick hadn't complimented her on her appearance yet. Not that flattery was his style; no one could accuse him of being sycophantic. But it would have been nice to have been told she looked pretty. She'd actually persevered with putting in contact lenses, but had Nick even noticed that she wasn't wearing her glasses?

'I'll have to get changed,' she said stiffly, ignoring Nick's question and trying to disguise the tears swarming at the back of her throat.

He looked vaguely sympathetic for a moment. 'Can't you just sponge it down?'

She shook her head. Even as she took most of it off with the tea towel, she could see that some of it had seeped straight through the delicate material.

'I guess that's what you have those burp cloths for.' Nick adjusted his immaculate, light grey tie. 'Should have been more careful myself, really. Guess I was just lucky.'

Amy nodded mutely, stroking Lucas's head as he gurgled in her arms. His upset was over, while hers was just beginning.

'What time is your mum dropping off Joseph?' Nick frowned at his watch. 'I want to leave in about half an hour.'

Their eldest son, who was three, had been staying overnight with his grandmother. It was his regular Friday-night treat, which Mikey was eager to be a part of. 'Why can't I sleep at Nana's, too?' he would pipe up every Friday afternoon when Amy dropped off Joseph. But Amy would fob him off with the usual excuse that Nana had a bad back and couldn't bend down to change a nappy.

She'd hoped this might spur Mikey along with his potty training, but there'd been no evidence as yet. The main reason that Mikey didn't stay at his grandmother's was that Amy didn't think it fair to saddle her mother with two lively, mercurial little boys for a whole night rather than just one.

'Mum should be here any minute,' Amy mumbled, just as the door buzzer went. 'That's probably her now.'

'Or Paul.'

Amy's brow puckered. 'Why would Paul be coming here?'

'I suggested he tag along with us. Well,' Nick shrugged as he pressed the switch to open the main door to the apartment block, 'there's room for him in the Espace, too. What's the point of him having to drive and not being able to drink tonight?'

'Hasn't he heard of taxis? Or hotel rooms?'

'Rosewood Grange was already fully booked by the time he got his arse into gear, and why should he mess about with a taxi when we're driving back this way ourselves?'

'*I'm* driving,' Amy reminded him.

'Oh come on, babe, don't be like that. You know you don't like drinking when you're breastfeeding.'

'That's not the point. Does Paul realise we're not staying for the evening reception?'

Nick glanced at his shoes. 'Well, I thought we could stay for a while.'

'But the kids—'

'Will be perfectly OK. They'll enjoy it, you know they will. If you take along their pyjamas then it won't matter if they fall asleep on the way home.'

Just then, the front door – which Nick had obviously left on the latch earlier when he'd gone to fetch the mail from the box in the lobby – clicked open. There was the sound of scuffling footsteps along the hall. The door to the main living area swung back and a young boy ran in, a Spider-Man rucksack draped round his shoulders which he swiftly deposited on the sofa. He rushed over to wrap his arms around Amy's thighs, then tugged fondly and playfully at Lucas's foot.

Amy ruffled his soft, fine hair, which was the evocative colour of a field of wheat and should really have been trimmed before today. 'Where's Nana?'

'She dropped me off outside. Said she had to go, said she'd call you tomorrow.' Joseph took a breath. 'It's all right, 'cos Paul was coming in. I wasn't on my own.'

As he said this, Amy looked up to see Nick's oldest friend

amble into the lounge, hands tucked casually in his trouser pockets. He was tall; almost as tall as Nick, and possibly the better looking if you liked the dark, Latin type. Fortunately for Amy, she didn't.

When she'd first set eyes on Nicholas Burnley and Paul Faulkner Jones, surrounded as they had been by their minions, like two young lords, it was Nick who had commanded her attention. There was something golden and glorious about him, sun-kissed and special, which Paul, with all his mysterious swarthiness, lacked. In another setting, Amy realised, Nick and Paul might have been rivals, but the fact that their families had known each other for years and were partners in business had cemented the bond between them from infancy.

Perhaps it was the physical contrast between them that had made them stand out from the other boys at that school disco. Or maybe it had been the unchecked confidence they'd both exuded. Amy had hardly been able to believe it when, later that evening, she'd crashed into them in a corridor, spilling the embarrassing contents of her handbag at their feet. She'd felt mortified. A complete ninny. Yet Nick had been charming and attentive, and by the end of the night had asked for her number.

She'd never expected him to call, had only thought he was being polite . . . But thirteen years, and three kids later, here they were.

'Hello, Amy,' Paul was smiling now, 'you look—' As he noticed the stain on her collar, his mouth clamped shut and the smile vamoosed.

'I've got to get changed,' she said tersely. 'Come on, Joe.' She ushered the boy towards the bedrooms. 'Let's get you ready, too.' She realised that Mikey had been quiet a long time. Silence, though welcome, was usually far more worrying than clatter.

She found him in the nursery bedroom he shared with

Joseph, hiding inside the wardrobe, clutching the scrap of old fleecy blanket he liked to keep close at hand.

'Doing a poo.' He sounded strained as he pulled the door closed again.

'Urghhh.' Joseph pinched his nose and pulled a pillow over his head.

Taking a deep breath, Amy went into the master bedroom, left Lucas in the cot to blink and coo at his mobile and chill out to Brahms' 'Lullaby', and returned to the nursery to deal with Joseph and Mikey. They were soon dressed and ready, and Amy shooed them off to the lounge, where she could hear them leaping excitedly on to Paul, only to have Nick rebuke them for crumpling Paul's shirt.

Right, she sighed, staring at herself in the mirror, and trying to be quiet because Lucas had dozed off. It was her turn. Again. Even though it was February, she felt as hot as if they were in the grip of a heatwave. It was all the rushing about. Her make-up had slipped, and her layered, shoulder-length, chestnut hair had gone flat, with a clumpy fringe. There wasn't time for another shower, so she'd have to make the best of it.

She wished her mother had come in, not rushed off like that. But Paul wasn't Elspeth's favourite person, and Amy couldn't claim any differently herself. In fact, if it wasn't for Faulkner Jones Burnley Limited as a whole – everybody swanning about as if they were in *Dynasty* and nepotism and shoulder pads were the in thing – her life with Nick would probably run a whole lot smoother.

2

Elspeth Croft let herself into the small terraced cottage, sweeping aside the straggling frond of ivy overhanging the porch. She really would have to call that man who'd cut it back so expertly last time; it was well overdue.

The cottage didn't have a hall – not even a little one – and Elspeth stepped directly into the lounge. It felt cold, in spite of the warm buttermilk walls and terracotta soft furnishings. Which meant that her younger daughter, Tilly, was out, because when the teenager was home the electric fire in the lounge was always on full blast, regardless of which room Tilly was in, and sometimes regardless of the season.

With a shiver, Elspeth switched on the fire, left it on a low setting and went through into the kitchen-diner beyond. She filled the old-fashioned, whistling kettle and placed it on the gas hob, preparing the teapot while she waited for the water to boil. Tilly had no doubt gone shopping in Mold with her friends. In addition to a few of the usual high-street shops, there was a market there.

As Elspeth drank her tea, she slowly unwound her long, striped scarf and shrugged off her coat. Heat was creeping back under her skin, seeping into her blood as if injected intravenously. Another welcome sensation came over her, and she crossed the room to the corner where the upright piano was squashed, lifting back the lid and smiling at the keys as if reunited with old, dear friends.

Her husband had given her this piano as a wedding present.

It was the only substantial item of furniture, if you could dare call it that, which she'd brought with her to this cottage when he'd died fourteen years ago. Elspeth had fled the large, old family house in Cheshire and uprooted her two daughters to 'the middle of nowhere', as Amy had once referred to this unassuming North Wales border village. She had been exaggerating, of course. Chester was less than twenty minutes away by car, so her old haunts hadn't exactly been denied her.

Elspeth knew that she'd been selfish, though, and hadn't been thinking about either Amy or Tilly when she'd upped sticks and come to Harrisfield. She had been propelled by her own grief; that dark, oppressive, all-enveloping misery. Wallowing in it for so long that when she'd finally emerged, bit by bit, it was as if she were living with two strangers.

Amy had already been too deeply involved with Nicholas Burnley for Elspeth to intervene without a battle, and considering he was smart, enterprising and well connected, everyone would have thought her mad anyway. And as for Tilly, she had no longer been a playful, chunky toddler but a tall, skinny child with quiet grey eyes and a maturity and independence at odds with her age. So like her father in many ways, it was both painful and fascinating to be around her.

Now, all these years later, Elspeth had acknowledged that her family's current situation wasn't how things would have turned out if her husband had still been alive. It was her own fault, and not a day went by when she didn't regret it.

George had been a good husband, a man of principles, and he would have wanted nothing less for his daughters. Instead, so far, there was just Nick, and Elspeth only pretended to get along with him for Amy's sake, and these days, for her grandsons'. As far as she was concerned, he wouldn't know a principle if it walked right up and boffed him.

Putting down her 'World's Best Nana' mug on a coaster on the window sill, Elspeth ran her fingers lightly over the piano keys, practising her scales. They were second nature to her, though. She'd been playing since she was a girl. It would be easier to forget how to breathe.

The day stretched ahead, as empty as any other Saturday, and she would fill it as she always did. A little music for pleasure, and then she would sit down in front of a very different keyboard, at the PC in the opposite corner of the lounge, getting on with work as if it was a weekday.

The only good reason for her to have accepted the invitation to the wedding today would have been to use it as an excuse to dress up. She'd helped Amy pick out a new suit in the department store in Chester, dismayed that her daughter should be so thrilled, as if it was a rare treat, when Nick could technically buy her an outfit like that every month of the year.

Of course, the only wedding Elspeth was keen to go to at the moment was Amy's, really, and she wondered at her own motives for that, considering who Amy would be marrying. Maybe it was this whole cohabiting thing; George would never have condoned it. But Elspeth couldn't see Nick making an honest woman of her daughter any time soon. Although he had proposed four years ago when Amy had fallen pregnant the first time, they had never got around to setting a date.

'There's no rush. I'm not waddling down the aisle in a dress from Mothercare,' Amy had stated defiantly, even though Elspeth had noticed in a pregnancy magazine left lying around the flat that Amy had circled an advert for special maternity occasion-wear.

After Joseph had been born, Amy had seemed to find her vocation in life all over again, quitting her job as a nursery nurse and devoting herself to her own child. She had rushed into a second pregnancy, hoping for a girl. When Mikey had come along, Elspeth had been convinced that Amy would go through it all again, just to get the daughter she longed for, whether Nick was in full agreement or not. Although as it turned out, Lucas – not Lucy, as the ultrasound had predicted – had been an accident. Apparently.

And no wedding, not as yet.

'I'm too busy with the kids to organise it,' was Amy's current excuse. 'And it's the twenty-first century, Mum. It doesn't matter if the boys are Burnleys and I'm still a Croft. When Nick and I *do* tie the knot, I want the whole shebang, and I'd like to have been involved in it. The last thing I want is Nick's mum finding an excuse to stick her oar in and take over.'

Elspeth's fingers hovered over the piano as she thought about the children's other grandmother. Stormily, she began to bang out some Beethoven. Rowena was an ice queen. Beautiful yes, but cold. She'd worked her way through two husbands already, Nick's father being the first, and today she was about to ensnare her third.

Elspeth didn't have to wonder how she managed it. In spite of once having been accused of putting the flint back in Flintshire, Rowena was in possession of a substantial amount of money – the basis of any sound romance, thought Elspeth sardonically. And then there was that villa in southern Spain near Valderrama. You had to take that into account, considering her new husband-about-to-be was eleven years her junior . . . and a golf fanatic.

The wedding had gone without a hitch, and the evening reception was drawing to a close. Amy sat in a quiet, smoke-free corner of the bar with Mikey's head in her lap and her hand gently jiggling the pram, endeavouring to keep the baby in a lulled state. Snoring softly, Mikey squirmed to get comfortable, smearing dribble over his mother's skirt.

Frustrated, Amy heaved a deep sigh. They should have gone home hours ago, but Nick had fobbed her off every time she'd suggested it. 'The kids aren't complaining, are they? On the contrary – Joseph's loving it. Don't be a killjoy.'

Joseph had made friends with a boy twice his age, and as cohorts they had totalled up enough scrapes to bring on an ulcer in any mother. The old country house hotel was a perfect setting for a civil wedding ceremony and an elegant reception, but it was way behind the times in catering for small children.

OK, so there'd been a high chair for Mikey at the formal wedding breakfast, but there were no nappy-changing tables in the Ladies or Disabled toilets, let alone the Gents. At least Mikey wore pull-on nappies, but Amy had had to lie Lucas on his mat on a sofa to change him, which had attracted a few disapproving glances, especially from Isabelle Faulkner Jones.

Stuff her, Amy thought now, as Paul's mother wafted past, her dark hair in a gravity-defying chignon and her olive skin taut and smooth over strikingly high cheekbones. She offered Amy a watery smile, before joining her husband at the bar.

Heaven knew where Paul and Nick had got to. Maybe they were still in the main reception room where the wedding breakfast and the dancing had taken place. She just hoped Nick had been paying attention when she'd asked him to keep an eye on Joseph. Paul, who was usually quite good with the boys even when he'd had a drink or two, wouldn't be much use tonight. And in her heart of hearts, Amy didn't like to count on him much, anyway. But his attention had been diverted all day by a leggy redhead called Francesca with the air of a young Nicole Kidman about her. Even though she was also single, she didn't seem quite as smitten by Paul as he was by her. She was a colleague of the groom, according to Paul's dad. 'A terrific little estate agent, a real rising star.' Paul had demanded to know why he'd never met her before.

'Because we all know what you're like,' his mother had chided him, her American accent still strong, even though she'd lived in England most of her married life. 'We can't introduce you to a pretty girl without wondering if we're throwing her to the lions.'

Paul's dad had chortled, Nick had snorted and the new Mrs Rowena Penn had sniggered, smoothing a hand over her stunning, rather youthfully tailored, wedding dress.

Nick had slapped Paul on the back in support. 'You go for it, mate. Don't take any notice. After all, you haven't been out with anyone for at least . . . let me think . . . four days, is it? Not since that Natalie or Nadia from Bar Lounge.'

'Natasha,' Paul had corrected him. 'And that was over a week ago.'

'A week,' Nick had echoed teasingly. 'How have you coped?'

'Nicholas, don't be facetious.' His mother had censured him, but it was a token gesture. He was still everyone's golden boy.

'You'll have your work cut out with Francesca,' Paul's father had warned him. 'I've heard she's extremely selective when it comes to her men.'

'Well, odds on Paul's been out with her before the end of the month,' Nick had concluded, grinning.

Amy released her grip on the pram, at long last. Lucas was flat out. Gently, she stroked Mikey's hair. He stirred in his sleep, wiping his nose with grubby fingers. There were probably enough bacteria under those nails to contaminate Chester's water supply for a week. Amy sighed fondly, then looked up as Nick breezed into the room. He always seemed to develop a swagger when he'd been drinking, as if his natural cockiness was magnified by the alcohol.

'Right,' he announced, 'we can go whenever you're ready.'

'I've been ready for the last couple of hours.' Slowly, Amy lifted Mikey's head off her lap and heaved herself to her feet. 'Where's Joe?'

'Saying goodbye to my mum.'

'And Paul?'

'Oh, he's not coming.'

Amy's eyebrows reared upwards. 'What do you mean? He hasn't pulled that Francesca already?'

'Not quite,' Nick grinned. 'But he's making a bloody good effort. The bar's open late to residents of the hotel, so the "party" isn't over just yet. Paul's decided to take a room rather than fart about with a taxi later.'

'I thought you said the hotel was full?'

'Er – did I? That's what Paul had told me, but I guess they must have had a cancellation or something.'

Amy frowned. 'So if he's staying here, why did we have to hang around?'

'He's only just decided to do it. I'm sorry, babe, are you tired?'

'Just a bit.' She couldn't help sounding narked.

Paul and Francesca Courtney entered the room. His arm was hovering around the region of her back, but not quite touching it. He raised his hand in greeting at his parents, and then grinned as he steered Francesca towards Amy and Nick. Still without touching the girl, noted Amy. Like a sheepdog guiding a lamb to the slaughter, or something equally disturbing.

But as they came closer, Amy decided she liked the look of Francesca. The redhead might seem beautiful and serene at first glance, but there was something in her face that was about as lamb-like as Hannibal Lecter. Perhaps she would be the one leading Paul to his doom for a change, rather than the other way around. About bloody time someone did, thought Amy.

'You've got gorgeous children.' Francesca addressed her directly. 'I meant to tell you earlier, but I think I've been rather monopolised today, so I never got the chance.'

'They're like a brood of angels,' added Paul, quite earnestly, ignoring Francesca's obvious dig at him.

Amy regarded him with suspicion. This was news to her. 'Well, they do take after their father . . .'

'Only in looks,' Paul went on. 'The rest of the time, they remind me of you.'

'Is that when they're throwing wobblies or chucking up everywhere?' winked Nick. 'Now don't look at me like that.' He put his arm around Amy and squeezed her jovially. 'I'm just teasing. Anyway, you know what you're like when you've had too much Chardonnay.'

She couldn't remember the last time she'd had too much Chardonnay, and she would be fairly surprised if Nick could. If she had been drinking, the likelihood was that he had, as well, and his faculties – particularly his memory – were always conveniently affected.

Paul seemed to realise that Nick was slightly the worse for wear now, too. He glanced nervously at Francesca. 'I just meant that the boys have many of Amy's better traits,' he tried to explain. 'They're very . . .'

'Go on.' Nick seemed to be daring him.

Paul looked at the floor, as if the Persian rug could provide him with inspiration. 'They're very . . . *angelic*, I suppose.' The rug had clearly failed to help.

Amy was too tired to analyse this now, although she remembered that Paul had once referred to her patronisingly as a goody-two-shoes, after a brief argument at a party when Amy had warned everyone they were going to wake the neighbours. Yet that was several years ago. She'd never particularly thought of her children that way, though. Especially not when one of them woke her up at three in the morning. They were unquestionably less loveable in the middle of the night than the middle of the day, unless they were ill and couldn't help it.

'I think you ought to take that as a compliment,' Francesca murmured, clearly amused.

'I'll take it and run.' Amy fished out the keys to the Renault Espace from her handbag, and heaved up the rucksack containing nappies, wipes and other baby paraphernalia. 'It was nice speaking to you.' She nodded at Francesca and then nudged Nick. 'Come on then, let's make a move.' She looped the rucksack over the handles of the pram and lifted the brake with her foot.

Nick nodded, and scratched his head as he looked down at his second son, lying comatose on the sofa with a travel rug over his legs. 'What about Mikey?'

'What about him? I doubt he's going to wake up if you just carry him out.'

Amy was right. Nick bundled the boy into his arms, blanket and all, and transferred him to the car. Even the cool blast of night air, or the elaborate strapping into the child seat, didn't rouse him.

'You get the car going,' Nick told Amy. 'I'll go back in and find Joe.'

Amy nodded, gingerly lifting Lucas out of the pram and laying him in his baby carrier, hoping he wouldn't wake up either.

Nick was gone five minutes. Amy had already driven the Espace out of the parking space and was waiting impatiently on the stretch of gravel by the main steps.

'I think Paul might actually be getting somewhere at last.' Nick was smirking as he climbed in the front passenger side, after depositing Joseph in his own child seat. 'He's introducing Francesca to his folks already.'

'I thought they already knew her.' Amy glanced over her shoulder to make sure Joseph was also strapped in properly. Her eldest son smiled at her drowsily. 'And anyway, they were talking to her earlier, weren't they?'

'Oh, yeah,' said Nick. 'You're right. Well anyway, it was all looking very cosy, if you know what I mean.'

'So maybe she's the one then,' said Amy, as she pulled out into the enveloping darkness of the country road.

'The one what?'

'Who'll finally give Paul a run for his money.'

Nick didn't reply. He was slumped in his seat. He would probably be asleep before they reached the A55.

'At this rate,' Amy went on, wetting her lips carefully, 'he'll be hitched before we are . . .'

Again, Nick didn't say anything. His face was in shadow. A sideways glance didn't provide Amy with any clues.

'Is today the kind of wedding you want?' he asked at last, hardly brimming with enthusiasm.

Amy looked at her engagement ring, the solitaire diamond catching the light and flashing with a familiarity that vexed her. She'd been wearing it on its own for longer than she'd imagined she would when Nick had first given it to her.

'I'd prefer it to be in church,' she said. 'But you already know that.'

'Well, it's Mum's third time. I could hardly see her walking up the aisle in a flowing white gown with flowers in her hair. Could you?'

Amy knew Nick wasn't very impressed with his mother's latest choice of husband. At least he had done his duty and supported her today, even if he'd only gone through the motions as if he were an ordinary guest, not the bride's son.

'It would be *my* first time,' Amy reminded him. 'And I'm not greedy, I only want the one.'

'But we're hardly the model Christian family, are we? I mean, three kids out of wedlock, as your mum would say. And that's the only reason you want a church wedding – because you know Elspeth would never go for a basic civil ceremony. It's the only reason you wanted the boys christened, too.'

'No, it isn't. And you and your mum can't talk, you just wanted to throw a big party each time. A three-month-old's hardly likely to remember it.'

'I've never got to choose the godparents, though, have I?'

Amy didn't put her foot down often, but she had about that. Intractably. 'Only because you'd choose Paul. And I'd rather they didn't have any godfather than have him.'

'So they've got your baby sister and your mum's fat friend.'

'Carol isn't fat, she's just big-boned. And Tilly won't be a child for ever. They're great godmothers. And how did you manage to get me off the subject of weddings?' she frowned.

'I was just trying to point out that we hardly go to church regularly.'

'*You* never go at all, unless you have to. But getting married in one would be nice,' said Amy flatly.

She felt Nick's hand squeeze her knee. 'Things aren't bad as they are, though, are they? And if Lucas was a bit older, he could remember the day his parents got married, otherwise Mikey and Joseph would have that advantage over him.'

Amy harrumphed softly, frustratedly. 'Do you think that really matters?'

She was aware of Nick nodding in the shadows, before slurring with a yawn, 'I do.'

3

The noon sky seemed to pour in through the Velux window, down into the top-floor flat of the late-Victorian house, and on to the papers strewn on the large, square desk. But Paul wasn't working on the architectural designs that lay half finished, even though he'd promised his father they would be ready by the end of the day. He was standing by the French windows that gave directly on to the small roof terrace, staring out over the river without really seeing it.

He'd known Francesca Courtney for a couple of weeks now, and he couldn't recall anyone having been this . . . *ambivalent* before when it came to going out with him. Of course, he could give up right now and retain his pride – if only she wasn't already orbiting his head so that he couldn't even concentrate on the work he normally thrived on.

Paul frowned out of the window, trying to dissect what it was about her that had hooked him. Redheads weren't normally his type. Freckles and carroty red hair were a little too Orphan Annie-like, in his opinion, yet Francesca carried it off with an amazing grace, as if she'd been doing it all her life. Which, Paul realised with a self-deprecating 'Doh!' a moment later, she had.

There was something almost Pre-Raphaelite about her, as if she'd walked out of a painting by Rossetti. Proud and strong and hauntingly serene. A dominant woman, like his mother. The type that he ran a mile from – when he was obviously in his right mind.

The night of the wedding he had escorted her to her room, and for once been content with a brief kiss on the cheek. The chaste, unlingering sort, with no promises attached. But it was better than nothing. They had met for breakfast the following morning, but that had been with his parents, and the conversation had mainly focused on business.

'I'll call you,' he'd told her, as he'd carried her bags to her car after checking out.

'OK,' she'd shrugged, managing to make that sound agonisingly ambiguous, as if she hadn't made up her mind yet whether she fancied him or not.

And over the next few days, Paul *had* called. But how many times? It was galling to realise he'd lost count. He'd been met with her answering machine at home, her voicemail on her mobile, or some junior clerk at work who would tell him – with a hint of malicious amusement – that Miss Courtney was out of the office.

Francesca had finally deigned to call him back. 'I'm sorry, Paul, but I'm really busy this week. How about dinner on . . .' he'd guessed that she was consulting her diary '. . . actually, can you make that lunch, next Friday?'

He'd muttered that that was fine, gutted to acknowledge that he would take any crumbs she scattered in his direction.

'I fancy a Spanish tapas bar,' she'd suggested. 'They're always fun, in a clichéd kind of way, and seeing as you know the lingo . . .'

'Actually, I don't,' Paul had admitted. 'I'm familiar with English, naturally. Some Welsh. And a smattering of schoolboy French, but otherwise . . .'

'Your mother, though, I thought I'd heard—'

'Oh, you heard right. But I wouldn't ever mention it to her. It's never been a secret, as such, but she still doesn't like to own up to that half of her ancestry.' Paul had grimaced, glad that Francesca couldn't see him.

A Spanish immigrant mother who had once worked as a maid wasn't something Isabelle was proud of, even if that mother had died when Isabelle was only three. The whole Faulkner inheritance might have been denied her because of it. At one point, Paul knew, it had been touch and go. Fortunately, as a young girl, Isabelle had managed to charm her Protestant grandparents and had reinstated her father, brother and herself firmly in the bosom of the family. Possibly, thought Paul cynically, by renouncing the Roman Catholic faith she had been baptised in, forgetting how to say the Our Father and Hail Mary in Latin, and insisting that everyone use the French form of her name rather than Isabella.

'Well, even if you're not,' Francesca was boasting now, '*I'm* a demon at ordering *calamares y patata frita*. That's the Spanish version of fish and chips, to you.'

Paul had hoped for something a little more exotic. But Francesca had made the whole thing sound like a challenge, in such a provocative manner, he hadn't known how to respond. As if she had the rare ability of reducing him to a gibbering adolescent. Also something shared by his mother on occasion.

Now, as he drew closer to coming face to face with her for the first time since that night at Rosewood Grange, Paul turned away from his modest view of the Dee, the one with the crippling mortgage, and hurried into the small bathroom to check himself out one last time in the mirror.

He'd only shaved a few hours ago, but already a shadow was materialising on his jaw. And the collar of his shirt was curling upwards slightly. It was the only one ironed. Not that he'd done a decent job in the first place – nerves, he supposed, because he liked to think of himself as an expert – but there was no time to have another go.

As he headed through the lounge area to the front door, the phone on the coffee table began to ring. His stomach knotted. What if it was Francesca calling to cancel? Before he could pick it up, the answering machine clicked into action. After a brief pause, Nick's voice crackled out, 'Hi, Paul, are you there? Paul . . .? Shit. OK, then. I'll try your mobile.'

Paul's hand wavered over the handset, then curled into a decisive fist. He headed towards the front door again, but then his mobile began to vibrate in his pocket. Frowning, he debated whether to answer it. Nick's voice had been odd; maybe something was wrong. Besides, Paul could talk as he walked to his car. He took the call, hitting the button an instant before it would have diverted to messaging.

'Brilliant timing, mate. I'm on my way out.'

'This is important,' said Nick crisply.

Paul evoked an image of Francesca drumming her fingers on a table and glancing at her watch. 'So's this.'

'I need to meet up.'

'Is something wrong?'

'No – not exactly.'

'So no one's at death's door then?'

'No, nothing like that.'

'Then it can wait.' Paul sighed, relieved, dipping into his pocket for the keys to his Audi TT.

'No,' said Nick a third time. 'Actually, it can't. I need to see you right away . . . My plane leaves in four hours.'

Elspeth stared unseeingly at her computer screen. She'd been sitting in a meditative state like this on and off all afternoon. Now she needed the loo again. That was what came of downing a pot of tea, meant for two, all on one's own. But there was an addictiveness to the whole ritual of tea-making. It filled entire minutes with something other than mundane work in a delicious, guilt-free way. Even popping to the toilet seemed part of the procedure – a necessary function to punctuate the monotony of typing and formatting another CV.

Elspeth was pushing back her little, wooden office chair when the front door blew open. At least, it seemed to; perpetrated by a gust of cold air from Siberia. According to the weather girl on the news this morning, there'd be gusts of bitter, icy Siberian wind all over Great Britain. And now there was one in Elspeth's living room. She tugged at the woolly scarf around her neck for comfort.

'Hi, Mum.'

The gust of wind was followed by Tilly, bundled in a puffy black anorak, thick black tights and chunky lace-up boots. There was probably a skirt under there, too – somewhere. She dumped her bulky black rucksack in the middle of the living-room floor. All this dark attire seemed to bleach her heart-shaped face of colour, apart from the ruddy lipstick and coppery blusher.

Elspeth sighed. She'd long given up nagging her daughter not to wear make-up to school. Even at home, there were only fleeting glimpses of Tilly without blusher and mascara on, almost as if she applied it the minute she woke up in the morning, with a mirror under her duvet.

'Good day at school?' asked Elspeth.

'OK, I suppose.' Tilly unzipped her anorak, but didn't take it off. 'Mum, it's freezing in here!' She immediately bent down to switch on the fire. 'Why do you do this? You don't have to be a martyr. We're not that hard-up that we can't afford to put on the heating.'

Elspeth wrapped her ribbed cardigan around her. 'I wouldn't call us hard-up, at all. But you know I don't feel the cold,' she said nonchalantly.

'Which is why you wear thermals, a jumper *and* a cardie,' Tilly pointed out.

This was a favourite sparring ground of theirs. Elspeth secretly enjoyed it. Even bickering could be a welcome form of communication. Why would married couples indulge in it so frequently, otherwise?

'I'm just careful with the pennies, as they say.' Elspeth stood up. 'Would you like some tea, love?' Any old excuse.

Tilly nodded, rummaging through her rucksack. 'I've got some history homework. Mind if I use the PC, or are you busy?'

Elspeth couldn't help smiling. This was an even better excuse to procrastinate than making tea. It was one of the reasons she hadn't bought Tilly her own computer. 'No, love, you feel free.'

'I'll have some hot chocolate, actually,' Tilly added. She was already flicking through a book about the social and economic history of Great Britain. Gripping stuff.

'No problem. I'll just nip to the loo first.' But as Elspeth reached the foot of the stairs, someone knocked on the front door. Through the diamond of opaque glass in the wood, she could make out the outline of a man. 'What does Jonathan want now?' she grumbled, going across to yank open the door, which had a tendency to stick even with a strong blast of air behind it.

'He'll probably hang around now till Amy gets here,' smirked Tilly. 'Saddo.'

'Sshhh,' hissed Elspeth.

But it wasn't her next-door neighbour. To her surprise, it was Paul Faulkner Jones.

Something about his face reminded Elspeth of an old work colleague of her husband's, who had come round unannounced on the morning George had died.

Elspeth felt chilled, as if the Siberian wind had permeated her bones. Paul had never turned up like this. Not on his own.

'Elspeth,' he muttered, 'can I come in? I need your advice . . .'

'Advice?' she echoed raspily.

Tilly swivelled round in the chair. 'What's wrong?' She fired the question Elspeth was too terrified to ask: 'Has something happened to Amy or the boys?'

Paul was shaking his head. 'They're fine. It isn't anything like that. Oh God.' He jabbed a hand through his dark, slightly spiky hair. 'It's Nick.'

Elspeth clutched at her scarf, apprehensive for Amy's sake. 'What about him?'

'He's all right. Not hurt or anything. It's just . . .' Paul contorted his face. 'Right now, he's on his way to Manchester airport.'

Elspeth paused to take this in. 'I didn't know he was going away. Amy didn't mention anything. Is it business?' Faulkner Jones Burnley was based in the North West, but as a premier housing developer, they seemed to be expanding all the time. That still didn't explain why Paul was here, though. Aware that she was babbling agitatedly, as if to halt the flow of something terrible, Elspeth reluctantly shut up.

'He rang me earlier,' Paul went on. 'Wanted to meet me right away. He said it was important. It couldn't wait. I went to Bar Lounge, and there they were, just sitting there . . .'

'Who?' Elspeth had never been a fan of Paul's, but she felt a pang of sympathy over his struggle to get the words out. He seemed to be choking on them, as if they were making him nauseous.

'Nick and Anneka.'

'Anneka?' prompted Tilly, her brow crumpling like a Roman blind.

'Anneka Shaw,' said Paul. 'She's the designer we use for our showhomes. At least, she *used* to be Anneka Shaw . . .'

Elspeth suddenly wanted to shake him, to get the words out. He was a foot taller than her, though, and she still felt slightly sorry for him.

'I guess she's Anneka Burnley now.' Paul stared morosely at the carpet.

'What do you mean?' Elspeth frowned. This was so confusing. Paul was normally such a smoothie, so sure of himself.

It was one of the reasons he grated on her. 'Smarmy,' her husband would have said.

'They got married,' explained Paul. 'This morning. At the registry office in Hawarden. Just Nick and Anneka, and a couple of her friends, for witnesses.'

Tilly was on her feet, glaring at him. 'Are you having us on?'

'Paul,' Elspeth went on, wringing her hands, as she always did when she was nervous or anxious, 'I don't understand. Is this some sort of joke?'

Paul's dark brown eyes – almost black, and glossy like a puddle of oil – flashed defensively, as if saying, *What do you take me for?*

'I came here first because I have absolutely no idea how I'm supposed to tell Amy,' he admitted hoarsely. 'I can't begin to say how I hate Nick right this minute for landing this on me. Or for doing what he's done.' His voice filled with anger and a distressing, childish desperation. 'But I've got no choice. Nick and Anneka have gone. They're on their way to catch a plane to the States.'

Paul pulled a creased envelope out of his pocket: 'I've got a letter he's written to her. Amy. But how am I supposed to just hand it to her without telling her first? It explains everything, apparently. How he's been seeing Anneka for the past eight months. How he's been hiding it from everyone – including me – and how he's so much in love "it's crucifying him", and he couldn't see any way out, except like this.'

Paul's voice seemed to break inopportunely, like a choir-boy's, but in reverse. 'I've been his friend practically all my life. He's the brother I never had. But right at this moment . . .'

Elspeth put a hand to her mouth. Even her younger daughter was lost for words. This was horrible. Unbelievable. How were they even going to begin telling Amy? She'd been with Nick since she was a teenager. She'd given him three gorgeous, amazing children. He was her first love, and to her mind, her last. And he'd just walked out, as easily as if he'd popped to the shops for a pint of milk. It seemed that way to Elspeth. And although the basic circumstances had been different, the sense of déjà vu crashing over her was exposing a wound that was still raw and painful, even fourteen years later.

Tilly had been too young to take it in properly, but Amy had felt the loss of George as keenly as Elspeth. A massive coronary at work. Dad slumped over his desk, never to regain consciousness. Even the paramedics, arriving on the scene in minutes, hadn't been able to save him. And Elspeth had had to tell her this.

Elspeth had had to sit her down, take her hand, and tell her that the man she idolised and adored was never coming back.

PART TWO

'Why, sometimes, I've believed as many as six impossible things before breakfast.'

Lewis Carroll, *Through the Looking-Glass*

4

'I'm really sorry, but I can't accept this card.'

'What . . .?' Amy blinked at the girl at the checkout, absently taking in that she had frosted pink lipstick, too much blusher, and silver hoop earrings, as large as Lucas's fist. Distantly, although it was only an arm's length away, she could hear the baby start to grizzle in his plastic trolley seat. 'I always use that card here . . .'

'There seems to be a problem with it,' the girl added quietly, glancing at the queue building behind Amy. 'We can take a debit card, or a cheque,' she suggested. 'Whatever you think best . . .'

Amy couldn't think. But then, over the past few days, her brain hadn't seemed able to function outside of its ordinary, mundane parameters. She got on with things that had been programmed into her.

Sometimes, after giving the kids a bath and putting them to bed, she would look back over that last hour with no real recollection of how she had got through it. It had just seemed to happen, to wash over her, requiring little effort other than the physical.

Shopping had been one of those things. Her hand just stretched itself out and put the necessary objects into the trolley. Veg, fruit, bread, milk . . . But today, she had hit an obstacle. As if someone had clicked their fingers and brought her out of a trance, leaving her totally disoriented.

'Cash, even?' the checkout girl was prompting hopefully.

She seemed nice, although Amy had always been intimidated by girls who were pretty and knew it. 'Trashy,' her father would have called them, because of the excess make-up and jewellery. In Amy's experience, they had just been popular, at school and at work. Girls with confidence, and a hard edge. But this girl had kind eyes. She had fussed over Lucas as Amy had pushed the trolley past.

Amy scrabbled about in her bag. There was only a five-pound note and a few coins in her purse. She didn't have her chequebook with her because she never used it for shopping, and her debit card had gone missing in the flat when she'd stupidly left it lying around and Mikey had got hold of it. It was either 'posted' under the sofa or lying at the bottom of a toy box, probably safer than if it was in her handbag.

As the realisation sank in that she had no means of paying for all the groceries already packed in plastic bags in the trolley, her head seemed to swim and her heart to thump violently.

Just then, though, as if out of nowhere, a hand came to rest on her arm. 'Amy, is everything OK?'

She blinked up at the man who must have pushed his way through the queue to reach her. He had peppered brown hair, a neat goatee to match and a familiar expression of concern.

'Jonathan,' she muttered, 'I . . .'

But her mother's next-door neighbour was intelligent enough to assess the situation for himself. He handed his credit card to the girl behind the checkout. 'Here, put everything on this.' He gestured to Amy's shopping, and then unloaded the contents of his basket on to the conveyor belt. 'I guess this is one way of jumping the queue . . .'

He smiled at the girl behind the checkout, who said especially warmly, and not at all in parrot fashion as she handed him the receipt, 'Thank you, sir. Goodbye.'

'Come on.' He took hold of Amy's trolley, something noble

about his demeanour and the way he held his chin – until he started blowing raspberries at the baby. 'Ssshhh,' he said soothingly, as Lucas stared up at him with surprised eyes. 'Hush now, your mummy's here, she hasn't abandoned you.' He seemed to falter, as if he'd realised what he'd said. 'Sorry,' he turned to Amy as they approached the exit, 'I didn't mean . . .' Jonathan stared ahead.

Amy couldn't speak. Literally.

'Where are you parked?' he asked softly, as they came out into the thin, March sunshine.

Amy pointed towards the Mother and Baby section. She'd managed to nab a space there, for once. It was often full, although a few of the cars never appeared to have a trace of an infant passenger. Their owners obviously felt they had a God-given right to be there, regardless. Amy had used to gripe about it to Nick, even though she secretly suspected he parked there himself when he was on his own.

Nick . . . His face loomed in her mind. The crookedness of his smile as one side curled up and the other down. The Pacific blueness of his eyes, and the gold of his hair, as if Rumpelstilt-skin had spun it himself.

As she fumbled with her keys, Amy felt a mass of tears press upwards into her throat. The thought struck her that she hadn't even thanked Jonathan, and the enormity of what he'd done, without question or complaint, only added to her wretchedness.

The car keys fell from her hands, the plastic keyring with the photos of the boys in one side and Nick in the other, smashing on to the tarmac.

'Amy' – Jonathan retrieved the keys – 'you can't drive like this. I'm taking you to your mum's. We can sort something out about your car later, when you're feeling up to it.'

Again, she couldn't speak. Every faculty seemed to be freezing over, as if an icy mist were creeping up on her.

Jonathan opened the car and took out Lucas's infant carrier before locking the car again. With the carrier perched on top of the shopping, he started pushing the trolley across the car park, leading Amy to his slightly neglected, but practical Volvo estate.

'You just have to show me how to strap this thing in,' he said, carefully placing the now babbling Lucas into the baby seat. 'It's been so long since I had to do it, and they all seem different anyway . . .' He tailed off, as Amy shakily pointed to a sticker on the side showing how the seat belt needed to be routed.

'Now come on, in you get,' he said, opening the front passenger door. 'I'll put the shopping in the boot.'

Like a robot obeying his instructions, Amy climbed in. 'The boys,' she managed to mutter, as Jonathan finally swung himself in beside her. 'Joe and Mikey . . . They're at nursery. I'm meant to be picking them up later . . .'

'Right.' Jonathan started the car. 'We can sort something out. Maybe your mother can go for them? But I suppose we need those other seats still in your car?'

'Not really,' said Amy. 'She's got a couple in hers.'

'So that's sorted then.'

'You don't have to do all this,' said Amy, sounding flat and emotionless. 'It's too much . . .'

'Please,' he stated emphatically, 'I want to help.'

'But all this farting about—' She stopped. That was one of Nick's expressions, not hers.

'It's no trouble. It's not as if I don't know what's involved. I'm a parent, too, remember.' He glanced at her as he drove out of the retail park. In spite of the fog that seemed to be enveloping her brain, she was vaguely aware of a hollowness to his voice.

Jonathan lived alone in the terraced cottage beside her mother's. Since he'd moved there, five years ago, there hadn't been any sign of an ex-girlfriend, let alone a child. Although he'd made it common knowledge in the village, it was still easy to forget that he was a dad. He seemed so much the staid, jumper-clad bachelor; unassuming and almost forty; dull and predictable. Nick had always rolled his eyes when Jonathan had appeared at his window to check who was driving up the private gravel lane that led off from Harrisfield's short High Street.

'Why doesn't he just get a life?' Nick had used to grumble as he parked the car.

And now, as Amy sat beside her mother's neighbour in his musty old Volvo, she realised with a sharp, stark clarity – like a blaze of light piercing the mist – that Jonathan Simmons *had* had a life once.

Just as she had.

5

'There's obviously no one in.' Francesca swept aside a spiral of hair from her brow. 'Come on, Paul, I'm cold.'

Paul pressed his finger for the third time on the intercom button. 'It's gone eight. She wouldn't be out this late with the kids.'

'So maybe she's giving them a bath and can't come to the door.'

'Amy always tries to have them down by now. It gives her a few hours' respite before she goes to bed herself.'

'It must be even harder for her now.'

'That's why I wanted to check she was OK.' Paul frowned. He walked around the side of the building, up to the edge of the canal, where he craned his neck to see if he could make out any light in the ground-floor apartment. It seemed to be in darkness. Yet Amy's Espace was parked in its allotted space under the car port.

Francesca, shivering in her thin dress and matching coat, shrugged her exquisitely proportioned shoulders. 'Maybe she's staying with family. Didn't you say her mother lived in Harrisfield?'

'They can't all be staying with Elspeth.' Paul shook his head, walking back towards the car. 'I wouldn't have thought there'd be enough room.'

'So other family then,' Francesca suggested.

'There isn't any other family. Not round here, at least. Some second or third cousins down south somewhere, I think, but they're not close.'

Francesca slid gracefully into the low-slung car. Her deportment was nothing if not excellent. No wonder his mother was enamoured of her. 'Hasn't Amy got any friends?' she persisted. 'Other mums from some toddler group or something.' She was growing impatient now. 'You can't pretend to know everything about her, Paul. Nick was your friend, not Amy.'

'Amy's my friend, too!' he protested, revving the engine a touch too aggressively.

'For appearance's sake, maybe. Because of Nick.'

Paul indicated left, heading towards the centre of Chester. Francesca was right, of course.

He had told her the full story, about knowing Nick since they were kids, and how they'd met Amy not long after she'd moved to Harrisfield.

A few schools in the Flintshire area, ranging from lowly comprehensive to posh and private, had come together to throw a disco every term for the combined sixth-formers. On this particular occasion, it had been St Stephen's turn – Paul and Nick's home turf – and the most illustrious of them all. Amy had recently joined the more middling Rosewood High. She'd been dragged along to the disco. It had been obvious she'd felt out of place and wasn't enjoying herself.

Paul had first noticed her because he'd never seen a more miserable wallflower. But he'd been too busy with a drop-dead brunette from a school in Flint to ask Amy to dance out of pity or courtesy, and he couldn't remember if the thought had even crossed his mind at the time.

They had actually met properly when she'd collided with him and Nick in the corridor leading to the toilets. By the streaks in her make-up, it was clear she'd been crying. In a fluster, she'd dropped her little handbag and a couple of tampons had slipped out. Ever the gent, Nick had got to the bag first, although Paul had chivalrously been reaching down, too. By this point, Amy's face had been beetroot red, but Nick, particularly chilled that night, had instantly put her at ease.

Even though she had been fairly attractive back then, if not conventionally sylphlike, Paul still hadn't been able to understand why his best friend had started seeing her.

'She's different,' Nick used to say, shrugging. This had been true enough. She was far more naïve and Pollyanna-like than any girl Paul had ever met. If you could stomach that hero-worshipping philosophy of hers where Nick could do no wrong and Paul was to blame for every misdemeanour. And even though the relationship had cooled while Nick had been at university – at least on Nick's part – they had picked up where they left off the minute he was back home and installed in the family business.

Paul had counselled his friend that Amy was 'nice' and 'sweet' and, in his more cynical moments, 'homely', but that was the crux of the problem as far as Paul was concerned, because in his eyes this made her predictable and boring. It had been hard to accept that someone like Amy could be Nick's ideal woman. 'You and I – we're too alike,' Paul had told him. 'You know that. We need someone to add spice to our lives, not just our curries.'

The fact that Nick hadn't rushed into an official commitment with Amy, apart from asking her to move in with him when he'd bought his first flat, had boded well, and five or so years had drifted by without any hint of a wedding being organised. But then Joseph had come along, as well as that solitaire diamond, and suddenly there they were – a family. Paul had finally, ironically, resigned himself to the fact that Nick was in it for the long haul.

'What time's the table booked for?' Francesca was asking, trying to divert his attention. He knew she was well aware that he'd made the reservation for eight thirty, later than usual because he'd wanted to drop by on Amy first.

Paul sighed, ignoring her question. 'Listen. Sorry I'm not myself. It's just when all this blew up—'

'But that's how long we've been going out,' she reminded him. 'When all this "blew up". So I've got no idea if this is your usual self or not.'

'Well it isn't. I'm not normally so . . . preoccupied.'

'It's understandable.' She shrugged again. 'You're feeling responsible.'

'Am I?' Paul jerked at the steering wheel slightly.

'But it's not your fault. You're feeling swamped by guilt, and it's Nick who's to blame, not you.'

A grim smile touched his lips, albeit briefly. 'Force of habit. Amy's always blaming me. I hadn't wanted to be there when Elspeth told her, but I knew I had to.'

'And I didn't mind being stood up. Well,' Francesca pursed her lips, 'of course I minded at the time. But I'm here now, aren't I? And when all this is over . . .'

Paul glanced at her. 'Do you think it'll ever really be over?'

'Of course it will. Amy'll come to terms with it sooner or later, even if she's in some sort of denial now. Nick will get back from honeymoon, and they'll reach some mutual agreement over when he'll get to see the kids.'

'It sounds simple when you put it like that.'

'Well it needn't be as complicated as you're making it out to be. Just because Amy's not at the flat, that doesn't mean anything terrible has happened. She might even have gone away herself, with her mum and the boys, or on her own.'

'It hit her hard, though.' Paul could remember her reaction all too vividly. He'd only thought people could turn that shade of grey when they were dead.

'Well it was bound to. It still wasn't your fault, though. You didn't leave her for another woman.'

'I've been meaning to go round before.' Paul backed the car into a space directly in front of the restaurant, and thanked the gods for being kind; he could keep an eye on it out of the window. 'I should have done. But what with work and . . .'

'Me?' Francesca murmured.

'And you.' Paul risked another smile. 'Maybe that's part of the problem – why I couldn't bring myself to face her sooner. Everything's going right for me.'

'Don't beat yourself up over it! If we all went through life feeling guilty for being happy when we knew other people weren't . . .' She paused, as if searching for the right words. 'Well then, it would make a mockery of happiness. We'd be devaluing it.'

Paul stared at her, regarding her with a mixture of awe and admiration. There hadn't been many people in his life to have exacted his respect that way. As well as being a vision to look at, Francesca Courtney was intelligent, sensitive and shrewd. She understood where he was coming from, and he hadn't felt understood in a long time, if ever.

Unable to resist the impulse, he leaned across and planted a firm kiss on her lips. 'Thank you,' he muttered.

'What for?'

'For finally dropping the "treat him mean" routine.'

'Who says I'm not lulling you into a false sense of security?' She grinned tantalisingly and kissed him back, tasting of the Sauvignon Blanc she'd been drinking when he'd arrived at her flat in Boughton earlier to pick her up.

Elspeth lunged for the trilling phone. Only a metre or so away Lucas was asleep in his pram. Elspeth had just got him off, after trundling the pram up and down the High Street three times.

'Yes?' she said breathlessly. At least all this pacing up and down with Lucas and running around after Mikey and Joseph would keep her fit. Eventually. When she got over the exhausted stage.

'Elspeth, it's Paul.'

'Oh.' Her natural warmth plummeted several degrees, and she spoke before she could stop this becoming evident in her voice. 'What do you want?'

'I know I'm probably something of a *persona non grata* at the moment, but . . .'

'I'm sorry.' She feigned civility as best she could. 'I didn't mean to be rude.'

'I'd feel the same in your shoes. The last time we spoke—'

'—you were breaking my daughter's heart.'

There was a pause. 'Indirectly,' he corrected. 'I was just the messenger.'

'And I suppose you're calling now because he's been in touch. Is he back from . . . honeymoon now?' She said the word 'honeymoon' through gritted teeth; it seemed so distasteful in this context. 'As far as he's concerned, Amy and the boys could have starved – messing around with their finances like that.'

'Nick?' Paul sounded confused and defensive. 'No . . . No, I haven't heard from him.'

Elspeth didn't believe him for one second. 'Amy always said you lived in each other's pockets.'

'That was one of her favourite complaints,' Paul agreed. 'On the other hand, I didn't know he was seeing Anneka. He managed to keep that a secret from me.'

'So you say.'

Another pause. 'Nick didn't say how long he was going to be away exactly. But that isn't why I was calling. I went round to the flat last night. Amy didn't seem to be in, but the car was there. I was worried –'

'How noble.' Elspeth couldn't batten down her sarcasm.

'I know I could have gone round sooner,' Paul ploughed on.

'I guess that Amy probably won't want to see me, but . . .' Elspeth sensed him shrug, at a loss for the right words. 'I *am* involved. Nick saw to that.'

'As I'm well aware, although I have to say, I've never understood it. Why didn't Nick just let Rowena do his dirty work? She's the boys' grandmother. Virtually Amy's mother-in-law – or was, before this Anneka materialised. I'm just surprised she hasn't stuck her beak in before now.' Elspeth bit her lip. Grief, this wasn't like her at all. She had been brought up to be more civilised. George would be turning in his grave. The lack of sleep was obviously doing strange things to her brain.

'My mother spoke to Rowena the other day,' Paul was explaining. 'She probably won't be back from Spain until June.' Yet another pause. 'I'm pleased the kids have at least one grandmother they can count on.'

Soften me up, why don't you? thought Elspeth sourly. It won't work. I'm not one of your . . . your floozies. 'Paul, I appreciate you calling,' she fibbed. 'But the reason no one was at the flat yesterday is that they've been staying round here.'

'All of them?' Paul seemed surprised.

'Of course, "all of them". They haven't got anyone else. Amy couldn't cope on her own, pretending nothing was wrong.' Elspeth cut herself short, before she could add that her daughter was still refusing to talk about what had happened, even with her. It was none of Paul's business to know how badly Amy was taking it. What if it filtered back to Nick?

'Isn't it a bit of a . . . squeeze?' Paul persisted.

'We're managing, thank you,' Elspeth retorted, unleashing her tongue again. 'She's better off here, anyway. Everywhere you turn at the flat, there's something to remind her of him. If it wasn't for the kids, she probably would have trashed the place. Cut up his suits and smashed up his CD collection. Something along those lines. And I wouldn't have blamed her.'

'Amy would never do that,' Paul protested. 'She isn't capable.'

Elspeth felt anger churn even more virulently in her stomach. Even people who had known her daughter for years seemed to be under the misconception that Amy was some sort of meek little drudge who would never harm a flea.

Elspeth wanted to yell to the world that that wasn't the daughter she had reared, the daughter George had doted on. Yes, Amy Amanda Croft was a good person, but how was it that people could make this sound disparaging? It was Nick who had rendered her submissive, and Elspeth had been helpless to do anything about it; or so she had persuaded herself at the time.

Now, remorse struck her at the notion that she had been apathetic and weak for allowing things to get so bad. For letting Amy put up with Nick's brashness and egotism. If he had been abusing her physically, Elspeth would have stepped in. But why had she just stood by and watched him quietly erode her daughter's confidence and spirit?

'Amy is more than capable of slashing a few suits,' Elspeth glared down the phone, wishing Paul were standing in front of her so he could fully appreciate it.

'Nick must be . . . very trusting then,' he replied, still sounding doubtful that Amy would be able to inflict that much damage.

'If Amy hadn't been as trusting of *him*, Nick wouldn't have been able to keep quiet about Anneka for as long as he did. But that's to his credit, if you want to see it from his point of view,' Elspeth continued acerbically.

'Which I don't!' Paul was starting to sound as if frustration were getting the better of him. 'I don't agree with what he's done. I'm on Amy's side.'

'For the first time ever. Which, I'm sure you'll agree, is a bit late. She's hardly going to start seeing you as some kindly benefactor or avuncular confidant.'

'Sorry?'

Elspeth was aware that she was talking the way her husband would have done. Even after all these years, she could slip behind the shield he had forged for her as easily as if he were still there. Perhaps because her own feelings were in disarray, it was easier just to believe in what George would have thought of all this. He wouldn't have had much time for the young man on the other end of the phone, Elspeth was convinced of that.

'Look,' Paul was saying, 'could you please just tell Amy I called. If she wants to talk, she knows where she can get hold of me. I know that sounds clichéd, but I really mean it.'

That was Paul all over, thought Elspeth disdainfully – one ridiculous cliché. From his rakish, black sports car, to his playboy bachelor pad overlooking the river, which probably housed a plethora of chrome and leather, capped off with a six-foot-wide waterbed.

'I will,' she said, having no intention of doing so. 'Goodbye,' she added, and put the phone down.

6

Amy could hear the voices of her sister and eldest son through the bedroom wall. It was only plasterboard, put in by the previous owners to divide one large room into two smaller ones.

'What you doing?' Joseph was asking.

'Curling my lashes,' replied Tilly.

'Does it hurt?'

'Nah . . . Looks worse than it is.'

Amy stared at the ceiling and tugged at the duvet, drawing it up over her shoulders.

'Are you ready for nursery?' Tilly asked.

'Mummy calls it school sometimes. I'm ready, but Mikey's brushing his teeth. Nana's going to take us again. Mummy's not well yet.'

Amy squirmed in her mother's bed. She had been sleeping in here during the day – and lying awake most nights – since that afternoon at the supermarket when Jonathan Simmons had come to her rescue. Her mother had insisted that Amy have her room. 'Joseph and Mikey can have the spare room, with the mattresses and sleeping bags, and I'll use the sofa-bed in the lounge, with the travel cot next to me.' Elspeth wouldn't hear otherwise.

'Nana says she can drive you, too,' Joseph told his young aunt now.

'Um – I think I'll get the bus as usual,' said Tilly nonchalantly. 'It's a bit out of Nana's way.'

There was a moment of silence, broken by Tilly scrabbling about behind the door, probably for her rucksack.

'Will Mummy get better soon?' Joseph asked suddenly.

Amy held her breath.

'Of course she will,' said Tilly at last, without sounding convincing.

'When Daddy gets back from holiday?'

'Er . . .'

'I want to go back home. My toys are there.'

'You've got some here . . .'

'I want my Spider-Man.'

Amy closed her eyes.

It had been her mother who had gone back to the flat and packed a couple of suitcases with what she perceived as the essentials. Elspeth had insisted, as with most things lately. But it wasn't as if Amy had felt railroaded into staying at Mews Cottage. She had given in without much of a fight, detaching herself from Jonathan and Elspeth's discussion as if she were merely an impartial onlooker.

Firstly, Jonathan explaining what had happened at the supermarket, and how Amy had been in no fit state to drive. Next, Elspeth insisting on writing him a cheque to cover the cost of the groceries, and declaring that there was nothing else for it – Amy would have to come and stay with her, in spite of the cramped conditions they would be under.

It had been easy to slip into this semi-catatonic state. No one had stopped her. On the contrary, they had closed the bedroom door and let her get on with it. The only time her mother pushed her was when she brought in a tray of food and cajoled Amy to try to eat *something*.

Rubbing her stiff neck, Amy heaved herself upright in bed. She reached out and fumbled for her glasses on the cluttered bedside table. They were poking out from beneath the box of tissues. Amy put them on and blinked around, catching sight of her reflection in her mother's antique cheval mirror. Her father had bought it as a gift the Christmas before he had died, but her mother would still have sold it if Amy hadn't intervened.

Amy had always imagined that a bereaved partner would hang on to every last scrap belonging to their late loved one; every gift they had ever received, every memory. But her mother had virtually done the opposite – getting rid of almost everything, as if it was all too painful to look at and always would be.

Amy's reflection in the mirror was like Medusa on a bad snake day. She glanced away quickly, and tried to work out what day of the week it was.

Her hand reached out instinctively for the tissue box, but then it struck her that she wasn't crying. The box was only half empty, and she hadn't noticed her mother replenish it. Somewhere along the line, the tears had dried up, but she couldn't remember when.

It wasn't as if she was numb inside. There was still a grey heaviness weighing her down, and the ache in her belly was raw and grating. But the supply of tears seemed to have run out, and she wasn't certain if that was a good thing or whether it had been better to bury her face in a wet pillow and expel as much misery as possible in one go, before the next wave hit.

Suddenly, she became aware of the silence, as loud in some ways as the voices that would drift through the walls and door. Had everyone gone? How long had she been sitting like this, staring into space?

Amy retrieved her dressing gown from the floor and shrugged it on over her thin nightie. She shuffled to the toilet, and a minute or so later was negotiating the rickety staircase to the lounge. She wasn't tall, or even average height, but she still had to bend her head at the last step to avoid the solid, black ceiling beam at the bottom.

There was no one there. It reminded Amy of a ghost town. The radio was tuned quietly into Classic FM in the kitchen, and the video in the lounge was still playing Mikey's Tweenies video, albeit on mute. Amy blinked at Jake and Milo having an argument, as Bella stomped about and Fizz tossed her dreadlocks. Before she became absorbed, merely for the sake of having some kind of distraction, Amy switched it off and drifted into the kitchen.

There were cereals scattered over the small round table, and the two elder boys' melamine bowls with Bob the Builder and Thomas the Tank Engine emblazoned on them were still there on the plastic tablecloth, each standing in its own puddle of milk.

At least she'd never had to endure Barbie. Amy was grateful for that much. It would have been the major downside to having a daughter. She'd had enough of that particular doll and all her assets when she'd been young herself. Few little girls would grow up feeling secure about their looks when their first role model was a cute, pert blonde with a minuscule waist, endless legs and long shiny hair. Amy had found consolation in the discovery that even Barbie's luscious locks could be reduced to a mass of frizz, particularly when subjected to Mummy's hairdryer.

Amy picked up the bowls and carried them dripping to the sink. Bugger. That hadn't been clever. With a paper towel, she wiped up the drops on the floor and was just flipping back the lid of the bin when there was a knock on the front door. Amy looked up with a frown. Someone was waving at her through the lounge window. She pushed her glasses back up her nose and looked again.

It was Jonathan Simmons. Trying to pat down her matted hair, redolent of that long-gone, doomed Barbie, she went to open the door. Jonathan was dressed in smart navy trousers, a white shirt and conservatively patterned tie, with a scuffed leather jacket to ward off the chill.

'Hello,' muttered Amy, huddling into the dressing gown. 'On your way to work?'

He nodded. 'I was just going to my car when I saw you through the window. Thought I'd just check how you were. Your mother said you hadn't been well . . .'

If a broken heart could be classified as a sickness, she'd been at death's door. Still was, effectively, even though she found herself making the effort to ask, 'Would you like to come in . . .? I can make some tea.' But that was simply proof that she was definitely her mother's daughter, some of the time at least. Elspeth would make a brew at the drop of a hat. 'Of course, you can't,' Amy faltered. 'You're on your way to work.'

Jonathan consulted his watch. 'It's OK, I can spare ten minutes.' And he stepped inside before Amy could change her mind.

7

Paul's parents lived in a bungalow. But it was no ordinary lace-nets-at-the-window, pebbledashed affair. It had been designed by a Californian in the late Sixties. Even after having called it his home for over twenty years before he'd moved out, Paul often felt a faint awe as he turned into the crescent of block-paved driveway to be greeted by the sight of the sprawling white house with the red-tiled roof and the arched windows. As if he'd magically been transported from North Wales to Beverly Hills. It was perched dramatically above blooming herbaceous borders interspersed with unpronounceable varieties of exotic-looking, spiky flora, and a sweeping lawn, as perfect as any golf course green, with about as much upkeep.

Perhaps it was the fact that he had grown up here that had first inspired him to become an architect. He couldn't actually remember a particular defining moment. But he'd always liked drawing, and instead of doodling geeky cartoon characters with goggling eyes or hangdog faces like the other boys used to, he'd drawn buildings. Sketches from his own imagination, which had made his mother tut and his father smile.

This morning he was too knackered to register awe. He'd received his summons to come here yesterday evening from his mother, who had texted him, as she often did, asking him to come over first thing. Any ordinary mother would have phoned for a chat, adding affectionately, 'I need to talk business with you, love, would you mind popping over when you have a minute?' But then again, how many sons worked for their parents? A small proportion, Paul supposed. Including, of course, Nick.

Yet while Nick was always getting things right when it came to Faulkner Jones Burnley, Paul constantly seemed to be having run-ins with his parents and Rowena. 'We're building a three-bed semi-detached,' they might chide him, 'not a replica of Hampton Court.' Of course, they were exaggerating, but his idea of a three-bed house, for instance, was always more generous than theirs. As far as he was concerned, there was no point calling a room a bedroom if you couldn't physically fit a bed in it.

Nick deputised for his mother in the sales department, which was at the other end of the spectrum, as far as Paul was concerned. For architecture and design, you needed to have a soul. For sales, it usually helped if you didn't.

Of course, Francesca was an exception. She seemed to appreciate Paul's craft, and specialised in selling houses that appealed to a more discerning clientele. The spec sheets he'd seen on her coffee table certainly weren't advertising run-of-the-mill semis. And the prices they were going for . . . Francesca had had to wrestle them out of his grasp, accusing him of being too distracted.

'Can we talk flesh and blood, for a change – not bricks and mortar,' she'd said provocatively, pinning him to the sofa.

The recollection was making Paul hot around his Ted Baker collar as he let himself into his parents' house.

The hall was spectacular and took most strangers by surprise. Straight in front of the main door was a central atrium – the basic idea hailing back to the ancient Romans and their innovative villas. Light was refracted through a myriad of glass panes on to a solar-powered, continuously running water feature. There was a decorative cluster of brilliantly glazed, bespoke pots, lush with ferns and palms, and a stone bench that no one ever used stood at the far end.

Beyond the atrium was a wide passage leading to the kitchen at the rear of the house. Paul followed the enticing aroma of fresh coffee. Jamaican Blue Mountain, he guessed. His new shoes squeaked on the floor tiles imported directly from the Continent, which had replaced the dated shagpile that had carpeted the corridor when he'd been a boy.

His dad was in the process of pouring the coffee from the filter machine. 'Oh – hello, son. Your mother mentioned you were coming. Fancy a cup?' He gestured with the pot.

Paul shook his head, then nodded. 'Actually, I will. Make it a black one.'

'Late night?'

'Francesca cooked dinner at her place.'

Kendrick Jones registered respect. His face relaxed enough to wink. 'I'm impressed. I honestly didn't think you were going to crack that one.'

Paul smiled. He couldn't help himself. It was jarring, frightening and fantastic, all at the same time. 'I think she's taming me, rather than the other way around.'

'About time someone did. When I was your age, I'd already met your mother.'

'And she'd whipped you into shape, had she?' Paul regarded his father with fond amusement. There was something of a harmless lech about him, twiddling his sandy-grey moustache whenever there was an attractive young lady around, and flirting with her as if he were still in his thirties and divinely handsome.

Paul's parents had met when Isabelle had been on vacation in Europe with her grandparents and brother – a sort of grand tour, Paul surmised. The details were sparse; he couldn't help thinking he might have added to them himself unconsciously over the years . . .

Northern France, somewhere near Calais. A misty, rainy night. Two cars colliding on a bend – but at low speed, no one was badly hurt . . . Two families had come together that night. Two young tourists united by fate. An American girl from Boston, and a Welsh lad from Ruthin.

Paul wondered if it had been love at first sight – a physical thing or the recognition of two kindred spirits.

Kendrick's father, William Jones, had already established a thriving building firm in the residential property sector with his partner, Phillip Burnley, Rowena's first husband and her senior by almost twenty years. Kendrick, following in his dad's footsteps, clearly had prospects. Yet Paul couldn't help thinking that Great-grandpa Faulkner might have been expecting Isabelle to settle down with a clean-cut, wholesome, all-American boy back in Boston. A doctor or lawyer, maybe, who'd been to Harvard or Yale.

He'd never pressed his mother or father about it, though. Maybe if he'd been a girl with romance in her soul and a penchant for Mills and Boon, he would have asked. Or maybe if his parents had been more forthcoming . . .

Kendrick now sighed resignedly. 'I suppose "whipping me into shape" has been your mother's lifelong vocation.'

'The other being to marry me off one day?' Paul added archly.

'You know there's a bit more to it than that. But she'd like you to settle down with a nice girl, preferably one as ambitious as her. It's the grandchildren she's not keen on. Just look at Rowena.'

Paul felt his brow crumple. 'Rowena should consider herself lucky.'

'You don't have to tell me. I like those three boys. But I think your mother still remembers the day Nick brought the eldest two over here, before the little one came along. They dug up one of her cordylines and left chocolate stains on her bedspread. I never had the heart to tell her I'd caught them using the bed as a trampoline.'

Paul smirked. 'Boys will be boys. Buy them a proper trampoline and they won't go near it. Sod's law. But what about you, Dad? Wouldn't you like grandkids? Not that I'm promising anything, mind.'

His father studied the Denby cup in his hand. 'You've never asked me that before . . . Francesca must really be getting to you.'

'I'm not afraid of commitment.' Paul puffed out his chest defensively. 'It's just been easier in some ways to let everyone assume it. I guess it's right what they say, though, it is a case of waiting for the right girl.' He took a swig of coffee. 'I'm not saying that's Francesca, of course. It's still early days. But I can't say that she isn't the one, either.'

His father snorted. 'Well it's a start.'

'It's more than I hoped for,' said another voice. 'Why aren't you wearing your slippers, darling? I bought them especially for you at Browns.'

'A couple of quid at the market would have done me,' Paul murmured churlishly, glancing round.

His mother was standing by the door that led to her office. 'You've never worn anything from a market in your life!' It was the verbal equivalent of a cuff around the ear. 'How are you anyway?' She came over, offered him her cheek, then took the coffee cup her husband handed her without her even having to ask.

It was a double act that had fascinated Paul since he'd reached adulthood and had started embarking on relationships himself, if you could even call them that. His parents seemed so disparate in some ways, yet their life together, both the business side and the personal, ran like cogs smothered in WD-40.

'I'm fine, Mum.' It was Paul's customary reply. He would probably say it even if he was hobbling about with a broken leg. 'How are you?'

'The same as ever. It's your father I'm worried about. I think he's been overdoing it lately.'

Paul turned to his dad. He didn't look any different from usual. 'Well, if I were a doctor, I'd prescribe a well-earned rest, not more of those vitamin mixes you like concocting. For one, they don't mix well with caffeine.' Paul sighed, suddenly serious. 'Why don't you take a holiday, Dad?'

'I have. Your mother and I went to Egypt.'

'That was four years ago. It doesn't count any more. What about that Far East trip you're always talking about?'

Isabelle Faulkner Jones gave an empty laugh. 'An entire month off?'

'Why not?'

'Because I just can't spare the time, darling.'

Paul shook his head frustratedly. 'You could *make* time.'

'People who say that have too much of it on their hands.'

Paul gritted his teeth. This was familiar territory, and never much fun, least of all at half eight in the morning. 'Listen, Mum, you wanted to see me about something . . .'

'I did.' She sighed heavily. 'I think it's best if we go through to my office.'

Paul put his cup down by the sink. 'OK.' As he turned to follow his mother, his father called out after him.

'When your mother's finished with you, Paul, I'd like a chat myself. I've a new project I'd like to run by you. Your mother isn't keen, but she's not putting her foot down, either. And I spoke to Rowena last night, and she's given me the thumbs up.'

Paul glanced round with a flicker of interest. 'Oh?'

'Cherry Tree Farm, just outside Harrisfield – do you know it?'

'I've driven past it enough times. The main building's quite interesting, from a local heritage point of view. They do pick-your-own stuff in the summer, right?'

'The farmer's selling off a couple of the lower fields. Cash-flow problem, apparently. But, the good news is, they've already been designated for building.' His dad's eyes lit up like the Blackpool Illuminations. Paul was always slightly envious of how a new idea could generate fresh fervour in his father, even after all these years. 'I'm thinking, "four-bed, detached—"'

'"—executive homes".' Paul finished the description for him, trying not to sound disappointed. 'Double garage? En suite to the master bedroom with shower *and* bath?'

His father pointed at him, almost gleefully. 'That's my boy.'

Paul had a compulsion to really delight his father by skipping around the kitchen shouting 'Yippee' as if he were nine years old. He'd never done that when he was nine, though, so it would be ridiculous to start now. He knew the reaction his father wanted was more than just a bog-standard, 'Sounds like a good idea, Dad.' Yet suddenly today, for some reason, Paul's supply of phoney enthusiasm was on the wane. He really wanted to point out that at sixty-three it was time to start taking things a little easier; but he knew his dad hated to be reminded of his age.

'You can have our son all to yourself when I'm through with him,' said Isabelle. 'I have to pop into Chester anyway. That little boutique in Watergate Street was putting a suit aside, and I need to go in and try it on.'

'Yes, my love.' Kendrick sighed, and poured himself another coffee.

Isabelle led Paul through to her tastefully appointed office in the annexe where she conducted her own family's business affairs over the Atlantic. The Faulkner Publishing Group had been set up by Paul's great-great-grandfather in the early part of the twentieth century, although it had gone by a different name back then. Starting out as a simple little enterprise printing religious books, it had expanded and diversified and was still successfully snowballing, as far as Paul could tell.

The head honcho – in title, at least – was Isabelle's younger brother, Louis. But everyone knew he was a little too mild mannered to play such a vital role, and was merely a puppet in his sister's control. It was also common knowledge here in the UK that Isabelle was more interested in her American affairs than in Faulkner Jones Burnley, but no one had ever dared suggest she take her fingers out of one pie and keep them solely in the other.

Paul's mother ushered him into one of the easy chairs positioned in a welcoming manner by the window, before settling herself in another. It was less formal than sitting behind her desk, although she had been known to do that even with her own son.

'So?' Paul was oddly nervous. Something seemed different about this summons, and then he realised that his mother had yet to give a reason for it.

'Paul,' she threaded her hands together in her lap, 'I wanted to speak to you privately, as soon as possible, before I told anyone else. Including your father.' She seemed to hesitate. 'Of course, *Rowena* knows, but . . .'

'Rowena?' Paul felt thrown. 'Is this about Nick?'

'As his friend, you ought to be among the first to know . . . he's not planning on coming back to Faulkner Jones Burnley. In fact, he's not planning on coming back to the UK in any hurry, either.'

Paul blinked. 'I – I don't understand. He's only on honey-moon.'

'*Was*. Until Monday, when he started working for the Faulkner Group.'

Paul opened and closed his mouth.

'The marketing department, in the Boston head office,' Isabelle elucidated, suddenly leaning forwards and speaking ardently. 'Now don't jump to any conclusions, darling, saying that I headhunted him or meddled in something that had nothing to do with me. Nick approached me a couple of months ago. He was wondering if I'd have any use for him in the Faulkner Group. He was looking for a new challenge, but something altogether more radical than a simple change of scene at FJB. I was surprised, and, of course, I asked him how Amy felt about it. But he was strangely non-committal . . . Now we all know why.'

'But you've still gone ahead and hired him?' Paul's voice had an unmistakable tremor. 'And I don't understand . . . why didn't Nick tell me all this before he left?'

'Too many bombshells in one go, I imagine.'

'Or maybe because he's the biggest coward I've ever known . . .' Paul scowled abruptly. 'And I still can't believe your part in this . . .'

His mother shrugged. 'I don't want to be seen as taking sides, but Nick's amazing at what he does. You know that better than anyone. He could sell a Big Mac to a vegetarian, and even though publishing's a different industry from the one he's used to, I know he's sharp enough to adapt.'

'You really think it was a good idea to give Nick a job thousands of miles away from his family? How are they going to feel about that?'

'Anneka is his family, too, now, Paul. And as for the children, they're very young. The perfect age, really – they adjust so fast. Nick's assured me he'll visit as regularly as work allows. And when they're older, the boys can go over to see him.'

'So they won't even have a weekend father. It'll be a once-every-quarter one – if that.'

'Paul, darling, I think you're escalating the situation. I know that Nick's a very close friend and you're going to miss him, but he's entitled to make a new life for himself. It could be easier for Amy, too, this way – in the long run. Nick thinks it might be best to give her time and space to get over it. I'm inclined to agree with him.'

'What does Rowena have to say about it?'

'She's not happy about letting him go, but she's not dashing over to try to talk him out of it, either. She won't be begging him to come home. She accepts that he's an adult and can make his own decisions.'

'I meant about her grandchildren, and their mother,' said Paul bitingly. 'Doesn't she owe them anything? A visit, maybe?'

'Amy's hardly going to be overjoyed to see her; I really think the poor girl needs time, Paul, rather than attention. And the children are used to Rowena being away for half the year, so it's not as if they're missing out. They'll still be getting their "pocket money", the same as always, so don't make it sound as if Rowena's washed her hands of them.'

Paul shook his head, stunned and exasperated, resentment growing by the second. He hadn't been able to help missing Nick these past three weeks, but he'd probably clout him now if he laid eyes on him. And his mother had sounded about as sincere as a bent politician when she'd referred to Amy as 'the poor girl'.

'I think you're jealous, darling,' Isabelle stated suddenly, commanding his attention the way she seemed to know best – with a contentious remark.

'Jealous?' echoed Paul, with a feeble attempt at a sneer.

'As my only child, you know I've always hoped you'd show some interest in the Faulkner Group. Your cousins are hardly worth grooming to take over the company, even your uncle agrees with that . . .'

'Mum, I thought you'd know better than to dredge this up again, or try to use Nick as leverage. I'm sorry, but my ambitions are never going to lie in that direction.' Paul scraped back his chair and stood up, towering over her. He'd had enough of her for one day. 'If Nick's the sort of son you've always wanted, you're welcome to him.'

'Paul' – as he turned away, his mother threw another verbal boomerang – 'what about Amy? She isn't aware of Nick's new plans.'

Paul smouldered darkly over his shoulder as the comprehension hit. 'You want me to tell her – don't you?'

'I think it would be better coming from someone she considers a friend, rather than from me. I think she finds me a little . . . intimidating.'

Don't we all, Paul wanted to retort. Doesn't mean we're going to crumple in a pathetic heap at your feet chanting, 'We're not worthy.'

He felt a dismaying sense of déjà vu as he contemplated approaching Elspeth again, but then realised that he couldn't keep hiding behind her. Although he'd suspected that he would have to play intercessor again at some point, he hadn't imagined it would involve his mother rather than Nick personally.

'There's something else,' said Isabelle, gazing distantly out of the window as Paul intensified his glare. 'It's about Nick's flat . . . Would you happen to know if Amy has a good solicitor?'

8

'Are you sure about this? It's very kind of you . . .' Amy glanced sideways at Jonathan, who was in the driving seat yet again. 'If I'd had my car at Mum's—'

'You still would have needed someone to go to the flat with you. It's not the kind of thing you should do alone. At least, not yet.'

'I suppose it could have waited. It didn't have to be today . . .'

'If you keep putting it off, it might get harder rather than easier. Thinking about doing something like this is always worse than just getting on with it.' Jonathan shrugged. 'That's how I see it. Anyway, you shouldn't feel guilty on my account. I've got more time to take off than I know what to do with, and I've never taken a day's sick leave. They can't complain if I need to take an "emergency" day off without notice. Besides, I've never pulled rank since I was promoted.'

Amy chewed on a fingernail, only half listening as Jonathan droned on about his job behind the scenes in a bank. He was probably trying to distract her from dwelling too much on what she was about to do, but the subject matter was hardly riveting, at least, not the way he was telling it. Amy was also beginning to wish she'd left her mother more than just that hastily scribbled Post-it note: '*Gone to the flat to pick up a few things. Don't worry.*'

Inevitably, her mother *would* worry, and might jump straight back into her car and dash after her into Chester.

Venturing home was something Amy wanted – needed – to do without a biased onlooker. She knew Elspeth would pass comment on everything from the contents of the fridge to the fact that Nick's dressing gown was still hanging behind the en suite door.

Amy's resolve had been growing ever since she'd heard Joseph talking to Tilly that morning. In her struggle to make conversation over a cup of tea with Jonathan, she had mentioned she was going to get the bus into town, pick up some stuff from the flat and drive her car back to her mum's.

Jonathan had immediately insisted on taking her. 'What are friends for?' he'd argued, when she'd baulked at the idea.

Amy was dimly aware that her mother had accepted Jonathan's help to ferry the Espace from the supermarket car park where it had been 'abandoned', back to the flat, considering it hadn't been needed elsewhere at that time. Still, Amy hadn't thought of Jonathan as a friend in a conventional sense, just a kind do-gooder. She knew her mother and Tilly had never considered him a friend, either; not in a true sense. He was just . . . *there*. Part and parcel of living in Mews Cottage.

'The visitors' spaces are just over here,' pointed Amy, as they drove into the car park. Her heart started thudding as Jonathan switched off the engine. He turned to face her.

'Ready?'

She nodded, but couldn't move. 'What if he's back?' she muttered suddenly. 'What if he's been here?' Her hand on the passenger door handle, she stared up at her apartment block.

'But you haven't heard from him? I mean, if he were back in the country, he'd have got in touch somehow – wouldn't he? The kids, after all . . .' Jonathan tailed off. 'Amy, is the flat in both your names?'

She shook her head. 'I let Nick take care of all that stuff. It just seemed easier. He was paying the mortgage and the other bills. When I was working, before the kids came along, my salary was just a bonus . . . The bank account's about the only thing that's joint, and there are no savings in there . . .'

'What about the boys, do they have children's accounts, or—'

'Rowena's in charge of those. Something to do with tax.'

As Jonathan nodded knowingly, an immense sense of naïvety descended on Amy. She felt as fragile as antique bone china. The term 'common-law wife' charged into her head, barbaric and ugly. Did it really have valid legal connotations? And was she still theoretically a 'wife' at all if her 'husband' was now married to someone else?

'These last few weeks, I've been living in a bubble.' She inhaled deeply. 'I've been trying so hard not to think. Now, it's as if – as if my brain's out of practice.'

'You've got the key to the flat?'

Amy took it out of her bag and dangled it in mid-air, as if it were giving off an offensive smell.

'Then let's just see what we find,' said Jonathan firmly. 'Come on.'

He led the way, as Amy concentrated on the ox-like width of his shoulders. In the past, he had seemed so weedy. Perhaps he was one of those people who shone in a crisis. A natural leader who only came into his own when circumstances pushed him to the fore.

The flat seemed to be just as Amy could vaguely remember leaving it. If Nick had been here recently, regardless of whether he'd been in a hurry, the Lego wouldn't still be lying scattered on the lounge rug and the toilet seat in the small cloakroom wouldn't be up. He was a stickler for having everything in its place. If it had been up to him, the children's possessions – and maybe even the children themselves – would have been confined to the nursery. Amy had allowed this fact to skim over her before, but there was no reason to let it do so any more. Like everything else, she had to face it head-on.

'He wasn't cut out for this,' she said dully, scooping up the Lego and depositing it back in its box. 'You only have to look around . . . you can see what's mine and the kids' and you can tell a mile off what's Nick's.'

Jonathan surveyed the open-plan lounge, dining area and kitchen. 'There does seem to be a clash of personalities here.'

Amy snorted, with a derision directed mainly at herself. 'It's easy to kid yourself when you know the only other option is being on your own.'

She walked down the corridor leading to the bedrooms, Jonathan trailing behind. She could sense that he was taking everything in, absorbing the tiniest details from a fresh perspective.

'There was a time I kept pushing for a house,' she went on. 'The full works, you know – utility room, conservatory, garden . . . The garden was the big thing. But Nick said there wasn't really any need when I could just walk to a park. They've got swings there, and they're free.' She came to a shuddering halt at her bedroom door. 'I suppose buying a house just took us one step closer to marriage and "cosy domesticity". And Nick didn't want that . . . at least, not with me.'

'Amy, unless there's something here that you really need for yourself, why don't you just pick up the stuff you wanted for the kids? You don't have to put yourself through this . . .'

Jonathan had obviously changed his mind about the wisdom of them being here. He was just trying to be considerate and make this easier on her, but it only served to provoke Amy. Defiance hardened in her throat. She rattled the door open and stalked in. The bed she had once shared with Nick was a jumble of king-size, white percale duvet. Her mother evidently hadn't stopped to tidy up when she'd packed a few essentials, but then Elspeth had a slightly chaotic streak in her, too. Nick had used to lose patience with this, as if he blamed his 'mother-in-law' for passing it on to Amy.

Everything that Nick had left behind was still there, untouched. His suits, ties and shirts, the polished shoes, the various gadgets and gizmos, including his scientific-precision, projection alarm clock, which he'd shouted at Joseph for fiddling with all too often.

Amy stood in front of the open wardrobe doors and swallowed the urge to tear all of Nick's clothes to the floor. She knew she would only feel worse afterwards.

Jonathan was hovering close by. Amy turned to him, her hands cupping her face, the fingers pressing into her temples as if she had a headache that refused to budge. 'He wouldn't care,' she muttered.

'Sorry?' Jonathan took a cautious step closer.

'Nick . . . he wouldn't care if I trashed his stuff. He cares about *things*, possessions . . . If the kids touched them, if I put something in the wrong place . . . But in another way, he doesn't care at all, because I know he'd just go and replace everything with the equivalent – or better. I'm not sure if that makes him materialistic or not.'

'It certainly doesn't make him sentimental.'

Amy snorted again. She glanced around her bedroom of five years. 'I always thought *I* was – until now . . . The boys were babies in this flat. I tried to make it into as much of a family home as I could, but right now . . . I hate it. I totally hate it.'

Her supply of tears was clearly replenished; she could feel them swelling painfully in her throat, as if there wasn't enough room. But she'd broken down once already in front of Jonathan, and the more she allowed herself to feel weak, the more she would start believing it.

'Spider-Man,' she muttered, pretending she had some grit in her eye. 'Joe wanted his Spider-Man. Can you help me look for it?'

The toy turned up in the laundry basket. 'They sometimes

hide stuff in here,' Amy explained, picking up a couple of things for Mikey and Lucas while she was at it. 'They want to come home, you know,' she said softly, stroking the tuft of fur which was all that remained of Mikey's panda's right ear. 'Or Joe does. I don't know about Mikey . . . I don't know much lately when it comes to how they're feeling. I don't think I've taken them properly into account in any of this. They think their father's on holiday or working away or something. I've just been so wrapped up in myself . . .'

'It's understandable. But there's no point bringing the kids back here if you know you're only going to be miserable yourself. Your state of mind reflects directly on them. Besides, they're so young, Amy – they'll adjust soon enough to living at your mum's.'

'But we can't.' She sighed. 'We can't stay with Mum long term, there isn't enough room. It isn't fair on her or Tilly.'

'Elspeth doesn't mind, does she?'

'She'd never say, even if she did. Which she doesn't,' Amy conceded, 'because she's not that type of person. Mum thrives on being . . . put upon.'

'So what are you saying? If you don't want to live here—'

'I don't even know if I *can* live here. I probably have some sort of claim, because I've been with Nick for so many years, but I've no idea what his plans are . . . He might want to live here himself.'

The notion made her feel sick. She sat down on Mikey's low bed, trawling a hand through her hair. It felt greasy and tangled, which made her more depressed. She hadn't bothered to comb it particularly well when she'd got ready this morning. She'd mainly concentrated on pulling on some clothes, and hadn't even brushed her teeth. They were probably in cold turkey, considering how much she used to brush them in the past.

'Amy.' Jonathan sat down beside her and took her hand. It

felt limp in his, but she didn't pull away. 'At the risk of sounding patronising,' he continued, 'I just want to say that things will get better. This time next year, you'll look back and you'll feel some sort of relief – maybe even pride – that you made it through. Some days will be better than others, but you'll cope if you take it one step at a time . . .'

She couldn't bear any more of this. It sounded like the speech her mother probably had reserved for her. Even though it made sense, it also infuriated her. Amy didn't want to hear it when she already knew it for herself. One platitude after another, as useless and annoying as 'there's plenty more fish in the sea'.

She drew her hand away and clambered to her feet. 'Thank you for all this,' she muttered. 'For helping. But I know I'll be fine. I've got to be,' she concluded stoically, 'for the boys' sake.'

Jonathan gazed up at her mutely. His eyes were hazel and deep and caring, yet this only wound her up more. She wished it didn't when, basically, she ought to feel gratitude. It was Nick who had hurt her, not this man she hardly knew who had gone out of his way to be kind. Perhaps she wasn't a nice person any more. Perhaps what had happened gave her the right to be resentful and bitter. Perhaps . . . But she still felt guilty alongside everything else.

'Do you want to go home soon?' Jonathan asked, then checked himself, 'I mean, back to your mum's?'

Amy nodded. It would have to be home for now, until she worked out what she was supposed to do with the rest of her life, apart from be a mother. Maybe that had been part of the problem, a reason why this had happened, even though thinking it made her feel worse. But was it fair to put all the blame on Nick? Had she stopped acting like his 'babe' once she had had babes of her own? Together, as a couple, they had shared something special once, but she couldn't remember the last time she had thought of their relationship with that warm, tingling glow that meant she cherished it above all else.

Being left this way was like being knocked off a known trajectory into an unknown one. But as Amy loaded a few bags and plastic storage crates into her car a while later, recalling thankfully that the Espace, at least, was registered in her name, she realised that no path from cradle to grave could ever be truly prepared for. There was usually something just around the bend, on its way to hit you. As if you were just a hedgehog, and life was one long road to cross.

Elspeth was in a tizzy. A few seconds ago, Mikey had snatched away the remote control from Joseph, who had turned round and thumped Mikey, who had fled bawling into the kitchen. The commotion had woken Lucas, now grizzling in the pram. And the ruddy phone was ringing.

Elspeth didn't know how to prioritise the situation. As a mother, she'd only had to deal with one baby or toddler at a time; and as a grandmother, she hadn't had all three at once on her own before this thing with Nick. How on earth did Amy cope? Especially after several nights of broken sleep. The cumulative effects were taking their toll on Elspeth like a bad bout of flu.

Just as she scooped up the baby from the pram, the front door opened and her eldest daughter and Jonathan Simmons walked in laden with crates and bags. The phone was still ringing, somehow sounding more imperious than ever.

'Amy!' cried Elspeth. 'Thank God. I was wondering where you were.'

'Didn't you get my note?' Amy unburdened herself of her cargo and crossed the lounge to the telephone stand.

'Note?' Elspeth glanced round. 'What note? I popped upstairs when I came home, to see if you needed anything, and when you weren't there—'

'On the kitchen table.' Amy pointed through the door. 'I thought you were bound to see it.' Frowning, she picked up the phone. 'Hello? A darkness crossed her face, like a storm brewing.

Elspeth clutched the baby tighter. 'Who is it?' she mouthed.

'No,' Amy was saying, 'no don't come here. I'll come to you . . . Yes. Yes, I'm sure . . . Of course I'm up to driving, I'm not an invalid . . . I'll see you later.' She slammed the phone down and crossed the room to take the baby.

'Amy,' Elspeth spoke out loud this time, 'who was that?'

'Paul.' Amy snuggled Lucas's head into the crook of her neck. 'He wants to see me. I said I'd go over to his . . . Apparently he's heard from Nick.'

'Oh, love!' Elspeth felt indignation swell in her breast, accompanied by the fervent desire of a lioness to protect her cub. 'I'll go with you—'

'No!' Amy shook her head emphatically. 'There's no need for you to be there. And there's no point putting it off, either. I have to get things sorted as soon as possible.'

'I don't mind—' Jonathan began to offer, but Amy cut him short, too.

'I'm fine. There are some things I have to do on my own.' Lucas had stopped whining; Amy gently passed him back to Elspeth, then turned to Jonathan again. 'Thanks for today, for everything. Taking the day off and—'

'It's OK. Don't worry about it. I'd – I'd better go.' Jonathan glanced towards the door but didn't make a move to leave. Elspeth nudged him nearer to it with her body language alone. He'd clearly been generous with his time, but she didn't think it stemmed purely from the kindness of his heart.

As the front door closed behind Jonathan, Joseph started poking about in one of the plastic crates his mum had carried in. 'Yay!' he cried exultantly. 'My Spider-Man!'

Elspeth looked on as Amy kissed him on the head and then

bent down to pick up a small, scruffy panda. She took it into the kitchen, along with the tatty, grey blankie that had been draped over the sofa. Mikey was still sniffing loudly, but moments later, he seemed miraculously assuaged.

Amy came back out. 'I think I need to feel human again before I face Paul. So if there's enough hot water, I'll go up and take a bath.'

Elspeth nodded. She wished her daughter wasn't so bull-headed sometimes. It was bound to be a difficult, emotive confrontation. Paul always rubbed her up the wrong way at the best of times. Elspeth really didn't think Amy could handle talking about Nick and the future yet, but she also knew her daughter well enough to realise there was no point telling her so. She could only pray that Paul would continue being as tactful and considerate as he'd so far made himself out to be.

9

Paul was looking forward to this even less than that root-canal work he'd had last year, but it wasn't something he could put off. He had even cancelled a date with Francesca, although she had been exceptionally understanding and had offered him moral support, if he wanted it. Paul hadn't thought Amy would welcome his girlfriend's presence, however. The women had met only once, at Rowena's wedding, and the conversation was hardly going to consist of polite small talk.

Amy and Francesca probably didn't have that much in common, either. Francesca would hardly be an expert on which brand of organic baby food was the best. And Amy apparently didn't share Francesca's penchant for flimsy underwear. Nick had once drunkenly complained that Amy bought her cotton knickers in discount packs of three, in plain, stripes and polka dot, and they seemed to get larger every time.

Paul had laughed back then, but now as he went to unlock his door, he couldn't remember why. He liked loose-fitting, cotton underwear, too, so he could hardly talk.

'Hello, Paul.' Amy stood at the top of the flight of stairs which led up from the hall. The intercom was on the blink, and the main door was being kept on the latch. He'd warned Amy about it on the phone.

Behind her gunmetal-framed glasses, her eyes were fierce, glittery and red-rimmed.

Paul tried to put her at ease with his friendliest voice,

without sounding as if he was hosting some kiddies' TV show. 'Hi! Come on in.'

'Thanks.' She stepped inside, relinquished her handbag and shrugged off her coat. 'Sorry I'm a bit late.'

'Don't worry. I've got all night.'

'No hot date lined up?' Amy's lips belied her attempt at humour – there wasn't even the merest hint of a smile.

'No. Not even a lukewarm one,' he joked back lamely. 'Not that your company isn't appreciated—'

She lifted a hand. 'It's me you're talking to, Paul. You don't have to treat me any differently just because of what's happened.'

He sighed, tugging at the cuffs of his shirt. A nervous habit he was vaguely aware of but derived a strange, ritualistic comfort from; like scratching the side of his nose. 'You're right. And this shouldn't stop us being friends. Thirteen years – it's a long time.'

Amy turned to face him, her eyebrows rising until they were lost under her heavy, mop-like fringe. 'Please don't start with that nostalgia crap now. We both know we put up with each other for Nick's sake, and I wouldn't be here now if it wasn't for him.'

Paul blinked at her, slightly taken aback. Amy had always been detached around him and about as approachable as a cactus, but she'd never spelled out her antipathy like this. It wasn't as if he felt the same way in return; his feelings were far more ambivalent. She wasn't much fun, and certainly not what he'd imagined for Nick. Maybe, inadvertently, he'd always let this show. In which case, he couldn't blame her implacability, least of all now.

'OK,' he said slowly. 'I wouldn't have put it *quite* like that myself. I know I'm not your favourite person.'

'Well you've gone down slightly in the ranking of non-favourites. Nick's overtaken you.' She brushed back her fringe in an exaggerated gesture, and he noticed the engagement ring had gone.

Paul could recall the day his friend had bought it. Nick had been genuinely excited at the prospect of fatherhood – the fantasy rather than the reality, though. The trendy clothes and accessories from Mamas & Papas and babyGap, rather than the mustard-yellow nappies and emotional neediness. The solitaire diamond had been an extravagant, impulsive gesture, and it was Paul who was normally the one prone to that type of behaviour. Yet he remembered how he had tried to talk Nick out of it. Or at least, make him face up to the responsibility that accompanied such an action. In a way, Paul realised now, he'd been as much on Amy's side as Nick's. But it was no consolation to know he'd been right.

Amy chewed on a thumbnail. When she looked up again, her expression had softened marginally. 'Look, I'm not here to have a go at you. This is just . . . difficult.'

The last time he'd seen her, he'd been pulling the rug from under her feet. Tonight he was about to start playing advocate for her ex, so the atmosphere was hardly going to lighten up. Every time she looked at him, she would probably see Nick. Maybe, perversely, though, that wasn't such a bad thing. She seemed to need to let off steam, as if everyone had been tiptoeing around her these last weeks. No doubt they had.

'Don't worry about it,' said Paul. 'Listen, we might as well have a drink. I've got a Chardonnay chilling in the fridge . . .'

'Just a coffee for me, please.'

'Oh, sorry, I was forgetting.' Before he knew it, he was gesturing to his firm pectorals, which he was rightly proud of considering how much his gym membership cost. 'The breast-feeding, right? I suppose you want decaff?'

She was looking at the floor again. 'Actually, I don't want to drink because I'm driving. And I'd rather have normal coffee, if you've got it. I'm not feeding Lucas myself any more.'

'Oh.' Paul was surprised. The first two boys had seemed grafted to her chest.

'Mum's been really brilliant with him, and I haven't been well . . .' Her voice was tinged with regret. 'He just took to the bottle really, so that was that. He's on solids now, too.'

Paul recalled that this primarily involved baby rice, which looked nothing like the grown-up variety. 'Hungry lad?'

'Like his brothers.'

Paul smiled, remembering how cherubic Joseph and Mikey had looked as babies. Dimpled and rosy cheeked; like their mother, for that matter, although their Nordic fairness came from Nick's side of the family. Yet as Paul regarded Amy now, he noted that she had lost some weight. He wasn't sure it suited her if it meant the bloom had gone from her cheeks. Her hair was scraped back into a ponytail, except for her heavy fringe and a few reddish-brown wisps around her ears, and it made her seem paler and a little wasted away.

Paul went into the kitchen, strangely wistful, as if an era had come to an end. And in a way, it had. It might not have been the most equilateral of triangles, but it had existed, whether he and Amy liked it or not. Now the three musketeers, of a sort, had been disbanded.

Amy appeared in the doorway, leaning awkwardly against the frame.

Paul glanced at her as he took out clean cups from the dishwasher. 'Espresso? Cappuccino?'

She stared at the coffee machine. 'Haven't you just got normal? You know, out of a jar?'

This was a strange one. Paul deliberately never bought the instant stuff. All the messing about with filters impressed the ladies much more, in spite of what the TV adverts implied. 'Er – no. I *have* got tea, if you'd prefer.' But even that was loose leaf from Marks & Spencer's. He recalled Amy favoured those pyramid-shaped bags.

'Can't you just make an ordinary coffee with the machine?' she went on. 'In a big mug? Nothing fancy. It's just, I feel like something a bit stronger than tea. I haven't been sleeping well and I've got to drive back to Mum's . . .'

'I understand. It's OK. Leave it to me.' He wondered if they were both deliberately procrastinating. Skirting around the real reason for her being here.

'So,' said Paul, when the coffee-making was well underway. 'How are the kids doing?'

Amy folded her arms over her chest. 'Fine, considering. Did Nick ask?'

Paul nodded, but didn't look at her. 'Of course. He was wondering what you'd told them exactly.'

'Not the truth,' said Amy, with a scathing note. 'Not yet. It would confuse them too much, and they're muddled enough as it is. They just think he's away, and we're staying at Nana's for a while because I've been ill. But they want to go home. The problem is, I'm not sure the flat can ever be home again. Not for me.'

'That's one of the things I wanted to talk to you about.' Paul held up two mugs, and gestured with his head towards the lounge. 'Let's sit in there. It's more comfortable.'

Once they were settled facing each other across the coffee table, Paul ploughed right on, without stalling further. 'Like I said on the phone, I spoke to Nick earlier . . .'

His mother had passed on Nick's new number, and in his agitation, Paul had completely forgotten about the small matter of the five-hour time difference. Serve Nick right. And speaking to him while he was still half asleep had probably worked in Paul's favour.

'So where is he then? At Anneka's?' Amy spoke the other woman's name with less venom than he would have expected.

'No. They're, um, still in the US.'

'Oh.' She blinked. 'That's a long time.'

'Amy, I'm not sure how to say this . . . Nick's got a new job over there . . . in Boston . . .'

'I – I don't understand . . .'

'For my mum's company. The Faulkner Group.'

Her eyes widened sharply, as if the lids were spring-loaded. 'He's not coming back to Chester?'

Paul shook his head. 'Not at the moment. For holidays, of course, but not permanently.'

Amy was silent for a long while. She rubbed a hand over her face, pausing to adjust her glasses. 'I see,' she said at last, too matter-of-factly for comfort. 'So where does that leave me and the boys, apart from destitute?'

Paul rested his hands together, as if praying. He possibly was, in a roundabout way. 'Nick wants to sell the flat . . . He thinks it would be best if everyone made a fresh start.'

'Does Anneka own her own place over here, too?'

'I believe so.'

'So they want to pool their resources and buy somewhere nice over there. Bully for them.'

'Amy, Nick will give you half of whatever he makes on the flat. That'll be in addition to maintenance for the boys, which will be paid once a month. The Espace is in your name, he explained, so that's yours, no argument. But he's given me the authority to sell his Saab privately.'

'What about all his other stuff?'

'He wants it shipped over to him.'

She sat looking stiffer and more straight-backed than ever. 'Lucky for him it's all still intact. But if he expects me to sort through it—'

'No, not at all. If you want to just take your own things, I'll arrange to have the rest packed up and sent over. Anyway,' Paul slid a sheet of paper across the table towards her, 'these are the terms of the agreement. Just notes I made, after I spoke to him. You can have a solicitor draft up something properly, if you want.'

Amy scanned the paper. Her expression remained blank. 'This "maintenance" – would that go up, or is it a fixed sum? Kids tend to get more expensive as they get older, and the cost of living doesn't exactly stagnate.'

'I'm sure it's always open to negotiation. Of course,' he broached, 'if you were to marry again. Well, not *again*, but—'

'What about this?' she interrupted, jabbing a finger at the bottom of the sheet. 'Does he really reckon he'll get that much for the flat?'

'Actually, that's what Francesca's valued it at.'

Amy looked up at him. 'You're still seeing her?'

'There's no need to be surprised!' Paul was instantly on the defensive, but a moment later, gave way. 'Well, maybe there is, with my track record. But she's different.'

'What – out of your league?'

'You've probably got a point there.' Paul struggled not to grin. This definitely wasn't the time to gloat over his own love life. 'She's a bloody good estate agent, and she'll get the best possible price for the flat if you agree to put it on the market with her. Nick did leave that up to you, considering you're in situ, as it were, and he isn't.'

'Whatever.' Amy shrugged. Her eyes glinted unnervingly. 'So, is that it then? Is this how the last thirteen years are going to be carved up?'

Paul put his hands together again. 'I feel really terrible . . .'

'What about the small matter of the kids – doesn't Nick expect to see them?'

'Of course he does. He, er, hopes to be over in the summer sometime.' Paul despised himself for sounding so casual about it. 'And when they're older—'

'They can go and stay with him? How civilised. He can fly them down to Florida and Disney World. That's exactly what a doting dad would do. As well as buy them loads of expensive gifts for their birthdays and Christmas. Perfect! They'll love that. And it's bound to ease his conscience.'

'Amy . . .' Paul couldn't imagine feeling lousier than he did right now.

She leapt to her feet. 'I need to use your toilet, if that's OK?'

'Er, yeah . . . sure.' He pointed down a corridor leading off from the lounge. 'Just down there.'

'I think I can remember my way round, thanks. You've had enough parties here. Different hostess each time, mind.' Amy offered him a chilling smile, before swaying off down the corridor as if she'd been indulging in too much wine after all.

Paul leaned forwards, burrowing his head in his hands, his throat tight and dry. He didn't want to have to go through anything like this again. Ever.

Amy broke off more toilet roll and blew her nose. She'd had to seek sanctuary in the bathroom. The tears had been threatening to engulf her, and the last thing she could have stood was Paul's pity. It would have been mortifying to have him put his arm around her and cap off his performance of giving a toss. Now, as the tears subsided, she was left with a hard nugget of anger in her stomach.

There was a gentle rap on the door. 'Amy . . . are you all right in there?'

She scowled, and rammed on her glasses. 'Fine – thanks. I'll be out in a second.' She flushed away the last scrap of toilet paper and washed her hands, so Paul wouldn't guess what she'd really been doing. As she dried them on a black towel, she glanced around the modest-sized bathroom. It was irrefutably masculine, with its contrasting white and grey tiles and sleek chrome fittings, yet slightly tongue-in-cheek, too. Especially the pinstripe loo seat. She'd been tempted to get one with an aquarium scene once, but Nick had pooh-poohed the idea. He'd been a stuffy sod, at times.

By comparison, Paul was hardly Mr Tidy. His flat was a testament to that, Amy had always thought, although it probably hadn't been fair to judge it when it was crammed with partygoers. Nick used to blame it on Paul's artistic streak. 'He hasn't got his mother's head for order. Or his dad's, come to that.'

As Amy stared at a toothbrush holder shaped like the Venus de Milo, she wondered who Paul had got his sense of humour from.

Her gaze fell on a deodorant spray. It was a feminine one, pink and floral. Francesca's? Or just a spare? Paul probably had a horde of fresh, spare toothbrushes stashed away with his condoms. Men like him were so presumptuous.

There was another knock on the door. 'Amy, are you sure you're OK?'

'Yes,' she called back, her voice brittle. 'I'm not nosing around in your laundry bin, if that's what you're afraid of.'

'No, of course not . . . it's just . . .'

She opened the door. 'Just what?'

He stood there in his bare feet, hands jammed in the pockets of his chinos. 'You were taking so long . . .'

'Was I?'

'Amy, come on.' He trailed after her back into the lounge. 'You think you're the only one feeling sorry for yourself?'

She stopped in her tracks and turned to face him. No one had used that tone with her lately.

'How do you think *I* feel?' Paul demanded, all embarrassment and concern gone. So, realised Amy, she'd been right. The nice-guy persona had only been a front for the egotist she knew better.

'How *do* you feel, Paul?' she asked accusingly. 'Betrayed? Totally floored by the fact that you've given someone three children and their way of repaying you is by going off with someone else? Hey, I've got half a flat out of it, though. And a nice car. That's not bad going. I guess you're going to say you've got nothing.'

'Nothing but a shitload of hassle. I don't need this, Amy, but somehow I keep getting "volunteered" to do it. And yes, I do feel betrayed, in a way. I've known Nick as long as I can remember, and I thought I knew him better than anyone.'

'You're going to tell me again that you didn't know anything about his affair, aren't you?'

'I didn't! And I honestly don't know what I would have done if he'd told me, which is maybe why he did lie by omission. But I'm still gutted that he couldn't trust me. And I'm angry with myself for not seeing it. For not picking up on something that might have made it less of a shock when I finally did find out. I think you feel the same, too, it's just easier to take it out on me than on yourself. Or on Nick, considering he's not here.'

'You've got some gall!' Her whole body seemed to tingle with outrage. 'Acting like you've lost more than just a best mate. He'll be on the phone to you once a week, if not more. But my children have lost their *father*. And I've lost . . .' she couldn't bring herself to say 'everything', because that wasn't true.

In the beginning it had felt as if her universe had caved in, but now that the dust was gradually settling and she was looking around at the debris, quite a lot still seemed intact. She was suddenly angrier from her children's point of view than her own. They wouldn't understand what their father had done, not the way an adult could. Maybe they would even blame themselves, and that was so unfair her heart seemed to groan under the strain. She wanted to lash out at something and someone, and Paul was right, Nick wasn't there to take it. Paul was the next best thing, and it wasn't as if she would be losing anything more by it.

'I understand what you're going through,' said Paul now, with such fake pathos she wanted to slap him. 'If Francesca were to break up with me tomorrow . . .'

'You still wouldn't have any idea how I feel,' hissed Amy, afraid her voice would crack but still desperate to get her point across. 'Don't have the nerve to think a few weeks can come anywhere close to over a decade. It's just the novelty value with you now. Francesca's a little more sophisticated than some of your previous girlfriends, and you're flattered. But that's as far as it goes. You're incapable of long-term monogamy, and you've always resented the fact Nick settled down with me instead of playing the field like you. You could have had such a whale of a time together, but he saddled himself with me and then the kids, and you hated that. You were probably secretly jumping with joy when you heard he'd left me.'

'Right,' Paul tossed his head indignantly. 'Like his getting married is going to mean I get my mate back. The opposite, in fact. My only issue with you, Amy, was that I never thought you and Nick were right for each other. If you took it personally, that was up to you.'

'Well, you've been proved correct. Whoopee for you, Paul!' Amy was running out of steam. She didn't know what there was left to say, except, 'Maybe you even engineered this without realising. Kept him away a bit too often from his family, distracted him by showing him what a good time he could have without us.'

'You're saying I pushed him into having an affair?'

'Maybe not deliberately. I'm not sure you're that clever. But it's served its purpose. You've got me out of the way.'

'Yeah, and Nick's halfway around the world. Great. Just what I wanted. And I wouldn't say you're out of the way. Right now, you're more in my face than ever.'

Amy could have kicked him, but he wasn't worth losing her

last vestige of dignity over. It was just an amazing release to get out everything that had been festering inside her. That mass of negative emotion that she'd harboured towards him for so long was coursing out through the best slanging match she'd had in ages.

Nick had been the moody type with a maddening ability to sulk for days. Perhaps it was Paul's Hispanic ancestry that made him hot-tempered and tempestuous, but it was the level of altercation Amy thrived on herself.

'The problem with you, Paul, is that you've never grown up. You're still that same stuck-up, St Stephen's prefect I remember, except now you drive a flashier car. Your precious mummy and daddy probably still bought it for you, though.'

'And you're so grown-up yourself, are you? Coming out with unsubstantiated stuff like that? As for me being a prefect, Nick was head boy, if you recall. And what about his own cars over the years? Who do you think subsidised those?'

Amy was sidling towards the door like a crab on a mission. 'I'm not going to hang around and take any more of this. As from this moment, I'm out of your hair.'

'I wish.' Paul grunted. 'Unless you want to deal directly with Nick – or my mother, who you probably have more of an aversion towards than me – you're going to have to put up with me a while longer. At least until everything's sorted out. But maybe you do want to deal with Nick, if you feel you're ready . . .?'

Amy couldn't answer that. She knew Paul was just goading her now, but she really didn't know if she could talk to Nick herself yet. One day she would have to, for the children's sake, but right now . . . No, it would be better all round to go through Paul, she admitted to herself. And after their sparring match tonight, she doubted very much if she would ever feel inadequate in his presence again. The opposite, in fact. She hadn't found herself so empowered in a long time.

'Just tell Nick he's getting off lightly,' she snapped, tugging on her coat.

Paul opened the door. He looked satisfied with himself. Amy fought back another urge to wallop him.

'I'll tell him, but I'm not sure he'll listen,' he said. A final parting shot, except that now his voice had lost all bitterness and sarcasm and was resonating with something that sounded like sincerity – but the genuine article this time.

Amy glanced back with a frown, then told herself she'd just imagined it.

IO

'Elspeth, petal, you look shattered.'

The concerned greeting of her best friend rallied Elspeth a little. She untangled her long scarf and flopped on to the banquette, glancing around the pub. It wasn't so much sleepy as unconscious. She and Carol were the only ones there. Even the landlady was absent from behind the bar. Elspeth hoped this was only temporary. It was a little early in the day, but she was still gasping for a Baileys.

'So, how have you managed to sneak away?' Carol appeared to have a drink. Her customary white wine. So maybe there was life behind the bar after all, unless the White Stag had suddenly become self-service.

'Amy's got the kids. She's taken them to McDonald's, as a treat. That's why I called you. It seemed a good chance to meet up. I'm telling you, Carol, I don't know how she does it. She doesn't look the picture of fitness, I know, but she has to be, just to keep up with them.'

'She's feeling better then?'

Elspeth sighed. 'Seems like it. I'm worried she's still in denial, though.'

'Hmm,' said Carol pensively, and got up as the landlady shuffled into view. 'Your usual?'

Elspeth scrambled in her bottomless bag for her purse. 'I'll get these.'

'No, you won't. Stay right there. You deserve some pampering. I can tell you've been neglecting yourself.'

Elspeth sighed again, staring into the flames tumbling about madly in the wide, high fireplace, filling the small village pub with a searing warmth. She shrugged off her duffel coat-style cardigan and adjusted the collar of her blouse. They had had a brief spell of fine weather, as if to lull them into a false sense of security, before the temperature had plummeted to below average again. April showers had now set in with a miserable predictability, and the forecast for Easter was more of the same.

'If you're not taking care of yourself,' said Carol on her return with a generous dose of Baileys, 'it's no wonder you're not coping.'

'I didn't say I wasn't coping,' Elspeth frowned. 'I'm just not a spring chicken any more. I admire Amy more than ever, but she still can't manage on her own – not yet.'

'From what I can gather, she was managing all right before. Nick was hardly Dad of the Year when it came to helping her with the practical stuff, was he? The thing with Amy is, she's a natural with kids. It comes easily to her.'

'On top of everything else, though . . .'

'I know. But you're her mum, not her guardian angel.'

Elspeth stared defiantly into the creamy liquid in her glass, where the ice was already starting to melt. In the depths of her mind, a memory stirred. Something about God not being everywhere at once, which was why he'd created mothers. Except she had always upheld that God was omnipotent, so this had never made sense. Strangely, however, she was now starting to see a grain of truth in it. Maybe loving, caring mothers were a good reflection of what God was really like.

'I'm not about to throw Amy and the kids out on the street, am I?' she challenged.

'I didn't mean that.' Carol patiently patted the tight coils of her perm. 'Why do you always have to go from one extreme to another? All I'm trying to say is, when Amy's ready, you're going to have to let her go.'

'Where to exactly? The flat's on the market.'

'So she'll be looking for somewhere of her own then?'

Elspeth took a sip of her Baileys, but so crossly, she made a slurping sound. 'Amy's sure she'll have enough for a decent deposit if the flat goes for the asking price, but what is she supposed to live off? Nick's giving her an allowance for the boys, but Amy's hardly a financial wizard. He always took care of the bills, and I really don't think Amy has a clue how much owning her own place is going to cost. She'll need a job, and whatever it is, she's hardly likely to get the salary of the century. Most of Nick's money would go on childcare, so where would that leave her?'

Carol squirmed on the banquette, which meant that she had something important to discuss. 'Actually . . . I'm glad you called today. I was going to ring you myself, anyway.'

'Oh?' Elspeth regarded her suspiciously, but with affection.

She often wished Carol had been around when George had died, to have helped her cope with the immediate aftermath. But they had met only after Elspeth had come to Harrisfield. One Sunday at church, when Carol had bustled right up to her.

Elspeth had been trying to maintain her usual level of invisibility in the back pew, but Carol had introduced herself, and roped her into some cleaning rota, of all things. Elspeth, who had been attempting to live reclusively, but hadn't been finding it straightforward with two daughters to look after, had been too overwhelmed to resist Carol's friendship. It had soon become a vital part of her life.

'Well,' sighed Carol now, 'you know my niece Maria who runs Little 'Uns.'

'The children's day nursery?'

'Behind the church, yes.' Carol nodded, and fished out a hankie from her cleavage. She was built like an Amazon, and made the most of it, even though she was a couple of years short of sixty. 'Well,' she went on again, pausing to blow her nose, as if for effect, 'it turns out one of her nurses – or assistants, whatever they're called – is going to be moving away soon, and I was remembering that Amy used to work in a nursery in Saltney . . .'

Elspeth could see where this was heading. Shouldn't she be pleased? For Amy's sake, probably. So why wasn't she?

'It was before Joseph was born, though,' she pointed out, as if this was a major downside.

'That doesn't matter. She has the qualifications, and I'm sure she could get her hands on glowing references. Anyway, I've already had a word with Maria, and she's really keen to meet her. If Amy's interested,' Carol added, acknowledging that this was a crucial element.

'I don't know . . . As I said, if Amy went back to work, the childcare costs alone . . . *I* can't do it indefinitely . . .'

'Ah,' beamed Carol, tucking away her hankie again, 'but that's the beauty of it. Maria said there would be places at the nursery for the boys, at reduced rates. And she seemed to think Amy might qualify for some extra child benefit or other, considering her situation. Although I'm not sure myself, it might depend on how much she's getting from Nick. Anyhow, Maria's got twin girls. They're nearly a year old now, but they're at Little 'Uns, so she gets to see them whenever she likes. That would be perfect for Lucas, wouldn't it? Not to mention Joseph and Mikey.'

'But Joe and Mikey already go to a nursery. They're settled nicely there. I know it's only a couple of times a week, and mainly for them to let off steam . . .'

'That's in Chester, though. Hardly around the corner, unless Amy's planning on moving back to town . . . If she is, then it's probably not worth mentioning the job at Little 'Uns to her.'

Elspeth hadn't even considered that Amy wouldn't want to stay around Harrisfield once she eventually moved out of Mews Cottage. The possibility of Amy working in the village suddenly took on a more appealing perspective.

'I know it's even more upheaval for Joseph and Mikey,' Carol went on, 'but if their mum's working at their new nursery, they'd adjust really quickly. Kids are so . . . *bouncy*, I always think. They fit into new situations better than their parents, half the time.'

Elspeth sighed and drained her glass. Losing a father, however it happened, wasn't fun, it was tragic. Admittedly, the boys were young, just as Tilly had been when George had died. But did the fact that they couldn't understand what was going on make it any easier for them?

'So, do you want me to speak to Amy personally, or are you going to have a chat with her yourself? I can give you Maria's number.' Carol took a card out of her purse and offered it to Elspeth.

'*Little 'Uns Day Nursery, quality care for the pre-school child* . . .' In the top right-hand corner was a smiley yellow sun, with a rainbow arching out from behind.

'I'll speak to Amy,' said Elspeth.

She recalled that it had been Nick's mother who had wangled places for Joseph and Mikey at their current, elitist nursery in Chester. What would Rowena think of the boys attending an ordinary little establishment open to anyone, not merely the well connected? That notion alone was enough to spur Elspeth on with this new plan.

Besides, if Amy did decide she wanted to work there, then she would need to find a house or flat somewhere close by, for convenience's sake. That meant her choice was more limited. She would have to stay on at the cottage while she hunted around. Elspeth could keep a watchful eye on her, and help out without Amy feeling too smothered. It was a squash in the little terraced house, but it was a sacrifice Elspeth didn't mind making. In the long run, it was the best for everyone.

11

'Tilly? Are you all right?' Amy glanced out from the kitchen. Her sister was curled up on the sofa in front of the television, like a foetus clutching a cushion.

'Yeah.'

'Do you want anything to drink? More orange juice?'

'Nah.'

'You're very quiet tonight . . .'

'*EastEnders* is on.'

'Oh. OK.' Amy frowned and shrugged to herself. Tilly wasn't normally this unresponsive, but she'd been subdued for a few days now, maybe longer. Amy had casually mentioned it to their mother when she'd helped her cook tea tonight, but Elspeth had just dismissed it as moody teenager syndrome.

'She gets like this sometimes. You were just the same. And you've got it all to look forward to. Although maybe, with boys, they'll be moody in another way. A different combination of hormones or something.'

Amy wasn't so convinced that this was just a teenage thing, or PMT. It wasn't as if she and Tilly were the closest of sisters, but they had never been at each other's throats, either. The age gap had naturally been an issue, although when Tilly had been born, Amy hadn't particularly resented the sudden appearance of a rival for her parents' affection, at least, not her mother's. At fifteen, she had been long past the playing-with-dolls stage, but she had already known that she wanted to work with children when she left school, so a baby in the house had been ideal practice. When their father had died and they'd moved to Harrisfield with their mum, Amy had obviously felt the disruption more keenly than her two-year-old sister, who had rapidly adjusted to their new surroundings.

Had Amy drifted away a little then? Looking back, there seemed to be a whole chunk of Tilly's childhood that she could barely remember. Those years when maybe she hadn't even been that close to her mother – the early stage of her relationship with Nick.

Since then, Amy realised, she had been too busy to involve herself in depth in her sister's life. Tilly had become an aunt when she was just a child herself, but she'd taken it on with the relish for a new challenge that had become her trademark. Now that they were actually inhabiting the same space again, Amy was taking advantage of the opportunity to get to know her sister better.

It was funny how you could go through life accumulating assumptions about another person, until suddenly a change in circumstances forces you to reassess everything.

For some reason, Amy had assumed that Tilly generally confided in her when she couldn't face their mum, but it was becoming obvious that she didn't. There were probably more secrets stored away in that sixteen-year-old brain than in the files of MI5.

Elspeth came trudging down the stairs, tucking stray curls of greying chestnut hair into the knot which was habitually perched on her head like a bird's nest gone wrong. She seemed to have had the same hairstyle since the year dot, and no one had ever been able to persuade her to try something new. She came into the kitchen and put the empty Tommee Tippee bottle on the table.

'Lucas had it all, then?' Amy noted.

'Seven ounces. Then I popped him in the cot and he went off without a murmur. You've got him well trained there.

Mikey won't let go of his bottle, though. It's empty, but he's clutching it in one hand and his blankie in the other.'

Amy sighed. 'It's a security thing. He'll grow out of it again.'

'You mean, he already had?'

'Sometimes children regress. It's normal when they're under stress.'

'You make it sound as if he's got a meeting with his bank manager tomorrow.' Elspeth frowned and rolled up her sleeves, ready to start on the washing-up. 'It's not fair! He's only a child.'

'I've rinsed the dishes already,' Amy pointed out, steering Elspeth away from her current favourite subject. 'I know you don't normally do that, but it stops the water getting too scummy.'

'Fine,' said Elspeth grimly. 'Even though you had a dishwasher, you seem to be some sort of expert on washing by hand, so if you'd rather . . .?'

'I'll dry up,' said Amy, grabbing a tea towel. 'How many stories did you have to read Joe and Mikey before they actually agreed to put their heads down on their pillows?'

'Four, including that complete retelling of *The Three Little Pigs*. All too politically correct for my liking, but there you have it, it's the twenty-first century.'

'Yes, Mum.' Amy concealed her smirk by looking down at her flowery, fuchsia-pink slippers. House shoes, as Nick used to call them, although his had always been made of suede.

The familiar drum roll from the TV signalled the end of another episode of *EastEnders*. Tilly drifted into the kitchen, stretching the bottom of her already baggy sweatshirt. She opened the fridge, stared at its contents morosely for a few seconds, then closed it again.

'Were you after anything specific?' Elspeth asked, over her shoulder.

Tilly shrugged. 'Do you need to use the computer now, Mum?'

'You know I do. I don't get much chance these days, and I've already got a backlog. I had two people on the phone today who should have had work mailed out to them on Monday. I've always had a reputation for being so prompt . . .'

'Really?' Tilly arched her eyebrows.

'And you will be again,' said Amy firmly. 'I appreciate all your help these last few weeks, but everything's going to be fine from now on. *I'm* going to be fine. With this job at Little 'Uns, and the flat going on the market, it's like . . . like a whole new chapter opening in my life. I can't wait to get on with it.'

Her mother and sister both turned to look at her, sharing the same dubious expression. *Poor Amy,* they seemed to be thinking, sympathy swelling in their breasts. *Such a stiff upper lip,* Grandad Croft would have remarked, *as if your grandmother's starched it.*

But Amy didn't feel brave, or even as if she was putting on a show. She really did seem to be stretching at the seams, bursting to get on with the future. And in those still-frequent moments when she felt raw and hurt and alone, she would go to her room and indulge in a few tears before emerging again, all the better for it. Yes, she probably had something to prove, to her family, to Nick, even to Paul and his shoulder-padded, trouser-suited harpy of a mother. But that wasn't a bad thing if she went about it in the right way.

'You'll soon be back to normal here,' Amy re-emphasised to her mother, then turned apologetically to Tilly. 'I know you're not getting much homework done, either.'

'Well, what with the bloody Fimbles, and then Pingu . . . I know that penguin's cute, but I just wanted to wring his neck earlier. How many times can Mikey and Joe watch the same bloody episode without getting bored?'

'And how many times are you going to say the "b" word in

one night?' demanded Elspeth. 'Anyway, madam, you could have been getting on with some work this last half-hour, while I got the boys ready for bed.'

'Hel-*lo*.' Tilly looked chagrined. 'I always watch *EastEnders*. It's about the only adult thing on in this house any more. Besides, I thought kids were supposed to go to bed at six o'clock.'

'So did Nick,' said Amy frostily, jumping to the boys' defence, 'but when they're too young to read, you can't expect them to know what it says in a baby-care manual, can you? And I'm sorry about Pingu. Sometimes I just want to ram a cork in his beak myself, but I couldn't take the kids to the playground, it was peeing down.'

'Yeah, yeah, I know.' Tilly crossed her arms over her chest and slouched against the Welsh dresser.

'Surely you can do some reading in your room?' suggested Elspeth. 'Revision doesn't have to involve the computer, does it?'

'S'pose not.' Tilly yawned. 'I'll probably just end up crashing out on the bed, though. Lucas woke me up last night bawling his lungs out.'

Amy was struggling to keep her patience. 'Well heating up a bottle isn't as instant as shoving a breast in his mouth. He's got to wait.'

'I thought bottle-fed babies didn't wake up at night, especially when they were on solids.'

'That's a myth sadistic mothers like to spread, just to make the rest of us feel inadequate.' Amy threw down the tea towel. 'Might as well leave the saucepans to drain.'

'Might as well,' said Elspeth lightly. She hummed the first few bars of *Für Elise*, as she often did when she was caught up in a tense situation, probably without realising she was doing it. 'Are you both coming to church with me tomorrow, by the way?'

'I'm supposed to be meeting Keira,' said Tilly. 'She's over at her dad's for the day.'

'You can spare an hour, surely? It *is* Good Friday. And Keira doesn't get to see all that much of her dad, so I don't think he'd appreciate you waltzing over there and—'

'OK, OK. I'll go with you.'

'Good,' said Elspeth smugly. 'What about you, Amy?'

'I would, but what about Joe and Mikey? The service is too long for them, and so sombre. They'd go stir-crazy. Lucas could probably be distracted, he might even sleep in the pram, but . . .'

'I could look after them,' Tilly volunteered keenly.

'Of course you could,' said Elspeth, 'but you're not available. You're coming to church, remember? What about Jonathan?'

Amy felt as if her mother had dug her in the ribs. She jumped slightly. 'What about him?'

'He probably wouldn't mind keeping an eye on Joe and Mikey for a couple of hours. He could take them to the playground, or for a kick-around in the park.'

'I thought you said an hour – not two,' frowned Tilly.

Elspeth gave her a dark look, then turned back to Amy. 'Why not ask him?'

'Well, he's done so much already . . . But if it means that much – my coming with you, that is.'

'It does.' Elspeth looked as if the matter was settled. 'You'd better pop next door, then,' she added.

Amy glanced at the kitchen clock. 'What – now?'

'It's hardly late. Go on, it'll be bedlam here in the morning, as usual, and you might not get the chance.'

'OK . . . you're right. But I'd better put a different top on, this one's got dots of bolognese sauce over it.'

Tilly rolled her eyes dramatically. 'God forbid Saddo sees his precious Amy with a less-than-clean top.'

Amy rounded on her sister. 'I'd appreciate it if you used his proper name, thank you.' Tilly's attitude towards him, after all the little kindnesses he had shown them lately, irked her. 'If you took the trouble to get to know him, you'd realise he's not the sad, boring person you seem to think.'

'Oh, I don't think he's boring as such,' sniffed Tilly. 'He reminds me of Gollum in *Lord of the Rings*. Except the object of his desire isn't a lump of metal. I guess I call him Saddo out of habit.'

'Well the number of times I've asked you to stop . . .' chided Elspeth, but rather faintly.

'Yeah, right,' Tilly looked at her mother with raised eyebrows again. 'You've changed your tune.'

Amy wasn't one hundred per cent sure what was going on, except that she didn't seem to have a direct role to play in this exchange. 'Look,' she began haltingly, 'we can't just be bitchy about the man and then expect him to do favours for us.'

'You know he fancies you?' Tilly blurted out, with all the directness of Jeremy Paxman. 'He's fancied you for ages, even when you were with Nick. It used to bother Mum, but all of a sudden it doesn't seem to . . .'

Elspeth was staring down at the lino, twiddling with the toggle at the bottom of her fleece. At last, she looked up confrontationally. 'Of course it used to disturb me back then. Amy wasn't available. It wasn't . . . right.'

'Tantamount to coveting you,' Tilly went on, as if Amy was being deliberately obtuse, 'which breaks one of the Ten Commandments. That neighbour's wife business, although not completely literally. I thought it was a little obsessive, and it was only sad because it seemed he was just afraid. As if he liked you because you *weren't* available.' Her voice lost its edge, and Amy realised that Tilly had taken the time to consider Jonathan's situation, after all. 'Sometimes, it's easier to admire someone from afar. Someone you know you can't have. You stay in control, and stop yourself getting hurt over and over again.'

'Such a lonely way to live, though,' said Elspeth, frowning at Tilly as if she'd never expected such insightfulness from someone so young and inexperienced.

'Course it is,' shrugged Tilly. 'But people do it. They can go their whole lives doing it, just so they don't have to take risks.'

'I thought you were going to do something in the media when you left school?' Amy pointed out, trying to get off the subject of Jonathan fancying her. 'I didn't know you were into all this psychology mumbo-jumbo, even if it is trendy these days.'

Tilly shrugged again. 'Haven't decided, actually. And before I get any career advice from someone who isn't an expert' – she looked directly at their mother – 'I'd like to ask Amy what *she* thinks of Jonathan. It's her opinion that counts, after all.'

'Mine?' Amy fluttered a hand in front of her chest. 'He's just a nice, kind man.'

'With ulterior motives.'

'And what if he has?' Elspeth cut in.

'As long as they're honourable?'

'Hello,' Amy frowned, 'I'm right here, remember? And I'm not naïve enough to catapult from one relationship straight into another.'

'Does Jonathan know that?' Tilly speculated.

'Rebound relationships aren't always destined to fail, you know,' said Elspeth. 'It's how . . .' She tailed off and shrugged. 'Well, anyway, it isn't unheard of.'

'Look,' sighed Amy, 'Jonathan is just a friend—'

'Then, Sis, why are you blushing?'

'Tilly!' Amy was losing patience again. 'I'm not,' she fibbed. 'And as long as Jonathan knows that I'm not looking for anything remotely un-platonic, there's no harm in my being friends with him.'

Her sister nodded, but her tone was serious when she said, 'Just make sure you're straight with him, then. A woman only has to smile at a man sometimes and he thinks he's pulled.'

'I won't lead him on.' Amy paused, and glanced down at her attire. 'I'm still going to change my top, though . . . I don't want to set foot out of the house looking this mucky, even if I'm *not* trying to impress anyone.'

12

Someone must have once told Francesca that she looked great in grey marl. Most of the pyjamas she slopped around in were made of the same flecked jersey fabric. Other women might have looked drab, he reflected. Amy, for instance, had a cardigan and matching long skirt made of the stuff. She had worn it frequently enough, Paul reminisced, covering herself from neck to toe, looking like a giant baby penguin.

Once lately, in one of his darker moods, Paul had considered that he couldn't blame Nick for leaving. Immediately afterwards, though, he had reminded himself that there were three kids involved, and had conjured up Amy's face when he had told her that Nick had gone. There were more important things in life to deplore than your partner having a dodgy dress sense.

'More coffee?' Paul leaned over the back of his tan leather sofa.

Francesca wriggled and stretched luxuriously, redolent of a cat stirring from a nap. She'd been so engrossed in the latest Harry Potter novel, she might as well have been asleep as far as keeping him company went. 'Mmm?'

'Do you want more coffee, my love?'

She stared up at him. 'That's the first time you've called me that.'

Paul paused, to think about it. 'Is it?' He tried to be nonchalant but failed. To his awareness, it was possibly the first time he had called anyone that. He'd sounded just like his dad.

'I'd love a cream of asparagus Cup-a-Soup, actually,' Francesca was sighing, as if what he'd just said wasn't of any lasting consequence. 'But I doubt you've got any.'

There were times, realised Paul, when he seriously ought to listen to his subconscious when it was urgently trying to impart something, even if it was a revelation as sudden as his namesake's – aka Saul of Tarsus – on the road to Damascus.

'I'd have a permanent supply – if you were living here,' he said, in all earnestness.

Francesca blinked.

Paul came around the sofa to sit next to her. He grabbed her hands, kneading them nervously. 'So – why don't you?'

Her blinking was on the increase. She seemed genuinely taken aback. 'Why don't I what?'

'Move in with me. You're here practically all the time as it is, when you're not at work or out with your friends.'

'But what about Donna? She couldn't afford the rent without me.'

'It's not as if she's your best mate. You don't owe her anything, and she'd find someone else to share with, the same way she found *you* when you moved up North.'

Francesca pulled her hands from his grasp, and skittishly ruffled her mass of hair. The Harry Potter novel, a hefty hardback, slid off her lap and landed on the bare, varnished floorboards with a thud. Within seconds, there were three bangs from the flat below. Mrs Freddy Kruger, as Paul had nicknamed her – her real name was Freda Kramer – was prodding the end of a broom against her lounge ceiling, reminding them that she was there and they'd disturbed her. But then flushing the loo in his flat was a crime in her eyes, especially after eight at night.

'And that's another reason,' Francesca grumbled. 'If I had to put up with that fruitcake downstairs . . .'

'She's not that bad,' said Paul dismissively. In truth, he

wished she would move out as unceremoniously as she'd moved in last year. The students before her, with that noise masquerading as music, had been a hell of a lot more neighbourly, even if they'd made him feel his age.

'Paul, how long have we been seeing each other?' Francesca asked, sounding perturbed.

'Are you trying to catch me out? You know it's been seven weeks. The longest I've been out with anybody, unless you count Fiona Smollett. But that was at uni.'

'Well, I do count Fiona, considering that was almost a year. She must have been special.'

'She was . . . at the time. But she was a third year and I was a first, it wasn't conducive to a lifelong commitment when she graduated and buggered off back to Inverness. Anyway, it was a sort of education for me with her. At eighteen, I felt like I'd been around the block a few times, until I met her in the halls of residence and realised the girls I'd known up till then—'

'Yes, well,' Francesca cut in, 'you can spare me the details. I already know you honed your technique with her.'

'And I've since perfected it with you.' Paul gazed deep into her eyes. But it was a weird thing, he realised: eyes were strange things to look at for too long, even gorgeous green ones.

Francesca feigned retching. 'Your tongue ought to be preserved in formaldehyde. It'd be a tragedy to let it decay. And much as I'd love to spend my every waking moment listening to you—'

'Which you could. Well, almost. If you were living with me.'

'I don't see what's wrong with the way things are now. Like you said, I spend a lot of time here. I've got a few things of my own scattered about, to stop you slipping back inadvertently into bachelor mode.' She gave a helpless shrug. 'I just like knowing that I've got somewhere else that's *my* space.'

'A bolt-hole to run to if we argue? That's not a good enough reason to throw away money in rent. What's the point if you're hardly there?'

'Can't you just humour me?' She tugged at his hand, pouting silkily. 'Seven weeks isn't a long time in the grand scheme of things. Why won't you just be content with the fact that I'm here now?'

He sighed, deflated. 'I am. Forget it. I guess it was just a spur of the moment thing, I got carried away.'

'That doesn't mean it wasn't a good idea. Just a bit . . . rash. You're more impulsive than you realise, Paul. It might get you into deeper waters one day than you're ready for. I don't mean this time,' she said quickly, as he opened his mouth to protest. 'I know we're really great together.' She smiled, crumpling his stomach. 'But if that's the case, then surely it's all the more reason to take it slowly and savour it.'

He wouldn't refer to some of the times they'd already shared as taking things slowly. It had become enough again, though, that she was here on his sofa with him on this gloomy Easter Sunday, the rain drumming against the window and French doors, unable to penetrate the warm glow of his flat.

He stretched over to kiss her. A brief, butterfly kiss on her mouth. 'I'd better make the most of having you here now and all to myself, then. I'm only just fully appreciating the fact that we saw my parents yesterday. I couldn't have faced having to traipse over to theirs this afternoon.' His brow contorted at the thought.

As it stood, they had the rest of today and tomorrow left to their own devices. He felt like a child again, at the start of the school holidays.

'I know!' Francesca grinned lavishly. 'Dinner at the Chester Grosvenor. You can't say I'm not full of good ideas.'

'Considering my dad footed the bill, you worked a miracle. And my mother thinks you're the next best thing to sliced bread.'

'I am. I'm a freshly baked, sundried tomato and black olive focaccia. Speaking of which, what are you making me for lunch?'

'Er,' Paul slumped back on the sofa, 'that's, um, something I sort of overlooked.'

She narrowed her eyes in mock suspicion. 'What do you mean?'

'From the contents of my fridge and larder, it might have to be a Cadbury's Creme Egg on toast.'

'Paul!' Francesca leaned over to thump him, her foot catching a pile of magazines on the coffee table, knocking them to the floor. As she bent to pick them up, Mrs Freddy Kruger started banging again. Francesca glowered at the floor, then straightened up with a travel brochure in her hand. 'What's this?'

Bollocks. It was meant to be a surprise. Paul had hidden it at the bottom of the pile, though, when he should have been more thorough and locked it in his filing cabinet.

'The Maldives?' Francesca flicked through the glossy pages. 'It's an up-to-date one.'

Paul took a deep breath. 'I – um – was hoping that maybe, you know . . .'

'I was thinking of the Costa, myself,' she announced.

'The Costa?'

'Del Sol. Hasn't Rowena got a villa out there? And didn't you say she'd given you the run of it one summer for a couple of weeks?'

'Yes,' said Paul slowly, 'but I thought you might prefer somewhere a little more exotic. I was going to try and plan it—'

'—in surprise?' She pulled a face, only mildly apologetic. 'Just as well you didn't. I'm a nightmare on long-haul flights. A couple of hours from Liverpool or Manchester would be fine with me.' She tossed the brochure carelessly back on to the table. 'I was thinking of June, actually. Or early July. Before the kids break up for the summer. If that doesn't clash with Rowena, of course.'

Paul struggled not to let his disappointment show. It was only the destination that had altered, he told himself, and surely it was a good omen if Francesca had also been considering going on holiday together?

'Anyway, haven't I mentioned I've got a friend in Estepona?' she said casually. 'Jules. She's just set up an estate agency over there. I know her from way back, we met at secretarial college. She's really nice. I always knew she'd move on to grander things.'

Paul tried to remember. 'I don't think you've mentioned her before.'

'Haven't I?' Francesca flapped her hand. 'Well, with your memory . . . Anyway, we wouldn't be slumming it in Rowena's villa, would we?'

'Hardly. The pool alone's the size of this lounge.'

Francesca was starting to look as animated as a child waking up on their birthday. Paul had a sudden urge to indulge her. 'I'll look up flights on the internet later, if you like.'

'OK. We can compare diaries, see what dates are best for us.'

Paul wasn't sure he'd even written in his organiser as far ahead as May, let alone June. He wondered how Francesca managed to fill hers so rapidly. She went out on girls' nights at least twice a week, and most of them seemed to have been planned ages in advance, as if her social calendar beyond her relationship with him was a carefully balanced juggling act. Or maybe she was just referring to her work schedule, he speculated, wondering if she was the sort of person who thrived on looking busy, rather than actually being it.

13

'Typical, isn't it? It rains all day and then as soon as the sun goes down, it stops.'

'Mmm.' Amy looked sideways at Jonathan as she strolled next to him in the twilight. 'It's definitely been a wet Easter.'

That sounded so feeble, but after an afternoon of endeavouring to make conversation with a neighbour who all of a sudden couldn't seem to string more than two sentences together – as well as trying to include her mother, sister and the boys – Amy felt her reserves fast running dry. Which didn't bode well for this evening. Maybe it really could just be a 'quick drink', and then she could say she was too tired. She'd had an early start, all things considered, with Mikey and Joseph charging into her room just gone half six brandishing their Easter eggs and yelling excitedly.

'Tomorrow might be a fine day, after all,' Jonathan struggled on. 'The forecasters could have got it wrong.'

'A dry bank holiday? That's like saying there won't be any traffic jams.'

Jonathan snorted, in acknowledgement of her weak joke. 'Listen,' he slowed his pace even further – at this rate they would just about reach the White Stag by last orders – 'thanks for inviting me to join you at your mum's today. It really meant a lot.'

That was exactly what Amy hadn't wanted it to mean. The idea to invite him to join the family for Easter dinner had come about when she'd gone over to ask him if he could keep an eye on Joseph and Mikey while she went to church on Good Friday.

Jonathan had agreed to babysit without a murmur of hesitation. 'It's not as if I've got anything planned.'

Amy had surmised that he probably didn't have any plans for Sunday, either, which had made her feel sorry for him. Before being fully aware of what she was letting herself in for, he was invited over for Easter dinner and had offered to bring the dessert and wine.

Then there were those fancy chocolate eggs he'd turned up with – not part of the agreement. Hers had been especially large and decorative, with a fancy satin bow. All gloss and not much substance underneath, unfortunately. Expensive and shallow. A bit like the Faulkner Joneses, Amy had reflected darkly.

Jonathan had meant well, but she would have been content with a Smarties one; or just a packet of Mini Eggs, which were her favourite, and so moreish she used to stock up on them every Easter so she would have some stashed away for the rest of the year.

That particular tradition had passed her by this time. Food had lost its attraction, which was fortunate in one respect, as it could have gone completely the other way. She had more than made up for it today, though. Maybe that was why her stomach felt as if she were on a dinghy in lurching seas. Or maybe it was due to something else. The fact that this unexpected, why-don't-you-go-for-a-quick-drink, Lord-knows-you-deserve-it, jaunt to the pub felt ridiculously like a date.

Her mother had sprung it upon them the instant the children had gone to bed. It had come out of nowhere, with much background eye-rolling on Tilly's part.

'Amy needs a break and some grown-up conversation,' Elspeth had declared. 'Go on, Jonathan – do the decent thing and take her down to the White Stag. By way of saying thank-you for all the hard work she's put in today.'

'But this was *my* way of thanking Jonathan for looking after the boys on Friday,' Amy had interjected. 'And the egg must have cost a fortune, anyway . . .' She'd tailed off, fighting a losing battle. Before she could say, 'I should put on trousers, it's still chilly for a skirt without tights,' she'd found herself ambling down the lane towards the High Street, with cold ankles and a companion who seemed more awkward than quixotic.

He had reverted to that bumbling neighbour who had once been the butt of too many jokes in Mews Cottage. The natural leader, the gallant knight, the rock to lean on that had been so in evidence recently had disappeared behind a plain, woolly, brown jumper.

Amy couldn't help recalling the conversation she'd had with her mother and sister only a few days ago. It had been obvious this afternoon that Elspeth was trying to steer Amy in Jonathan's direction, just as Tilly was trying her hardest to pull her back. What Amy felt or thought didn't seem to come into the equation any more. Maybe that was just as well, though, as it seemed to be changing from one minute to the next.

It wasn't that she fancied him in some electrifying way. After the manner in which she had first fallen for Nick, she was convinced it would be impossible to feel anything like that again. In real life, at least. She had always been a hopeless romantic when it came to books and films, wooing the hero vicariously through the heroine. But then, taking into account the whole of womankind on the planet, she was hardly alone in having her pulse race when confronted with Mr Darcy, or experiencing a wild abandon when swept off her feet by Heathcliff.

What she felt right now as she walked alongside Jonathan was more a sense of security than anything else, as if she knew without a shadow of a doubt that this man would never hurt her like Nick had.

In some ways, rebounding into another relationship – in spite of what her mother had said – was the coward's way out. As far as Amy was concerned, and maybe it was the way her sister saw it too, it would simply be that she was too weak and frightened to be on her own. Proof that she had become reliant on having a man around, at least some of the time.

But then again, the knowledge that someone found you attractive, that they wanted to be with you . . . the feeling that that generated was so *nice*, so addictive, Amy realised she couldn't turn her back on it completely.

Jonathan wasn't ugly. Even that marginally crooked nose was an asset rather than a disadvantage. If she had a plastic surgeon at her disposal to sculpt him into the perfect man, Amy honestly wouldn't know where to start. He had warm eyes, a generous smile, a better than average physique, with only the slightest hint of middle-aged spread. In fact, even his age wasn't a problem, because it was hardly as if she were still in her twenties herself.

No, apart from being much . . . *duller* than Nick had been, although not necessarily in a bad way, Jonathan Simmons was a down-to-earth, quiet man, his potential probably overlooked by women because he wasn't conventionally macho. He didn't put himself about, as other men did, and as far as Amy was aware – although, of course, she didn't know what he was like at work, and she was assuming rather a lot – he hadn't been going out of his way to meet a possible partner.

'About this drink tonight,' she began, her voice slightly unsteady.

'Look,' he cut in quickly, 'I do realise that it *is* just a drink . . .' He seemed genuinely shocked when she touched his arm. They both stopped, and turned to face each other.

'I'm not in the market for anything . . . complicated or

heavy,' she heard herself say. 'But I appreciate everything you've done for me these last few weeks.'

Jonathan looked at the ground, shaking his head. 'Much as I miss being appreciated by anyone . . .'

'That wasn't what you had in mind? The thing is . . . the only man I've ever been out with was Nick, and what I'd consider the "going out" phase happened a long time ago. I'm seriously out of practice.'

'I haven't been out with anyone properly in at least five years,' Jonathan admitted. 'And even then, Niamh and I were living together, too . . . It was hardly "dating". We had a daughter. Well, we still do, of course . . . but . . .'

'Then I guess that puts us on a fairly equal footing,' Amy said lightly, then added, on a more sober note, 'I've got the boys to consider, though, and I don't want them getting confused or upset. I also wouldn't want people to get the wrong idea about me, or about us.'

Jonathan puckered his brow. 'And that would be . . .?'

'That I didn't care about Nick. Or that I haven't considered your feelings, and I'm just using you. They could think a dozen different things. And I wouldn't want you to get the wrong idea yourself.'

'Amy, your partner of thirteen years just walked out on you and your children. He's not dead, so you can't grieve him, and no one expects you to go into mourning.'

'Part of me has, though,' it struck her. 'Part of me feels as if it always will. But I'm not so much mourning *him*, as the plans and hopes I've been robbed of. Do you understand? Do you know what I mean? And just a few days ago, or even a few hours, I was ready to tell you – if you broached the subject,' she added bashfully, 'that I couldn't be anything more than just a friend . . . but—'

'What?' he asked, clearly on tenterhooks.

'I realised I couldn't give you an outright "no".' She sighed heavily at the smile that burst on to his countenance. 'Just as I can't give you an outright "yes",' she went on quickly. 'Not right now . . . not *today*.'

'But it would be fine to go out for a drink now and again?' he asked, taking her hand and squeezing it.

'I don't see any harm in that . . .'

'Maybe even dinner? Or the cinema?'

'It's no more than friends would do, anyway,' she nodded, ignoring the nagging voice in her head that sounded like Tilly.

Friends wouldn't stand around on street corners holding hands and staring into each other's eyes.

Amy quickly removed her hand from his and continued en route to the local pub. Jonathan easily fell into step beside her.

'Just don't let me get to you,' she murmured, without looking at him this time. 'Don't let me mess you about. I'm still not myself, whoever that is. There was so much I thought I could rely on . . . well, it just isn't there now. It's gone. And I need to move forward at my own pace. So if I start going doolally on you, if nothing I seem to do makes sense, just let me know, OK?'

'Amy, I'm not about to start shouting anything from the rooftops. For starters, I'd get too much stick at work if they knew I was seeing anyone – especially if it's not their idea of what dating ought to be. Most of the younger ones have grown up on a diet of *Sex and the City* and *Friends*.' He coughed diplomatically, looking as if he wished he hadn't said that.

Amy felt herself colour, and hoped it wouldn't show in the fast-fading light. In spite of her embarrassment, a trickle of excitement entered her bloodstream and warmed her a little.

It would be something to look forward to, wouldn't it? Dinners out, and the cinema . . . She hadn't been to see a film with Nick in years. Their tastes had been too diverse, and he had preferred to wait till something came out on DVD or Sky, anyway. Sitting in semi-darkness, munching popcorn, had been too twee for him, even if he was watching the latest all-action Hollywood offering, which was the only sort of thing he enjoyed, anyway. Amy suspected that Jonathan would be the kind of man who would happily watch her video of *Casablanca* with her.

They reached the White Stag, and he stepped aside to let her pass through the door first. Amy entered the rosy-hued, beery confines of the pub, feeling much less apprehensive about being here than she had when they'd set out from her mum's. One thing was certain about whatever lay ahead, she mused gratefully. Not just tonight but for the days and weeks to come. She would be treated like a lady, not a doormat.

14

Spring had a smell all its own, thought Elspeth. And once it was in the air, you knew winter was finally over.

She was hanging out washing in the small yard behind Mews Cottage. Her only regret about living here was the absence of a garden. No lawn flanked by flower beds, no fancy patio or greenhouse, no summerhouse or shed. None of the things she'd had when she'd lived with her husband in their large, family home in Chester.

When she had first come to Harrisfield, she'd been relieved that there wasn't a garden to fret about. It had been one of the reasons she'd chosen Mews Cottage over the other properties she'd viewed. Pottering about with a spade and fork, mowing the lawn, tending to the vegetable patch . . . that had all been George's department. She wouldn't have known where to start.

Over time, though – and finding it rather therapeutic – she had livened up the concrete yard with a display of glazed pots in various sizes and colours. On this warm, balmy day in early May, some of them were spilling over with ivy, pansies and busy Lizzies looking as if they were bopping to an inaudible disco beat.

Earlier this morning, Elspeth had unfolded the small, round wooden table and four matching chairs that she kept covered up during the winter, setting them out of range of the clothes line and dustbin. It was the best she could do, given the limitations, but it was a vast improvement on Jonathan's yard next door, which seemed to be a graveyard for bric-a-brac and unwanted furniture, as if he didn't know the way to the nearest charity shop or council tip.

Just as Elspeth was hanging up a cot sheet, she heard the back gate rattle and a female voice with an accent that definitely wasn't local call out, 'Hello . . .? Is anyone there?'

The brick wall at the rear of the property was so high that no one could poke their head over it unless they were in the Guinness Book of Records – or in possession of a stepladder or crate. Elspeth went to unbolt the wooden gate, which was the same height as the wall and afforded some privacy from the narrow alleyway running behind the cottages.

A young woman poked her head round, blinked at Elspeth for a couple of seconds, then erupted into a smile. 'You must be Amy's mum?'

Elspeth nodded. The woman was younger than Amy, and didn't look the type that her daughter would normally befriend. She was power dressed to the hilt in a fitted, grey suit complete with tan leather attaché case. Her flaming red hair seemed to be quite curly, but it was austerely tied back from her high-cheekboned, impeccably Estée Laudered face (or whatever brand of department-store make-up she no doubt used).

'I'm Francesca Courtney.' She waited for a flicker of recognition.

The name was familiar, although Elspeth couldn't quite place it. *Francesca Courtney* . . . Amy had mentioned her – but in relation to what?

Francesca's smile faltered. 'Amy's estate agent,' she prompted.

'Oh! That's right. Paul's . . . girlfriend.' Elspeth hesitated, then gestured towards a chair. 'Would you like a tea or—'

'No . . .' Francesca held up her hand. (Beautiful nails, a yard long, thought Elspeth jealously.) 'No, thanks, I'm fine.'

She didn't make a move to sit down, either. 'I was just passing through Harrisfield – there's a property I'm supposed to be seeing outside Mold – and I decided to drop by on Amy. I've got some good news for her, and I thought it would be nice to tell her face-to-face rather than over the phone.'

'Oh?' Elspeth felt her breath catch. 'Is it about the flat? Have you got a buyer?'

'Amy isn't in, is she?' Francesca glanced up at the house. 'Only I saw a couple of windows open at the front, but no one was answering the door. That's why I came round the back.'

Elspeth shook her head. 'I'm afraid Amy's at work. I could pass on a message, if you want. I was going to pop down there shortly, anyway. She left her lunch box behind this morning.'

'Really? Where does she work? I could take the lunch box to her myself. Kill two birds with one stone.'

Elspeth fended off a frown. It was clear that Paul's latest conquest was as far removed from being a bimbo as Pluto was from the Sun. She was professional to the core, and wasn't about to give any information away, even to her client's own mother.

'Well,' said Elspeth carefully, 'if you can spare the time . . .'

'Is it far – where she works?'

'Don't you know? Hasn't Paul mentioned it?' Elspeth dug for information.

Francesca shook her head. 'I've been in touch with her directly myself, you see, but she hasn't mentioned it, either. Not that she would, I suppose. Not to me. But I don't know if she's even spoken to Paul since she went to see him a while back.' She pulled a face, as if to say, 'Hardly surprising.'

Elspeth tried not to betray her curiosity, ablaze though it was. Amy hadn't said a great deal after she'd gone to Paul's flat that night a few weeks ago. The names she'd called him weren't repeatable. Yet, oddly, it was after that evening that Amy had started to come alive again, no longer hiding away but charging at life head-on, as if she were attacking Paul and whatever it was he'd said or done that had made her so defiant. Amy had confided only a few sketchy details about the financial settlement Nick was offering. Elspeth had wanted to hear more. Much more. But Francesca Courtney plainly wasn't going to be the one to fill her in.

'It's a shame Amy doesn't get on with him,' she sighed, and Elspeth's ears pricked up in anticipation. Perhaps she'd been hasty in assuming Francesca wouldn't blab. 'It would make all this intermediary stuff with Nick so much easier if she just buried the hatchet with Paul.'

'Well,' said Elspeth slowly, trying to be tactful in her choice of words, 'they've always been the same, so they're hardly going to change now. Anyway, you can't put all the blame on Amy. I know you're biased in Paul's favour . . .'

'And you're biased in Amy's. But—'

'But what?' said Elspeth. 'You're not going to try and tell me he's on her side in all this?'

Francesca looked a little ruffled by Elspeth's sudden sharp tone, as if she were a child chastised by one of her elders. 'It's Amy I should be speaking to about this, anyway.' She sighed, drawing the thread of conversation to a close. 'And I ought to be getting a move on, really. Where is it you said she worked?'

'I didn't,' said Elspeth, then berated herself for being curt. 'It's Little 'Uns Day Nursery, just behind the Parish Church, at the other end of the High Street. It used to be the old schoolhouse.'

'I shouldn't have any trouble finding it.' Francesca paused a moment. 'The lunch box then?' She raised her eyebrows pointedly.

'Oh . . . Of course.' Elspeth had forgotten. She went through the back door into the kitchen. 'Could you tell Amy I had to use the boys' Milk Roll. I've run out of her usual.'

'Er – Milk Roll. Right.' Francesca stared at the battered Disney World lunch box. A souvenir from Amy's holiday to Florida, the autumn after Nick had graduated from university. Looking at Francesca's amused expression, Elspeth wished she had swapped it for a plain Tupperware affair. But then she surprised Elspeth by confessing with an embarrassed little smile, 'Mine's a Harry Potter one. Someone at work bought it for me as a joke at Christmas. I'm a big fan, although it takes me ages to get through the books.'

'Well, I'm sure Paul keeps you busy.' Elspeth couldn't help sounding prim.

Francesca's smile stayed put, but Elspeth now detected an element of wistfulness about it. 'Paul's . . . amazing, really.'

Elspeth didn't reply. Paul was certainly something. Maybe Francesca Courtney would be the one to finally give him what he deserved – the sort of emotional hammering he'd no doubt dealt out himself in the past.

'Before you go,' Elspeth wet her lips, 'I was wondering . . . do you happen to know if there are any properties coming up for sale in Harrisfield?'

'*Just* Harrisfield, or—'

'Hereabouts, you know, not too far.'

'There's very little in this area on our books at the moment, but things can pick up around this time of year. Are you planning on moving somewhere larger?' Francesca glanced up at the cottage, as if she couldn't really believe it was large enough to house its current occupants.

'I know it might seem small,' sniffed Elspeth, 'but it's a Tardis really. And I'm not looking for myself. I was thinking about Amy and the boys.'

'Oh. She hasn't asked me to keep an eye out, but if she does, I'll make sure to keep her posted.'

'She's quite limited, in terms of her price range, I would imagine . . .'

Francesca's smile was almost furtive now. 'Well, I think she might be pleasantly surprised when she hears the offers I've had for the flat.'

'Offers?' echoed Elspeth. 'There's more than one?'

'They're like buses sometimes. Three come along at once. Well, in this case, two. But still great bargaining power for the vendor,' she added, with a hint of glee. Then she popped the lunch box into her own Tardis of an attaché case, and opened the back gate to let herself out.

'Amy, there's someone here to see you . . .'

The Little 'Uns Day Nursery garden was awash with sunshine. The children who were playing outside had been smothered in sun cream and wore uniform, French legion-naire-style hats. Amy had been helping an introverted little boy of sixteen months to use the multicoloured plastic slide. She clapped in encouragement, then glanced towards the back door. Maria was showing Francesca Courtney through. Amy's mouth gaped open, before she cobbled her wits together and endeavoured to look intelligent.

'I'll take the children back inside,' Maria offered. 'It's time they got cleaned up for lunch anyway.'

'Oh, er, all right.'

'Hi, Amy.' Francesca smiled. She looked rather pleased with herself. 'Is there somewhere we can talk . . .?'

Amy hesitated, then pointed towards a picnic bench in the shade of a tree. They headed over, making chitchat about the sudden fine weather. Beside Francesca, Amy felt disconcert-ingly conspicuous in the bright yellow T-shirt that all the staff members wore. It seemed sloppy and gaudy beside the sharp, grey business suit. However, a moment later, as Francesca tried to perch on the bench without having to swing her legs over, Amy was glad she was wearing cargo pants. She made herself comfortable and leaned her arms on the table.

The estate agent started rooting around in her case, but instead of pulling out some paperwork, she drew out Amy's lunch box.

Amy suddenly felt ten years old. 'How . . .?'

'I went to your mother's house first,' Francesca explained. 'She said she was going to bring this to you, so I offered to do it myself. I was just passing through Harrisfield and thought you might like to hear some good news . . .'

Amy stared at the lunch box gormlessly, then back up at the estate agent. This time, Francesca did pull out a sheet of paper from the case, and slid it across the table.

Amy couldn't seem to focus on the words and numbers; they danced in front of her eyes like the mischievous fairies who were doing exactly the same in her stomach. Get a grip, she told herself sternly. You're an adult, in spite of appearances. This is all supposed to make sense.

Francesca was waiting for a response. Those green eyes, flecked with gold, which had clearly mesmerised Paul, now held Amy in their beam. 'Well?' she said, almost breathlessly. 'What do you think?'

Amy forced herself to concentrate, looking down at the paper again. It consisted of scribbled messages, possibly jotted down while on the phone.

'When the first call came through, I tried getting hold of you,' Francesca explained, 'but your mum's phone was engaged and your mobile was switched off. Then when I got the second call . . .'

'These are offers for the flat,' said Amy, the penny dropping with a huge clunk. 'You've had two offers for the flat?' she added incredulously.

'Well, we had a few viewings over the weekend . . . It *is* a great flat, and there's been a lot of interest. There's so much space – you don't often get that with urban living.'

It *had* looked spacious, Amy concurred, once she'd cleared

out all the boys' things and her own and put what she didn't need to take to her mum's in storage. It was as if she and the boys had added another layer to the apartment, one which might have seemed superfluous to some people and wouldn't have made a great selling point to the sort of young professional she imagined would want to live there. What was left was Nick's, and apparently he hadn't organised the removal side of things himself yet. But Francesca had assured Amy that the flat would be more attractive with the basic structure of a home in place. Dark leather corner settee; metal-framed, king-size bed; beech-effect computer station; aluminium venetian blinds . . . the things that Nick had overruled her on. Modern, minimalistic and, in her opinion, soulless.

Francesca started droning on about which offer they were going to accept. Logical enough, it seemed. 'But when the first young man – Mr Collins – does find out there's been another offer, he might be willing to go higher himself,' she concluded.

'Like an auction?' Amy frowned. 'I'm not an expert in this house-buying business—'

'No,' said Francesca politely, 'so you can safely leave this to me. You're my client, and I'll get you the best price I can. It's in my interests, too.'

'And you'll do it . . . ethically?' Amy wanted reassurance, and didn't care if she came across as difficult.

Francesca bristled perceptibly. 'I've never done anything *un*ethical.'

In a career that could hardly be classified as long, Amy speculated. And nowadays, people seemed to have different definitions when it came to the word 'ethical'.

'As long as it's fair,' she persisted, trying to lessen the margin for error.

'When it comes to fairness,' said Francesca, obviously licking her wounded pride, 'I don't think you can lecture me.'

Amy rocked back slightly on the picnic bench, surprised by Francesca's counter-attack.

The other woman seemed to be studying the tree to her right now, as if she suddenly found it fascinating. 'I'm sorry. I shouldn't have said anything . . .'

As the shock wore off, Amy was feeling justifiably curious. 'But you did. And I'd appreciate it if you explained what you meant.'

There was a pause. 'Well, it can't make matters worse.' Francesca sighed, and looked back at her. 'It's about Paul, and the fact that you're being awful to him for no valid reason. Shit,' she hissed, 'he'd do his nut if he heard me saying this. But it's such . . . playground behaviour. I wish I could just bang your heads together.'

Amy stared at her in shock again, wondering where the posh, softly spoken Cheltenham girl had gone.

'First there's Paul,' Francesca went on, 'pretending he's not offended by your attitude towards him, when he's gone out of his way to help. And then there you are, acting as if *he's* the arsehole who ran out on you and that this is all down to him.'

'I – I know it's not his fault directly,' stammered Amy.

'Or indirectly. If it wasn't for him, you'd be fighting for a share of what was yours through a solicitor. As it stands, it's been Paul's influence with Nick that's saved you from an even bigger headache. And why he won't come out and tell you that himself, I wish I knew. He says he's got his reasons, but they don't seem to be doing him much good.'

Amy couldn't reconcile any of this with her last face-to-face confrontation with Paul. He'd been so self-absorbed and mindless of her feelings. And since then, there'd been only a few short phone calls, with both of them sounding clipped and strained.

'This doesn't make sense,' Amy floundered. 'Paul's just a go-between.'

'Is that why he's jeopardising a lifelong friendship? He's not simply a glorified messenger boy, Amy. He's been doing his best to craft Nick's messages, too. And that's for your sake and the boys', because Paul doesn't condone what Nick did and he never will.'

'Maybe he's just feeling a bit guilty,' said Amy lamely.

'If he'd known about Nick's affair,' Francesca wagged her finger schoolmarmishly, 'if he'd been lying to you all along, too . . . But Nick deliberately kept him in the dark, and I think that speaks for itself, don't you?'

Amy didn't know, her brain felt fuddled. This was too much to take in. Paul was the good guy? No . . . He wasn't capable of it; he didn't know what heroism meant. He was a caveman, pure and simple. But then again . . .

Amy distractedly opened her lunch box, blinking down at the child-sized sandwiches made with the kids' bread and not her own usual, nutty wholemeal. She wasn't hungry any more, and wasn't sure why she'd even looked inside. For something to do, maybe, while she tried to straighten her thoughts. Had she grossly misjudged Paul? Or was it Francesca – her faculties blurred by passion and goodness knew what else – who had got the wrong end of the stick?

'Anyway,' Francesca snapped shut her attaché case, 'I ought to be making a move. I've got an appointment at two.'

'Right,' said Amy quietly, 'well thank you for coming in person to tell me about the flat.'

'No problem.' Francesca didn't look at her as she stood up. 'I'll call you tomorrow then, keep you posted.'

'Great,' said Amy, without enthusiasm.

'Oh, er,' Francesca turned round, 'your mother said you might be interested in properties in this area . . .'

Amy frowned. 'I suppose I will be now.'

'Three-bed, four-bed?'

'I wouldn't want to stretch myself too much financially, even if a larger deposit means a smaller mortgage . . .'

'OK, then. I'll see if anything comes up that I think might interest you.'

'It's got to be a house, though. With a decent garden. I always missed that about the flat.'

'And it's not much better at your mum's, is it?'

'It's better than a lot of places,' said Amy loyally, wondering why it was fine to criticise her mother herself, when she always jumped to Elspeth's defence if anyone else did.

'I'm sure it is,' sighed Francesca, twirling a strand of stray hair around her finger. 'Now, I've really got to go. But like I said, I'll keep you informed.' She reached across the table to shake Amy's hand. A knee-jerk gesture between client and agent, which appeared to catch them both off guard, considering a major proportion of their conversation hadn't been business related.

Amy watched her teeter across the grass, the ground still slightly sodden from all the rain they'd had lately. Francesca's heels seemed determined to sink. Why hadn't Amy noticed that earlier? And how had Francesca Courtney managed to lose her mystique, that edge of sophistication? By letting down her defences and showing Amy that she was just a woman, too? Charmed by a man who would ultimately screw her up and let her down.

But as Amy gazed into the lunch box – her stomach so contracted she knew she wouldn't eat a single bite – she couldn't stop her mind from picking over everything Francesca had said . . . And the more it picked, the worse Amy felt.

15

'Dinner?' echoed Paul, slow to conceal his surprise. 'At your mother's house?'

'Well, I haven't got my own place yet,' murmured Amy, on the other end of the slightly fizzing phone line. It wasn't a great connection; maybe he was hearing things wrongly? Or perhaps she was supposed to be talking to someone else and had rung him by mistake. Except that she'd called him by his name when he'd first answered; and he couldn't think of anything that he could mistake for 'dinner' which would make more sense.

'It's . . . tricky,' she limped on. 'I need to talk to you, and apologise.'

'Apologise?' Paul leaned back in his chair, frowning up through the skylight. 'What for?'

'For acting the way I have. Anyway,' she said, more briskly, 'I have to go. Mikey's managed to get hold of Joe's felt-tips. He's probably about to redecorate Mum's lounge. You'll come over, then? You said you weren't doing anything on Friday . . .'

'Er – no, I'm not. Francesca's going out with her lot from work, so I'm at a loose end . . . I'll see you around eight thirty then.'

'OK.' She hesitated. 'I appreciate it. Goodbye, Paul.'

Still fazed, Paul stared at the phone after Amy had hung up. Then he picked it up again to ring Francesca and run it by her. A woman's brain was usually the only way to unlock the complex mysteries of another female. But he changed his mind. Best after the event, he decided. Francesca was a little too vocal on the subject of Amy and the kids, accusing Paul of being too soft at the same time as admiring him for his compassion; for want of a better word, he supposed.

Frankly, he didn't believe Nick ought to get away lightly with what he'd done; not simply to Amy, but to their friendship. Because when Paul had finally dared to put his motives for this 'compassion' under the microscope, he'd found he really was feeling profoundly betrayed on a personal level himself. *So much for brotherhood*, his offended ego had grumbled sulkily. And so much for their boyish vows to stick together through hell and high water. Nick's actions had desecrated all the good memories. Paul even found it tough drinking at their old haunts, and the idea of going to the Chester races without him come summer was depressing.

'Don't rush out and canonise me just yet,' he'd moped to Francesca.

'So you're getting back at him through Amy somehow?' she'd retorted, her smooth, gorgeous voice barbed with sarcasm. 'It isn't that you care about those children, or anything selfless like that?'

Paul had wavered, and Francesca had taken the opportunity to add, 'You might be slightly misguided, Paul, but that doesn't mean your heart can't be in the right place, too. With most people, it's in several places at once, and you're no exception.'

She knew exactly what to say and do, thought Paul, in total admiration. Francesca was one of the most truly wise people Paul had ever met, besides Tilly, Amy's little sister of the owlish, grey eyes. Unlike Francesca, she had the knack of making him feel stupid, as opposed to grateful and blessed. And she was half his age. He hoped she wasn't going to be there on Friday night. He'd be treading on eggshells, as it was, trying not to make some gaffe that would have Amy revoking the apology she'd claimed she needed to make.

Paul pinched the bridge of his nose between his thumb and forefinger, closing his eyes. There was a headache lurking behind them, threatening to have him reaching for some ibuprofen. Tension-related, no doubt. He wasn't comfortable about Amy saying sorry when there was no true need, and the more he dwelled on her doing it, the more apprehension seemed to heap itself upon him.

His only consolation would be seeing the boys again, although when he started to think about that in depth, he realised it wouldn't be so welcome after all. What did you say to a two- and a three-year-old if they asked you why their father had gone away, leaving them behind? 'He's a tosser,' would probably be met with blank expressions and a whole new set of questions.

Besides, thought Paul, it wouldn't go down well with their mother. Especially if they started repeating it at nursery.

'I'm afraid the boys are in bed,' said Amy, ushering Paul towards the sofa and wondering if his interest in them was sincere or whether he was simply playing the role of doting 'uncle'. 'Were you expecting to see them?'

He did seem genuinely disappointed. 'I – um – just assumed they'd be around. I forgot eight thirty was a bit late.'

'They've not long gone down. I just thought this would be easier without them, or I would have made it earlier. I've usually had dinner myself by now.'

'So have I,' admitted Paul. 'But don't worry, I'm not ravenous. I'll eat, of course. I *am* hungry. I'm just not . . . famished.' He stopped wittering and scratched his nose. 'How are you keeping, then? Have you done something different with your hair . . .?'

'No. Well, er, I've combed it.'

Paul nodded encouragingly, as if she'd said she'd been to a salon for a complete new look, but then a second later he was glancing around the lounge again, possibly searching for an escape route. 'So where are your mum and Tilly?'

'Here!' Elspeth's voice preceded her down the stairs. The hem of a long velvet skirt appeared first, followed by a cream Aran cardie and then a familiar stripy scarf. 'Hurry up, Tilly, or we'll be late!' The voice floated back up the stairs, impatient and flustered. Amy frowned; her mother had obviously forgotten about not disturbing the boys.

Elspeth reached the foot of the stairs and faffed about getting her mac off its hook. Amy watched with trepidation as her gaze finally rested on Paul. Was she going to be on her best behaviour?

'Oh.' She pretended to act as if she hadn't realised he was there, even though she had just replied to his question a moment ago. 'Hello, Paul.'

'Hello, Elspeth.'

'How are you?'

'Very well, thanks. And you?'

She slipped on the coat. 'Oh, you know, mustn't grumble.'

Amy resisted rolling her eyes. That was Tilly's prerogative. Elspeth was putting on her best jolly-hockey-sticks persona, so blatantly false it was cringeworthy.

Amy was aware that her mother didn't believe any of that 'twaddle' Francesca had come out with about Paul. 'If you're going to grovel to him,' she'd told Amy tersely, 'you'll excuse me if I don't stay and watch.'

'I'm not going to grovel,' Amy had argued. 'I just want to get to the bottom of it all. I need to know what's really been going on.'

'And if Paul *has* been on your side—'

'—then I'll thank him.' Amy didn't add that she would also feel compelled to apologise. Her conscience could be a merciless creature, at times.

'Going out?' Paul asked Elspeth now, as Tilly clattered down the stairs and acknowledged his presence with a nod. 'Aren't you staying for dinner . . .?'

'We had ours with the boys,' explained Elspeth.

'We're going to see that new Tom Cruise film,' added Tilly, casting a sideways glance at her sister. 'Thought we'd make ourselves scarce and not cramp Amy's style.'

Frowning slightly, Paul looked from Tilly to Amy.

It struck Amy that the situation did look rather staged, as if she'd engineered to have some private time with Paul; which she had, for an innocent and valid reason. A hot flush radiated upwards from her chest. She prayed it wasn't obvious. She could have clobbered her sister, who knew very well that only a sadomasochist would have designs on Paul Faulkner Jones. He was good-looking, she'd never disputed that, but in a sterile sort of way, as far as she was concerned. He didn't elicit the responses in her that he seemed to do in plenty of other women. There was a lot more to the chemistry of physical attraction than just noticing that a man was athletic and virile.

The sound of a car horn made Amy perk up with relief. 'That must be Carol.' She herded her mother and sister towards the front door. 'Have a good time. Don't binge on the popcorn!'

'We'll bring some back for you,' waved Tilly chirpily, then winked and inclined her head towards the house. 'Be good.'

Oh, for goodness sake. Amy shut the door with a shudder and a bang, then turned back to Paul.

He was looking warily at the baby monitor on top of the piano. Amy went over and turned up the volume. Lucas was definitely on the move in his cot. There was a lot of rustling going on, interspersed with the occasional coo. Whether he settled himself back to sleep on his own was another matter. Amy found herself waiting, almost holding her breath.

'Is Lucas's cot in with Joe and Mikey?' whispered Paul. 'Or in your room, or . . .?'

The corridor? Amy felt like adding.

'You don't have to whisper. The monitor's not two-way. And Lucas is in my mum's room with me now.'

'Right.' Paul's voice was still low. 'So where's your mum sleeping?'

'There.' Amy pointed to the sofa. 'It turns into a bed.'

Paul looked down to where his pert backside was resting. 'Must be a pain. Do you make it up every night and fold it back in the morning?'

Amy nodded. 'It's quite an easy sort of mechanism, though. And Mum only has to take off the pillow and duvet. The bottom sheet can stay on.'

'That's handy.'

'Yes, it is.' Amy frowned, and nibbled on her thumbnail, forgetting she'd varnished them yesterday. This wasn't how she'd envisaged the conversation going. The merits of sofa beds had hardly been on her 'to discuss' list. But she was beginning to realise there was a whole evening to get through; or at least, dinner. Her plan was rapidly showing its flaws, as it struck her that it would have been simpler just to have gone for a drink somewhere.

There was a pinging noise from the oven. 'That's the timer.' Amy jumped at the chance to change the subject. It seemed that the baby had gone off to sleep again, so she wouldn't be needed upstairs. 'The roast should be ready . . .'

'Something smells good.' Paul followed her into the kitchen.

'Beef. I know it's not a Sunday, but . . .'

'Yorkshire puds and horseradish sauce?'

Amy nodded.

'My fave! And your famous carrot and turnip?'

Amy nodded again. 'I'd hardly call it famous. There's not much to it.'

'Well, no one else's tastes like yours. I must have been missing your roast dinners without realising.'

'You did use to turn up unannounced a lot on a Sunday afternoon. I figured you were just too lazy to cook your own.'

'You know what they say,' Paul was abstractedly examining the bottle of red wine she'd placed on the table, 'the way to a man's heart . . .' He tailed off, and put down the wine.

Amy felt another hot flush coming on. The notion that she was reaching an early menopause seemed more favourable at that moment than blushing for some other reason connected with Paul. If only Tilly had kept her trap shut. Paul was looking increasingly uncomfortable himself, and it was probably her strong maternal streak that made her take pity on him, enough to put him at ease without stalling further.

'Paul . . . the reason I asked you here tonight . . . Well, after everything Francesca said, when she came to tell me about the offers for the flat . . .'

'Francesca?'

'Please don't take it out on her, Paul, she was only trying to help . . . Anyway,' Amy sighed, 'I think I need to say sorry for what happened the last time we met. I said some terrible things . . .'

'Amy, you had every right to be mad.'

'But not at you. You didn't do anything. Not anything that deserved the way I reacted. The opposite, in fact. You've been trying to help, haven't you? Really help, I mean. You've been arguing my case with Nick.' Amy swallowed the lump ballooning in her throat. 'My case, and the boys'. If it wasn't for you—'

'Nick would have seen sense,' Paul murmured darkly. 'With or without my help.'

'Would he?' Amy heard the tremor in her voice, and turned away to start dividing the roast potatoes between two warmed plates. 'He's one of the most self-centred people I know.'

'Worse than me?' snorted Paul, but he was looking at her with thinly disguised surprise, as if he'd never expected her to say something like that about Nick, even after everything that had happened.

'Let's just say, the scales have fallen from my eyes.' She came over to the table, brandishing the roast beef on an oval dish. 'I'm not saying you're perfect, mind. Just that I may have been a bit too hard on you over the years, and way too soft on Nick. Anyway,' she took a resigned breath, 'could you carve for me, please?'

'Haven't I always?' Paul took the knife like a pro.

'You did use to do it, didn't you?'

'Only way to check if the meat's done – trying it for yourself. No good just poking it about a bit to see if the juices run clear. That's for wimps.'

Amy shook her head at him. 'So that's why the meat never seemed to amount to much once it was cut up! A third of it was probably in your stomach. And at least wimps don't get gastro-enteritis.'

'When have you ever seen me throwing up?' Paul puffed out his chest, then deflated it. 'Actually . . .'

'Well, for starters, there was that stag night you and Nick went on last year – that old school friend's, Pip or Kip, or whatever his name was. You both came back to the flat just gone three, and you said you couldn't get a taxi home because you'd lost your keys.'

'They were in my pocket all along. *Doh!*'

'And then you were sick in my best saucepan.'

'At least I didn't pee in your sink.'

Amy couldn't help a small laugh dodging past her lips at the memory, even though back then she had been six months pregnant and fuming.

'Good times,' said Paul, oozing sarcasm.

'The best,' rejoindered Amy, on a similar note.

They both sat down to eat, absorbed in thought. Paul poured the wine.

'Listen,' he hesitated, with a forkful of food on its way to his mouth, 'you don't have to apologise for anything. And you don't have to thank me. My own motives haven't been purely honourable. I mean,' he bumbled on quickly, 'I'd like to think it's payback time for Nick. I'd like to believe there's some justice in the world.'

'He can't just walk out of our lives without giving something back – is that it?' Amy asked, as if Paul's clichés hadn't been clear enough. She sighed, hooking her hair behind her ear. 'When I think about what you said the last time we met, about being angry because he'd left you, too . . . You had a point. You've got every right to feel hurt.'

'I said a lot of things that night.' Paul frowned into his wine glass. 'But I acted that way for a reason.'

'What way?'

'Insensitive.'

Amy now paused with a fork halfway to her own mouth. 'Were you?'

'You know I was. You had a go at me for it. The thing is, though, I was so sure everyone had been treating you like granny's old china, it hit me that you might need . . . an alternative form of therapy.'

'A good old-fashioned slanging match?'

'The harmless sort.'

'I thought aggression was always meant to be bad?'

'Depends what's behind it. Anyway, did you feel better afterwards?' Paul took a sip of wine, and gave her a chance to think about it by gazing round the kitchen, looking as if he wasn't in a hurry for an answer.

He hadn't been to Mews Cottage very often, let alone had a meal here. He'd just tagged along with Nick sometimes, perhaps to pick up a heavily pregnant Amy (she'd never driven past eight months) or Joseph, after he'd been visiting his grandmother, or to run an errand with Nick on Amy's behalf ('I picked up some shopping in town for Mum, can you just drop it over to her?') en route to some Faulkner Jones Burnley development in Flintshire. He hadn't always come into the house, anyway; just waited in the car.

Thinking about it harder, though, one memory stood out among the others. Yet it wasn't recent, and it hadn't seen the light of day in years.

Nick had just passed his driving test – his third go, much to his mortification – and Rowena had rewarded him with his first car, a Peugeot 205 cabriolet. Paul had gone with Nick to pick up Amy on the way to another end-of-term school disco, this time at Rosewood High.

They'd shuffled into the lounge: Nick, Paul and some stick insect of a girl Paul had been seeing whose name he couldn't remember. Elspeth had called peevishly up the stairs, and Amy had come down wearing a long black dress with a low bodice, her hair piled up on her head in a jumble of glossy curls. She'd been wearing high heels and a truly dazzling smile – the sort that was impossible to fake – and Paul hadn't been able to help noticing that there were slits in her dress which reached daringly above her knees.

It was the first and only time she had seemed totally at ease with her figure, and the only occasion Paul had felt envious of Nick when it came to a girl. The first and last time Paul had wondered if he'd made a mistake by not asking her out before Nick had. The crazy thing was, Nick had been more excited by his new car than the fact his girlfriend had looked so amazing.

Paul shook his head. He hadn't been alone back then in doubting whether Nick was the monogamous type. So what had gone awry, after so many years of proving the sceptics wrong? When had things turned sour, on Nick's part, at least?

Because it seemed to Paul that Amy had been blissfully unaware that the relationship had been in trouble.

'Why are you shaking your head?' he heard her ask, and he looked up blankly. Back to the present day, and this odd little meal for two.

'You were shaking your head, as if you were thinking about something specific.' She seemed to think this sounded silly, and shrugged, 'Never mind, don't worry about it. And the answer's yes, by the way. Yes, I did feel better after I acted like a stroppy mare.' Her eyes crinkled at the edges when she smiled, coaxing him to smile back. 'And if that really was your intention, then thank you.'

Paul shrugged matter-of-factly. 'I just wish I could do more.' He helped himself to another spoonful of creamed horseradish. 'Wring Nick's neck, or something.'

'So you're a professional hitman now?'

'More of an amateur.' His own smile faded gradually. 'Amy . . . I've been meaning to ask . . . How are the kids doing – *really*? Do they know exactly what's going on yet?'

Amy stared down at her meal. She'd hardly dented it. She was still too wan, and although she had a soft, pale pink top on, lending a touch more colour to her face, she still didn't look as if her health had been a priority lately.

'They know more,' she sighed eventually. 'It's understanding it that's the problem. It's impossible to tell how much is really sinking in, or what damage it might be doing. Joe's gone very quiet, he doesn't talk about it. Mikey, on the other hand, recites the information you give him as if he's taking it all in. You assume he realises his dad won't be back for some time, although I haven't mentioned Anneka yet. Then, the next hour, or the next day or whatever, he's asking when will Daddy be home, or when are we going back to the flat . . .'

Amy shook her head. 'I have tried to tell them their dad won't be living with us any more, but that it isn't their fault; it wasn't because of anything they did. But do they believe that? Joe especially . . . And I've said we're going to look for a new house, with a garden to play in, but then Mikey asks if Daddy's going to come and live with us again there, because there'll be loads more room than at Nana's . . .'

It was harrowing to talk about this from the kids' point of view. And Amy was right. What effect would this have on them in the long-term? Broken homes, if they were still called that, might be commonplace these days, but did that make it any less of a tragedy for the individual families involved? Did it help to dilute the suffering? Paul cradled his wine glass in his hand, momentarily overwhelmed by the 'what if's corkscrewing through his head.

Had Nick's own childhood, primarily his parents' divorce, his father's long illness and subsequent death, and then his mother's remarriages, instilled a kind of ticking time bomb in him that had finally exploded, with far-reaching consequences for his own young family? Would he find it difficult to stay faithful to Anneka, too, in the long term? And would there be more children to be messed about and further loyalties to divide?

'You could screw yourself up thinking about it,' he muttered out loud. 'About the things in our past that make us the way we are, and the things we do to our children that'll shape their own lives, without us even realising.'

Amy was sitting up very straight in the fiddle-backed pine chair. 'When did you get to be so philosophical?'

'I've always been the sensitive type,' Paul smiled stiffly. 'I've just hidden it well.'

'Yeah, right.' Amy pushed the plate of Yorkshire puddings towards him. 'Go on, eat up, I don't want anything going to waste.'

'I'll eat if you will.'

'Bossy boots.' She picked up her fork grudgingly, but he was pleased to see her try.

The smell of home-made apple crumble slowly infused the air. Amy had popped it in the oven after the roast had come out. Paul was looking forward to it. He couldn't remember the last time he'd had a plain and simple dessert that hadn't come out of a packet.

'I've got custard or double cream?' Amy offered, as she cleared away the leftovers of the roast – not as much as Paul had originally feared. He was sure what remained wouldn't really go to waste. Amy was too resourceful for that.

'Custard, please. It'll remind me of school dinners.'

Amy wrinkled her nose. 'You miss those, do you?'

'Certain things. Why? Don't you?'

'Not really. But then I didn't go to a posh public school, did I? When I was at Rosewood, I used to take a packed lunch and go with my friend Samantha to the park to eat it. When it wasn't freezing cold or peeing down, anyway.'

'Samantha . . . I think I used to fancy her . . .'

'You fancied all the girls in my sixth form,' said Amy tartly, 'except me.'

Paul didn't answer immediately. 'It wouldn't have been fair on Nick, would it?' he said eventually. 'You were strictly off limits. The ultimate taboo. My best friend's girl? Never,' he shook his head emphatically. 'Not in my book.'

'Very admirable,' scoffed Amy. 'And I was only teasing.'

'I know,' said Paul quickly. 'And I didn't really fancy every single girl in your sixth form.'

'You just went out with them.'

'I never went out with Samantha.'

'No, that's true, but that's only because she knew better. She used to hear all the horror stories from me. And I heard them all from Nick.'

'He'd embellish them, you know. I was never as bad as he made out.'

'Don't diminish your reputation now, not after it's taken all these years to cultivate it. And the last I heard of Samantha before we lost touch, she'd moved down South somewhere. Suffolk or Sussex. With her husband and two kids.'

'Have you tried Friends Reunited?'

'The website? No . . . But then, we hadn't been that close in years, to be honest. She was great when I first moved to Harrisfield. Instantly took me under her wing. She lived round the corner and caught the bus with me. That's how I met her. But it was never going to be the friendship of the century. I've kept in touch with a couple of friends I went to school with in Chester, before Dad died. We meet up now and again, although we haven't for ages . . .' Amy shrugged. 'I guess that's how it goes sometimes. So effectively I'm partnerless, and friendless and—'

'Yeah, right.' He echoed her earlier retort with the same intonation she'd used herself. 'And I'm still the thorn in your side, the bane of your life. I could be a friend, too, you know.'

She placed a generous, steaming bowl of apple crumble and custard in front of him. 'That's a hard concept to grasp at this time of night, Paul, but I'll give it a go.'

He glanced at his watch. 'Is that the time already?'

'Meeting Francesca afterwards?'

Paul shook his head. 'Going home to my lonely flat and my lonely bed and . . . um . . . no. No, I'm not meeting Francesca. Nothing to rush off for, but if you want shot of me after dessert—'

'You know I wasn't implying that, so don't pretend to be offended. You can stay for coffee. I even bought some proper Colombian stuff for the cafetière I gave Mum last Christmas. It was still in its box up until a few hours ago. The cafetière, not the coffee.' Amy sighed raggedly. 'It was Nick's idea, actually. I should have known Mum would never convert from her regular English Breakfast.'

'My mother's the same, only in reverse. I bought her a

Bodum teapot a couple of years ago. That's probably still in its box, too.'

Paul grinned spontaneously, surprised at how easy making conversation with Amy had been this evening. He was willing to bet that they had talked more tonight than on any single occasion in the past. About to comment on this, he stopped with his mouth still open. 'Amy,' he murmured instead, 'there's some bloke looking through the window.'

'What?' She leaned over in her chair to peer around the kitchen door. Paul had a clear view of the lounge, while she didn't. 'Bugger.'

Paul squinted. The man was now trying to get Amy's attention, but she seemed to be trying to ignore the fact. 'Isn't that the bloke from next door?' asked Paul. 'The one Nick always used to say—'

'Yes,' she hissed. 'That's him, that's Jonathan.'

'Do you want me to have a word with him?'

Amy frowned. 'About what?'

Paul frowned back, unsure. 'I don't know . . . I'll tell him you've got a headache or something. I mean, what does he want calling at this time? Has he run out of milk or something? Nick used to say—'

'Yes, I know what Nick used to say,' Amy snapped, 'but Jonathan's got every right to call round.' She was looking rather red and shiny, as if she'd been exerting herself. 'He's been a good . . . friend.'

'I thought you said you didn't have any?'

'You see, that's your problem, Paul, you never know when to be serious. If it hadn't been for Jonathan lately . . .'

She was rising to her feet, smoothing back her hair, straightening her top . . . Paul realised with a jolt that Jonathan was possibly a little more than just a friend.

As Amy went to let him in, Paul leaned back in his chair and folded his arms over his chest. Well, well, well. Had the adoring little woman found solace at the loss of her beloved in the arms of another man? The notion disturbed Paul, and it struck him that he still viewed Amy as some angelic, wholesome, passive creature who would always belong to Nick, even if he no longer belonged to her, and even if she had finally proven that she was about as passive as uranium.

16

'Are you coming in, Carol, love, or shooting straight off?'
Elspeth clicked off her seat belt and turned to her best friend,
who was peering in the rear-view mirror.

'I don't know. What do you think, Tilly?'

Slumped in the back seat, the teenager was probably still
having palpitations over Tom Cruise, if Elspeth's own youth
had been anything to go by. She'd had a few heart-fluttering
moments over screen icons herself.

'Think we're back too early?' Carol went on. 'That film
wasn't as long as I thought it'd be.'

'I think we're way too early,' smirked Tilly, as Elspeth
glanced over her shoulder with a frown. 'But then Mum
did have us rushing home, so she obviously doesn't agree.'

'I don't know what you're on about,' said Elspeth, tossing
her head. 'I'm tired, that's all. It's been a long day.'

Tilly snorted. 'You just don't want Amy to be alone with
Paul longer than she has to be.'

'Oh, for grief's sake, you know why Amy wanted some
privacy with him. Why do you have to turn it into something
. . . lewd?'

'I'm inclined to agree with Tilly,' said Carol cautiously.
'You have been rather nervy this evening, Els, and you kept
looking at your watch all through the film.'

Which hadn't been easy in the dark, thought Elspeth, still
frowning. But she hadn't been able to help herself. She felt too
old to fully appreciate Tom Cruise. That supporting actor

playing his father had been much more her type. Sensitive, yet commanding, like George. A shame he'd been killed off in the first five minutes. If it hadn't been for those flashbacks . . .

'If you're not worried about Amy, then what's the big rush to get home?' Carol added.

'I am worried about Amy, of course I am,' said Elspeth, exasperated. 'But not like that. I'm just worried about how she's dealing with it all. It won't have been easy.'

'Mum, Amy's thirty-one. If she'd wanted you to be here tonight to fight her battles for her, she'd have asked you.' With a frustrated sigh, Tilly began clambering out of the car.

'You've got no idea what it's like,' Elspeth called after her. 'You're not a parent, you don't know how powerless you feel sometimes.'

'I do know. You keep telling me. And, Mum, Amy *is* a parent, three times over, so you definitely can't lecture her about it.' Tilly slammed the car door and stood waiting under the porch, her arms firmly crossed over her chest.

Elspeth sighed, too, sounding as frustrated as Tilly. 'I thought it was supposed to get easier once they grew up.'

'Hah!' Carol cackled. 'That's a particularly cruel belief. It helps sustain us through the knackering, no-time-for-ourselves years, and then dissolves like a mirage. But no one will ever convince us that they're not worth it. And at least we do get a little more time to ourselves when we haven't got to wipe their noses or tie up their shoelaces.'

Which meant that Carol must have a great deal of time to herself right now, considering that her offspring had well and truly flown the nest. Her son lived with his wife on the south coast near Bournemouth, and her daughter was a hairdresser in Manchester with a busy social calendar that didn't appear to involve many trips back to Harrisfield.

'I just wish I knew what Amy was thinking,' Elspeth sighed. 'We never get a chance to sit down and talk, just the two of us.'

Carol inclined her head towards the porch and the willowy figure hovering beneath it. 'And what about Tilly? She's had you to herself these last eight or so years. Have you had any time for the two of you lately?'

Elspeth shook her head slowly. 'But she understands why Amy and the boys had to move in. She gets on fine with her sister – only the occasional sniping session, but that's normal, isn't it? And she's brilliant with the boys.'

'She's also sixteen. It's all about finding your own space at that age, isn't it?'

'I suppose . . . But when Amy came to stay, I never even considered putting Tilly out of her room or insisting she share. And she's so mature for her age, she really doesn't mind the upheaval in the rest of the house.'

'So you've spoken to her about it, then?'

'No . . . not exactly . . .'

'Mum!' Tilly rapped on the glass. Elspeth opened the passenger door. 'Mum, are you coming in, or what? I'm not barging in there on my own when this is all your idea.'

'What's my idea? Not hanging around the cinema once the film was over? And we're not barging in, love, this is our home. I'm sure Amy and Paul have finished dinner by now.'

'The car's still there.' Carol pointed further up the lane.

'I can see that. And it's a good sign,' said Elspeth stiffly, privately wishing it had gone. 'It means they've probably sorted out their differences.'

'The day Amy and Paul sort out their differences,' said Tilly, 'will be the day I finally admit I'm not right about everything.'

'It would be almost worth sticking around for,' snickered Carol, slipping the car into gear as Elspeth climbed out. 'But I won't impose tonight, petals, even though I'm extremely tempted. I've got a husband and a cat to take care of . . . He'll be asleep by now, in front of the telly. I'll probably have to prise the remote from underneath him and carry him to his basket.' She grinned. 'Tiglet's such a clever thing, I'm thinking of sending in a video to *You've Been Framed*.'

Tilly gaped after her as the car reversed up the lane. 'What is she *on*?'

'Nothing. And Carol Caldicott's more sensible than you and me put together,' said Elspeth grimly. 'Now come on, what are we hanging about for? Haven't you got a key?'

'Actually, no. It must be in my other jacket.' Tilly sidled over to the window. Elspeth wondered how she'd resisted that long, considering there was a narrow gap in the curtains where they didn't quite meet in the middle.

'Well, I haven't got my key, either,' sighed Elspeth, 'so we'll just have to knock . . . What? What is it? Why are you gawping like that?' Elspeth took a few paces towards the window, herself, and peered into the lounge without compunction. It was her home, after all.

There, from left to right on the sofa, watching television, were Paul, Amy and Jonathan. Amy and Jonathan both looked as if they would rather be anywhere but there. Paul, on the other hand, had his legs stretched out and seemed to be quite at home. Elspeth went to the front door and knocked.

'I've never seen Amy move so fast,' giggled Tilly, still at the window. 'Here she comes . . .'

Amy flung open the door. 'You're back!'

For a moment, Elspeth thought she was going to hug them as they stepped inside; she seemed so overjoyed at their return.

'This looks cosy.' Tilly whipped off her coat and plopped herself on the sofa in the spot Amy had vacated. 'And what's this you're watching? A talk show, how fascinating.'

The girl could join the Royal Shakespeare Company, thought Elspeth, half cringing, half in awe.

'You know,' continued the teenager, 'when I saw you

through the lounge window, I thought to myself, this has to be the most innocent ménage à trois ever.'

Tilly would have had her mouth washed out with soap if she'd been living fifty years earlier and had known the great-grandmother she'd been named after, groaned Elspeth inwardly.

'And you're an expert on the subject, are you?' murmured Paul.

'No, but I bet—'

'Didn't you hear the car, love?' Elspeth asked Amy, cutting her younger daughter short. 'I thought you would have realised we were back. We forgot our keys, you see. Silly us.'

'I didn't hear anything. Not with the television on. I mean, it wasn't loud, so that we didn't wake the boys, but . . .' Amy shrugged. 'Maybe Carol was trying to be quiet, too.'

Jonathan rocked forwards on the sofa. 'It's my fault the TV's even on. I remembered I'd seen a trailer for this interview with—'

'—some politician I'd never heard of before,' said Paul cheerfully. 'It was interesting enough. But I still can't remember the guy's name.' He yawned, stretched and rose to his feet. 'Whoa, look at the time.'

'Lost track of it? Easily done.' Jonathan was clambering to his feet, too. 'Well, it was good to meet you at last, Paul. I mean, I knew your face obviously, I've seen you around, but—'

'—we'd never been properly introduced. You're right. We should all do this again sometime.'

'And I'm sorry again if I interrupted anything.' Jonathan glanced from Paul to Amy. Elspeth couldn't define the look on his face. She wished it was more disgruntled.

'Nothing important,' said Amy, smiling like the Cheshire cat on speed. 'It was a nice surprise seeing you.'

'And we're still on for lunch on Sunday?' Jonathan checked. 'I know a good family pub where we can take the kids.'

'That'll be nice for you,' said Paul.

'It'll be lovely,' said Amy firmly. 'Yes, Jonathan, we're still on for it.'

'Great, I'll see you then – if not before.' He hesitated, before leaning towards her to give her a peck on the cheek.

Elspeth held the door open as he went out. 'Why don't you come over tomorrow?' she suggested. 'If you're not doing anything, you can have tea with us. It'll be a takeaway as usual, seeing as it's a Saturday, but if you don't mind something from the chippy . . .'

Jonathan didn't need to be asked twice. 'Great. OK. I'll see you tomorrow then. Bye all.'

Tilly heaved a groan once he'd gone. 'Mum, did you have to? Can't we have a moment's peace without having to watch him leer all over Amy?'

'Jonathan does not leer,' Elspeth frowned sternly.

'To put your mind at rest, Tilly,' said Paul, 'I didn't notice him leer once tonight. He seems like a very pleasant chap, in fact.' Paul scooped his jacket from the row of coat pegs and slipped it on, patting his pockets. He fished out a dinky mobile phone, gave it a cursory glance – checking for messages, Elspeth supposed – and then returned it to his pocket, pulling out his car keys instead. 'A very pleasant chap,' he added, a dry smile skirting his lips.

From the sofa, Tilly suppressed a giggle.

'No, I mean it,' said Paul, with too earnest a frown to be taken seriously. 'Amy clearly finds him pleasant, don't you, Amy?'

'He's very pleas—' she began, and then stopped herself, as if she'd fallen into some trap. 'Look, we're not going *out* out. And if people took the trouble to get to know him . . .'

Paul touched her arm. 'Amy, I'm sorry. He does seem like a decent bloke, and even if it isn't anything serious, if he makes you happy . . .'

'He must do,' said Tilly. 'But that's not exactly saying much after Nick. What I want to know is if he makes the earth move when—'

'Right.' Elspeth's strained patience finally snapped. 'Could you come into the kitchen with me, please, Tilly? You can make me a cuppa while I tidy up. Goodbye, Paul . . . I imagine we'll be seeing you around.'

Paul nodded. 'Oh, you will.'

Elspeth couldn't make out what was being said as Paul took leave of Amy at the front door. His head was bent over hers, and whatever they were talking about, it seemed to drag on a bit. Elspeth rolled up her sleeves. Tilly had obediently put on the kettle, and was now clearing the table, which was amazing for her. She evidently didn't want to make herself scarce yet, curious no doubt to hear about Amy's evening at first hand.

'I've got a few things to say to you, Tilly,' hissed Elspeth, still watching Amy out of the corner of her eye. She was now locking the front door and drawing across the long curtain that kept out the chill at night.

'OK, Mum,' sighed Tilly, 'I know.'

'Well, I don't. I've got no idea what that performance was in aid of . . .'

Amy came marching into the kitchen. 'Tilly, you're really beginning to lose it. What was all that about back there?'

'I didn't like your attitude *or* your language,' said Elspeth, shaking her head at the teenager. 'You're only sixteen.'

'And you were flirting with Paul like a 25-year-old,' added Amy accusingly.

Elspeth stared at her elder daughter, surprised. This hadn't been the point, as far as she was concerned. It was Tilly's attitude towards Jonathan, and her risqué utterances, which had offended Elspeth. She hadn't been aware of any flirting, as such. If Amy had noticed, though, then it was cause for concern.

'Tilly,' said Elspeth worriedly, 'I'm aware that Paul's a very attractive young man. But on many levels, he's bad news, and I don't want you to start viewing him as . . .'

'Worth dropping my drawers for? As Great-grandma Mathilda might have said.'

'Tilly!' Never mind drawers, Elspeth almost dropped the leftovers of the apple crumble. 'What's got into you? You're just a child!'

'No, I'm not, Mum!' Tilly folded her arms together.

In spite of her slender frame, her younger daughter had fairly pronounced breasts, Elspeth realised, as if waking up to the fact for the first time. Perhaps it was one of those padded push-up bras creating that effect. But there were definite curves where her hips ought to be, and a bra couldn't do *that*. No, at sixteen, Tilly wasn't a child; but it had just been easier to suppress the knowledge the majority of the time, and just call her intellectually mature for her age.

Apart from slapping on make-up and wearing a short school skirt – usually with thick tights, practically like leggings, really – which was something all her friends seemed to do anyway, Tilly had never shown the slightest urge to stay out late, get drunk, smoke cigarettes, sneak around with a boyfriend or dabble with drugs, thank God.

It had always been books, with Tilly. Books and homework and the computer and an hour or so of TV. And when friends came round, admittedly not often these days – but then the house was so crowded anyway – they had never seemed the type to get into any trouble. They were nice girls, from nice families and nice homes, and even poor Keira had seemed to make it through her parents' divorce relatively unscathed.

Since hitting puberty, Tilly had been particularly outspoken, dramatic and fiercely intelligent, but at least this had come with its own reassuring predictability. For the most part,

Elspeth had been proud of her, but she was beginning to wonder if she had breathed a sigh of relief too soon.

'I'm just stating a fact,' Tilly went on to explain. 'Paul's attractive, you said so yourself. But he's way too old for me. And even if I did think throwing myself at him was a good idea, or theoretically possible, he'd never go out with a schoolgirl in a million years. Paul's not the type, and Amy knows that better than anyone.'

'I – I do?'

'You've got a good idea who he's gone out with over the years, haven't you? To some extent. And Nick liked to exaggerate, but did he ever once tell you Paul had got off with an eighteen-year-old or under . . .? No. Well, then, I seriously doubt he's been out with someone my age since he was my age himself.'

Amy didn't look placated by this. 'You were still flirting with him,' she insisted mulishly.

'It was just a bit of fun, not *flirting*,' argued Tilly. 'I've never given him much of a chance in the past. But after he's been on your side with this Nick business, he can't be all bad. I think you biased me against him over the years. By the look of it tonight, though, I'm preaching to the converted. You're warming to him yourself.'

'Not "warming" as such . . .' said Amy slowly, still frowning. She picked up a tea towel, even though there weren't any dishes that needed drying yet. 'But he's not shallow, if that makes sense. He looks and acts like he is, in some ways, but he isn't.'

Elspeth lifted her gaze to the ceiling. 'Heaven preserve me! Here are my normally sane daughters trying to tell me there are hidden depths to Paul Faulkner Jones. You'll be telling me next, Amy, that we're going to be seeing a lot more of him at Mews Cottage.'

'No . . . well . . . you might. He's like an uncle to the boys, and he's always been good with them . . .'

'He was also Nick's friend, not yours,' Elspeth pointed out tetchily. 'And he's not a proper uncle. Not family.'

'Actually,' Amy repudiated, 'that's not strictly true any more. I mean, no, of course he isn't family, but he *is* a friend. Francesca was right, you know. Paul hasn't been on Nick's side in any of this. He's spoken out on my behalf and the boys', and I'd rather let him stay and fight my corner with me than have to deal with Nick and Rowena all by myself.'

'But you wouldn't have to deal with Nick and his mother on your own, love,' said Elspeth ardently. 'I'm always here.'

'Mum, I appreciate it, really I do. Without your help . . .' Amy shook her head and shrugged. 'But you've got your own life, and I can't hide behind your skirts for ever.'

'You can hide behind Paul, though?' Elspeth couldn't help her scathing note. How was it that your own children could make you feel so useless? More than anyone else on this earth, they had the power to lift you up or pull you down.

'Mum,' said Tilly carefully, 'Amy's not hiding behind anyone any more. That's her point, I think. Paul's already been dragged into this, it wasn't his choice, either. So in a way, they're fighting it out side by side, on an equal footing.'

Elspeth watched as the two sisters exchanged a look of such empathy, it was both moving and painful. Fleeting though it was, it made Elspeth wish yet again that she'd had a brother or sister to share such moments with. An ally and a friend, even if you'd been biting each other's heads off only minutes before.

When George had come along, he had been all men to her, in some ways. Filling such a huge void in her life, his passing had only seemed to make the hole larger and her life more empty. Perhaps they had understood each other so well because they had both been only children. They had never wanted that for Amy, but it had been difficult for Elspeth to conceive again. Tilly had been a last-minute miracle, the result of numerous prayers and a romantic, rainwashed weekend in the Lake District.

The age gap between their daughters had always been a concern. But Elspeth was now realising that as Amy and Tilly grew older, their differences would only lessen. And that would leave her where exactly . . .? Somewhere on the outside again, looking in.

'I felt so bad when Jonathan turned up out of the blue,' Amy was confiding in Tilly. 'I hadn't told him about Paul coming round. It just hadn't come up yet.'

'Well,' said Elspeth sniffily, 'Jonathan was never going to ask, "By the way, is Paul coming round for dinner?" – was he? It was up to you to tell him.'

Elspeth knew this wasn't the right way to join in again, but she couldn't seem to just switch back into Caring Mother mode after it had been so casually dismissed.

'And I was going to tell him,' said Amy, clearly ruffled. 'But it seemed better to do it after I'd found out the truth. Once I'd apologised to Paul and cleared the air.'

'Oh, you didn't stoop to that, did you?' Elspeth shook her head despairingly. 'What about all the trouble he's caused you over the years?'

Amy was staring out of the kitchen window, but it was so black in the yard, only their reflections were being bounced back at them. 'I wouldn't call it "trouble". Nick was hardly Mr Innocent, himself. And I don't think Paul's done anything to me that would have stopped me saying sorry to him tonight. I honestly believe he's never acted with any vindictiveness.'

Elspeth sighed. In her heart of hearts, she knew that Amy was probably right. Paul was only a product of his parents, and with a mother like Isabelle, he had done well just to stay of sound mind.

'It was weird, though,' Amy was addressing Tilly again. 'I would have thought Paul would have leapt at the chance to make a run for it when Jonathan turned up. I think he was too surprised at first.'

'Stunned that you'd even look at another man so soon after Nick, probably,' said Tilly, squirting washing-up liquid into the sink. 'Men can be like that. Very territorial. Dates back to the apes, I guess.'

'Territorial,' repeated Amy. 'That's exactly it. That's how he was. As if he owned the place and had more right to be here than I did, even. Definitely more right than Jonathan. Well, you saw him, how he'd made himself at home. It was so awkward. Jonathan just didn't know what to say, so he started going on about this interview on TV he wanted to see. Paul even had the gall to suggest he go home to watch it. Politely, of course, in a very . . . veiled sort of way.'

'And I thought you said he wasn't vindictive.'

Amy turned to face Elspeth again. 'It wasn't like that! He wasn't deliberately rude. It was as if – as if he couldn't help himself. Anyway, he didn't have anything to rush home for. I suppose he might have been feeling a bit lonely.'

'And jealous,' said Tilly, 'that you had company,' she added quickly.

'Jealous that you could find another man more appealing than him, more like,' interjected Elspeth scornfully. 'You know, Amy, that's probably been his problem all along. You chose Nick over him, and he couldn't stomach it.'

Amy was staring at her, open-mouthed. So was Tilly, for that matter.

'Paul was never in the running, Mum. It was Nick I wanted from the start, and in those days, he actually wanted me back.'

'I wasn't implying Paul was after you in that way,' said Elspeth, wishing she hadn't gone down this road. How did you explain to your own daughter that she wasn't alluring enough? 'It's just, if you're used to girls falling over themselves to get to you, it might feel like a huge rejection when one of them doesn't. When she chooses someone else instead. Whether you fancy that girl yourself or not.'

'So seeing Amy with Jonathan tonight raked up all those old feelings, is that it?' summarised Tilly.

'You don't actually believe all that, do you?' Amy appealed to her sister.

'Mum's got a point. And the crux of it is, Paul might not even realise it himself.'

Amy was doing her best impression of a goldfish, soundlessly opening and closing her mouth. But she soon recovered and said, 'I think you've both gone mad. Paul was perfectly normal when I said goodbye to him just now. And if he doesn't realise he's feeling that way – all wounded pride, or whatever – then how is he supposed to act on it? Subconsciously?'

'You said it yourself,' answered Tilly, 'he couldn't seem to help it. That spells subconscious to me.'

'Oh, for goodness sake.' Amy stalked out of the kitchen. 'I'm going to check on the boys and then I'm going to bed,' she called peevishly over her shoulder. 'Leave the dishes. I'll do them first thing in the morning.'

'Talk about overreacting.' Tilly shook her head as she picked up the first of the dirty plates piled up by the sink.

'Do you think so?' frowned Elspeth. 'Well, your sister still has a lot of issues to resolve . . .'

Tilly looked at her with those clear grey eyes that were so like George's, it was almost as if Elspeth had been transported back in time. Her husband used to look at her like that, quietly amused, and a tiny bit pitying sometimes.

'I wasn't just referring to Amy, Mum . . .'

17

Summer crept up on them, and then crept away again after a day or so, as if it had changed its mind.

It was on a blustery day in late June that Amy went to view the house in March Street. To say that it was love at first sight would be pushing it, but it was the most hopeful she had seen so far.

Very nearly the only one she would have seen, if Francesca hadn't managed to persuade her that Buttercup Meadow – a small, relatively new development between Harrisfield and Mold – was worth taking a look at. The houses there were all under three years old. Amy felt familiar with it even though she had never personally been there, because Nick had talked of nothing else when he had been involved in selling off the thirty or so plots. Buttercup Meadow was a Faulkner Jones Burnley initiative. Amy soon realised that, in her eyes, this didn't work in its favour.

There were two houses in the estate on the market, both three-bed and owned by professional couples with expanding families who wanted to upgrade to more prestigious homes with downstairs studies and larger en suites. At least, that was what Amy had surmised. They had seemed cagey with her, considering. Maybe the fact that she was a single mum with three kids immediately had them assuming she was living off benefits and a house at Buttercup Meadow was simply a pipe dream.

'My ball will go over the fence a lot,' Joseph had predicted, forlornly staring round the small trapezium-shaped garden of the first house. Amy had wondered where she could fit in the little swing, slide and wooden patio furniture she had envisaged acquiring, without knocking through to next door.

'There's no room for Daddy to play on his 'puter when he comes back from holiday,' Mikey had pointed out, looking around the 'master' bedroom.

The corresponding bedroom back at the flat had been large enough to house a computer desk along with the king-size bed, cot, double wardrobe and modest dressing table. Nick had kept his laptop at the workstation when he wasn't using it elsewhere. Amy had pointed out a couple of times that if they moved somewhere larger, he could have his own study, as he'd used to before the children had come along. But a house that size had clearly been too much responsibility for Nick to face.

'When you're washing us in the bath,' Joseph had muttered, peeking around a bathroom door in one of the Buttercup Meadow houses, 'you'll have to kneel with your legs around the toilet.'

Amy had looked at him in alarm, but when she'd peered around the door herself, she had understood what he meant. The sink, bath and loo were positioned around the cramped space in a haphazard fashion, as if someone had just pointed and said, 'There, there and there,' without logic or practicality coming into it.

'Neither of the houses was right for me.' Amy had phoned Francesca at the office the following day. 'They were both very appealing in their own way, but . . .'

'You know Paul was the chief architect involved?'

'Yes. Yes, I was aware of that.'

Amy could recall how moody he had been while he worked on the project. His father had overruled him on so many aspects, Paul had eventually snapped and told him to design the whole thing himself. But they'd quickly sorted it out, and

Paul had been back on the job. Amy had taken that to mean
that Paul's parents had bribed him, presumably with that
skiing holiday he'd gone on soon afterwards.

'I think he did a good job,' Francesca had declared
proudly, 'considering how limited space can be on these
new estates.'

'Well, maybe if they stopped trying to cram in so many
houses . . .' Amy had mumbled, but Francesca hadn't seemed
to hear her. 'Haven't you got anything else on your books?' she
had asked, more audibly.

'Nothing suitable. Your requirements are very restrictive.'

'If it comes to it, I'll broaden my search. But Mum insists it's
fine to hang on a while longer.'

Francesca had sighed. 'So Harrisfield it is, then.'

'It's ideal in so many ways . . . My mum, my job, it's got an
excellent junior school, a nice High Street . . .'

'OK, OK, I'll see what I can do, even if it's bumping
someone off,' Francesca had joked, in a brittle fashion. 'Leave
it with me. I'll be in touch.'

But when the call came through from the estate agents
towards the end of June, it wasn't from Francesca. It was a co-
worker of hers, explaining that Francesca was on holiday but
that she'd left instructions for him to contact Amy asap should
anything come up. There was a house in Harrisfield – semi-
detached, Victorian and in need of some work, but apparently
it had three good-sized bedrooms. An immediate viewing was
recommended, even though it was at the top end of Amy's
price range.

She left the kids with her mum this time, and took Jonathan
with her. The immediate drawback as they turned into March
Street was that it was actually a cul-de-sac, with an obvious
dearth of parking spaces. Most of the red-brick houses had
three front steps that gave directly on to the pavement. No
front gardens, let alone driveways.

'Those steps aren't great for the buggy. And I'm rubbish at parallel parking,' groaned Amy. Nevertheless, she managed to find a vacant spot and coaxed the Espace as straight as possible to the curb. 'I suppose I'd get better with practice.'

'Isn't it peculiar how you can live in a village for years, but you still don't know every part of it,' remarked Jonathan, climbing out of the car.

'It is a bit tucked away,' Amy reasoned. March Street was just off a street, off a street, off the other end of the High Street from Mews Cottage. Even her mother hadn't heard of it, and she'd gone to ask the lady in the newsagent's for directions on Amy's behalf.

'We should have walked here,' said Jonathan. 'It's not that far, and we could have timed how long it would take.'

'I suppose,' said Amy. 'It is quite windy, though. And it looks like it might rain later.'

'Nothing we couldn't have handled. Hardly a trek in the Himalayas. Anyway, which one's number five? I can't see a "For Sale" sign.'

Amy had already spotted it, nestling unremarkably between three and seven, but there was no number anywhere. An iron plaque attached to the brickwork beside the green front door pretentiously referred to it as 'Willow View Villa'.

A middle-aged woman in a tweed skirt and twinset answered, almost as soon as they knocked.

'Hello, yes,' she said in a breathless, impatient voice, which wasn't as posh as her attire. 'Croft, yes? I'm Mrs Ash. You're the first of my viewers. Come on in. The others are due in fifteen minutes.'

'The first?' Amy stepped inside. 'I assumed we'd be your only viewers. At least today.'

'Oh?' The woman frowned. 'No, no. You're my first so far, but that nice young man at MacIntyre and Bright assured me that there's already a lot of interest.'

Damn. Amy frowned at Jonathan, who was furtively running his finger along the dado rail, scooping up dust.

This wouldn't have happened if Francesca had been around, but it wasn't as if Amy hadn't been aware she was going away. The last time she'd spoken to Paul, he had mentioned that they would be staying at Rowena's place in Spain for two weeks.

All right for some, she grumbled to herself now. And while Francesca might have left instructions for that nice young colleague of hers to keep Amy informed of anything appropriate coming on to the market, it clearly hadn't stopped him blabbing to other potential buyers, too.

'This was my mother's house,' Mrs Ash explained, ushering them up the stairs. 'She passed away recently.'

'Oh, I'm sorry,' began Amy, but the woman flapped her hand, cutting her short.

'I'm afraid my mother couldn't look after this place on her own, judging by the state of it. It was as much a shock to me as it probably is to you. I live in London. It was impossible to come up often enough to be of much use.'

'So 1996 was the last time you bothered, then,' Jonathan muttered under his breath, discreetly gesturing to an old *Woman's Weekly* topping a pile of yellowing magazines.

Amy elbowed him in the ribs. 'The bathroom's a good size,' she said, trying to find something optimistic to say about the grimy, Seventies' turquoise suite. 'And the bedrooms,' she added, 'I'm sure they'll look big, too, once all the . . . um . . .'

'Once all the junk is out of the way,' tutted the woman. 'Yes, I know. I've made a start on it, but . . .'

The accumulation of a lifetime. And often it was of no use to anyone, mused Amy, not even your own offspring. Unless it was valuable, of course, then everyone would want to get their mitts on it.

She sighed dispiritedly, and glanced out of a rear window,

only to stop in her tracks and move closer. The view didn't seem to belong to this house at all. Amy was instantly reminded of *The Secret Garden*, one of her favourite books as a child.

Instead of wooden fences, which seemed commonplace these days, there were brick walls dividing the March Street properties. The gardens were long but not too narrow, and in the one directly below the window, creepers and climbers and roses and goodness knew what else seemed to grow on every side.

Amy sometimes watched gardening programmes on TV if she got the chance, but she hadn't had much of an opportunity over the years to practise what she'd learned, unless it involved house plants or window boxes.

In the centre of this particular garden was a stone bird bath, with creamy yellow flowers entwined around the base. The low evening sun glimmered on a small York-stone patio, and the lawn was a lush, vibrant green, looking recently mowed. It wasn't the most toddler-friendly of play areas, but there would be ways around that without harming the overall integrity too much.

In the wall at the far end was a wooden door, which appeared to give on to a footpath. Beside the footpath ran a stream, and on the other side was a row of willows, which clearly gave the house its name, although it wasn't the only one that could claim it for a view. The willow branches trailed in the water and swayed in the wind like a Hawaiian girl's skirt.

'Before you ask,' said the abrupt, tweed-skirted woman who had inherited this vista but seemed to care nothing for it, 'that is a public right of way, yes. But my mother kept the gate padlocked, for security. There's side access to the front too, of course, on the left.'

'Did your mother have a gardener?' asked Jonathan. 'Only . . .'

'No,' sighed Mrs Ash. 'She just loved that garden more than the house. I think it was where she spent most of her time, unless the weather drove her indoors. There's a little potting shed just round the corner; you can't see it from here, but she kept all her tools and gardening things in there. Those will all be sold off with the house, if that's your sort of thing. I've got no use for them myself.'

'The lawn,' began Amy, 'it looks recently—'

'—mowed? Yes. That's the neighbours. The ones on the right. Nice couple, early sixties. They got on well with my mother, and they've been looking after the garden since she passed away. To be frank, I think they must have been helping her while she was alive, too. At least with the more strenuous stuff.'

'That's very kind of them,' said Amy, putting it down as another plus point on a gradually mounting list.

'Good neighbours are in such short supply these days,' Jonathan winked.

Amy pulled a face at him as the woman led them back downstairs.

Beyond the dust and clutter, a few interesting original features were still evident, such as the fireplace and the panelled doors. And the tiles on the kitchen floor looked antiquated but charming if you liked that sort of thing, which Amy did.

'Mother should never have ripped up that lino,' sighed Mrs Ash. 'But you could always lay some of that fake wood down, I suppose. That's very popular these days.'

Amy would gladly replace the carpet in the lounge and dining room, which consisted of threadbare swirls of crimson against a darker background; but she would keep those patterned tiles over wood laminate or lino any day.

Just then, the doorbell sounded loudly, and the woman hustled them back up the hall. 'That'll be the other couple,' she said briskly. 'Well, it was nice meeting you, Mr Croft' – she shook Jonathan's hand – 'Mrs Croft' – she shook Amy's.

'I'm not Mr Croft,' said Jonathan. 'Amy and I aren't married.'

'Oh.' The woman paused, tight-lipped. 'I see.'

Amy frowned. What if Mrs Ash was some kind of puritan who would refuse to sell the house to anyone who didn't meet her strict criteria?

'Er – Jonathan's a friend,' Amy interjected swiftly. 'I wanted his advice. He won't be living here. It's just for my children and me. I've got three boys. Their father isn't . . . with us any more,' she added, like a postscript.

'Oh,' said the woman again. 'I'm sorry to hear that. And so young . . .?'

'Yes, he is. Was. Ahem. We'd better go. Thanks for showing us around. We'll be in touch via the agency.'

Amy and Jonathan nodded briefly at the young couple who exchanged places with them on the front step, then they made their way back to the car. Amy opened it, and was about to climb inside when Jonathan tugged her back.

'You fibber,' he murmured, sliding an arm unexpectedly around her waist. 'On two counts.'

'Really?' Amy looked up at him, eyes wide and ingenuous.

'You made it sound as if you were a widow.'

'I might as well be, for all the use Nick is. And if that woman looked at me more sympathetically because of it . . . I'll just have to pray she doesn't mention it to anyone from the estate agents. Hopefully, the spec sheet will arrive in the post tomorrow. I think I'll bring my mum back for a viewing. And Tilly and the boys. I'll have to tell them not to mention Nick, not that they probably would, I suppose. Well, the boys might. That could be awkward.'

'You told that Mrs Ash we weren't a couple,' Jonathan pursued his point, cutting her prattling short. 'Lately, I was under a different impression.'

Amy glanced towards the house, and tried to wriggle from his hold. 'Ssshhh, she'll see us. And then our cover's blown. Anyway, I didn't mean it like that.'

'Well, then,' he said slowly, consulting his watch, 'why don't you come back to my place? The boys will be in bed by now, you don't need to worry about them. I can open a bottle of wine . . .' He leaned towards her, his lips pressing down on hers – a sensation she was becoming accustomed to. And even though it didn't set off any fireworks, it was pleasant enough in a mild, tingly sort of way.

Amy backed off again, glancing at the house, hoping the woman hadn't spied them. 'I don't know . . . I'm quite tired . . .'

'We can always skip the wine, if you'd prefer.'

'Actually, a mug of cocoa in front of the telly would be lovely, if that's on offer . . .'

Jonathan hesitated. 'Of course it is . . . Although I haven't got any cocoa.'

With a small smile, Amy motioned for him to get in the car. 'Then you'll just have to prove how much of a gentleman you are,' she said archly. 'Hop out at the Co-op and buy me some.'

18

'I don't want Cornflakes,' harrumphed Joseph, folding his arms over his chest. 'I want Shreddies!'

Elspeth sighed. 'But I haven't got any Shreddies, sweetheart. They ran out yesterday – remember?'

'Well, buy me some.'

'I will later, when I go to the supermarket. This morning, though, it'll have to be either Cornflakes or toast. Or Lucas's baby muesli, which doesn't have any added sugar, but somehow manages to taste as sweet as anything.' Elspeth scrunched up her face with revulsion, commenting dryly, 'Still, Lucas likes it. Or at least, he likes smearing it around his tray. That's the main thing.'

'You could have eggs, Joe,' suggested Tilly, leaning against the kitchen counter, scraping charred bits off her wholemeal toast.

'I don't like eggs. I like Mummy. I want my mummy *now*.'

'I want Mummy now, too,' said Mikey, his bottom lip wobbling over his bowl of soggy cereal.

'Where is she?' glowered Joseph.

Elspeth exchanged pained glances with Tilly. 'She's um—'

'Right here,' said Tilly, her face clearing. She straightened up and gestured towards the lounge.

Amy was coming through the front door. Her clothes looked crumpled, and her hair clearly hadn't been near a comb or brush as yet this morning. She ventured into the kitchen, biting her lip and looking unprepared for the whoops of delight from the older boys.

'Mummy, where were you?' demanded Joseph, retreating into petulance as quickly as he'd burst out of it. 'I went in your room this morning and you weren't sleeping there.'

'Oh.' Amy made a circle with her lips, holding it for a couple of seconds. 'I . . . was . . . er . . .' She looked as helpless as if she were on stage waiting for a prompt.

'You were staying with a friend,' piped up Tilly.

'Er – yes.'

'Who, Mummy?' asked Mikey, wrapping his arms around one of her legs and almost throwing her off balance.

'An old friend,' said Elspeth, following Tilly's lead. 'No one you know, poppet.'

'It was a last-minute thing,' said Amy. 'I'm really sorry I wasn't here earlier. But, look, I'm here now. So – has everyone had breakfast yet? *No?*' Her eyebrows somersaulted histrionically as she pretended to be shocked. 'And why not?'

Elspeth watched with pursed lips as her daughter negotiated her way around the kitchen, moving from child to child and back again, and finally praising when all three had some food in their stomachs. It was an art form, and Amy was exceptionally good at it.

'Right,' she sighed, with palpable relief. 'It's brush your teeth time!'

Joseph and Mikey slid down from the table, groaning. Tilly grabbed their hands.

'I'll take them. I've still got to brush mine.'

Elspeth now stared as Amy wiped down Lucas, took off his plastic bib and undid the high-chair straps. She lifted him out and held him tight against her chest, closing her eyes briefly. He chewed on her chin – an early attempt at a kiss.

'So,' Elspeth sucked in her breath, then let it out again portentously, 'where have you been exactly?'

Amy jiggled the baby on to her hip and with her free hand started putting things away in the fridge. 'You know very well I was next door,' she murmured. 'You can hardly claim you were going to send out a search party.'

'That's not the point. You popped in here yesterday after viewing that house and said you were just going to be over at Jonathan's for an hour or so. If I'd have known what the "or so" stood for, I might have been more prepared.'

Amy slammed the fridge door shut. 'It wasn't planned, Mum.'

'You're not footloose and fancy-free, you realise. You haven't been in years. And if you didn't mean it to happen, then at the very least I hope you were . . . responsible.'

Amy frowned. 'You think that Jonathan and I . . .?'

Elspeth knit her brows, and picked half-heartedly at her toast. She had only managed a few bites so far, even with her favourite Rhapsodie de Fruit jam.

'You're a grown woman,' she said tersely, 'and I'd sound foolish if I started preaching to you, especially after your relationship with Nick. I'd just prefer to have some sort of warning in future.'

'Like what exactly? Excuse me, Mum, I'm feeling a bit horny, so I'm just going next door to have it off?'

Elspeth winced. She hated hearing it phrased like that. 'Not quite so obviously, perhaps.'

Amy opened the back door, uncovered the wooden playpen in the yard and scanned it rapidly for anything untoward before depositing Lucas in it. He immediately pounced on some squeaky building blocks with a gleeful gurgle, as if they were long-lost friends. Amy came back in, leaving the door wide open to let in a beautiful, serene morning, as if the wind last night had blown away every last trace of cloud from the sky. She collapsed into a kitchen chair, tugging a hand through her hair.

'It's expected of you to sleep with your boyfriend, isn't it?' she said gloomily.

Elspeth pushed away her toast. She really didn't have the appetite for it today. 'I suppose that's the culture we live in, at least in this part of the world. Not that I'm saying it's right. It's just something we can't seem to get away from. Sex is everywhere. I imagine it must be difficult to swim against the tide . . .'

'It is. And I don't know how much longer I can put it off, or come up with different excuses.'

'You mean . . .?'

'I fell asleep on the sofa. And my neck's killing me.' Amy rubbed it with a moan, as if to make her point. 'Why Jonathan couldn't have just woken me up . . .' She shook her head, and winced. 'He covered me with a blanket and left me to it, told me this morning that I'd looked so peaceful, he hadn't had the heart to disturb me . . . I could have had a real go at him, but I didn't have the heart, either. He was all chirpy and cheerful, fussing around me, making tea . . .'

Elspeth sighed. 'He cares about you a lot, love.'

'Too much sometimes. It's stifling. And he's getting impatient, even though he claims he isn't. I can tell. He's frustrated. Not just because I won't put out—'

'Amy, that's a terrible term! It sounds as if you're under some sort of obligation.'

She lifted her head blearily. 'Aren't I? And then there's the fact that we're not very public about our relationship, and the kids aren't properly aware of it yet. When we take them out, I won't even let Jonathan hold my hand or make it obvious to them that we're more than friends.' She groaned heavily. 'It wasn't supposed to get this complicated.'

'You know, it's not really been that long since Nick left . . . Maybe you've rushed into this whole thing.' Elspeth felt more than a smidgen of guilt.

'I just thought it would be good to have someone around who cared. Not family, I mean, just someone impartial, in a way. Someone who didn't have to say that you looked pretty, or that you were special, unless they really meant it.'

'We'll go to any lengths to boost our self-esteem, won't we?'

Amy let out a stilted, mirthless laugh. 'I do care about Jonathan, and I want to keep seeing him . . . I just don't want to rush into anything too physical. I don't feel ready.'

Elspeth had never discussed the facts of life with her daughters beyond the standard clinical details, mainly involving towels and tampons, rather than condoms and caps. She had been aware of Amy's sexual activity with Nick, because she'd found the pill in her room by accident, but she hadn't sat her down and discussed it with her. It had never been the sort of thing her own mother had been comfortable talking about, and that might have had a bearing on why Elspeth had nearly landed herself in hot water the summer before she met George.

At least Amy hadn't been so naive at such a tender age, and it hadn't been likely that she'd find herself in the same predicament, although Lucas's conception was still debatable. It was funny how the pattern of reticence was being repeated, though; even now, after all these years. Presumably, Elspeth found it difficult speaking to her own daughters about these matters because her own mother had rarely spoken about them to her.

'Amy, can't you just explain to Jonathan how you're feeling? He seems an understanding man.'

'He is. And I probably could. It isn't that I haven't tried, I guess, but the words don't seem to come out right. I can't help thinking how he went through hell when Niamh walked out on him and took their daughter with her. Sally-Ann was only four. He moved here just to get away from the house they'd shared, and all those memories . . .'

'He's over it now, though, isn't he? It hardly happened yesterday, after all.'

'He's still in touch, but you know they're in Ireland now. He hardly gets to see Sally-Ann . . . I really think Tilly might have been right when she said Jonathan was shielding himself from getting hurt again, so he kept women at arm's length, or admired them from afar . . . I feel so lousy, letting him take such a huge risk with me . . .'

Elspeth didn't get a chance to reply. There was the sound of pounding on the stairs, and Joseph and Mikey came roaring into view, pretending to be dinosaurs.

Amy glanced at the clock, yelped and jumped to her feet. 'Yikes, look at the time! I need a quick shower. Thanks for this chat, Mum . . . And, listen, on another subject entirely, if I get a letter from MacIntyre and Bright, open it for me, will you? It'll probably be a spec sheet for the house. Ring me at the nursery and tell me what you think.'

'Oh, OK. You quite like this house, then?'

'It's got potential. But I really want you and Tilly to see it. And the boys, too, of course. So if I can arrange another viewing later today, before tea, would that be all right with you?'

'Why the big rush?'

'I don't want to take any chances. It's a good location. I reckon it's only five minutes' walk from the primary school. And other "local amenities", as the spec sheet will probably point out. Plus it's got a few original features. You know what some young couples are like: they want to get their teeth into a meaty renovation. This is just that sort of house.'

'So it's got character?' asked Tilly, strutting into the kitchen with her shirtsleeves already rolled up and striped school tie askew.

'And cobwebs, by the bagful.'

Elspeth felt a niggle of doubt. 'Amy, if it needs a lot of work, are you sure this is the right place for you? With the kids under your feet, it won't exactly be easy. And I never put you down as a DIY kind of person. It won't be cheap if you bring people in.'

'It won't be cheap even if I don't. But listen,' she tapped her watch, 'I've got to have this shower right now, or I'll be really late.'

'Look at me, Mummy,' snarled Joseph, 'I'm a T-Rex! I'm going to *catch* you and eat you ALL up!'

Amy smiled as she hurried through the lounge, and instead of saying, 'Not right now, darling,' as Elspeth had expected, she dazzled her son instead by asking, 'Isn't there a new theory, about the T-Rex being a scavenger rather than a predator because of its small arms?' She ruffled his hair and vanished up the stairs.

A goggle-eyed Joseph ran into the kitchen, Mikey trailing behind with his panda under one arm and blankie under the other.

'Nana,' gasped Joe, 'what's a preddy-tor and that other thing Mummy said?'

'Grief,' exclaimed Tilly, impersonating Elspeth, 'don't they teach you kids anything at nursery?'

Paul glanced at himself in his rear-view mirror before climbing out of the car. Behind his Oakley sunglasses, he seemed lean, glowing and happy. But beyond this aura of good health, still fresh from his fortnight away, he wasn't quite so certain that he was feeling as content as he looked.

At least it was a bonus to have flown back to some excellent British weather. A heatwave, no less. The school holidays weren't due to start in earnest for another week or so, but people were already flocking to the beaches, clogging up the coastal roads and sending ice cream sellers' profits soaring.

Paul had had his fill of sun and sea for now, though. Back in Spain, when Francesca hadn't wanted to be lying prone on a towel on the beach, she'd been lounging by the pool at Rowena's villa. And when she hadn't been there, she'd been getting mullered with her friend Jules. And on those infrequent occasions when they weren't pissed up to their eyeballs, they were racking up their credit card bills at *El Corte Ingles*. And the main topic of conversation besides handbags and shoes and which waiter was the fittest? Apartments and villas and rentals and leases and celebrity clients and the fact that Jules had been on some rich nob's boat a couple of times. 'He's always appearing in *Hola!*, you know,' Jules had gushed once when they'd stopped shopping for long enough to have a coffee, and Francesca had lapped it up with a startling lack of intelligence, Paul had thought. As if she'd left her brain behind on the plane.

Most of the time, even while carrying all their 'bargains' for them, he had felt like a third leg. Superfluous. An encumbrance. He had even gone as far as to take off by himself on a couple of mornings, in the jeep they'd hired to get from the villa to the beach, driving up into the mountains to Ronda one day and over the frontier into Gibraltar on another. Not a barrel of laughs on your own, but then making sketches or taking photographs of 'dilapidated old buildings' hadn't been Francesca's idea of fun and frolics.

It was only at night that she truly seemed interested in him and actively sought his company as more than just someone to tag along with her wherever she wanted to go. At night, when it was still hot and sticky, yet in a more sensuous sort of way, she would come prowling for him in her diaphanous baby-doll nightie. 'What're you doing out here on your own?' she would pout silkily, in a Lolita-ish way that disconcerted him, staring as he dipped his legs in the pool.

'Thinking,' he would murmur, and she would inform him that thinking was for back home, and while home was out of sight and out of mind they had to cherish their fleeting time together. By which she had obviously meant making love everywhere in Rowena's villa, bar the broom cupboard.

Paul sighed, removing his sunglasses and reminding himself that now wasn't the time or place to relive those particular memories. For one, he probably wasn't wearing enough deodorant, and it was hot enough as it was.

Taking a deep breath, he approached the converted old schoolhouse behind Harrisfield Parish Church. A large placard of a rainbow and a beaming yellow sun loomed above the main entrance, declaring that Little 'Uns Day Nursery was the perfect place for the pre-school child.

Paul wished he'd gone somewhere like this when he'd been a pre-schooler himself. Instead, before starting at St Stephen's, he had a dim recollection of a governess-type nanny he'd shared with Nick, who had never let them play outside or watch *Playschool* on TV.

As instructed by a notice next to the door, Paul rang a buzzer, and waited. The door latch clicked, and a girl of about eighteen or nineteen greeted him in the brightly painted hall.

'Hi.' She smiled warmly. 'Polly's dad, right? Your wife rang to say you'd be collecting her, but as you've never been before, I'm afraid I need to see some ID . . .'

'No,' said Paul, scratching his nose. 'I'm not Polly's dad. Or anyone's dad. I'm just—'

'PAUL!' hollered a familiar voice. Joseph came charging out from a room on the left, almost bowling him over. 'What'ya doing here, Paul? Hey, come and see this castle, it's got *pirates*!' He started tugging him back into the room with him.

'Joe,' said the girl firmly, 'you know we can't just invite strangers into the nursery, we need to know who they are.'

'But I do know.' Joseph crumpled his brow, confused. 'Paul's Paul.'

'It's OK, Krissie.' An attractive brunette walked out from the side room. She was about Amy's age, but cooler, with an air of seniority about her. 'I'll take care of this.' She also smiled at Paul. Most females did when they first met him. 'Hi, I'm Maria. And you are . . .?'

'Paul Faulkner Jones. I'm a friend of Amy's. I was wondering if she was free. I probably should have called first.'

'Oh, I don't think that'll matter too much.' Maria looked him up and down unashamedly and appreciatively. Paul's smile dissolved in discomfort. He vowed never to eye up another woman, at least not overtly. The boot wasn't so brilliant on the other foot.

'Krissie,' said Maria again, 'can you cover for me in there? I won't be long. And Joe, do you want to come out into the garden with us for a few minutes?'

'Yay!' Joseph grabbed Paul's hand and started dragging him down the corridor. 'Mummy's out here. She's with Mikey's class. We've got a new 'normous slide for the bigger boys. Come and see!'

Paul grinned. Nick's kids were exhausting, but he'd missed them.

He was led out into a large, irregular-shaped garden at the rear of the old schoolhouse. Toddlers seemed to be running around all over the place; on foot, on plastic bikes or horses and in red and yellow cars, some even two-seater. There was a trampoline, a swing and two slides. Joseph immediately made a beeline for the larger one. Among all this haring and tearing about, Paul could see three women in bright yellow T-shirts who were presumably there to attempt keeping order. One of them was wobbling around herself on a larger tricycle, laughing. Paul stared as she tumbled to the ground, only to be leapt upon by four little people, one of whom was her son Mikey.

Maria smiled again, looking far from apologetic. 'She does get rather involved in her work, as you can see.'

'That's a good thing,' Paul agreed, his eyes straying back to

Amy. 'When you find someone that passionate about their job, you do everything you can to keep them. That's what my mother always says, and she knows what she's talking about, believe me.'

Maria nodded. 'You're right. Amy's my most passionate employee. I'd pay her double before I'd let her leave, but don't you go spreading that about, least of all to her.' She wagged her finger at him, then inclined her head in Amy's direction. 'Well, if you want to speak to her, I think you'll have to do your best knight-in-shining-armour routine and rescue her from the dragons' lair. There are quite a few of them, as you'll have noticed, so I'd tread carefully.'

'Actually,' said Paul, sheepish all of a sudden, 'I was hoping to whisk Amy away for a spot of lunch. Is she due a break soon?'

'No.' Maria's mouth widened into an enigmatic grin. 'She had it earlier. But I'm sure we can work something out. I'll check who's in the staff room. I'd hate for Amy to miss a good whisking.' And still smiling mysteriously, she left Paul to do the gallant thing.

19

'I can put the top up, if you prefer?' Paul gestured to his car.

'On a day like today?' gasped Amy. 'You've got to be kidding!'

'But you always used to say—'

'Yes, well, that's only because you never offered me a ride in it, you sod.' She slid in, rubbing against the leather and lamenting, not for the first time in the last five minutes, that she was rather sweaty.

Her 'Little 'Uns' T-shirt was clinging to her damply, as was her fringe; but at least the latter was a wispy one now that she was persevering in growing out the old, heavy, Dulux-dog look. She pulled out her scrunchie and gave the rest of her hair a shake, fanning it behind her for a moment before twisting it back into a loop at the nape of her neck.

'Warm, isn't it?' Paul stated the obvious as he revved the engine.

'Not as hot as Spain, I'm assuming.' Amy gave him a sideways glance. 'So, how was your holiday?'

'Oh, you know . . .'

'Is Rowena's pad as plush as ever?'

'What do you think? She's had a hot tub put in. And a sauna.'

Amy whistled admiringly, concealing how easily she took umbrage at the way Rowena threw her money around.

'I reckon it was all the new fella's doing,' Paul added.

'The lengths some people go to for love,' said Amy lightly.

'Well, talking of vacations, it's my turn to skive off work as from tomorrow. For a few days at least.'

'Oh?' Paul turned the car into Harrisfield High Street. For some strange reason, he wouldn't tell her where they were going, except that it wasn't far. Amy was intrigued, but so far successfully keeping her impatience in check.

'You're going on holiday, too?' Paul went on. 'With Jonathan?'

'I wish.' Amy hesitated, because that hadn't sounded as she'd meant. 'Well, not with Jonathan.' She hesitated again. Now she'd gone totally the other way. 'Of course, a holiday with Jonathan would be *nice*, don't get me wrong. It's just not on the cards right now . . . No, I'm simply aiming to enjoy this weather from the concrete luxury of Mum's back yard. I know for a fact that there won't be a proper going-away holiday this year. Not if I'm going to buy this house and take care of all the stuff that needs doing.'

'Francesca told me about the house in March Street. She's delighted that you had your offer accepted.'

'Hmm. Funnily enough, it wasn't formally accepted until you came home from Spain and Francesca was back in the office. Which makes me wonder if she kicked some ass and behaved a little unethically, even though I'd asked her not to.' Amy tried not to sound punctilious, but failed.

Paul shrugged in a blasé manner. 'I wouldn't know . . . But then again, you didn't need to raise your original offer, did you? So it's hardly likely there was any gazumping. Maybe that Mrs Ash who'd inherited the house from her mother was holding out for more lolly. Maybe all that was needed was someone to point out the error of her ways.'

'So you do know what's been going on!' cried Amy, almost accusingly. 'But if that was the case, do you realise how much I owe Francesca? That Mrs Ash needed bringing down a peg or two.'

'Or a few grand,' smiled Paul. 'I understand Francesca also did a little bartering on your behalf.'

Amy nodded. 'I couldn't believe it! How did she manage it?'

'I don't know all the details. There *was* another offer, apparently, but it was lower than yours, anyway, and there was a long chain involved. Francesca explained to Mrs Ash that you'd had to rethink your own because of the condition of the house and the amount of work required – something to do with a rough architectural estimate. She highlighted the fact that anyone else considering making an offer would find themselves in a similar situation, especially after having a survey done, thus complicating the entire conveyancing process and possibly delaying it. Basically, Francesca made your offer sound so heaven-sent, Mrs Ash probably realised she should just take the money and run.'

Amy was shaking her head, part in disapproval and part in awe. 'But Francesca's stake in all this goes down, too, doesn't it? Or am I just being thick? I know she was doing this as a favour to me, and I really appreciate it, but I hope she doesn't get into any trouble. If you can think of any way I can repay her . . .'

'She's a chocoholic, if that helps. Although, thinking about it, she's trying to cut back after the holiday.'

Without much warning, just a couple of ticks of the indicator, Paul swung the car on to a dusty, unmade track. 'I think it's just up here . . . Yep, here we go.' He pulled over and parked in a spot where the track widened sufficiently for two cars.

'Here we go, *where*?' asked Amy, looking around blankly as Paul jumped out. 'It's a field.'

Beside them was a grassy meadow, at the far end of which a house rose up on a hill, red and imposing, with an abundance of chimneys. Cherry Tree Farm, as it was now called, was a familiar landmark if you were directing people to the village.

Amy was vaguely aware that in its heyday, when landed gentry had swanned around these parts, it had been loftily known as Harrisfield Hall.

'Are you coming or not?' Paul called back to her, as she sat in the car, perplexed. 'Oh, and bring the picnic. It's in that plastic bag by your feet. Hope you haven't squashed it.'

Amy checked in the bag as she picked it up, and saw that the two packs of bacon, lettuce and tomato sandwiches were still intact. Huffing and puffing, she trailed after Paul, who had taken off his jacket and was holding it over his shoulder while attempting to climb a stile. She shook her head at him.

'You're the only person I know who'd wear a suit on a picnic. Armani, is it?' She was thankful for his sake that he'd drawn a line at wearing a tie.

'You know it isn't. You took up the trousers for me, remember?'

Amy peered at them more closely. 'Oh, yes.' One time last summer, when Paul and Nick had been on their way out, she'd noticed the hem had gone on Paul's left trouser leg. While the two men had faffed about, bemoaning the lack of decent tailoring in this day and age, Amy had taken out her sewing box like a good little woman from Jane Austen's time, and battening down her exasperation, had set to work.

'It's the only time you've ever asked me to take my pants off,' Paul grinned.

Amy tossed her head, and overcame the compulsion to topple him from the stile. 'You knew very well that I meant your trousers, not your boxer shorts, but you had to turn it into a big joke.'

'I know, I know,' Paul choked. 'I'm sorry.'

Frowning, Amy followed Paul over the stile, declining his offer of help and just handing him the sandwiches to hold. Climbing was a fairly easy feat in her cropped jeans and Clarks

Springers, and she smugly pointed this out to him as she landed on the other side.

'I still don't get what all this is in aid of,' she grumbled, straggling after him as he led the way to a clump of trees, a short way along the edge of the field. 'Aren't we trespassing? I've never understood this hiking business. Do you have to stick to designated paths or—'

'No idea. But my dad owns this field now,' announced Paul abruptly, standing on a small knoll and gesturing to the meadow. 'And the one just next to it, over there.'

'Your dad?' blinked Amy.

'Well, Faulkner Jones Burnley would be a more technical way of putting it.'

Amy shook her head, almost pleadingly. 'Don't tell me . . .'

'It wasn't my idea,' Paul assured her swiftly, looking grim. 'Not that it ever is.'

Amy gazed around at the expanse of long, tufty grass. It wasn't the prettiest of places, but she could think of far worse. At least it was green.

'So go on, then,' she sighed. 'Tell me the worst.'

Paul sighed himself, and quickly went on to detail his father's plans for the 'prestigious' Cherry Tree estate, as if keeping it brief would lessen the impact.

'So really,' he concluded, 'building won't actually start until September at the earliest, I'd say. I'm still working on the plans with my dad, and then we have to get them approved and . . . I'm sorry. This is crap.' He flopped on to the grass under the shade of a tree. 'Even the sandwiches are rubbish,' he added, tearing open a pack. 'I just grabbed them from the garage shop when I filled up. They're prob-ably stale.'

Amy paused, then flopped down beside him on the grass and opened up her own pack. 'They don't look that bad. And it seems like ages since I had my salad. I'm starving.'

'Salad?' Paul glanced at her. 'Don't tell me you're on a diet? You don't need it.'

'I'm not, not a calorie controlled one, anyhow. I love my food too much. It's more a programme where I eat as much as before, so long as whatever passes my lips is healthier than a doughnut.'

'You measure everything you eat against a doughnut?' frowned Paul. 'What about all those people who've made millions devising diet plans?'

'I'm not going to jump on the bandwagon, if that's what you're thinking. Just look at me, I'm hardly a great advertisement. It's not stood me in good stead to be five-foot-three with a J. Lo bottom and Dolly Parton . . .' She coughed bashfully. 'Not after three kids, at any rate.'

'I think you're being too hard on yourself,' said Paul, with authority. 'You look totally in proportion to me, and that's what counts.'

'What – your opinion, or the fact I'm in proportion? And I know very well that in your eyes I let myself go once I had Nick in my clutches, or at least, once I was installed in his first flat. I *know*, because you told Nick, and Nick told me. Which was nice of him, I thought.' She gave Paul a gritty smile, and just as he mustered a protest, she cut in again, 'But you were right, so I can't hold it against you. I did let myself go. I did what countless women – and men – do when they get too complacent.'

'Amy,' he stammered, 'what I said to Nick . . . What I really meant by that—'

'I was a frump, Paul. There's no getting away from it. And as I said, I'm not going to blame you when you were right.'

Paul started to protest again. This time, she let him. 'Amy, that doesn't excuse Nick. Even if you hadn't shaved your legs for months, or you'd put on twenty kilos – which as far as I'm aware,' he went on hastily, 'you never did – he shouldn't have treated you the way he has. You're the mother of his children. You deserve more respect.'

She stared at the ground, and then at the sandwich crusts she'd so far discarded in the packet. They were so hard, they were practically inedible. 'Let's just leave it at the fact that I'm making more of an effort these days.'

Paul flicked some crumbs off his trousers. 'To impress Jonathan?'

'No!' countered Amy. 'For myself. For my own sake.' She refrained from adding, 'So that I feel like the woman I'm supposed to be,' because that sounded too intimate. It was enough to have said all that she had; particularly to Paul, of all people. But it was becoming apparent that she could more than tolerate his company these days. She could actually – miraculously – enjoy it.

When they'd eaten what they could of their 'picnic', Paul stood up, and brushed down his trousers again. Then he held out a hand to her. The knowledge that he would be supporting her full weight put her off accepting it, but he took her arm anyway as she clambered to her feet. He scooped up their rubbish, emptied it into the plastic bag and swung it awkwardly in his hand.

'Listen, there is a good reason for my bringing you here,' he admitted, 'and it wasn't just to give you inside information on my dad's plans. I don't know if you know your local history, or whether you've got a good sense of direction . . .'

'You've lost me.' She looked at her watch. 'And, incidentally, I've got to be getting back soon.'

'I know, but this won't take long. It's just this way.' And he started leading her further along the edge of the field towards a copse at the other end.

Once the cool shade of the trees had enveloped them, Amy thought she could hear the sound of running water. But it was so soft, like a whisper, she wasn't sure if it was just the breeze rustling overhead. Then a stream came into view. By the state of its banks, it appeared to be running at only half its capacity, probably due to the dry weather. There was a footpath on one side, and as Paul led her along it, the blue-black slate roofs of some houses came into view. It was only when she saw the willows, that Amy twigged where they were.

'That's March Street!'

Paul nodded. 'You didn't know it was built by the March family back in the nineteenth century, did you? Then again, not many people do. It doesn't seem to be of any great historical interest. Maybe if they'd been famous celebs of their day . . .'

'And who were the March family when they were at home?' asked Amy, on tiptoe, as she tried to work out which of the houses was number five.

'They owned Harrisfield Hall – aka Cherry Tree Farm – from eighteen fifty-one to sometime in the early 1900s. March Street was built for their labourers and the families of domestic staff. It was all very philanthropic. Over time, as the village grew, the street merged with it.'

Amy, who had been listening avidly, regarded Paul with a mixture of deference and surprise. 'How come you know all this?'

'Because, funnily enough, I like architecture. And old buildings. In fact, I prefer old buildings to new ones. If you were to ask me whether I'd want to faithfully restore a crumbling mansion, or design, from scratch, a luxury hotel and leisure complex . . . well, you'd probably be surprised at which I'd go for.'

Amy gazed at him searchingly. 'I dare say I would. But then, how could I be expected to know better?'

Paul sighed. 'You couldn't. Then again, I don't even think my parents would. You've got a better excuse than they have.'

'Well, they've got an excuse, too, if you haven't told them. And talking of parents, is this why you brought me here? Because that estate your dad wants to build is just on the other side of these trees?'

It was his turn to look at her with admiration, although she wasn't sure which of her statements had extracted that response. 'It was the main reason,' he nodded. 'I wanted to make you aware of it, in case it cast things in a different light and made you think again about whether you really want to buy this house.'

'That's the problem with most villages, though, isn't it? They're always evolving. You implied yourself that March Street must have been quite rural once.'

'I suppose. And it's up to you. But I don't know how it might affect things at the local school if there's a sudden influx of kids in the area . . . You'll need to take all that into consideration.'

'Well, Joseph's already got a place at the nursery class in Harrisfield Primary for September, and when it comes to future admittance, siblings of existing pupils have priority, so Mikey and Lucas should be OK. We're already on the list at Harrisfield Surgery, and the dentist in the High Street, thanks to Mum really. She took so much in hand when I first came to stay . . . But the main point is, Harrisfield's become my home again, and whether you built a new estate at this end of the village or the other, it wouldn't put me off.'

Paul nodded again. 'I'm glad. Like I said, it's your decision. There's bound to be mixed feelings about the estate; there always is. Faulkner Jones Burnley are used to it, it goes with the territory. But I wanted you to know about it from me first, not your solicitor further down the line. All these trees are staying, my dad can't get rid of them even if he wanted to, they're protected. So you won't have your view ruined, and the building work shouldn't affect you. I doubt you'll hear much noise from here.'

Amy reached out to touch his arm, but drew back, afraid it would seem condescending rather than reassuring. 'It's fine. Honestly. You seem more worried about it than I am.'

'I guess people have to live somewhere.' He frowned, and looked away, before turning back to her a moment later, his face so clouded over he looked positively grey. 'Amy, listen. There's one more thing I've got to tell you. I'm just not sure how to go about it, or even where to begin . . .'

Suddenly, there was a lump in her throat, as if she'd swallowed thin air and it had turned into a heavy, cloying toffee. 'It's about Nick – isn't it?'

'He's coming back to the UK for a couple of weeks. At the end of the month. Rowena and her husband are out there at the moment; they have been since they left Spain. They're all flying back here together.'

'Well,' Amy shrugged, with as much insouciance as she could fake, 'if Rowena wasn't at her villa, and she wasn't here in this country, I knew the chances were she was visiting Nick. Is Anneka coming back with them?'

Paul nodded. 'Nick wants to see you . . . and the boys, of course. He thinks it's time you were on speaking terms again . . . His words, not mine.'

When she didn't immediately reply, he continued, 'Amy, I'll be there, too, if you want. You don't have to meet him alone, or on your own with the kids.' She still didn't reply, so he went on, 'I really don't mind. No, in fact, I want to be there. I'm still on your side, this doesn't change anything.'

'Doesn't it?' Amy tore her gaze away from his face, which oddly required more effort than usual. She looked down at the dirty buff suede of her shoes, not quite so smug about them as she had been earlier. Even in a heatwave, boots would have been a better option for this trek.

'He was your best friend for thirty years,' she reminded him.

'You've been my friend – properly – for how long? It's one thing speaking to him on a phone . . .'

Since Nick had left, Amy had known she would have to face him one day, but now that it was imminent, her fears seemed to have changed. Now her most pressing concern seemed to be how Paul's present allegiance might switch once Nick had a chance to smooth-talk him face-to-face. Yet . . . shouldn't she be more anxious about how the children were going to react?

'When you actually see him again,' Amy limped on, utterly convinced that Paul was underestimating his loyalty to the past, 'it could change everything.'

20

'How about this?' Elspeth asked Carol, holding up the jersey top emblazoned with the latest fashion slogan.

Pursing her lips, Carol shook her head. 'Too young for Amy, and too old for Tilly. Do you actually know what it means?'

Elspeth folded it neatly, and returned it to the pile on the shelf. 'I'm not a complete prude. But it's a pretty colour, don't you think? Greeny-blue, but not quite turquoise.'

'If you knew what it really stood for, you wouldn't even have noticed the colour. Let's get out of here, Els, this isn't the sort of shop you're after, trust me.'

'But all the ones we've been to so far have been our sort of stuff – far too . . . *prissy* for them.'

'Speak for yourself,' Carol huffed, good-naturedly. 'I haven't worn anything "prissy" since I was fifteen. Cleavages and prim-and-proper don't go. Sluttish, on the other hand . . .'

'Well in that case, what was so wrong with that top back there? It was hardly low-cut. I thought Tilly would appreciate it.'

'I'm not even going to try to explain it to your tender ears. That top wasn't even sluttish, Els, it was downright rude. No, what you want for Tilly is something sporty, with an authentic logo.'

Elspeth looked grumpily up at the sky, biting her tongue. That was why they were here, she wanted to snap, and not down the market. She had set her heart on something sophisticated yet casual for Amy, and hip and trendy for Tilly. Her elder daughter had been moping about again the last week or so, and could probably do with a morale boost, and her younger just deserved an overdue treat for working so hard on her exams.

This out-of-town designer outlet, bursting with famous labels, had to be the perfect place to find what Elspeth was looking for. You would have thought so, at least. But they'd already been here nearly two hours, and she'd never felt further from achieving her objective.

'What about this?' Carol pointed at a two-piece outfit in the window of a shop Elspeth had never heard of before. 'Amy would look gorgeous in it. That's just the sort of cut that would flatter her figure without making it too obvious.'

'Do you think so?' Elspeth was dubious. 'She's about to come face-to-face with her ex.' Elspeth couldn't stop herself sounding acrimonious.

'Precisely!' said Carol, her enthusiasm boundless. 'She'd knock him dead in that.'

'It's only afternoon tea at Rowena's house, not a cocktail party,' Elspeth sneered. Uttering that woman's name made the hairs rise on the back of her neck, more so now than ever. 'And the last thing Amy needs is to have Nick sitting up and taking notice again.'

'The last thing she needs, maybe. But what about what she'd like?'

'Everything's complicated enough without there being any whiff of a reconciliation. And it would be extremely unlikely anyway, considering his wife's coming back with him,' Elspeth reminded her sardonically.

'But would Amy forgive him, anyway?' Carol cocked a finely plucked eyebrow, and jostled a vacillating Elspeth into the stylish boutique. 'Could she really pretend that all this never happened?'

Elspeth frowned as her friend led her to the rack where the same outfits as the one in the window were hanging. 'I think Amy's telling me the truth when she says she doesn't want Nick any more. Things have gone too far for that. Besides, she's got Jonathan to consider now. He's such a nice man . . .'

'And Nick would have to get a divorce. That's hardly straightforward. But – is Amy being truthful with herself? When she actually sets eyes on him again . . .' Carol pulled out the skirt and top in Amy's size and passed them to Elspeth. 'She might *want* to be over him, so she just keeps telling herself that she is, using Jonathan as an excuse. Which is bad news when Nick comes swaggering back into the country with that big bleached grin of his and that streaky blond hair. If he had her drooling at first sight, how's she going to resist him now?'

'Because she's a grown woman, not a ragingly hormonal eighteen-year-old!' Still frowning, Elspeth examined the price tags and did a quick calculation in her head. Expensive, but not exorbitant. And it was a stunning outfit. The sort of thing Amy might keep for going out of an evening to a fancy restaurant or club. Not that she went anywhere like that very often – or at all, recently – but hadn't she mentioned that Maria and the girls from Little 'Uns were planning something along those lines for her birthday, which was coming up fast?

'Amy's ruled by her head these days,' Elspeth continued starchily, 'not her heart or her hormones. She knows she can't let Nick worm his way back in, and if it wasn't for the boys, she wouldn't have to bother with any of this. It's the only reason she's got for even agreeing to speak to Nick and Rowena, as far as I can see. But if she's not going to stoop to their level, what choice has she got?'

Carol sighed, which meant she was aware there was no choice at all. 'So, are you getting that for her?'

'It isn't what I had in mind, but it would sort out the

question of her birthday present. She could wear it on her night out with the girls.'

'So we're still looking for something smart rather than slinky for Granny Rowena's?'

Elspeth nodded, feeling decisive for what seemed the first time in over an hour. 'Yes, we are. But we'll stop for a quick cuppa first. My treat.'

'It had bloody well better be,' groused Carol.

By the time they sat down to a late lunch, over two hours later, Elspeth was exhausted but satisfied. It felt as if someone were using her feet as a couple of pincushions, but her spirits were now soaring over her successful shopping spree.

After splashing out on the skirt and top for Amy, and stopping for a welcome cup of tea, she had found herself on a roll. She hadn't indulged in any serious retail therapy since before Christmas, so after seven months of just popping into Help the Aged, Asda or Woolworths without exceeding her self-imposed allowance, this spending frenzy was a worryingly liberating experience.

'I'd understand you fretting if you were destitute or in debt,' said Carol, voraciously attacking her baked potato with prawns. 'But you're minted! You didn't have to buy that scarf from the charity shop last week, you could have bought one today from Liz Claiborne.'

'But I like this one.' Elspeth fingered the diaphanous, lilac fabric. 'I don't care that it only cost fifty pence. And you know very well that I'm not rolling in it. It's only because George was so good with money that I've got any of my own now.'

'I know, I know. What I don't know is why you go round pretending you haven't. That "job" of yours, for instance. It's not as if you enjoy it, so why inflict it on yourself?'

'Because, however many different ways you manage to phrase the question, my answer's always the same: I'd be bored if I didn't.' Elspeth munched on her tuna and sweetcorn baguette and rummaged around in one of her shopping bags. She pulled out a pink sweatshirt with white writing scrawled across the front and back. 'I hope Tilly likes this,' she sighed, spreading it over her arm.

'She'd better, at that price. But don't start getting it all out now; you might get food on something. Honestly, Els, I'd forgotten what you're like. You can revel when you get home.'

'No I can't, because I'm hiding it at yours. I'll get mobbed the minute I walk back into the house if they see me with all these bags, and the boys will think I've bought them toys, or something they can appreciate more than those shorts and T-shirts.'

'OK, OK. You can pretend you're the hard-up little widow to your own family, too, but when all this new stuff starts appearing in their wardrobes, I think they're going to start getting suspicious.'

'I do not pretend to them.'

'Yes, you do. Even Amy probably hasn't a clue what you're worth.'

'What I'm "worth"? You make me sound like Rowena,' scoffed Elspeth.

'Maybe not as bad, but you could be driving round in one of those Mercs yourself. It wouldn't break the bank.'

'No, but it'd seriously dent it. I'm happy with my Skoda, thanks very much. And it's silver, just like her car. It's even got a badge. Anyway, have you heard of the term nest egg?'

Carol pulled a face and stared out of the window at the other shoppers strolling past with their arm-loads of bags. 'I under-stand that bit, and I'm sorry for going on at you. You're right to be careful. I suppose it's just this "business" of yours – maybe if you were happy doing it . . .'

'Well, aside from my English degree and my music, desktop publishing's what I'm qualified in.'

'It was just an evening class, though. And not your first choice, if I remember rightly.'

'Well, if they'd done flower arranging on Wednesday nights, I might be working in a florist's now.'

'Or making wedding bouquets from home . . . Wouldn't that be lovely? All those orchids and roses.'

'I'd prefer wreaths myself. There's a better success rate with funerals than marriages.'

Patting her tight perm, the curls barely quivering, Carol pouted at her defiantly. 'That's what I like about you, Els. Your quirky sense of realism. Considering you were happily married for eighteen or so years . . .'

Carol was right, in a way. Elspeth did seem to be growing more disillusioned as time passed. There were lots of reasons, she'd dare say, and Amy's relationship with Nick – before the break-up, not simply afterwards – was unequivocally one of them. Because a healthy and natural reason for having a partner was to provide mutual support; to build your self-assurance, not have it sapped out of you.

What kind of person would her daughter be now, Elspeth wondered, if Nick hadn't come along? What would she be doing with her life? The irony didn't escape Elspeth that it was probably precisely what Amy was doing now. Raising children of her own and working with other people's. One way or another, she had found her niche.

As Elspeth tucked into her baguette, she couldn't help contemplating what her own existence would have been like if she hadn't met George. Not just if he hadn't been snatched away from her when he had, but if he had never charged heroically into her life in the first place.

It was unsettling to think along these lines, as if she was being disloyal somehow. But as Carol had told her countless times, Elspeth was one of the most devoted wives she knew. 'Just a shame,' she would add, 'that technically you're not married any more.' And because it was Carol saying this, Elspeth appreciated that she wasn't being cruel or crass. She was only saying it because she cared.

'If something else came along, for instance,' Carol began now, settling back in her chair, 'wouldn't you be interested? Not a man, I mean, nothing like that. But a change of career, perhaps.'

'If I didn't know you better . . .' Elspeth narrowed her eyes warily. 'You've got something in mind, haven't you? Come on, out with it. What sort of hare-brained scheme do you think I'd be stupid enough to go for?'

'It's not my idea, as such. In fact, I'm surprised Amy hasn't mentioned anything.'

'Oh, that again!' Elspeth shook her head. 'The music teacher job at the nursery. That's what you're on about.'

'So you do know. And it isn't a teaching role, exactly. It's not showing a three-year-old how to play "Chopsticks" on the piano. Nothing like those private lessons you used to give.'

'They were such a long time ago, anyway. I haven't got any recent experience with children.'

'You're a grandmother – doesn't that count? And what about being able to sing in tune, and play an instrument, and just basically adoring music? You've got it into your head that Amy's the only one who's great with kids, but you've got a way with them, too. And if anyone can show them how to use different musical instruments – the percussion sort, you know – and how to have fun with song and dance and rhythm and rhyme – it's you!'

'Well, if I'm so good, how come Amy and Tilly never learned to play anything?'

'We're not talking child prodigies here. It's not your fault if Amy and Tilly are both tone-deaf, and take after their father on that score. All Maria wants is someone to come in about three or four hours a week, on different days or whatever's best for the person involved. Nothing strenuous, and nothing that'll involve taking sole charge of a dozen kiddies at a time. The assistants will always be there.'

Elspeth wrinkled her nose self-deprecatingly. 'She needs someone younger, not an old fogey like me.'

'Els, the last person she tried a few months ago was this girl fresh out of college. You couldn't get much younger. She pinged a triangle a few times and made the children sing "Old McDonald had a Safari Park", trying to think of as many different jungle animals as they could. All well and good in moderation, but not quite what Maria had in mind.'

'Oh, I still don't know . . . It would involve a lot of pre-paration; coming up with a good enough variety of songs and maybe researching out-of-the-ordinary instruments, from dif-ferent countries. And then it would be best to tie in each session with the themes they're working on at the nursery at different times – like shapes and colours, or phonics and maths for the older ones. So whoever was doing it would need to liaise reasonably often with Maria. It sounds time-consuming to me, whatever you say.'

'And it sounds to me as if you're already bringing an extra dimension to it, which just makes you even more perfect. You're coming up with things even Maria probably hasn't thought of. That's why she needs someone special for the job, not just one of her nursery nurses singing "Incy Wincy Spider" *et al* with the children once a day.'

'I couldn't take all that on board, Carol. Not on top of what I already do. And if it didn't work out . . .'

'If you weren't happy at Little 'Uns, you could just go back to doing what you're doing now.'

'I've got people relying on me, though. You can't wind up a business like that, however modest, and then just expect to take up where you left off.'

'You can call it a sabbatical, if that'll help. And you'd have to finish whatever you're working on now, of course. But you wouldn't have to take on anything more after that. And if there are any regular clients you'd like to keep, just in case . . . well, you'd probably still be able to find a little time to do some proof reading or editorial stuff, or whatever it is you enjoy most.'

Elspeth sat back with a heavy sigh. 'You've got an answer for everything, haven't you? You've got it all planned out.'

Carol spread her rosebud lips – still with a faint trace of crimson lipliner – into an exultant beam. 'Don't I always?'

'Mmm,' conceded Elspeth implacably, 'but I haven't said "yes" yet. I haven't even said "maybe". I'm only promising to *think* about it. So you can wipe that smile off your face, Mrs Caldicott. It's extremely irritating.'

21

It had been just over five months since Amy had last set eyes on him.

Her parting memory of Nick was when he had supposedly left for work that Friday morning in late February. Casual, nothing out of the ordinary, kissing her briefly on the top of the head as she munched on her toast and fed the children theirs. He had been well aware that a few hours later he would be marrying another woman and wouldn't be there that night to tuck his children into bed. Not that he'd ever played the dominant role in the bedtime ritual, but a swift cuddle and a two-minute story was better than not being involved at all.

In the sunlight flooding through the watered-silk stateliness of Rowena's formal reception room, Nick's hair looked burnished and his skin rich as honey. He appeared to have been pacing the room, but had stopped as Amy walked in. Like a classic romantic hero, he now stood in impressive isolation with his elbow propped against the marble mantelpiece, his cleft chin proud and his stance arrogant. He was as mesmerising, if not more so, as the hour she had first met him. But her heart this time – instead of melting as it had in that narrow, spartan, public school corridor – froze over.

'Hello, Amy,' he murmured soberly; and then, with a slight nod, 'Hello, Paul.'

Nick looked past her, and Amy glanced round, realising that Paul hadn't just led her here, he had followed her in.

She was aware that the two men had already spoken since

Nick's return the day before yesterday. Paul had confided that much earlier as Amy had arrived with the children, deposited on Rowena's front steps by an anxious, clucking Jonathan.

'I can stay, if you want.' Jonathan had squinted up at her from the driver's side of his Volvo, which had looked more battered than usual next to Rowena's husband's new Land Rover. 'If you need me—'

'I'll be fine.' Amy had cut him off gently. 'Thank you for the lift.' Understandably, she hadn't been in the best of moods for driving today. 'I'll call you later – when we need picking up.' And as if out of some sense of duty and gratitude, she had bent down and given him a kiss, albeit a lukewarm one.

'So he's a taxi service now,' Paul had remarked dryly, as he'd led her and the boys into the Regency-style – Faulkner Jones Burnley – house on the outskirts of Chester, set in an acre and a half of traditionally landscaped grounds. 'Is there no end to the man's talents?'

Amy had shot Paul a damning glance. Yet as the regal Rowena had swept into the hall to greet them – her slightly greasy husband Conrad trailing behind, like the latest fashion accessory – Amy had instinctively swayed closer to Paul again.

As if she had just stepped on to a fairground ride but wasn't sure what to expect, she had found herself herded with the boys into the huge conservatory at the rear of the house. There, they had been plied with refreshments, and Amy had been subjected to a galling Spanish inquisition regarding their welfare.

'I understand you took Joseph and Michael out of that excellent nursery school I found for them and put them in an ordinary little one in Harrisfield. Was that wise, Amy?'

Amy had swallowed the bile rising in her throat, struggling not to let rip in front of the children. 'It was more affordable. And practical, considering I work there, too. I don't live in Chester any more.'

'But I thought Nicholas was paying you an allowance. Doesn't that cover the nursery fees?' Rowena had tutted under her breath, as if Amy was obviously lacking in the ability to handle the family finances; either that, or she was keeping some back for herself.

But before Amy could explode, Paul had intervened by reminding Rowena that three hungry, growing lads were sure to keep any supermarket in business.

After sandwiches and cakes, accompanied by Ceylon Orange Pekoe for the adults and barley water for the boys – which Mikey hated and unceremoniously spat out – Rowena had suggested the children go outside with her and Conrad. She had had a permanent wooden sandpit constructed while she'd been away, and couldn't wait to show off what a clever, brilliant grandmother she was. She had scooped Lucas into her arms ('He looks just like his father at the same age! He's got nothing of you about him, has he, Amy?') and beckoned to the older boys to follow, enticing them with talk of plastic diggers and rollers and how they could pretend to run their own Faulkner Jones Burnley construction site from her back garden.

'Every bloody time,' Amy had hissed under her breath, once they'd gone. 'She spends months away on the Costa del Sol, without so much as a postcard, just the odd phone call, and then expects to pick up where she left off . . .'

'It must seem ten times worse this year.' Paul had sighed, looking grim. 'I don't know how you do it.' He had stared at Amy across the rattan and glass coffee table. Spontaneously, it seemed, he'd reached across and squeezed her hand. 'And I don't care what Rowena says,' he'd smiled reassuringly, 'Lucas definitely has your eyes.'

She'd taken a deep breath, staring down at his fingers lying over hers. 'So, where is he then – Nick? And where's Anneka?'

'She's gone to visit her parents in Kendal for a few days.'

His reluctance apparent, Paul had stood up. 'Nick said he'd wait for you in the lounge . . .'

And so here she was. Facing the man she had lived for, and lived with, for more years than some couples were even married.

'Hello, Nick.' It was a battle to keep her voice steady. 'How are you?'

'I'm . . . good.' He glanced at Paul again, who in turn glanced at Amy.

'You don't have to stay,' she assured him, sounding anything but certain. 'Really. I'll be OK.'

'Well, well . . .' By Nick's tone, he seemed to be trying to break the ice. In the present company, it was as futile as attempting to use a feather instead of a pickaxe. 'This is a turn-up for the books – Paul and Amy, speaking to each other.'

Paul regarded him witheringly. 'Nick, cut it out. Someone's got to look out for her.'

'Excuse me,' Amy interposed, a spark of feminism igniting in her breast, 'I can look out for myself.'

Paul turned back to her. By his wounded expression, she immediately realised she had acted like an ungrateful cow.

'I'm sorry,' she said quickly, 'it isn't that I don't appreciate . . .'

'It's fine. I can take a hint.' Paul threw one final warning glance in Nick's direction, and then closed the door behind him with a sickening thud.

Amy stared over her shoulder at the classic white panels and the doorknob with the handpainted roses. This was not the start she'd been aiming for.

Blinking rapidly, she turned back to Nick. 'Paul – he's – well, he's been good to me and the boys. I owe him a lot.'

'I'm aware of that. And it's nice to know where his loyalties lie.'

Amy frowned. Anger burst fiercely into her heart, retaliation hot on its heels. 'There are more important things than so-called loyalty. If Paul had stuck by you in this case, he couldn't have reconciled it with his own conscience.'

Nick trawled a hand through his thick, sun-streaked crop. 'Do you think any of this has been easy for me, Amy? Do you think I wake up every morning free from regrets?'

'No.' Amy forced herself to admit that even Nick wasn't that cold-blooded. 'But then not everyone goes around abandoning their children as easily as you did.'

'Amy, what I meant to say . . . I think about you and the boys every day. Leaving the way I did – it was the hardest thing I've had to do. But I was torn . . . I couldn't keep up the act any more.'

'Right.' She grunted derisively. 'So how exactly did you think I'd react? By racking up a massive Visa bill? It would have been nice to have had some sort of warning that you didn't trust me that way.'

He couldn't look at her. 'If I'd been in your shoes . . .'

'Well, you weren't. And if I'd been in yours, I'd have definitely been more generous from the start. I wouldn't have needed anyone to arbitrate, least of all my so-called best friend.' Amy neglected to add that Nick would never have been as naïve as she'd been if the roles had indeed been reversed.

'This business of "maintenance" – it was all so new to me, Amy . . .'

'And I was an old hand at it, was I?'

She sank down into an armchair. After the first threat of tears, her eyes were now curiously dry. She looked down at her fingernails, which she'd painstakingly manicured yesterday evening, and had succeeded in keeping flawless even while getting the kids ready this morning.

'Anyway, things like this happen all the time,' she uttered stonily. 'The planet's littered with failed relationships. And it's not as if we ever stood before God, vowing to love each other till one of us popped our clogs. I guess I know now why you never wanted to make it official. You knew you wouldn't be able to stick it out with me. In one way, that makes you quite honest. I still can't respect you for it, though. As soon as the kids arrived, it stopped being about you and me, or what we once might have had.'

'Amy, I really did care about you. I still do, in many ways. Yes, it was the real thing. I know it was. We were good together.'

'A long time ago perhaps . . . for the wrong reasons.'

'I – I don't understand. *Why* were they wrong? We were attracted to each other, weren't we? That's usually how it starts. There was always something about you.' He paused to study her. 'You're looking great now . . . But that's the way, isn't it? At the beginning of a new relationship.'

Amy twitched in the armchair, as if he'd poked her with a pin. 'What?'

'Paul mentioned it. I don't think I was supposed to tell you . . .' Nick made a show of biting his lip.

'What did he say?'

'He let slip that you were seeing someone.' A flicker of amusement crossed Nick's face, before he appeared to suppress it, perhaps for etiquette's sake. 'Jonathan Simmons . . . "Saddo", as your sister used to call him. I always knew he had a soft spot for you.'

'It's not serious.' She felt compelled to put Nick straight, even though she didn't owe him an explanation. 'He's been around when I've needed him.' As Amy said it, she started to feel her own conscience stir into activity. 'That doesn't sound fair on him, I know, but—'

'You couldn't be expected to think straight after what I put you through.' Nick hitched up his chinos at the knees, and sank into the armchair opposite hers. 'And, Amy, some people don't mind being used. Although, I know you, you're probably racked with guilt over it. You shouldn't be. I know how men think, and someone like Jonathan Simmons only comes into their own when they're playing the saviour. He's been waiting for this opportunity for years, and if it wasn't with you, it would have been someone else, eventually. Someone vulnerable. He's crap with women normally, isn't he? Not surprising. You only have to look at him. But no one could blame you for seeing him in a whole new light when he was the only person around to tell you how great you are.'

Amy blinked, floundering for a reply.

Nick sighed. 'It's the boys I'm worried about, though. Any relationship you have has a direct bearing on them. I don't want them unnecessarily confused.'

Her eyes narrowed. She couldn't believe Nick's nerve. Acting like a Relate counsellor, when all along . . . And yet . . . there was a grain of truth in his words. She agonised over it, and then finally, astonishingly, acquiesced.

'You might be right, up to a point, although I've been taking the boys into consideration all along. But what about you, Nick? You started it all – you and Anneka. You confused them most, when you left the way you did. I so wanted to be strong for them, but in the beginning . . .' Amy couldn't let him know just how badly she'd taken it.

Nick pressed his hands together, flattening the fingers and palms in a near-perfect mirror image. He drew his index fingers up to his chin. 'The children,' he murmured. 'I can't wait to see them . . . I thought this time apart might help everyone. That's one of the reasons I left it so long. I wanted to give you space to get over it, to let the children adjust to my not being around all the time. Barging back into your lives after only a few weeks, with a stepmother in tow . . .'

It was the first time anyone had referred to Anneka that way in front of Amy. She felt her stomach churn.

Nick did look serious about longing to see the boys. But it was one thing saying it. He would probably only last five minutes in their company before fleeing back to Amy, begging for a respite.

'You haven't even asked me how they are,' she upbraided him coldly.

'I didn't need to. I asked Paul yesterday. I ask him every time we speak, without fail. Why do you think I'm back, Amy? Anneka wanted to visit her folks, yes, but I probably would have stayed in Boston. I'm busy enough, Lord knows. But I've been missing the boys like crazy. I needed to see them . . .'

Nick was now staring in a melancholy manner at the textured ivory carpet, as impractical as it was eye-catching. 'I know I haven't been first-grade father material. And I'm not trying to say I've changed. I'm never going to be the sort of dad they deserve, but unfortunately for them, I'm the one they've been saddled with.'

A part of Amy longed to inform him that it was too late to turn back the clock. He had put the children through too much. Even the baby had been affected. She wanted to point out that Lucas might not even remember him. Five months might seem a lifetime, at that age. Nick couldn't just hurt his sons like that and then imply he was the only salve that could heal them.

Then again, that wasn't what he was implying, was it? It was simply the sort of hypocrisy she had come to expect, even though she hadn't called it that while she'd been with him. On the contrary, she had probably indulged it. Today, right now, he actually seemed to be casting stones at himself. Amy hadn't anticipated that. She had come into the enemy camp prepared to handle the Nick she knew – selfish, self-centred, impatient – not the Nick slouched opposite her with that pitiful look of remorse. This wasn't the way she'd rehearsed it.

She had been going over everything in her head for the last

two weeks. Her tactics were age-old, yet they'd required careful implementation.

One: look as sensational as possible, without going overboard – i.e. no ball gown and diamonds for a simple afternoon tea.

Having taken the time to blow-dry her hair in stages, she had used her sister's ionic – whatever on earth that meant – ceramic straighteners, to make her layers especially sleek and glossy. Then she'd put on her smart, A-line, pink skirt and timeless white top, with a contrasting blue linen jacket her mum had lavishly splashed out on. It made her feel less mumsy and more businesslike. Womanly and attractive, but not overtly so. Even her feet in flat, beaded flip-flops, had been pumiced to a smooth silkiness, and the toenails painted to match the varnish on her hands.

Two: appear cool, calm and collected, even if you're not and no one else is, either.

Three: never let on how you really feel, if what you're really feeling means exposing yourself to pain again.

But what good was having a strategy? What good was learning your lines if the ones you'd memorised suddenly belonged to a different play? And what message was she sending out by finding herself going over to Nick and perching on the armrest of his chair? Rowena would probably have a fit, considering she had always been a great lover of informing the children that armrests were for arms not bottoms.

How was it possible to feel strong and weak at the same time, frowned Amy, as she almost found herself patting Nick's shoulder? To feel as if she had the upper hand, but that things had spiralled out of her control?

'If you're so desperate to see the kids,' she heard herself say, 'you should go and find them right now. We could sit here and talk for hours without getting anywhere, and it can wait . . .' It was only her pride, after all, arguing that it couldn't.

Nick seemed to hesitate, then slowly heaved himself to his feet. 'Do they know about . . . Anneka?'

Amy nodded. 'They haven't known long, though. Only since I heard you were coming back to the country. But they're only little. Remember that, Nick. Joseph isn't even four yet. What they've been told and what they understand are probably two separate things.'

Nick reached down and squeezed her arm. 'Thank you, Amy. You were always too good for me,' she thought she heard him murmur. Or it might have been, 'You were always good to me.'

There was a world of difference.

Amy didn't want to have to start analysing it now. Her own behaviour was bad enough.

Less than a minute after Nick had made his exit into the garden through the French windows, the knob of the door leading to the corridor rattled, and cautiously the door creaked open. Paul peered round it. He blinked at her for a moment, then enquired, rather sheepishly, 'Truce?'

'Nick and me?' Amy felt thrown.

'No, er – us, actually. I'm sorry about before . . .'

'Oh, that . . .' She bit her lip. 'It was my fault.'

'I just spotted Nick outside with Rowena and the boys – and as you weren't there yourself . . . I thought you might need a friendly ear.'

'Do you think I should have gone with him?' Amy hadn't been sure she had the bottle for it. And with Rowena there, too . . .

She was still beating herself up over it, though, as if she had failed her children when they needed her.

'I don't know . . .' said Paul uncertainly. 'The kids might cling to you and ignore Nick. Would that be a good idea . . .? Anyway, about earlier . . . it wasn't your fault. I can get too overprotective. And edgy. It's being around Nick again . . . He has this knack of getting under my skin.'

It seemed as if Paul was blaming himself for it, and wanted to blame Nick instead.

'You shouldn't feel bad about anything,' Amy assured him. It was only fair that she lighten his burden. He could have walked away from all this if he'd wanted to; if he'd been a different kind of person. 'Fraternal-type bonds like yours don't just snap overnight. Maybe if you keep reminding yourself that you were never going to agree one hundred per cent about everything, it might be easier to deal with. There was bound to be a time in your lives when you'd clash really drastically. I don't expect you to suddenly hate him.'

'What if I want to, but I just can't?' Paul shook his head. 'You're right, though. Pearls of wisdom, as always. Sometimes – well, a lot of the time lately – I envy Joe, Mikey and Lucas, for having you as their mum. I'd have killed for someone like you.'

Amy hesitated before replying, 'Really?' It was a strange sort of compliment to receive from a man. Paul was only trying to be kind, of course, attempting to slap on the balm in one lavish dose, but Amy couldn't help feeling disconcerted and slightly disgruntled.

'I'm jealous of them for having each other, too, I guess,' Paul went on, oblivious. 'If my mum had been different, less ambitious, I suppose, she might have wanted more kids. It wasn't like Rowena: a case of not being able to. She just didn't enjoy being pregnant or having the mess of a baby to deal with. And I know because she's told me – once too often. I was the child she wanted to follow in her footsteps, and that was enough, she didn't need any more. In hindsight, she obviously did.' Paul let out a short, hollow chuckle. 'She should have had at least a couple more, as a safety net.'

Men were funny creatures, mused Amy, struggling not to let her hand reach out and reassuringly stroke Paul's back. Somehow or other, the ones she knew best always seemed to turn the focus of any conversation back on themselves. It was as if she was destined to play the role of mother with all of them, not just her children. But maybe that was her own fault? Look at her now, for instance, straining towards Paul because right at that moment he seemed particularly needy and insecure. Was that another reason she'd first gravitated towards Jonathan, and towards Nick less than five minutes ago?

Twitchily, she rose from the armrest of the chair and walked towards the French windows, her arms folded over her chest. The voile drapes swayed and fluttered like a bride's veil, the sunlight bleaching them a blazing white. Amy peered through the gap, but from here she couldn't make out the sandpit, which was probably next to the wooden swing and slide that Rowena had had installed last year.

'I came here today expecting a showdown,' Amy admitted, sensing that Paul was somewhere close behind, in spite of her efforts to put some distance between them. If he honestly wanted to help, he'd have to shut up about his own Oedipus complex, or rather his lack of it, and listen. 'When I saw him,' she continued, 'Nick . . .' she shrugged despairingly. 'I could have easily throttled him. I could have clawed his eyes out. I could have . . .'

'Run straight back into his arms, if he'd just said the word?'

Amy swung round, indignation stoked, nostrils flaring. 'Why do you have to go and assume that? What makes you think I still want him?'

'I don't . . . I just . . . You were with him so long, Amy . . . I didn't think your feelings could just evaporate.'

'So I'm still hoping he's going to wake up one day and realise he made a huge mistake?' Amy folded her arms over her chest again. This time she was shivering, as if it wasn't twenty-five degrees outside. 'Well, I'm not. I don't need him. I hate to admit that I once did, because that isn't the same as love. But when he first noticed me, when he picked me out from all those other girls he could have had, he made me feel . . .

amazing. Better than I was. Special. And I needed that. I needed it, because I'd just lost the man who'd made me feel like that since I'd been born.' To her dismay, her voice seemed suddenly on the verge of breaking.

Paul was standing so close she could smell the faint trace of his aftershave, and even a hint of mintiness on his breath. Tears were clouding her eyes. Maybe her other senses had already started to compensate. Touch, above any other. His hands were on her shoulders now; they seemed to burn straight through the linen and cotton, directly into her skin.

'Hey,' he muttered softly. 'It's OK. Even the strongest mums sometimes cry in public.' He was trying to be facetious, to defuse the tension. 'Well, except mine. But she doesn't count. I'd rather be your kid any day.'

'That's the problem.' With this whiney note in her voice, she sounded pathetic. 'That's what I'm trying to get at. I'd just lost my dad, and meeting Nick – he was like Polyfilla, I suppose. He filled the cracks. But why did he pick *me*? Because I was some sort of mother figure?'

'He's got a mother, though.'

'Technically. But we both know what Rowena was like back then. And by the look of husband number three, she's no better now. She likes the *idea* of motherhood . . .'

'More than mine, at any rate.'

Amy sniffed, and futilely attempted to dry her eyes with the pads of her fingers, until Paul handed her a Kleenex.

'It's clean,' he attested. 'I haven't used it. I just get a touch of hayfever this time of year, so I keep a couple on me, in case. Not very macho, I know.'

Amy sniffed again, in thanks. 'Just because Rowena enjoys the perks of being a mum, that doesn't mean to say that she's any good at it, though. She likes the idea of being a gran, too, but her main way of expressing it is to buy the boys expensive gifts. And she was like that with Nick. The clothes, the cars, the deposit on the first flat.' Paul had alluded to it himself once. 'As if to make up for the fact that she wasn't really there for him when he was growing up.'

'So you're saying Nick viewed you as a substitute?' Paul seemed doubtful.

'Not consciously. But you only had to listen to yourself, the way you were going on just now. It's not that I mind people thinking of me as naturally maternal. It just isn't the best foundation to base a lifetime commitment on. So maybe that's why Nick never did, because when the kids came along, I stopped mothering him.' Amy gazed down ruefully at her frosted candy-pink toes.

'What about *you*, though? How was it that you stopped "needing" him? When did that happen?'

Amy shrugged helplessly. 'I don't know exactly. But I must have.'

Paul loomed over her, still looking confused. 'So you never actually loved him? Is that what you're trying to say?'

'It seemed real at the time, so I can't say if I did or didn't. My attraction was genuine.' But how many different types of emotional adhesive kept a couple together? 'Knowing what I know now – apart from the kids, of course, they're a separate issue – if I had to do it again, waste my twenties like that . . .' She shook her head. 'Nick's not what I want. I can't help thinking there's got to be more to it.'

'More schmaltz, you mean, *à la* Hollywood?' Paul looked cynically amused.

Amy looked away. 'Whatever that is. The kind of emotional attachment a bloke like you probably doesn't believe in. Unless Francesca's converting you . . .'

'Well, it doesn't sound as if Jonathan's converting you, if you're still no nearer to figuring it out yourself.'

'Speaking of which,' Amy remembered, relieved to veer the

conversation on to a different track with the minimum of effort, 'I've a bone to pick with you.'

Paul looked wary. 'You have?'

'You told Nick about him.'

'Oh.' Paul screwed up his face momentarily, partly in apology, Amy guessed, and partly defensiveness. 'That. I know you asked me not to, but it – um – slipped out. Anyway,' he pulled his back straight, 'don't you want him to know you're managing fine without him? That you've moved on? Regardless of whether it's serious or not?'

'The fact that I'm coping without Nick has nothing to do with Jonathan.' Amy hesitated, and frowned. 'Well, in the beginning it did.' She felt like an ungrateful cow again.

'Nick was winding me up,' Paul explained. 'Harping on about how wonderful Anneka was, and how great the job in the Faulkner Group's going; how he's already en route to bigger and better things, and has masses of stuff to discuss with my mother. I felt sick listening to him, and Jonathan just popped into my head. I mentioned him as a dig. Unfortunately, Nick seemed to find it . . .'

'Funny?' Amy prompted grimly. 'Look, if you've got issues to sort out with him on a personal level, about him working for your mum and filling your boots or whatever, I'd prefer it if you didn't drag me into it.'

Paul looked duly chastened. 'You're right. And that *is* another reason he's getting to me. I don't want to work for the Faulkner Group myself. I never have, never will. But somehow, the fact that Nick does seems to nark me.'

'Well, when it comes to your mum, he's hogging the limelight that's rightfully yours.'

Paul's brow crumpled. 'But I've never been that kind of son. I've never set out to please her.'

'We all want to please our parents at some level. You might not have wanted to go into publishing, but you went to work for Faulkner Jones Burnley. Is that really what you would have done if you'd had a completely free choice?'

'Yes,' said Paul, without seeming to give it any consideration.

'Then I'm wrong,' Amy shrugged. 'My mistake.'

'What are you on about?' A scowl flashed briefly across his countenance.

This time, she'd deliberately managed to steer the dialogue back to Paul on her own. But it didn't seem to be a subject he was comfortable to discuss. Not right now, at any rate, and not in depth. Which was a pity, because it was an aspect of him that she was beginning to find fascinating.

'Why do women always try to make everything so complex?' Paul grumbled.

'Because some things actually are,' Amy pointed out, as the sound of distant wailing reached their ears. Oh, hell. 'What's happened now? I bet Joe's pushed Mikey off the swing.'

They both hurried out of the French windows, fighting aside the flapping voile.

'Maybe they've tried to bury Nick in the sand,' smirked Paul, as they walked swiftly across the lawn. 'I tried it once when we were about eight, on a school trip to Llandudno. I think he's had a hang-up about it ever since.'

'He always did just want to stick around the pool when we went on holiday. Hated going to the beach,' Amy recalled. 'So it's you I've got to blame for that, too, is it?'

And the look they shared was nothing short of conspiratorial.

22

'Will my daddy be here soon?'

Amy looked down at the four-year-old with the wiry, red curls crammed into two fat bunches. With her round, freckled face and retroussé nose, Mandy Driscoll was just the sort of girl Amy had once imagined having. Her own hair had a tendency to go more gingery in the summer, and a light dusting of freckles would materialise on her nose. If Nick's blondness had been thrown into the bargain . . .

But now, that was never going to happen.

'I'm sure your daddy will be here soon, Mandy,' she assured the little girl, who already had her yellow, Little 'Uns rucksack slung over her shoulders.

'He's being a long, long time.'

Amy glanced at the clock on the wall of the small office. It was getting quite late. Even Maria had had to leave because she was going out with her husband that night and needed to get ready in time to give the babysitter a full briefing. Amy, because of her age, qualifications – and experience as a mother of three, she suspected – had already adopted a senior role at the nursery, and Maria was relying on her more and more. Such as now. Amy had volunteered to stay behind with Mandy, whose father hadn't arrived at the usual time to pick her up. They had tried phoning him at work, but he had already left, and his mobile kept diverting to messaging.

Twenty minutes after the last member of staff bar Amy had left, there was the sound of a car rumbling to a stop outside, and the familiar shock of flaming red hair appeared outside the window.

'Daddy!' Mandy jumped up and down.

Amy hurried to let him in. 'Hi—'

'Sorry, sorry, *sooooo* sorry.' He was short of breath as he scooped up his daughter and cuddled her. 'Massive delay on the M56,' he gasped. 'Accident – jack-knifed lorry – my phone out of battery. I am so, so—'

'It's fine.' Amy smiled. They had to make allowances for this kind of thing. Mr Driscoll was a single parent, his wife having died from leukaemia when Mandy was one. 'She's had a lovely day, and she ate everything. Oh – and here's a foot painting. I'm afraid her feet will need a good soaking in the bath. We couldn't get all the green off.'

Mr Driscoll laughed and relaxed. 'Lucky our carpet's green, too, then.'

After fending off another apology, Amy watched from the door as he strapped his daughter into the car seat. 'Enjoy your weekend!' She waved as they drove off.

Amy sighed and closed the main door again, thinking about her own start to the weekend. She didn't have to worry about the boys this evening. Her mother and Tilly had picked them up an hour ago and were taking them to a family pub with indoor and outdoor play areas and a sickly ice cream machine. Being a Friday, it would probably be heaving, but that was how the older boys liked it – when there was a gaggle of children to befriend or terrorise, depending on their mood.

Amy's own plans for the evening were a lot less stressful than a tussle over the last high chair, or breaking up a ball-pit brawl, but she still felt as if her nerves were frayed. She would rather just be going home to some cheese on toast and a night in front of the TV. But alas, she was only going home to get changed, tidy up her hair and go next door to Jonathan's. He was cooking tea for them both. Amy predicted that it would probably be spaghetti bolognese. It had been shepherd's pie last time, and they were the only two dishes he seemed to know how to prepare.

She also predicted that he was going to go on about that long weekend away with her and the kids. It was all his idea, and she hadn't even said yes to it yet, even though he was talking about a late deal for the August Bank Holiday, which wasn't far off. Maybe he thought plying her with overcooked mince and rubbery spaghetti would have her melting into submission, but it wasn't that simple. This trip obviously involved taking the relationship to a new level – installing him as some kind of stepfather figure in the children's lives.

As for their real father, Jonathan had seemed to welcome Nick's return, rather than feeling threatened by it. Amy had found it odd and disturbing at first, until she'd realised that Jonathan saw it as a milestone; because if Amy could get through it relatively unscathed, then the most difficult aspect of the past hanging over them would be dealt with. After that, it would be far easier to give herself body and soul to a new relationship.

Amy hoped this didn't mean he had gone out and bought condoms. But when everyone on TV and in the tabloids seemed to be jumping into bed with each other at the drop of a pair of knickers, and when she could scarcely pretend to be all virginal and then run home to her children, it was becoming harder and harder to put off what was fast becoming the inevitable.

Amy fetched her bag from the office, and was about to set the alarm when the sound of sharp rapping against glass made her jump. A man was peering in through the main door, trying to attract her attention.

It was Nick.

She stood staring at him, frozen with her fingers over the alarm keypad. He seemed agitated. Not quite himself. His hair looked as if he'd been distractedly jabbing it over and over again with his fingers, so that now it was standing on end in a different, less deliberate way than when he used gel.

With more than just a twinge of apprehension, Amy opened the door. And without waiting to be asked, Nick stepped inside.

'I – I wasn't expecting you,' Amy stuttered, more from surprise than anything else. 'I thought you were having the kids on Sunday.'

'I am. It's you I needed to see. I wanted to catch you on your own. I've been waiting for you to come out, but . . .' Two lines were etched vertically between his eyebrows as he frowned at his watch, as if to imply that her timekeeping was as erratic as ever.

'Can't it wait?'

'It's never going to be a good moment for this.'

'Look, I know we didn't get to talk much the other day, not about maintenance and alimony, if it's even called that, as we weren't married. But you're here for another week, at least, so I'm sure that's long enough to iron out anything we're not happy with. We'll make an appointment, or does that sound too formal?'

'It's going to take more than ironing anything out to get my life back on track again.' He let out a low moan. 'I used to feel I had some sense of direction . . . Now, apart from the job with the Faulkner Group, I feel as if I'm swimming in circles.'

Amy frowned and glanced out into the lane behind the Parish Church. Nick must have parked further down, she couldn't see his hire car from here. But wherever he had been waiting, he must have had a clear view of the nursery entrance. She hoped no one had noticed and found it odd. In this day and age, even good-looking, relatively young men in Fred Perry polo shirts were suspicious if they were caught loitering around nurseries or schools.

'Nick, I'm not sure why you're here, but I haven't got time for this now. I'm not in the mood, either.'

He ignored her. 'Can we talk through here . . .?' He poked his head around a door leading to one of the playrooms. Before Amy could answer, he had walked in. 'This is nice,' he mumbled, scanning the gallery of pictures and other handi-crafts festooning the walls. 'Joe did that one, then?' He pointed to what was supposedly a self-portrait, consisting of various facial features made out of odds and ends and pasted on to a paper plate, including yellow wool for hair. It bore their eldest son's name. Nick never would have recognised it otherwise.

'He's still young, I know, but it's becoming clear that art isn't his strong point.' Amy sighed, then added, with a mother's staunch defiance, 'He does try, though.'

'He's stubborn,' said Nick, 'just like you. And I mean that in a good way.'

'Oh, I doubt I'm anywhere near as determined,' she shrugged, then wondered why she was putting herself down again in front of him. Had she been guilty of downgrading herself all along, so that Nick had started to believe the myth she had presented, rather than the reality?

He perched on one of the low, square tables, and stabbed at his hair again. 'I don't know . . .' he sighed exasperatedly. 'I feel as if I don't know anything any more. Not even how to be happy.'

Poor dinkums, thought Amy darkly, but managed to con-tain herself.

'You said you were happy with your new job, didn't you?' she probed instead.

'Oh, I am, I am. Although I'm not sure that's the right word. I've just felt . . . displaced since I left you and the boys. And I'm wondering – really I am – if it wasn't a huge mistake . . .' He was frowning, those trademark lines carved on his brow again, and he seemed to be talking as much to himself as to her, as if he were lying self-absorbed on a psychiatrist's couch.

Amy waited for a flood of warmth, for a rush of 'whoopeeee' to tingle through her. But instead, she felt cold again. 'What about Anneka? Your wife. You married her quickly enough. You must have felt more for her than you ever did for me.'

Nick paused, but even taking time out to consider his next words didn't make him any more diplomatic. 'Where did that go, then? That feeling? It hasn't been a barrel of laughs, settling down in Boston, restructuring our lives like that. Yes, all right, it's been an adventure. And she wanted it as much as me, I didn't have to force her into anything. But before that, when she worked for FJB, she had purpose, I guess. Direction. That was one of the things I was first attracted to. And now . . .'

Amy didn't really want to hear all the intricate, intimate details, but there was something emerging that was obvious to her, if not to the thick-skulled, thick-skinned Nick. 'So she's not working at the moment?'

'No. Problems with her visa. I mean, the flat looks great. We're renting, but she got the go-ahead to work her magic on it, and she was in her element for a while, but . . .'

'Now she's bored. So – no, don't tell me, let me guess – she's "changed"?'

'Uh-huh.' Nick regarded Amy as if she were the Oracle at Delphi. 'She's so . . . *clingy* now. Doesn't like me working late or going out for a few drinks afterwards. Hates me playing golf, which is part of the job really – thrashing out deals, you know – even at weekends. Won't make the effort to socialise with other wives or girlfriends, even though we've gone round for dinner at colleagues' houses. She's just . . . caving in on herself, and I can't seem to do anything about it. I even thought this trip might help her re-evaluate things, but she hasn't come back from her parents' yet, and I can't work out what she's trying to tell me over the phone. She's speaking, yes, but she's not making a huge deal of sense.'

Amy shook her head, perching stiffly, awkwardly, on the table next to Nick. 'Do you realise who *you're* talking to?' She didn't make any attempt to cover up her irascibility this time. 'A few months ago, you more or less left my life in tatters . . . But here you are now, after my sympathy vote. Sometimes, Nick, you take my breath away.'

He swivelled to face her. 'Amy, I'm not after sympathy, or forgiveness or advice.'

'From where I'm sitting, Nick, you're after all three.'

Before she knew it, his hand came to rest on her cheek. 'When did I stop appreciating you?' he murmured, brushing her hair back over her shoulder. 'When did I stop seeing how pretty you are . . .?'

Amy felt an old, familiar sensation in the region of her stomach: a small explosion of lust that shivered through her like a shockwave. Nick had always had that effect on her. Yet it was nothing compared to the alarm bells clanging in her head.

She immediately slid away from him, her shorts slipping easily across the shiny Formica. 'Nick, you're only saying these things because you thought your new life was going to be better than your old one. You pictured yourself walking off into the proverbial sunset, but if you want to keep it like that, you've got to work at it. Just because it doesn't come easy, that doesn't mean it's wrong.'

'Amy, you're so sensible. I should never have taken that side of you for granted.'

'No,' she said petulantly. 'But you did. And it seems to be your biggest failing. You go through life taking everyone who cares about you for granted, even your own children. And right now you're doing it to Anneka. You ought to be jumping in a car right now and haring up the M6 to wherever it is her folks live exactly, not that I'd ever condone speeding, you know me. You ought to be trying to save your marriage, because right now it sounds as if you're just letting it go down the pan. And that's apathy and laziness, not to mention the fact that you're spoilt, and I don't deny that maybe I had something to do with that.'

'Spoilt?' he choked, taken aback.

'I'll grant you that you miss the kids,' she continued, 'because there are lousier fathers than you out there. But please don't try and pretend you want me back, or everything we once had.'

'Don't *you*?' Nick looked fazed, incredulous even. 'If Anneka wasn't in the picture.'

'But she is. And even if she wasn't . . .' Amy shook her head. 'The last thing I want is to go back to that flat; even if we could, considering we've sold it. And I couldn't start over again somewhere else with you, either. There's nothing to start.'

'Amy, I know I hurt you—'

'You see, even now, you're not pressing me because it's what you really want. You said yourself that you don't know. You're only trying to convince me because you honestly can't believe that I'm knocking you back. And, Nick, that's what I'm doing. Really. For my sake, and the kids', I won't go into reverse.'

He stood up, his hands seemed on a hair-jabbing frenzy as he paced the room. 'So what am I supposed to do?' she heard him mutter, and then louder: 'What the fuck am I supposed to do, Amy?'

'Go back to Boston and take Anneka with you,' she said firmly, without hesitation. 'Start appreciating her more. Every single facet, not just the ones you fell for. I need to believe you left me and the boys because it was a grand, sweeping passion. Because you couldn't live without her. Anything less . . . and it diminishes what we had. If you could leave me so easily, over nothing of any real value . . . that just makes *me* feel worthless.

It makes me feel as if the children don't really matter. Anything less than truly, madly, deeply, just turns our thirteen years together into a joke.'

As she spoke, she became aware that it was all true; not bluff or bravado. It was how she felt. Another reason for believing in the sort of elusive, epic love she had spoken to Paul about only days earlier.

Nick had finally stopped pacing. His face seemed closed. He wasn't even frowning. His hands fell to his sides and hung limply. 'If that's how you want it.' But by his voice, he was neither admitting defeat nor sounding as if he was actually going to do as she'd suggested. 'We still need to talk, Amy. You said it yourself, there are details to work out. Not now, obviously.'

'No. It's getting late.' Amy wondered dimly if spaghetti could burn.

'So when? If we don't set time aside, it won't happen.'

'Tomorrow night? Unless you're planning on going up to the Lake District . . .'

'I'll give Anneka a couple more days. If she's not back . . . I'll go then.'

'Fine.' Amy bit her lip. It was clear that if he did drag himself up the motorway to see his wife, it wasn't likely to be the kind of emotional plea that would win an Oscar on the big screen. 'So tomorrow night, then . . . At the White Stag?'

'If you don't mind village gossip?'

'Harrisfield isn't that bad. And I'd rather do it on neutral territory, not at your mum's or mine.'

Nick nodded peevishly. 'Whatever you say. Then maybe you could show me this house where you're planning on bringing up my children, whether I have a say in it or not. I'd at least like to see it from the outside.'

He could be dramatic if it suited him, realised Amy.

'OK,' she agreed. And as she did so, an idea began to form,

nebulous to start with. She felt her spirits creep upwards as it took shape and form. 'Nick, I know you don't work there any more, but you've still got connections at Faulkner Jones Burnley, haven't you?'

He blinked at her; nonplussed. 'Aside from my mother?'

Of course. Amy kicked herself for not having thought of it before, although to be fair, the 'doting' grandmother had been out of the country.

'Why bother asking me that?' Nick narrowed his eyes at her.

Amy shrugged. 'I'll tell you tomorrow.' She needed time to think it all through. Besides, she wanted a witness around. 'It's nothing that can't wait. One thing, though . . .' she added, as if it was an afterthought.

'What?' The lines were there again, chiselled above Nick's nose and lending balance to the cleft in his chin.

'You might want to bring Paul with you, if he's free . . . You've got to admit, he's done a good job mediating up to now . . .'

23

As the elderly gentleman finally made it off the zebra crossing, Zimmer frame, flat cap and all, Elspeth eased the car out of neutral and proceeded up Harrisfield High Street in the direction of the A55.

For a Saturday afternoon, traffic was light. She would be at the antiques fair in Chester with plenty of time to have a good scout around. She hadn't been to one in ages, and was quite looking forward to it.

Her main objective was to find something of interest on a music stall she'd heard might be there. Nothing fancy or fragile, but hopefully unusual enough to appeal to the older children at Little 'Uns. Maria kept a few percussion instruments in one of the numerous cupboards at the nursery, and there was an old piano in one of the playrooms. Elspeth was simply aiming to expand on that.

A week ago, after trawling through every single charity shop in Mold, she had come home with some hand puppets, a marching drum, a plastic trumpet, a rattle with bells attached – the sort you found on pet collars – and a small xylophone. She'd hidden them all in a red opaque crate with a snap-on lid, out of sight of Joseph and Mikey.

There wouldn't be anything quite as cheap on offer today, but there might still be some bargains to be had. Anyway, Elspeth had learned how to barter from her husband, and had retained the skill ever since. She would have to consider anything she bought as an investment in her trial run at Little

'Uns, but it would be paid off soon enough. There had been one session this week, with the two-year-olds, and it had gone far better than she'd imagined, except for Mikey asking her twice to wipe his nose for him, behaving as if the other children weren't there.

Last weekend, Elspeth had managed to pin down Tilly – who had a lovely voice for reciting, and was often asked to do it at school – to record a couple of fairy tales (*Little Red Riding Hood* and *The Gingerbread Man*) with gaps for the children to make the relevant sounds, either vocally or with their instruments. While the tape had been playing during the session, Elspeth had encouraged the toddlers to pretend to be the characters from the story, using the hand puppets, or some masks she had made one evening with Amy's help.

'Over and above the call of duty,' Maria had raved elatedly, after the children had filed away noisily for lunch. 'Not just music, but drama, too.'

'I've always thought they went hand in hand.' Unaccustomed to being fêted like that, Elspeth had coloured bashfully, and poked restlessly at her hair. 'We all know the effects of a powerful soundtrack.'

'The majority of children love music and dancing, but most of the time at home they're only exposed to it on the TV or radio.'

'Some parents get embarrassed easily, I suppose. Amy, on the other hand – well, she's quite brazen about that kind of thing. And when the Tweenies or the Fimbles are on, she always joins in with the songs. Lucas seems to be showing a keen interest in music already, so she wants to encourage it, to see if he takes after me.'

'I can just visualise her now,' grinned Maria, 'prancing around your lounge pretending her topknot's twitching. Oh, the joys of modern parenthood!'

Elspeth had proudly carried her little stash of puppets and

instruments home in her large canvas shopping bag, before returning them to the crate and cramming it into the small cupboard under the stairs.

Her euphoria had lasted for days. In fact, she was still on a high now, although perhaps reality was beginning to settle in, and niggly doubts starting to augment again.

After all, she couldn't say if she'd made the right decision based on one session alone. Carol and Amy had managed to persuade her to try it out, but ultimately she would need to convince herself that it was worth pursuing.

Creating an entire repertoire alone would be time-consuming – one of the arguments she had used from the outset. She couldn't keep churning out the same old stuff. Admittedly, unlike a school, children came and went at Little 'Uns like library books, to meet parents' shifting childcare needs. But some of them started there as babies and didn't leave until they went into full-time education. Elspeth didn't want to bore the poor loves to death.

Still, she was only dabbling at the moment, and it couldn't hurt to try something different. Life didn't stand still. She only had to look at her daughters to appreciate that much.

Elspeth shifted smoothly into fifth gear as she cruised along the dual carriageway. The sun was shining, a Mozart violin concerto was playing, the grass in the fields was a sparkling, brilliant green. Life was like a luscious peach, and Elspeth hadn't felt that way in a long time.

Of course, it wasn't all blooming and rosy when you scraped at the skin a bit, unfortunately. Try as she might, she couldn't escape the knowledge that Mews Cottage wouldn't be the hub of her daughters' universes for ever.

Tilly had done very well in her exams. Although not as exceptionally as she might if she'd had more peace and quiet to revise, Elspeth accepted with a twinge of regret. The teenager was bound to sail straight through sixth form and on to university. The cottage would seem dead with her gone, at first.

But why fret over something that wasn't imminent? It would be Amy and the boys Elspeth would have to part with first, although it was a consolation to know that they wouldn't be going far. The fact that Amy would be exchanging contracts soon meant that the purchase of 5 March Street was progressing without any unforeseen hiccups. Although there had been one surprise, albeit a positive one. Something which Elspeth hadn't seen coming, and nothing short of a coup, when you analysed it . . .

When Amy had spoken to Nick about it, he had apparently looked at her as if she'd asked for the moon and the stars, but Amy had stood firm. She wouldn't have asked if it wasn't for the boys, and when you saw it from their point of view, it wasn't taking liberties at all. Joseph, Mikey and Lucas bore Nick's surname as well as Amy's; although, unlike Paul's mother, Amy would have instantly dropped her maiden name as soon as she'd had a wedding ring on her finger. If Rowena wanted to prove her financial worth as a grandmother once and for all, this was the best way to do it.

'When we lived in the flat, you just had to click your fingers and there were chippies, plumbers and electricians at your disposal,' Amy had reminded Nick. 'And no call-out fees then. It was all charged to the company.'

Elspeth had to confess that she'd been surprised, but in a good way, by her daughter's counter-attack, and the way Amy had brought her old bugbear of Faulkner Jones Burnley into it.

'If I don't ask for a lot,' she had argued, when she'd returned from the White Stag and recounted what had happened to Elspeth and Tilly, 'I won't even get a little. This way, I can save myself a hassleload of DIY or hours thumbing through the Yellow Pages . . . And Paul said he'd be happy to help,' Amy had relished informing them. 'He said he'd actually been thinking about offering his architectural skills – for free, of course – but he hadn't wanted to seem forward. After all, it's my house, and I'm not after a major renovation.'

Amy had beamed, looking jubilant. 'Paul was great helping me convince Nick. Did I mention that already? It's hardly going to amount to tens of thousands to do up a three-bed semi, he pointed out. It's a period property, admittedly, but there's nothing too wrong with it. And if Faulkner Jones Burnley can't spare a few grand or whatever, then they're in serious trouble.'

Elspeth sighed, as she rolled to a stop at some traffic lights. Was it her imagination, she wondered for the umpteenth time, or had her daughter's spirits soared even further since Jonathan had gone to Dublin?

It could just be coincidence that it had all happened around the same time as this Nick business, but Elspeth wasn't convinced.

The matter of Jonathan's departure had come about the evening she and Tilly had taken Joe, Mikey and Lucas to the family pub with the children's play areas and the sickly ice cream machine (not an experience Elspeth wanted to relive in a hurry).

Amy had been round at Jonathan's for tea when, unexpectedly, he'd had a call from his ex-girlfriend Niamh. According to Amy, he had turned very pale, and after hanging up the phone, he had sunk down at his little kitchen table and explained that Niamh had found a lump in her breast. She was having tests . . . She wanted to see him.

'If there was anyone else she could call . . .' Jonathan had struggled to justify it; even to himself, it seemed. 'But there isn't. And she's worried about Sally-Ann . . .'

'You have to get over there as soon as possible,' Amy had advocated. 'Sally-Ann's your daughter. You can't let her down if she needs you.'

And so, the following Tuesday, after straightening things

out with work, Jonathan had left. Driving off in that car of his, which had seen better days, to catch a ferry from Holyhead to Ireland.

At first, Elspeth had noted that he had called Amy every evening, but now the calls seemed to be dwindling.

'Aren't you jealous?' Tilly had frowned one day, from under her curtain of recently dyed, 'raven' hair. 'You must be abnormal.'

Amy had shrugged. 'What's to be jealous of? He's Jonathan, not . . .'

'Paul?' Tilly had prompted, helpfully. 'Now, much as I've come to appreciate Mr Faulkner Jones's finer points, I still wouldn't trust him in the commitment stakes, and if I were Francesca and he was getting all up-close-and-personal with me, I'd seriously consider hiring a private detective, just to be on the safe side.'

Sometimes, thought Elspeth fondly, Tilly was a veritable little fruitcake. It was easy to imagine her in sixty years' time, butting into everyone's business like a shameless, outspoken Miss Marple.

As for Amy, it was as if a load had been lifted from her shoulders lately, which only went to highlight yet again what a negative influence Nick must have been. Yet it didn't bode well for Jonathan, either.

Elspeth wished she hadn't nudged her in his direction, especially at such a susceptible time when Amy couldn't really have been thinking straight. With the wisdom of hindsight, Elspeth ought to have stood well back to allow things to develop naturally. The knowledge that she might have precipitated another ill-fated relationship didn't exactly have her turning cartwheels.

She sighed again as she finally found a parking space, and climbed out and locked the car, squinting in the sunlight at a huge banner advertising the indoor fair.

For now, she thought firmly, she would take everyone else's advice and concentrate on herself for a while. Maybe even treat herself to some jewellery, while she was here. Why not, after all?

A new – or rather, an old – pendant, maybe. Or a brooch to pin on a scarf. She had a box full of trinkets, but there was always room for one more, and she was definitely aiming to start wearing them again, once Lucas wasn't around so much. Being strangled by a ten-month-old, who was desperate to cut a tooth on your sterling silver locket, wasn't quite how she'd envisaged grandmotherhood.

'Mum' – Amy teetered into the back bedroom in the sort of high, pointy heels that had been in and out of fashion for decades – 'are you sure you're going to be OK tonight?'

'Of course I am,' said Elspeth calmly. 'Aren't I always?'

'But this is different. You'll be completely on your own. Tilly isn't here to help.'

Elspeth sighed histrionically. 'Woe is me!'

'What's a "woe"?' asked Joseph, straightening his arms in the air as Elspeth slid on his pyjama top.

'Um . . . it's being sad,' said Amy.

Mikey instantly turned to his grandmother, two worried little lines etched on his brow. 'Are you sad, Nana?'

'No, of course not,' laughed Elspeth. 'It's just something grown-ups say. I was trying to be funny.'

Both Joseph and Mikey regarded her as if she had been anything but. Amy opened her arms and beckoned for them to snuggle up to her.

'You look pretty, Mummy.'

'You smell nice, like that po-porry up on the shelf in the toilet. Are you going to read us a story?'

'I'll read you a quick one, and then tuck you up in bed. Remember, Nana's just downstairs if you need her, but I know you're going to be big boys for her and sleep all night – aren't you?'

They nodded, like golden angels.

'Have you both done wee-wee?' Amy checked.

They nodded again, halos twinkling.

'But in the dark,' confessed Mikey, in hushed tones, 'it still comes out in my nappy.'

'Well, you're still learning,' his mum reassured him. 'But when it's light again, remember to ask Nana for the toilet and put your pants back on. You're doing very well without a nappy in the daytime.'

Elspeth smiled at them from the doorway. 'I'll be in the kitchen, then.'

Amy nodded. 'I'll be down in a mo.'

When her daughter came downstairs five minutes later, Elspeth was scraping scrambled eggs on to a slice of toast.

Amy's heels tappety-tapped across the kitchen floor. 'Are you sure you'll be fine, Mum . . .?'

'It's no bother. You look lovely, by the way.' Elspeth should have said it before. Now Amy would never believe her, even if it was the truth.

'Oh, I wouldn't go that far . . . but I really do love the outfit. Thanks, so much.' Amy hugged her tight, and Elspeth squeezed her back.

'You have a brilliant party, love.'

'It's not a party, as such.'

'Well, a girls' night out, isn't that what they call it?'

'Something like that.' Amy's smile seemed to widen. It was obvious that she was looking forward to it. How long was it since she'd been out on the tiles in Chester like that? Too long, calculated Elspeth. And to cap it off, a couple of old friends would be joining the group, too. One of them had recently split up with her boyfriend and lived alone in Handbridge. She had invited Amy to stay over, considering it was going to be a late night anyway. They might even be able to walk back from wherever they ended the evening, rather than queue up for a cab.

'So I'll see you sometime tomorrow afternoon, then,' said Amy, faffing around with her bags at the front door. 'Lynette said she'd do a big fry-up for brunch, if our stomachs could hack it. But it'll be nice to catch up, at any rate. It's been ages. I'll leave my mobile on all the time, except if we have to switch them off in a club. Mind you, I could have it on vibrate in my bag, like a kind of pager.' She tapped the black-and-gold handbag that seemed no bigger than a purse. 'I can usually feel it. It's like an earthquake. And if I do, I can go outside and call you back.'

'Amy, love,' Elspeth shook her head at her, 'there won't be any emergencies. Don't worry. I won't need to call you. You just enjoy yourself – but don't drink too much.'

'That's what Dad probably would have said.' Amy sighed and checked herself in the little oval mirror by the front door. 'Huh! Like I *could* get hammered any more. Three glasses of wine and I can't even stand up. Well, slight exaggeration, but you know what I mean.'

Elspeth regarded her with bewildered amusement.

'So, I'll leave you the keys for the Espace,' Amy jabbered on, 'in case you need to drive the boys anywhere. And where are your car keys, Mum . . .?' She started patting the pockets of all the garments hanging from the pegs. 'Oh, here they are, got them. Tangled up in a tissue – euch. You're hopeless.' Amy smiled back at her affectionately.

She really did look a picture tonight.

For a moment, Elspeth contemplated taking a photo, but Amy was as coy as Joseph in front of a camera. She would probably pull a face and spoil it, anyway. Like mother, like son.

Just then, the phone began to trill. Amy hesitated at the front

door – perhaps in case it was Maria or Lynette – as Elspeth
went to answer it.

'Hi, Elspeth, it's me.'

'Oh, hello, Jonathan . . .' She looked at her daughter, who
instantly gestured at her watch and shook her head. 'I'm – er –
afraid you've just missed Amy . . .'

'Have I?'

'She's going out in Chester, with the girls.'

'Oh, that's right, for her birthday . . . I'd forgotten.'

'I'll tell her you called, though . . . Er, how are things at your
end?'

'Oh, you know . . .'

Elspeth didn't, which was why she had asked. 'How's
Niamh?'

'Bearing up.'

'Good, good. I know she doesn't know me, but send her my
regards, won't you?'

'Er, sure.'

'Any idea when you'll be home?'

'No, I'm afraid. Not exactly. Can you tell Amy I called?'

'Of course I will,' Elspeth reassured him again. 'Are you
going to ring again on Sunday, her actual birthday?'

'Um,' he sounded non-committal, 'I'll try . . .'

Odd, thought Elspeth, putting the phone down after they'd
said their goodbyes. He'd seemed so indifferent.

Amy was still loitering by the front door. 'What did he have
to say?'

'I don't know why you didn't just speak to him yourself,'
Elspeth bristled.

'He wouldn't have kept it short with me.'

'He might, considering his mood.'

'What mood?'

'He didn't seem very . . . with it,' sniffed Elspeth. 'Anyway,
he'll try and call back on Sunday.'

'Right.'

'Although you'd have thought he'd more than just "try", seeing as it's your birthday . . .'

Amy shrugged. She didn't seem too fussed, Elspeth noted. 'It's difficult for him, Mum. It can't be pleasant, finding out someone close to you has cancer.'

Elspeth reared up a little. 'I understand that part, Amy. But Niamh isn't close to him. Or hasn't been, at least, for the last five years. In fact, she probably hurt him more than Nick hurt you. I can't help thinking that if I were in your position—'

'Yes, well, you're not.' Amy's voice was sharp, but not hurtful. 'And it's getting late.' She frowned at her watch again, then rippled her fingers in a small wave. 'I'll see you tomorrow, Mum, OK.'

Elspeth watched her shut the door behind her, then turned to stare at the phone, screwing up her brow as she ran through her brief conversation with Jonathan again. Aside from Amy's own apathy towards the relationship of late, something wasn't right on his part, either.

As only a parent could, Elspeth started to fret about whether this was a good thing or not. It would depend, she supposed, on what it was, and how it might affect her daughter.

Suddenly, she jumped, as the phone began to ring again.

'Hi, Mum,' Tilly greeted her in a lilting, happy voice. 'Just calling like you asked me to. I'm at Keira's mum's house.'

'That's quick. Public transport can't be so bad, after all.'

'No, it was OK. So I'll see you sometime tomorrow, then.'

'You just have a nice time. Say hello to Keira's mum for me.' Not that Elspeth knew the svelte, sophisticated divorcee that well. Keira's mother always managed to make her feel gauche.

'Will do . . . Listen, Mum, my mobile's almost out of battery, and I forgot my charger, so don't bother to call, there'll be no point. I just didn't want you to worry, OK?'

'Well, Keira's number must be in this phone's memory anyway. If I need to get hold of you for anything . . .'

'Yeah,' Tilly sounded vague, 'think so . . . See you tomorrow, Mum. Byeee.'

The phone went dead before Elspeth could reply. She put it down, tutting good-naturedly. She was on the verge of picking it up again, just to reassure herself that Keira's mum's number was definitely there if she needed it, when she heard rustling from the top of the stairs. She tutted again, but it wasn't as if she hadn't been expecting it. The boys were more than likely to be hyper tonight.

'The coast's clear!' she called up quietly, so as not to wake Lucas, who had been settled in his cot for the last hour. Then she realised that neither of the escapees would understand what she meant, so she clarified it for them. 'Mummy's gone!'

Joseph and Mikey scampered excitedly down the stairs. 'Can we make that card for her now, Nana?'

Elspeth sighed, glancing at her eggs on toast, but her light supper didn't look all that appetising any more.

'You promised,' Joseph reminded her.

'Yes, I know I did, poppet.' Although she'd really been talking about the following morning. Elspeth opened one of the drawers of her Welsh dresser and pulled out some pink card and a craft box full of crayons, cotton wool, stickers, glue, plastic scissors and the other odds and ends she collected for the boys.

Mikey screwed up his nose. 'Pink's for girls,' he said in disgust.

'Mummy's a girl,' Joseph pointed out scornfully. 'Ooooo, glitter, can we use it, Nana? Can we? I want to make a big star shape.' He proceeded, for some reason, to draw around his hand – and over it – with a chubby felt-tip pen.

'When's Mummy's birthday properly?' asked Mikey.

'It s'not today,' said Joseph superciliously.

'Well,' said Elspeth, 'it's on Sunday, which is the day after tomorrow. So after two big sleeps, it'll be Mummy's real birthday, and you can give her this card you're going to make.'

'Will she have a cake? How many candles will the cake have? Will it have a dinosaur on it?'

'One candle. That's all she wanted. Just something to blow out and make a nice wish over. And flowers rather than a dinosaur, I think.'

'Mummy's old,' Joseph informed his brother. 'A hundred and something. I'm going to be four, Nana. I'll have four candles.'

'Yes, I know, darling. You'll be a very big boy then.'

Elspeth looked on in dismay as glitter was sprinkled not just on the card, but over everything on the table, including Mikey's blankie, which had already been smeared with glue. She sighed, yet again.

Yes, the hazards of being a grandmother were, without a doubt, outweighed by the joys. But sometimes even the joys required an incredible amount of clearing up after.

24

'Same again, mate?'

'Huh?' Paul jumped slightly, and returned his attention to the small group of colleagues from Faulkner Jones Burnley. They were all men under thirty-five; more or less single; out to have a good time. He was probably the most heavily involved out of all of them – a realisation that made him feel as if someone had suddenly pulled the knot in his tie tighter.

He nodded, and swallowed hard. 'Same again – definitely.' Keeping up with the lads was a strain in itself these days, but one he couldn't quite seem to relinquish.

Francesca still regularly went out with the girls, after all, and encouraged him to stick with his own mates, too. Trouble was, they weren't the sort Paul would go running to with a major personal crisis, and he never saw them outside work or a pub or club.

Since Nick, in fact, there hadn't been another close comrade on the horizon. Not surprising really, considering how long they had been friends. And Paul had started to wonder if one of the reasons his relationship with Francesca was lasting so long had something to do with that. Did loneliness have to be diagnosed before a person tried to find a cure for it? Or had he, without being conscious of it, attempted to plug the gap that Nick had left?

'Come on, Paul,' said a voice to his left. He felt himself jostled good-naturedly. 'It might never happen.'

'What if it already has?' he responded automatically, sounding glum, even to his own ears.

What if he'd misread all the signals and was even now stringing Francesca along to some unknown, ill-advised end? Why was he always *thinking* about her these days rather than *feeling* anything? As if his heart – God forbid anyone was a mind-reader around here, it would be too embarrassing – had washed its hands of her. Paul groaned to himself self-deprecatingly. Even his analogies were confused.

'Isn't she here yet?' asked Dan, who tried too hard to be the clown of the group, but subsequently put most women off with his stupendous lack of tact.

'Who?' Paul frowned.

'The birthday girl. The reason we came here and didn't just stick to what we know.'

'Amy?' Paul shook his head. 'Can't see her . . . Anyway, that wasn't why I wanted to come. I don't want to gatecrash her own thing. I just thought you'd all appreciate my getting tickets for this place. It's opening night, for Pete's sake. Didn't you fancy trying something new?'

'Yeah,' grinned Al, 'we all know you've got connections, but it's a bit . . . quiet for my taste.'

Paul cocked an eyebrow. 'It's heaving.'

'I was talking about the music. Subdued, don't you reckon?'

'You mean, you can hear yourself talk?'

'Tacky, though.' Spencer, the tall, weedy one with the badly fitting specs and an amazing ability to pull in spite of his apparent nerdishness, shrugged as he glanced around. 'Is it trying to be Indonesian, Polynesian – or neither?'

'I'd go with the Hawaiian connection,' sighed Paul. 'The name's a giveaway, don't you think?'

'Hula Palace?' Al shook his head. 'I *mean*.'

'There are some benefits to opening night,' Dan pointed out, his eyes popping wider. 'Exemplary totty, for starters. Just take that lot.' Practically salivating, he leered over Paul's shoulder.

Paul looked round, and almost dropped the remnants of his current pint.

There was a group of girls a few yards away, standing on a wide raised section, separated by a railing. The girls' skirts were so short, it was obvious they had some cheek, in more ways than one. Their elevated position meant the onlookers at ground level would get more of an eyeful than anticipated.

It wasn't anything Paul hadn't seen before. Even the fact that the girls were among the youngest in the bar wouldn't normally have bothered him. He preferred over twenty-one places, himself, rather than just over eighteen, to filter out the more immature and giggly types. But each to their own, unless it was illegal.

No, it was the fact that one of them was Tilly Croft that had rendered Paul speechless.

Little Tilly of the owlish grey eyes – except they were even more heavily lined with kohl and mascara than usual. Was she even seventeen yet? Too young to be here, in any case.

He was only viewing her in profile as she talked animatedly with one of her friends, but as she leaned across to speak to another, her skirt rose up to reveal practically everything there was to be seen from the rear.

Spencer was already psyching himself up to make a move. 'I'm going for the brunette,' he announced, straightening his jacket. 'Great little arse.'

Tilly was the only brunette. The other girls were various shades of blonde, from natural mousy streaks to glaringly fake platinum.

Paul felt ill. 'No you don't.' He yanked Spencer back.

'Huh?' Spencer looked at him vacantly. 'What's wrong?'

Dan was smirking. 'Fancy her yourself?'

Paul shook his head, infuriated. 'I know her. She's just a kid. She's still at school.'

'So?' Spencer still looked blank.

'And she's a family friend,' Paul elaborated stiffly. 'She shouldn't be here. Excuse me.'

Frowning so earnestly it seemed to weigh his brow down, he wove his way to the stairs and up on to the platform, slaloming past one group after another until he reached Tilly's. When her gaze fell on him, she blinked for a moment in unconcealed surprise, before her face lit up in a wide, intoxicated grin.

'Paul!' she exclaimed rapturously, stumbling forwards in her heels and draping an arm around his shoulder. 'Hey, guys,' she turned to her group, who were giggling even more profusely now, 'this is Paul. *The* Paul. Say hello nicely now. Are you on your own?'

He gestured vaguely to the lads down below. 'Tilly,' he mumbled, as he tried to dodge the fumes of alcohol on her breath, 'what the hell are you doing here?'

'Don't be like that,' she said sweetly, twiddling his tie. 'We're just celebrating passing our exams. No big deal.'

The others all cheered. Paul instinctively hushed them, aware that down below, Dan and the others were watching avidly. Without thinking it through, he tugged at Tilly's skirt.

'You're wearing a thong,' he hissed reprovingly, as if he were forty years old and her dad.

She seemed to jump, and jerked backwards slightly, so that suddenly his hand was flat against her bare buttock. Her flesh was soft and warm. A blush seeped hotly up from his collar, as she stared at him oddly and pressed herself closer to him.

Paul could hear the girls sniggering and the lads guffawing, but they sounded distant, as if they were dissolving in the wave of panic that suddenly gripped him. On the other side of the circular bar, he had caught a glimpse of Amy flapping a twenty-pound note at a barman. Oh, shit. Oh, bollocks.

He tried to prise Tilly off him. But in his experience, women always seemed to acquire the clinging ability of leeches when drunk. This one was no exception. Even after years of fending them off, Paul was no closer to working out how to do it without the girl in question falling flat on her face. One thing was certain, he couldn't let Amy see them like this.

'Do your mother and sister know you're here?' he asked Tilly, trying to sound like the voice of authority again, rather than just incompetent.

She rolled her eyes, still provocatively attached to him. 'What do you think?'

No, then.

'So how. . . ?'

'She's staying at mine,' said the tallest girl in the group, whose medium-toned locks could be either natural or artificial – it was a tough call. 'Hi,' she said silkily, extending her hand, 'I'm Keira.'

'Hello, Keira.' Paul was crisp yet smooth, realising that this girl wasn't quite as pissed as Tilly, and might prove crucial. 'So do your parents know where you are?'

'My mum got me the tickets for this place. As a sort of congratulations present. I'm seventeen next month. That's practically *eighteen*, she says. It's not as if we don't all look old enough.'

Paul stared at her sceptically, before reminding himself that he had no claim to the most conscientious parents in the world, either.

'Paul,' said Tilly, from somewhere close to his ear, so that her breath washed over him like warm rum, 'you mustn't tell Mum or Amy – *please*. We're only having a laugh, and s'not as if I'm out like this all the time.'

'Right,' he nodded, his voice dripping sarcasm, 'well, why don't you tell Amy yourself? She's right over there.'

'What?' Tilly suddenly stood bolt upright, as if someone

had stuck a broom handle down her back. 'Where? Oh, fu—' She bit her lip. 'Where?'

As she swayed on the spot, looking around wildly, Paul reached out to steady her again. Thinking fast, he pulled her a few yards away, behind a pillar, out of sight of the other side of the bar. She leaned against it, staring up at him again.

'Paul, are you having me on?' She was still slurring slightly; yet, on a more hopeful note, her eyes were showing a glimmer of their former intelligence. 'Why would Amy be *here*? She never said . . .'

'Because I wangled her some extra passes at the last minute,' he explained impatiently. 'She told me she might come, she might not. It depended what time they finished having their meal.'

'Oh, shit.' Tilly rubbed a hand over her face, then clutched at the lapel of his jacket. 'Paul, what am I going to do?'

Stop pawing me, for starters, he wanted to snap. It would be bad enough if Amy caught her here in this state, but if she found them both like this . . . Paul felt stone cold. He grabbed Tilly's hand and peeled it away from his jacket, just as Keira tottered over.

'The best thing,' said Paul, 'would be to leave right now.'

'Leave?' frowned Keira. 'But we haven't even been here that long.'

The two girls embarked on a noisy, squawking discussion, as Paul glanced around nervously. At last, Keira sighed and rested a hand on her hip in a stroppy but surrendering manner. She tossed her head as Paul shepherded them quickly towards the door, relief flooding through him.

'Shouldn't I tell the others—' Keira began, but he cut her off.

'Are they staying at yours, too?'

'No, but—'

'Then just wave,' he said briskly. 'They'll get the hint. You can call them later.'

He suspected, however, that at any moment Keira and Tilly's phones would ring in stereo, probably with some jangly ringtone of the current chart Number One.

Just as they were almost out of the door, Tilly lost her footing and stumbled back against his chest. She stared up at him through her clumpy, dark lashes.

'I'm sorry,' she whined, 'this is all my fault. I'll make this up to you. Really, Paul . . .'

He frowned. She still wasn't quite as compos mentis as he'd hoped.

'Right,' he said, 'fine, good, whatever.' And just to get her through the door at top speed, he put his arm around her waist and hauled her out alongside him.

If only it wasn't so crowded in here, frowned Amy, looking around the large, modern, high-ceilinged bar. With its split-level design, and beautiful young people draped around chrome railings or on leather couches as if they were part of the decor, Amy felt as if she'd trespassed into a glamorous photo shoot.

Hula Palace had been scooped out of an old building near the canal. As its central feature, it boasted a circular bar made out of some bamboo-like material with a thatched canopy, looking as if it belonged on some tropical island paradise. Amy was convinced it was a fire hazard, and couldn't get it out of her head. Her imagination kept drifting off, conjuring up an image of half a dozen hulking firemen bursting in and closing the place down, before erupting into their own version of the final scene from *The Full Monty*.

Then again, Amy was aware that she wasn't exactly sober. Which made her wonder if there was ever a point when you were drunk and you stopped realising you were drunk, or were you always dimly aware of it?

Anyway, if it wasn't so akin to a tin of sardines in here, Amy might have had some chance of spotting Paul. Not that he had been definite about coming; he'd just said he might try and drag the lads along, just as she'd been non-committal herself about whether the girls would agree.

But a few of her gang had been determined to go on somewhere after the meal, and had leapt at the possibility of some opening-night freebies (amounting to a mere cocktail each, basically). It seemed as if Paul might have had more trouble convincing his lot.

'Looks like your mate's at it again.' Maria nudged her, and Amy glanced round to see Lynette in another clinch with a bloke she was guessing was a total stranger.

'She never used to be this bad,' Amy recalled wistfully. 'It's splitting up with her boyfriend . . . It's got to be.'

'Well you haven't turned into a self-professed snogaholic, have you?'

Amy considered the comparison. 'No . . .' she said slowly, sipping her drink, 'but maybe that's because I've got kids and she hasn't.'

Although Amy suspected that if the roles were reversed, things would be no different, at least on her part. She had never had the compulsion to go around snogging a variety of different men, although admittedly Nick had been on the scene. But to her, there was something about kissing someone's open mouth that was sublimely intimate. She hadn't quite got into the full passionate spirit of it with Jonathan yet, let alone a man whose name she didn't know.

'Could be worse, I suppose,' Maria shrugged. 'At least a snog can't get you up the duff.'

'S'pose not.' Amy looked around the bar again with a sigh. 'And I'd know about that.'

'He's not here, is he?' asked Krissie, the youngest of the Little 'Uns cohorts, bopping up to them in her minuscule black dress, which barely harnessed her best assets. A paper cocktail umbrella was now tucked into her curly hair extensions.

'Who?' asked Amy nonchalantly.

'That bloke. The posh-sounding what's-his-name. The one who got you the invites.'

'Paul Faulkner Jones,' smirked Maria.

'Oh, him.' Amy shrugged. 'Can't see him . . . Then again, he only said he might come. He didn't promise—' Her breath snagged in her chest.

Having decided that Paul probably wasn't here yet, she had taken to glancing at everyone coming into the bar, and a small group was entering right now. It was a couple going out at the same time, though, that had seized her attention.

Amy froze, in shock.

The man was holding the girl close, smouldering down at her seductively, and the girl was looking up at him in an obvious, wanton fashion. Yet the whole thing was so unbelievable, and just a brief glimpse before they vanished outside, that Amy wondered if she had hallucinated the whole thing.

'You OK?' Maria sounded worried. 'You look like you're going to throw up . . .'

'I know I've been drinking,' Amy muttered, still reeling and staring in the direction of the door, 'but I'm not going mad. I couldn't have imagined it . . .'

'Imagined what?'

'I *couldn't*,' said Amy, suddenly galvanised into action.

In her woolly state of mind, she couldn't fit all the pieces of the jigsaw together, but as a sudden outrage whipped through her, she swung round to Maria and thrust over her drink.

'Listen, if I don't come back, tell Lynette I'll call her later. She's still eating that bloke's face off.'

Maria's strong, dark brows crumpled in confusion. 'If you don't come back,' she repeated. 'Where the bloody hell are you going? The loo?'

But Amy didn't reply. She was already hurrying away. Down a few steps, and then a battle through the throng of bodies to get to the door. By the time she was outside herself, barely conscious of someone asking if she was all right, there was no trace of the couple she had seen leaving the bar.

The cobbles in the alley sparkled in the glow of a street light. Amy felt a hand on her shoulder and swung round. It was a doorman; so wide-shouldered in his smart DJ, he looked like a caricature.

'Everything OK?' There was an air of concern about him. Why did men always assume she required rescuing?

'I need a taxi,' she burst out, deciding she'd take advantage, anyway. She added, in case he rightly assumed that she'd been drinking, 'This is an emergency – one of my kids is ill . . .'

God forgive her for lying, and bringing the children into it, but it worked. She wasn't quite sure how it happened, but what felt like seconds later she was sitting in the back of a black cab. It had probably been hovering at the kerbside all along, but in her delirious state, she hadn't noticed. She closed her eyes. Her head started spinning.

The harder she tried to erase the image of Paul and her sister, the more indelibly it seemed to stamp itself on her mind. Their intentions had been obvious. Tilly had lied about tonight. But then again, why had Paul bothered to get Amy tickets if he'd known . . .?

Amy shook her head, and hugged her little handbag against her. None of it made sense. But she knew what she had seen, and it had nothing to do with the wine she had consumed in the restaurant or the two and a half pina coladas she had knocked back at the bar.

'Where to?' said a male voice, so impatiently, Amy suspected it wasn't the first time he had asked.

'Sorry?' she muttered, opening her eyes and realising that although the cab was running, it was still stationary.

'Where to, love?' asked the driver, looking over his shoulder at her suspiciously. 'I thought it was an emergency. One of your kids—'

'Oh,' said Amy, 'yes. Paul's flat, I need to get to Paul's flat.'

'Right.' The cabby seemed more annoyed by the second. 'Is that another new bar,' he asked, his voice barbed, 'or just your boyfriend's place?'

'This really is urgent,' glared Amy, on the defensive. But this time, she remembered to give a proper address. 'It's by the river. And he's not my boyfriend.'

'Whatever. Just next time you have a barney, don't bring me into it.' The cab rattled off.

Amy was fast becoming indignant with the world in general. Dipping into her handbag, she pulled out her small, wallet-style purse. 'Look,' she snapped, brandishing a photograph. 'I really do have kids, see! And this *is* an emergency, even if it hasn't got anything to do with Joe, Mikey or Lucas. Right this minute, a pig of a man might be trying it on with my sixteen-year-old sister.'

The cabby surveyed her dubiously in his rear-view mirror. He put his foot down slightly. 'You've got a complicated life, love,' he muttered. Although a moment later, she thought he changed that to 'love life'.

Amy closed her eyes again, sinking into a strange, dragging despair. If things had indeed seemed complicated at the start of the evening, they were positively indecipherable now.

25

Paul had just finished brushing his teeth, when he almost sent the brush flying at the sound of violent hammering on his front door. It sounded as if someone was trying to break it down.

The intercom system was on the blink again, so the main door downstairs had been left on the latch. Any weirdo could have got in, which was why Paul had already installed a Fort Knox-style lock on his own door. On the other hand, Mrs Freddy Kruger could have flipped, once and for all; no longer content with just banging on the ceiling with her broomstick.

Paul glanced down in alarm. Impatient to hit the sack, he had peeled off his clothes the minute he had come home.

He hurried into the bedroom and grabbed the T-shirt and shorts he sometimes wore to bed if he was cold, tugging them on agitatedly. Just as he finished dressing, a more familiar noise started from the flat below.

Now, if that was Mrs Freddy Kruger venting her frustration on her Artex, then who . . .?

It was unlikely to be Francesca. She was driving up from Gloucestershire this evening after a few days away, visiting her family. She had already called earlier to say she'd be too tired to stay over tonight and would see him tomorrow. Besides, she had a key. Why use a battering ram?

Paul ventured down the hall, trepidation swilling in his veins. He was about to call out, when a voice bayed furiously, 'I know you're in there! It's no use hiding. Open this door right NOW.'

'Amy?' Paul blinked in surprise. Without hesitating, he let her in.

She barged straight past like a Pamplona bull who'd spotted something red behind him.

'OK, where is she?' Flinging down her little bag on the side table by the coat rack, Amy swivelled to face him, hands on her hips. She glowered at him for a couple of seconds, then turned her head slowly to the corridor on the left. 'Silly question,' she muttered, as if to herself. And before he knew it, she was charging down it.

His bedroom door was the first on the right. Amy virtually kicked it open as wide as it could go. Paul was right behind her, gobsmacked. He watched as she took in the large, empty bed with the crumpled duvet and out-of-shape pillows. She seemed to falter slightly, before she was off again, pushing past him into the corridor, only to fling open the bathroom door.

It wasn't until she had checked every single room, and even out on the roof terrace, that she finally started running out of steam. When it looked as if she might actually start opening cupboards, though, Paul finally recovered and intervened. He grasped her by the shoulders, while she squirmed and refused to look at him.

'Amy' – he shook her gently – 'have you been taking something?' Paranoia could be the effect of a few things, the majority of which he couldn't see her using willingly. But he had to ask.

'You mean drugs, don't you?' she snapped, finally looking him in the eye. 'Of course not! I'm not stupid.'

'Someone might have spiked your drink . . .'

'Only the barman. And I'd have thought that was a firing offence, myself.'

'I'm sorry I asked . . . I just wondered what other reason there might be for you to come here and rampage around my flat, acting as if I've kidnapped someone. I know Nick said you couldn't hold your drink, but I've never seen evidence of that. Up until now, I suppose,' he added, in a mumble.

'Paul, just shut up and tell me where she is,' Amy demanded, still looking furious, yet confused now, too.

He sighed. 'Who?'

'You know frigging well I'm talking about Tilly. I saw you leave the bar together, and you were hardly—'

'Oh, bollocks.' He said it under his breath, then realised it was scarcely the reaction of an innocent man. He let Amy go, but prayed she would stay still rather than charge off again. It would be easier to explain himself if she remained in the one spot for long enough. He frowned. 'You saw us, then?' Shit, he was incriminating himself further with every sentence.

'Only when you were leaving together. You pig,' Amy seethed. 'So what happened after that? Did she come to her senses and blow you off? And why did you take her to that bar in the first place if you knew I might be there?'

Paul saw a speck of hope, and snatched at it. 'Exactly,' he pointed out. 'I didn't. I was there with my mates when I saw her with hers. Anyway, she didn't have any idea at first that you were there as well, so—'

'So what were you trying to do? Cover for her?'

'I – er – no . . . Well, yes, in a way.' He paused, and scratched heatedly at his nose. 'Didn't you ever do anything like that when you were her age, Amy?'

'What, flaunt myself around bars in a gymslip and a blouse three sizes too small for me?'

'If you put it that way . . .' Paul shook his head. 'Come on, though, you're being a bit harsh. OK, so I can't say I totally approve of what she was wearing.' He almost referred to the incident with the thong, then decided Amy wouldn't take kindly to hearing he'd fondled her little sister's bum. 'But it's peer pressure – and fashion. That's what all the girls seem to be parading around in, not to mention the older women.'

'Well, you'll never see me in anything like that.' Amy arched her head disdainfully.

Paul twitched an eyebrow. Amy, in a thong? Probably just as well. However, he couldn't resist appraising her present attire, rating her as if he were setting eyes on her for the first time.

To be fair, it was a pretty hot outfit in itself, although in a less obvious and more elegant way than Tilly's. The fitted, sleeveless top was scooped and low, flatteringly showing off smooth, lightly tanned shoulders, not to mention a hint of bosom, as pert as a balcony – although that was probably her bra's doing. The matching skirt was short but not too short, exposing enough leg to leave a man hankering for more, whether there were barely existent knickers at the end of it or not. Along with the narrow, high-heeled shoes, it was the most attractive, feminine get-up he'd seen her in in a long time, and it was clear that, even if she hadn't lost any extra weight recently, she was fitter and more toned than in recent memory.

Her glossy, chestnut hair could easily be classified as long now, expertly layered with a feathery fringe that framed her round face rather than weighing it down. And there was something else that was different about her these days . . . Paul rubbed his jaw as he tried to pinpoint it.

'You're not wearing glasses,' he blurted out loud, as he realised what it was; then instantly bit his lip, because he might as well have admitted that she used to remind him of Velma out of *Scooby Doo*. At least, a few years ago, when she'd been going through an orange phase.

Amy looked thrown. 'Er . . . no.' She hesitated. 'I've got special contact lenses. I can sleep in them and everything. Great for working with the kids at nursery, aside from dodging blows from my own bunch . . .' She frowned again, looking piqued. 'What's that got to do with you and my sister, though?' she flung at him reproachfully. 'You're trying to change the subject.'

'No!' He swiftly denied it, because he hadn't been – not intentionally. 'I've only just noticed, that's all. You know what men are like. Not very observant at the best of times. You've worn lenses on and off in the past, anyway, so I guess it wasn't a major makeover . . .' He felt as if he was digging himself in deeper every time he opened his mouth, but he couldn't seem to stop. 'You're looking different these days, anyway. Very nice, in fact. I was just trying to work out what you'd changed apart from your hair and um . . .' He gestured to her outfit, realising that in the digging stakes, he'd hit rock bottom.

'Well, thanks for noticing.' She was nothing short of acrimonious. He couldn't blame her. 'A woman always relishes being called "nice".'

'Better than nice, I mean,' Paul laboured on. 'You're looking—'

'Oh, it's all right. I don't honestly expect compliments from you.' She heaved a gritty sigh. 'What I do expect is an explanation for why you were all over my sister like a rash.'

'Me?' Paul smarted. It was beginning to really bug him that Amy couldn't let it go, or accept that his motives had been as far from devious as left was from right. 'Why is it always my fault? Why can't you even consider that Tilly may have been to blame? It wasn't me who forced the alcohol down her neck, and I wasn't the one who lied to my own mother about what I was up to tonight. I know how it might have looked, but I was just a prop to keep her upright, as well as the guy who realised she shouldn't be there in that state. So I took her and her friend home in a cab. Well – to Keira's home, which was on my way here anyway. I wasn't in the mood to go back to the bar after that. I couldn't face you, I'm sorry.'

'Keira?' Amy shook her head. 'I didn't see her . . . But then, I didn't have the best view in the world . . .' She groaned, as if everything had suddenly become clear. 'I should have known she still had to come into this somewhere. I don't trust that madam one bit, even though Mum thinks the sun shines out of her backside. This whole thing was probably her idea.'

Paul didn't comment. He didn't even point out that Amy had deflected the blame away from Tilly again.

'My only mistake, in fact,' he thought it might be judicious to add, 'was that maybe I should have marched your sister over to you the minute I saw you.'

For a long moment, Amy seemed deep in thought. 'She was flirting with *you*, wasn't she?' she asked at last.

'Uh-huh.' Paul tried not to sound as if he was bragging.

'I knew she liked you that way. She tried telling me it was harmless, but—'

'Amy, it is harmless. I'm never going to act on it, and neither is she, not really.' Again, he thought it best to avoid mentioning the thong incident. 'Tomorrow morning, Tilly's going to wake up with a massive headache. And if she remembers what happened, she'll probably be too embarrassed to ever mention it. It's up to you where you take it from here . . . whether you tell your mum or not, or whether you just talk it through with Tilly yourself.'

'What do you think I should do?'

'Me?' Paul grunted. 'I'm hardly the person to ask. Parenting's not my forte, you might have noticed, and I've never had a sibling to contend with.'

Amy stared up at him. 'I guess not.' She still seemed troubled. 'Look . . . I'm sorry for earlier . . . But you can see my point of view – can't you?'

'Why you jumped to the wrong conclusion?' Paul still felt hurt to a degree. 'I can understand how it might have looked,' he conceded.

It was, to be fair, the very reason he hadn't wanted her to see him with Tilly like that. Yet he couldn't exonerate Amy so easily. He couldn't let her walk out of there without somehow, perversely, making her pay, even if it was just in some infinitesimal way.

Amy now shrugged back sheepishly. 'I thought you'd understand. You can't blame me, really. After all . . . I know what you're capable of.'

'Actually . . .' he said slowly, smiling to himself, 'you don't.'

Amy stared out over the quiet river. It was so deliciously warm out here still, and so peaceful.

She'd never comprehended how Paul's cluttered roof terrace, with its plethora of plants in terracotta tubs and its eye-level view of other people's chimney pots, fitted in with his contemporary, sybaritic, almost James Bond-ish approach to life.

All right, so there was a narrow view of the Dee, but it was nothing spectacular. She'd never seen the attraction of standing out here during one of his parties, even with the authentic, antique hurricane lamps burning invitingly in a row, or while sipping a glass of chilled, freshly squeezed orange juice (she'd either been driving or pregnant, or both). It had always been crowded and noisy and stuffy, but tonight . . .

With only a couple of candles burning in the lamps and a mug of coffee in her hand, this place seemed just about the most magical spot on the face of the earth. And even more oddly, it fitted Paul like a supple leather glove.

'You can sit down, you know.' He spoke from behind, still with that peculiar note of wry amusement that had been flitting in and out of his voice ever since he had insisted she stay for a conciliatory drink.

She looked round, as he gestured to the space beside him on his wood and wrought-iron bench. It looked just like the ones in the park behind Harrisfield's small library.

'In a minute,' she said dreamily. 'I'm just enjoying your view.'

'Mmm. From where I'm sitting, it's not half bad.'

Amy pursed her lips as she realised he wasn't referring to the Dee. 'Corny, but cute.'

'That's me.' He grinned rakishly, and after a pause commented, 'You look tired, though.'

She sighed. 'I suppose I must be. It's only when I stop these days, that I realise how knackered I actually am. I don't know how I've managed to stay up this late tonight. I guess I must have really wanted an evening for myself. Mind over matter.'

'Sit down then, before you keel over.' Paul took her arm and coaxed her down on to the bench. 'I know how you feel, anyway. I can't seem to hack the pace myself these days.'

'That's domesticity for you. You're settling down, Paul. Not to mention growing up.'

'More like growing old,' he snorted. 'Anyway,' he shifted position on the bench to face her, folding one leg at right angles over the other, 'have you managed to get through to Maria yet?'

Amy picked up her mobile from the ledge where the hurricane lamps stood. She tried again.

'It just rings and then goes to messaging. I'll send a text, to be on the safe side, even if it takes me half an hour. I hate them. There's not a lot else I can do, though. I haven't got Lynette's mobile number, only her landline. Maria's the only mobile I've got listed here – out of all of them at the bar.'

Paul took hold of her wrist, turning it slightly to glance at her watch. 'There's no point going back to Hula Palace, either, everyone'll be getting chucked out at any minute.'

'Someone will get back to me,' said Amy, trying to sound confident.

Maria had already left a cranky, garbled message, demanding to know where Amy had got to. When Amy had called back, she'd typically got no answer because Maria only seemed to hear her phone when it was virtually next to her ear, which was hardly ever.

'I left a message, anyway,' Amy added. 'Told her where I was, and not to worry, it was a long story. But I asked her to call me back, or get Lynette to, at least. I've got this image of me camping out on Lynette's doorstep, waiting for her to get home.'

'Without a tent or sleeping bag?' Paul tutted disapprovingly. 'You can borrow mine, if you like.'

Amy glanced up from tapping in her text message. 'You've got a tent and sleeping bag?'

'Er – no.'

'Didn't think camping was your style. Maybe when you were a student.'

'I think I preferred the five-star lifestyle even then.'

'You don't look very "five star" right now. More like a B&B,' scoffed Amy, glancing very briefly at his sloppy jersey shorts. It was refreshing to see him looking scruffy for a change.

Even on a hot summer weekend he always seemed to have a collar stifling him, albeit on a short-sleeved linen shirt. And his shorts were always the more tailored variety, nothing baggy or garish; always subdued, with just one zip at the fly, rather than half a dozen scattered all over to conceal a multitude of pockets and secret compartments.

'Beauty and the Beast.' Paul grinned, tugging at his grubby T-shirt, and then nodding at her own outfit.

Amy felt herself blush. It started in the region of her chest and spread upwards like warm sunshine. She concentrated on sending the text message to Maria. If she didn't hear back soon, her only option would be a taxi to Harrisfield, which would cost the earth at this time of night. She couldn't expect Paul to drive her all the way home. He looked knackered himself, and besides, he'd no doubt been drinking earlier, too.

In spite of joking about it, she didn't much fancy going back to Lynette's just yet and risking having to wait on the doorstep. Her mum's car was parked outside Lynette's house, fine, but the keys were in her overnight bag in the guest room. Even if they'd been in her handbag, Amy wouldn't have fancied 'camping out' in a Skoda, either.

'I'm a bit stuck, really,' she acknowledged ruefully. 'I'll try ringing Lynette's, see if she's home yet . . .' But when she did, the answering machine picked up instantly. Amy had no option but to leave another message. 'This is such a pain.'

'Stop trying for a while. Just relax.' Paul extricated the mobile from her grasp and put it back on the ledge. 'I'm sorry I even asked if you'd spoken to anyone. You seemed quite chilled up until then.'

Amy gazed round the roof terrace again. 'You're right, I was. I should be more . . . spontaneous sometimes, don't you think? Sometimes I get bogged down in the detail.'

'Eh? You're talking to an architect. Detail means everything to me. Anyway, if you weren't an organised sort of person, you wouldn't be able to juggle everything as well as you do.'

'Ha! Appearances can be deceptive. I don't juggle as much as throw everything up in the air and hope for the best, usually with my eyes shut.'

'Yeah, right, you're not convincing me. And I'd say you acted pretty spontaneously tonight. Charging over here like a woman on a mission, desperate to save your sister from a fate worse than death. There would have been far worse fates, you know.'

Amy frowned primly. 'It wasn't a laughing matter, Paul.'

'It wasn't – back then. What about now, though?'

Amy stubbornly refused to look at him. She stared at a carefully potted geranium, instead. 'I suppose there might be the tiniest reason to find it slightly funny. Only slightly, mind. And this is the last time I'm going to apologise for getting the wrong end of the stick.'

'As opposed to your sister getting the right end?' Paul grinned.

'Oh, you . . .' Amy almost hit him. 'You're vile, d'you know that?'

'I've been called worse. Anyway, she would have been in good hands.'

This time, Amy did lash back. Paul intercepted her, though, barring her way with a martial arts-style manoeuvre that meant her intended slap on the wrist seemed to just bounce back into her lap. His lightning-quick arm draped itself along the back of the bench, and he chuckled so cheekily, Amy sat in stunned, annoyed silence.

'Sorry,' he relented, 'I'm being a bastard to you, aren't I? And it's virtually your birthday . . . Well, in about twenty-four hours . . .'

Without any warning, Amy suddenly felt his hand in her hair. It was the hand belonging to the arm on the back of the bench, so it was only inches from her head, anyway, but it was the last thing she had expected. She froze, uncertain of what it meant. His fingers were playing with a tendril of hair close to her ear, while his eyes just seemed to be staring at her as if she were a mirage in a desert.

A voice in Amy's head told her to move, stand up, get away, but something else in her dismissed that as nothing but blind panic. Even when his face loomed so close that the features blurred, Amy remained pinned to the bench by her own will, rather than anything else. Even when his lips brushed against hers, and a crazed warm rush tumbled around in her stomach, Amy couldn't move because she didn't want to.

As if in slow motion, he sat back again, and tenderly hooked her hair behind her ear. 'See what Tilly would have been missing?' he murmured, as another devilish grin swept across his countenance.

With a sickening jolt, Amy realised that it had all just been a continuation of the joke.

'I'm sorry . . .' He started laughing. 'I wish you could see your face. You don't know whether to hit me or—'

'Hit you, definitely,' she scowled, biting back the full extent of her anger because getting too upset would mean she had taken his actions seriously, at face value. It was bad enough that she probably resembled a lobster in a pot of boiling water. 'You're more than a bastard,' she stammered, 'you're a – a—'

'OK, OK, I give up.' He flung up his hands. 'But you started it. Coming round here and accusing me of all sorts. I'm going to forgive and forget it now – and I mean it this time – but you've got to promise not to take this out on me at some distant point in the future when we're both old and grey.'

Amy took a deep breath. 'Me? Bear a grudge?'

'Besides,' he twiddled her hair again, 'you can consider it a birthday kiss, seeing as I haven't bought you a present yet, and, being a useless male, probably won't get around to it. If I do, it'll be bubble bath, anyway.'

'I'll count myself privileged.' Amy wondered if her legs would work properly if she tried to stand up. The wine and pina coladas seemed to be having a delayed effect. In order to test her other faculties first, she reached for her mobile phone.

Paul got to it first, though, and clutched it in his fist. 'On a really serious note – deadly serious, I mean, all joking aside – I've been thinking . . .'

Amy frowned. 'You? Thinking? Well, it must be serious then.'

'You're supposed to stop joking, too,' he frowned back sternly.

'I'm sorry, I didn't realise. Continue.'

'I can lend you an old shirt of mine – fully laundered, in case you were wondering – and I've a brand new toothbrush somewhere, untouched by human gums. I think Francesca's got a suitably girly deodorant in the bathroom, too, so you're sorted for the morning . . .'

It was the first time he'd mentioned Francesca all night, and Amy immediately found herself scrambling to her feet, which now felt adequately sturdy, even in heels. It was disquieting how his girlfriend's name had acted as an antidote to the alcohol, but it had.

'What are you on about?' said Amy exasperatedly. She tried to make a grab for her phone, but Paul held it just out of reach.

'The fact that I've solved the problem of your sleeping arrangements. And if you want, I'll send a text to your friends to that effect.'

'Paul Faulkner Jones, if you want to get me talked about at work . . .'

'I'll even mention the futon in my spare room,' he assuaged her. 'Although I'm sure you can get yourself talked about at work without my help.'

And, to add fuel to the fire burning indignantly in her breast, he winked.

26

Groggily, Amy opened her eyes, and panicked that something was seriously amiss with her vision. The whole room seemed a mass of stripes. She blinked, and rubbed her eyes; gently, so as not to dislodge her lenses. Relief danced through her as she realised her eyesight was fine. There were vertical blinds at the windows, and the narrow wooden slats were open a fraction, letting light slant in.

But relief soon turned to something far less welcome. Amy managed to sit up, in spite of her aching limbs, and edged up the futon to look outside. She tried turning the thin pole hanging down, to open the blind further, but it was tangled with the string that lifted it completely. She had to content herself with cautiously lifting a slat with her finger and peeking into the bright August morning. It was so dazzling, Amy realised it couldn't be that early. Her watch had to be somewhere around here . . .

She groped around for her clothes, which would have been hanging up if she'd been more conscientious last night, but instead were lying in a muddle on top of the sheets. Her watch and jewellery were tangled among them.

'Bugger.' It was nearly eleven o'clock. But before she could change, there was a hesitant knock on the door. 'Er . . .' She dithered in alarm as it was slowly pushed open. The shirt she was wearing had a button missing at the top, and wasn't quite long enough to cover up her cellulite satisfactorily at the bottom.

To her even greater consternation, it wasn't Paul's head which poked itself around the door, but his girlfriend's.

'Oh – you're up.' Francesca smiled and came in with a mug of steaming tea, which she put down on the stool that doubled as a bedside table. 'I was going to wake you. It's getting late, and Paul wasn't sure if you had to be anywhere.'

Still in shock, Amy mumbled a meek thank-you for the tea.

'You're probably surprised to see me,' Francesca went on, still in that same light tone. 'I was surprised myself when I turned up at ten to find Paul was still flat out. Late nights don't usually affect him like that. Sorry I missed it, by the way. It sounded interesting.'

Amy made a non-committal 'hmm' noise, wondering how much Francesca knew.

'Your birthday's tomorrow, though, isn't it?' Paul's girl-friend breezed on.

'Officially,' Amy mumbled; 'I'm a bit like the Queen.'

Francesca smiled politely. 'Anyway, Paul sent me to ask you what you'd like for breakfast. We've got—'

'Toast will be fine,' Amy interrupted, becoming even more ruffled at the use of 'we'.

'It'll have to be brown, if that's all right, Paul's run out of white. You know what men are like about grocery shopping.'

'Brown's fine. I'll, um, just get dressed first . . .'

'You don't want a shower?'

'No, it's OK. I have to go back to my friend's house to get changed, anyway. I'll only have a quick wash now, freshen up a bit.'

Francesca nodded. 'Well, I've left a clean towel over the bath. Paul *has* come to grips with his washing machine, you know – just about.'

'I'm sure he's very competent,' said Amy, musing as to why she was the one rallying to his defence and his girlfriend the one putting him down.

'See you in a little while, then. I won't put the toast on just yet. And don't forget your tea.'

No, ma'am. Amy frowned after her, grumbling.

Five minutes later, after trying to fluff up her hair and then flattening it again when she speculated who she was trying to look presentable for, Amy ventured down the corridor towards the kitchen. She was aware of being overdressed, and carried her shoes in her hand, swinging them idly to belie how tightly strung she felt. It was a direct consequence of walking barefoot, she realised, that led to her inadvertently overhearing the conversation taking place in the kitchen.

Neither Paul nor Francesca could have heard her coming, and even though they were talking in low voices anyway, Amy could still make it out.

'Aren't you . . . jealous, at all?' Paul was asking. He sounded strangely guttural.

'Of what?' Francesca responded, possibly with a shrug. 'Why are you acting so guilty, Paul? It's not as if I walked in and found you in bed together. You spent a whole night with another woman under the same roof, but you still managed to keep your hands off her. If anything, I'm less jealous after this. And you said it yourself – it's just Amy.'

Amy ground to a halt, pinned to the spot by the weight of her plummeting heart. But it was the reason behind this sinking of her already low spirits that vexed her. It didn't seem valid just to say that her self-esteem had taken a knock. There was more to it. Far more . . .

Paul strode out of the kitchen, only to rear up with a 'Shit!' as he confronted her. 'Sorry,' he looked genuinely rattled, 'you made me jump.'

She prayed there was nothing in her eyes to betray her, even as she gazed into his. If Paul had looked dishevelled and tired last night, he was positively ravaged now. It was as if he hadn't slept, or only the bare minimum. He was still in his T-shirt and shorts, unshaven, with his hair sticking up on one side. He looked as rumpled as his duvet, and would be just as easy to throw herself at.

Francesca leaned around the door. 'Oh, hi,' she said brightly. 'I'll pop the toast down, then.'

'No, um, it's OK,' Amy wavered, 'I think I ought to be making a move anyway . . .'

By the chagrined look on Paul's face, it was obvious that he realised Amy had eavesdropped.

'You can't leave without eating something.' His demeanour was now abrupt. 'And if you're going straight to your friend's place, I'll drive you there. I just need five minutes to put some clothes on.'

'No! It's OK,' Amy protested, 'there's no need, it's just across the bridge, really. How long could it take on foot? Fifteen, twenty minutes, max?'

'Dressed like that? You might get a few odd looks at this time of day.'

'I wish I had something here that might fit you,' Francesca sighed, and Amy grudgingly came to the conclusion that she wasn't being deliberately bitchy. 'That really is a gorgeous outfit, but Paul's right, it's hardly Saturday-morning-about-town, is it?'

'Depends on the town,' Amy volleyed back. 'But I suppose you've got a point,' she conceded a moment later, lapping up the awareness that if style-guru Francesca really did think the outfit was gorgeous, Amy couldn't look too bad in it.

Unfortunately, this led her to dwell further on the hypothesis that Paul didn't view her as anything other than 'just Amy', which effectively meant that in his eyes she wasn't a sexual creature, or a woman in a complete sense.

Last night, when she'd looked as feminine as she felt she possibly could, he had kissed her on the mouth for the first time ever, and although it had been too restrained to be classed as a snog, it had still elicited the intended response from her. Whereas with anything else in a skirt this might have led to other things, though – with Amy, Paul had seen it as a joke, a bit of a laugh. He had teased her, without a motive on his mind other than mild – and on his part, innocuous – revenge.

But it hadn't been harmless or innocent on her part. It had been tantamount to opening the Pandora's box that she had been dragging around with her for . . . That was another problem. How long *had* she been dragging it around? Not years, it wasn't quite that dire. But was it months, or just a few weeks? And how far gone was she really? Slightly infatuated, moderately infatuated, very infatuated – or . . .

Amy tried to snap out of her introspection by concentrating on buttering her toast.

'Jam, marmalade or honey?' chirruped Francesca.

The woman was so damned cheerful, sulked Amy, settling for the blueberry jam and slapping it on the bread in big, angry dollops. It was as if every part of Francesca Courtney, from her dark russet eyelashes to her French-manicured fingertips, was gloating: *He's mine!* And revelling in the triumph. She was so self-satisfied. So perfect. So . . . here.

'Right.' Paul was back, sporting loafers, dark trousers and a pristine white shirt in a casual, crinkly material. His hair appeared to have wax in it now, making the sticky-up parts look intentional. Even his stubble seemed neater. 'Oh,' he frowned at Amy, 'still eating?' It was obvious he wanted her gone. It would be a waste of his day with Francesca, otherwise.

Amy ate quickly in spite of her heaving stomach, and as she shoved in the last mouthful, she slid down from the stool at the breakfast bar. Misjudging the distance to the floor, though, she reached out to steady herself and just happened to grab Paul . . .

Amy stared in horror at the jammy fingerprints on his shirt. So did he. Usually, he was remarkably calm about stains, as if he'd discovered some miraculous washing powder or dry-cleaning agent. The boys had got all sorts on him, and he'd seldom flinched, unlike Nick. Today, by the look on his face, she might as well have rubbed black dye into his sleeve.

'I'll go change – again.' He thundered off.

Francesca handed Amy a napkin. 'It's not personal. Paul can't take his drink like he used to. It seems to turn him into a grumpy old git.'

Amy struggled not to glower at her. How dare Francesca imply she had a history with Paul when in the grand scheme of things, she had only known him five minutes!

History was putting him to bed after his twenty-first birth-day party, when his parents had buggered off to bed them-selves and everyone else was too comatose. History was staying up all night playing bloody Pictionary one New Year's Eve, because he wanted to see the sun rise on a new millen-nium. Not to mention nursing him through countless bouts of flu – or whatever the male equivalent of a cold was called – because he preferred to convalesce on her and Nick's sofa rather than his own bed. History, realised Amy, was there to be rewritten, or at least glossed over, because back then, if she'd had a crystal ball, she would have looked at herself now and laughed hysterically, in derision.

'Your phone's been emitting strange noises, by the way,' Paul informed her crisply, returning in a fresh shirt.

'Really?' Amy looked around. 'Where is it?'

'It's—' He hesitated, patting his pockets, which were clearly empty, then glanced automatically at Francesca, who didn't seem to be paying attention anyway. 'Er, I've heard it,' he muttered, 'and I know it wasn't mine.' He absently lifted a cushion off the sofa, while Amy stared at him, perplexed.

'You had it last,' she reminded him. 'You sent that text message for me.'

'Um – did I?'

Amy realised that he was still embarrassed to mention last night in front of his girlfriend, in spite of Francesca's cavalier attitude towards it.

Paul wandered out on to the terrace, then distractedly drifted in again. 'I'll check the bathroom,' he murmured.

Amy was sure it wasn't in there. She would have seen it. And it was a ridiculous place to have left it, anyway. She was voicing her thoughts when he strode back in, brandishing the phone.

'Your battery's low,' he told her. 'And you've got some missed calls.'

'It wasn't in the bathroom, though, was it? I didn't see it—'

Her mouth clamped shut at the dour look that crossed his countenance. It struck her that it had probably been somewhere in his room. He had promised to send a text to Maria's mobile, and that had been the last Amy had seen of it. Maybe it had spent all night under his pillow. Closer than Amy would ever get, at any rate.

She handled it gingerly, as if it were some precious artefact from an archaeological dig, rather than a run-of-the-mill Nokia with a metallic Winnie the Pooh cover.

'Lynette called,' she murmured, scanning her missed calls. 'And Tilly . . .' Amy turned to Paul, momentarily forgetting he was in a mood. 'She doesn't know yet that I saw her last night . . . What do you think she wants?'

He shrugged. 'Give her a call and find out,' he said gruffly. 'Here, use my phone.' He picked the handset out of its cradle and handed it to her.

Amy wandered out on to the terrace. When she came back in a few minutes later, she felt resolved to sort out one mess in her life, at least.

'She's still at Keira's. She was angling for a lift back. I said I'd pick her up in an hour. But I think I'll take her for a coffee, rather than straight home.'

Paul checked his watch. 'I'd better take you over to Lynette's then, so you can get yourself organised and work out how you're going to broach it with Tilly. I assume that's what you've decided.'

Amy registered woefully that he sounded more like a solicitor this morning than a friend. She nodded. 'I think I've being neglecting my sisterly duties lately.'

'I know what you mean,' Francesca sighed, as she flopped on to Paul's sofa with a TV guide. 'I hadn't been shopping with Sophia in ages, so we went into London on Thursday. I'm talking *serious* retail therapy. My Visa's still in shock.'

Amy thought she heard Paul mumble something under his breath about the 'real world', but she couldn't be certain. She barely had a chance to grab her handbag and say thank you for the toast, before he'd whisked her out of his girlfriend's sight and down the stairs to the threadbare-carpeted hall.

'I am so sorry—' Amy began, but he cut her off.

'No,' he said, without meeting her eye, 'I am. I meant to get up earlier, in case Francesca came round without calling. But last night . . . I couldn't sleep for ages, then when I finally did . . .'

'It's OK,' said Amy, shielding her eyes as they stepped into the blazing sunshine. 'I couldn't sleep, either.'

He turned to her abruptly, a strange, hounded look on his face. 'Couldn't you?'

'No,' she shrugged, blinking up at him. 'It's the caffeine, isn't it?'

He gazed at her for an interminable moment, then fished his sunglasses out of his pocket and slipped them on. His face took on an expressionless look, like the Terminator. 'You're right.'

'We should have had decaff,' she added lamely.

Paul turned away. He led her to his car, blipping it open. 'Decaff,' he echoed. And he drove her to Lynette's house in Handbridge, managing not to utter another word until they got there.

27

'Watch out, it's melting on this side!' Tilly swooped with a tissue, saving Amy's denim skirt from getting blobbed with soft-whip, vanilla ice cream.

'Knew we should have stuck to a cappuccino.' Amy frowned at her Flake 99 as it melted faster than she could lick it.

'Too hot,' said Tilly, curling her bottom lip outwards and puffing at her fringe, which lifted momentarily like a fluffy black wave before cascading down again over her brow.

'How come you've nearly finished yours already? I haven't even got to the cone yet.'

'Practice. There's an ice cream van that parks outside the school every lunchtime – in term time, of course.' Tilly woefully patted her hips. 'Forget being offered weed by pervy men in parkas. It's the Flake 99s I've got to watch out for.'

'You never put on weight,' said Amy sourly, but with affection, privately concerned about these dubious blokes in parkas and the blithe way Tilly referred to them. 'Mum says you've got Dad's metabolism. And I've got Grandma Cullen's.'

'I've got a lot of Dad in me, according to Mum. It would be nicer if I could remember him.' Tilly adjusted her sunglasses as they slipped down her nose. 'Sometimes,' she hesitated, 'it's like you and Mum belong to this exclusive club. You've got all these memories stored away up here,' she tapped her head, 'and I've got to settle for old videos or photo albums.'

Amy frowned behind her own dark glasses. 'Do you re-member anything about him?' she asked her sister frankly, finding it disheartening that they had never taken time out to talk like this.

'Vague flashes, I guess. But it's hard to know what I really *am* remembering first-hand, or what I've heard about, or dreamed, or seen in photos.'

Amy looked towards the bandstand, as a cacophony of musical sounds blasted the air. The band paused, and a moment later burst into 'All Things Bright and Beautiful'.

It had been Tilly who had suggested coming to The Groves for an ice cream. Amy had parked opposite the racecourse, and together they had strolled along the bustling riverbank, lingering near the pleasure boats – where business was clearly booming today – and the rows of benches by the bandstand. They had been fortunate that an elderly couple had been vacating a seat in the shade as they walked past. Tilly had instantly nabbed it and Amy had queued up at the nearest kiosk.

'I'm sorry if you feel left out sometimes,' she said now, with complete sincerity. 'We don't mean to do it.'

Tilly sighed resignedly. 'It's just the way things are. And for all *I* know, you might have felt outside of things when you left Harrisfield to move in with Nick.'

'You and Mum did seem cosy together, just the two of you in Mews Cottage.'

'Yeah, it was good. Nice to have her to myself. But then . . .'

'Out popped Joe, and the dynamics changed, yet again,' Amy nodded in assent. 'And then I went and moved back in, bringing my tribe with me.' She put an arm around her sister's shoulders. 'But you've been brilliant about it. I couldn't have handled a mass invasion like that at your age.'

It was a white lie, of course, because she would have enjoyed nothing better than a gaggle of little children to fuss over. Her sister could probably see right through it, but it was the sentiment that counted.

'My age,' repeated Tilly. 'Sometimes I feel older than you and Mum. I've put up with everything that happened since Nick left, because I had to. Because if it was bad for me, then it was ten times worse for you and the boys. But if I hadn't been able to just lock myself in my room sometimes, or see Keira . . .'

'You still managed to revise, though. And you did really well.' Amy stopped short of saying she was proud, in case she sounded patronising.

'Yeah, I did OK. And don't get me wrong, I'm really glad you're only going to be moving five minutes away. I can come round and hog your sofa whenever I like, or at least when Mum's watching something crappy on TV.'

'So, what was last night in aid of, then?' Amy probed. 'Were you trying to prove something to us?'

'You weren't supposed to ever know about it,' Tilly pointed out tetchily. 'And you've already promised not to tell Mum. As far as she's concerned, everything went as planned last night, OK? I stayed at Keira's, you stayed at Lynette's, end of story. And you've got to make sure everyone sticks to it, even if you have to ring round half of Harrisfield.'

'Yes, I know, I know. But if I'm going to be part of this mass conspiracy, I'd like to hear a bit more about what went on. Whose idea was it to go out like that, anyway? I understand Keira's mum got you the invites—'

'Amy, does it matter? I have been in pubs before, you know, and I don't just mean the ones that let kids in. I have passed myself off as eighteen, and I have been drinking. I just haven't been pissed. Not like last night, at any rate.'

Amy inhaled deeply. She'd never done anything like that at sixteen. And those school discos she'd used to go to had operated a strictly no-alcohol – not to mention no-smoking –

policy; if you were caught with some, you were practically treated like a criminal. She could still remember those ghastly 'alternative' fruit punches. But that was another lifetime.

'So,' Amy wet her lips and hoped she didn't sound too naïve, 'have you got a boyfriend?'

Tilly was quite unabashed about it. 'Currently, no.'

'But you have had one?'

'A couple,' she shrugged. 'Nothing heavy. And no one you'd know.'

'So . . . what did these dates entail?'

Tilly grunted. 'You'll make a great mum one day.'

'I am a mother,' said Amy, arching a brow. 'Or did those pina coladas wipe away all memory of your beloved nephews?'

'I meant, of a girl. Because there'll always be that double standard, won't there? People always seem to worry more about daughters.'

'I'll never have a girl, Tilly. Three boys is enough for one lifetime.'

'You will have another baby,' her sister proclaimed knowingly. 'You won't be able to help yourself. Your brain will turn to a broody mush and wham, bam, that'll be it. And it won't necessarily be a boy, will it?'

'Tilly—'

'Come on, you're only turning thirty-two tomorrow, and you don't seem menopausal to me yet. You'll meet someone sooner or later, and you'll go all gooey-eyed over him and decide you want his babies.'

'Huh, very likely. What books have you been reading lately?'

'Advanced physics. No, honestly, you will get over Nick.'

'I already have. And now there's Jonathan . . .' Amy paused and sighed. 'I'm with Jonathan.'

'You're not with him!' Tilly remonstrated, screwing up her face. 'You're nowhere near it. He's only just come into your head because we were on the subject of boyfriends. You don't fancy him. And that isn't because he's not OK-looking, because he is. You just don't gel. You never have. Second to Nick, he's the last bloke you ought to have another kid with.'

Oh, help. Amy closed her eyes and threw back her head. Tilly was right. So disturbingly, hitting-the-nail-on-the-head right. When *had* she last thought of Jonathan? At some point yesterday evening, admittedly, but not while someone else had been kissing her, however briefly. Not while she'd been lying on a spongy mattress with half a dozen planks of wood pressing into her back, her mind bearing her off into the adjacent room and the arms of a man she had once wished never existed. She'd fought her imagination at every turn, but it had been a long, hard, and ultimately futile battle.

'It's over,' declared Tilly. 'And Jonathan probably knows it, too. That's why he's not even bothering to call much any more. Sometimes people break up and it hurts everyone involved, and sometimes . . . sometimes things just die a natural death, and no one gets hurt very much at all.'

'You *are* Dad,' said Amy sullenly. 'You're as sharp as Dad was, anyhow, but without the parts that made him just that little bit too Victorian. He'd have made a great psychologist, if he'd wanted.'

'But life insurance paid more?'

'No,' Amy repudiated. 'He just judged people too much. Expected more than they could give. Morally, that is. There never seemed to be any room to make mistakes.'

'Well, you and Mum are Victorian enough for one family, so I can't imagine things being any worse.'

'We are not Victorian. We just . . . don't . . .'

'Look, I get embarrassed too, you know. I'm just not made of eggshells. And I know you're gagging to ask outright – but the answer's no. No, I haven't had sex yet. And that isn't because we didn't have condoms or because I'm not on the pill. I just didn't want to. Like I said, I've had boyfriends, but nothing serious. Just hanging out on the bus before school, or at Keira's, that kind of thing. And it wasn't that I lied about it, it just wasn't worth talking about. I wasn't going to bring them home for tea or anything like that. They'd have definitely got the wrong idea then. You see, now and again it's OK to be the geek, although usually it's not. And everyone knew the exams were important to me.'

'I know what you're saying,' said Amy, who didn't really.

She'd never been as academic as her father had hoped; not that he'd ever pressed her on it. On the contrary, he'd used to say that if there was an exam in it, she would get an 'A' for the biggest heart. But it would be more like a 'D minus' today, she acknowledged morosely, if she was prepared to let a man cheat on his girlfriend, or blot out the fact that, purely on a technicality, Amy was still involved with someone else herself.

'Anyway,' said Tilly, 'it's your turn now. I've spilled all the beans there were about last night, so—'

'Not quite. And actually it was Paul who spilled the beans, and a few more than you've accounted for.'

Tilly made a groaning noise, like a wounded animal. 'Paul. Shit. I'll crap my pants next time I see him. It's hazy, but I know I made an idiot of myself . . .'

'Do not let Mum hear you talking like that.'

'I never do. And she's the last person I'd be telling all this to. You know how she reacts when you mention Paul. Even if she didn't mind me going out to clubs and stuff.' She sighed. 'I wish she'd just chill a bit. Keira's mum doesn't seem to care.'

Amy watched a little girl toddle in front of them, chasing a pigeon while her father kept tight hold of her safety reins.

'I'd rather someone did care, to be honest. And, Tilly, I'd feel a whole lot better if, in future, you can talk to me if there's anything bothering you . . . Anything you can't tell Mum about. That's what I'm here for.'

'Yeah, OK, "Big Sis". I'll try and remember. Thing is, it's like a gut reaction for me to keep things in. As if I know Mum's going to come down harder on me because she let you get away with too much.'

'If you mean Nick, Tilly, I was eighteen when . . . Well, you know. Mum didn't have a huge say. And you know what she was like back then, anyway. You remember . . .?'

'I remember she was sad a lot. And quiet.'

The sisters sat quietly for a while themselves. Amy didn't really like the road they'd gone down. She wanted to return to the Here and Now, not the Back Then. Besides, something Tilly had said was preying on her mind.

'Do you really think Mum dislikes Paul these days?' She asked the question as if she'd just plucked it out of nowhere and the answer didn't actually matter a great deal. 'Or is it just a front,' she went on, 'a habit she's slipped into? Don't you think he might be growing on her?'

'What, like a wart on her chin?' Tilly sniggered. 'Maybe, a bit. Although I reckon he'd have to run into a burning building to rescue her before she'd admit it. But he isn't such a bad bloke, is he? I mean, take last night. I was basically throwing myself at him . . .' She groaned again. 'But he obviously cares about Francesca. Either that, or he doesn't fancy me – which is highly unlikely,' Tilly added, tongue in cheek. 'Then again, I've always said he prefers women nearer his own age. And then he took us home in a cab, which was sweet, I thought. Keira's got a real crush on him this morning.'

Amy was grateful for the sunglasses to hide behind.

'But what about you?' Tilly demanded, swinging round on the bench and leaning closer, as if there was some huge, juicy secret to be divulged.

'What about me?' said Amy squeakily.

'Well, I know you got it into your pathetic head that I'd

copped off with him, but that doesn't explain why you ended up spending the night round his flat.'

'I already told you. I couldn't get hold of Maria or Lynette. I didn't have a lot of choice.'

'But Francesca wasn't there?'

'No, she turned up this morning.'

'And Paul didn't try it on with you?'

'With me?' laughed Amy, too quickly and shrilly.

'Well – why not?' Tilly was now peering over her sunglasses, her gaze boring into Amy like a drill. 'What's so funny about that?'

'Because Paul and I – we—'

'You're friends now, aren't you?'

'Yes,' spluttered Amy, 'exactly. But just because Paul and I aren't sniping at each other any more, that doesn't mean it's going to go the other way. You said it yourself, he must really care about Francesca. They're practically living together. And it wouldn't surprise me if one of these days a colossal rock turns up on her left hand.'

Tilly leaned back, looking surprised. 'You think it's that serious?'

'Yes,' snapped Amy candidly, and was taken aback by the intensity of the pain she had feared would hit. The gauge to measure her infatuation pivoted dangerously into the red.

'Wow. Well, you ought to know as well as anyone.'

Amy had had enough of these insinuations. 'And why's that, then?' She stood up, brushed down her skirt and glanced left and right along the riverbank, as if deciding which way to go next.

With wide eyes, Tilly looked up at her, too ingenuously to ring true. 'Are we going already? I was enjoying the band.'

'Right. If they were Blur or Blue, or whoever's currently in favour, then I'd believe that.'

'Amy, I'm sorry, I only meant that you and Paul do seem close now . . .'

Amy gritted her teeth as she stared at the Dee. Paul's flat wasn't far from here. She wondered what he and Francesca were doing right now, slamming the brakes on her imagination as it reached his bedroom door.

'Don't you think you've strung the joke out long enough?' Flicking back her hair in what she hoped was a nonchalant gesture, she turned to her sister again. 'It's sounding tired.'

'I wasn't joking. I was just trying to say that you and Paul are quite good friends now, and I think that's a positive thing. He's been really brilliant offering to help with the house, and he was great support for you when Nick was over. Mum does appreciate all that, I'm sure. So what I meant was, if he's confided in anyone about this thing with Francesca, then it's likely to be you, isn't it?'

'Well,' replied Amy – who knew diddly-squat and had just been guessing when she'd referred to an engagement ring – 'he hasn't.'

'Oh,' said Tilly slowly, 'don't you think that's odd?'

'Why? I don't tell him much about Jonathan and me.'

'That's probably because there isn't much to tell. And knowing you, you'd be too coy to divulge anything remotely connected with sex, anyway.'

'Well, maybe Paul just wants to play his cards close to his chest, too. Or maybe he knows I get embarrassed easily.'

'It's just . . . if things were going as well as you assume they are, then I think he'd be more inclined to broadcast it.'

Amy made a show of rubbing her fingers together, grumbling that they were sticky from the ice cream and lamenting that she didn't have the nappy bag with the wipes on her.

'Sometimes, Tilly,' she said at last, knowing she couldn't remain evasive for ever, 'you can be over-analytical. You go too far. People's feelings – their motives, I suppose you could call them – can be more subtle and less clear-cut than you think they are.'

Tilly shrugged. 'Yeah, I guess. But take last night, for instance, when you saw me with Paul. Your only instinct was to protect me, right? You thought I was in over my head, and put on the big sister act to save me.'

'I wish I had some bread to throw to the ducks . . .' Amy murmured, as if her attention was a million miles away from what Tilly was saying.

'It wasn't that you were jealous—'

'Jealous?' reared Amy, like a skittish horse.

'Of course not.' Tilly shook her head solemnly. 'That would be far too analytical, even for me . . .'

Yet as they headed back along The Groves in the direction of the car, Amy couldn't help gaining the impression that her sister's brain was working overtime. And the worry was that instead of putting two and two together and coming up with five, Tilly's quick, perceptive and cunning little mind would end up smack, bang with an accurate four.

28

'So, do you think they're OK? Do you think the boys will like them?' Jonathan gestured to the two Disney watches for Joseph and Mikey, and the Eeyore wall clock for Lucas. 'I suppose Joe's learning to tell the time at school now.'

'Were you at the Disney store in Chester with Sally-Ann and Niamh?' Amy picked up a Donald Duck watch in its case and examined it in more detail.

Jonathan nodded. 'Sally-Ann's got a thing for *The Little Mermaid*. Loves the story to bits.'

Amy smiled, and put the watch back on the kitchen table. 'Well, I'm sure the boys will appreciate them, but you really shouldn't have.'

'Why not? I know things are different now . . . but . . . Well, the kids mean a lot to me, and this birthday party—'

'Are you sure you won't come? Wouldn't Sally-Ann enjoy it?'

'She's a bit old for it, probably. The Little Mermaid's one thing, jelly and ice cream's another.' Jonathan pulled a face, and took a tentative sip of the tea Amy had made. It had cooled down sufficiently now. He took a larger dose, as if it was a welcome panacea.

'This is Rowena we're talking about,' Amy reminded him, unable to stop herself sounding terse, 'and she's getting caterers in. There won't be any home-made trifle or sponge cake on offer, unless Mum carries out her threat and bakes something herself.'

Jonathan's lips broadened into a weak smile. 'I don't know how Rowena ever agreed to this.'

'It was her idea in the first place, actually. I don't relish the thought of it one little bit, but I don't want to make a fuss, either. And I'm not going to hide away, or let that Faulkner Jones Burnley bunch think I'm still pining for Nick . . .'

'It's a difficult situation. I think you've done well to stay on speaking terms with Rowena, considering.'

'It wouldn't be fair on the kids if I didn't. She's still their gran, whatever Nick's done. Anyway, the boys are getting their separate little parties, too, with their own friends. Just because they've got birthdays relatively close to one another, they shouldn't be treated like triplets.'

'But Rowena still decided to host this joint thing?'

'Just because she can. Although Mum reckons it's purely to piss her off; she's got a huge bee in her bonnet about it. But it's more a case of Rowena showing off her grandchildren to her own friends than to get one up on Mum.'

'What about trying to prove that she's the hippest granny in the North West?' Jonathan's tired, lined brow twitched in amusement. 'She must get off on people telling her she doesn't look old enough.'

Amy smirked as she loaded the stacked-up lunch things into the dishwasher.

Jonathan had dropped by unexpectedly just as she'd put Lucas down for his nap and had been psyching herself up to tackle some housework. It was a Saturday, her second here in March Street, and Elspeth had picked up the two older boys, intending to let them loose in the park. Amy – who had taken a week off work to get her family organised and settled in the new house, and was now trying to establish some sort of routine – knew that there was a bath to be scrubbed and a toilet to disinfect, but Jonathan's arrival had postponed her plans.

Her date with those new eco-friendly cleaners she had bought would just have to wait.

It was funny how things had panned out since Jonathan had come back from Ireland, Amy contemplated now, as she closed the dishwasher and sat down at the kitchen table herself. Understandably, there had been a certain amount of awkwardness at the beginning, and she couldn't say that it was entirely rosy now. The fact that he wasn't coming to the boys' party, but had still bought them gifts, smacked of guilt, whether he was conscious of it or not.

The kids didn't really go on about him much. She had tried to explain why he had had to go away in the first place, and by the look of it, they'd simply got used to his absence. It wasn't on the same scale as Nick leaving, not by a long shot. And by the time Jonathan had returned, in September, there had been more pressing matters to deal with.

Joseph had been starting in the nursery class attached to Harrisfield Primary; grown-up and serious in the basic navy-and-grey uniform the younger pupils wore. Amy had shed a surreptitious tear as she'd kissed him goodbye on that first day, mildly reassured by the knowledge that some of his classmates hailed from Little 'Uns as well. He did seem to be settling in fine, though; chattering non-stop when he got home from the afternoon sessions, explaining how so-and-so had done such-and-such, and who had done what to who.

It hadn't been the best of times to complete on the purchase of 5 March Street, but that couldn't be helped; it had been one of those things. An upheaval, naturally, but thrilling, too. Her own house, in her own name. Her signature in black and white. Amy Amanda Croft. She was now officially a home-owner.

But it had brought with it an unavoidable problem, as well. An architect with so many ideas he hadn't seemed to know where to start.

He had finally pinned Amy down over a pub lunch, and together, with a clumsy, stilted atmosphere between them – which Amy could understand on her part, but not on his – they had whittled his ideas down to the basics.

And so, Amy had busied herself packing up her things at Mews Cottage, while the Faulkner Jones Burnley crew had set to work on 'Willow View Villa'. By early October, Amy and the boys had moved in, marking their territories with a mounting excitement.

Bunk beds here, a play area there, a bookcase with Amy's knick-knacks on show rather than hidden away in boxes as they had been at the flat . . . She had had to buy some new furniture, of course. At least some rudimentary pieces to start with. But she had had plenty of hands on deck to assemble it.

Everything had come together so smoothly when it could have been so stressful, against the backdrop of a house that had been sympathetically, albeit hurriedly, restored and re-decorated.

Amy was all too aware of the debt she owed Paul.

He was still being remarkably blasé about it. 'I've had fun,' he would shrug. 'It's made a change from the usual starting from scratch.' And it wasn't as if he hadn't been busy enough anyway, with the development taking off at Cherry Tree Farm.

'There must be some way I can thank you,' Amy had argued.

'Just let me be here to see Nick's face when he steps inside for the first time.'

She had already shown Nick from the outside, during his visit in the summer, and she could tell he hadn't been impressed. He probably wouldn't appreciate anything about it when he viewed it properly, but she hadn't had the heart to say that to Paul. Perhaps Nick had always complimented him whatever the job, so that Paul would unwittingly be expecting that same pat on the back now.

Evidently, old houses with history weren't Nick's thing, and if he brought Anneka with him – provided they were still together by then, thought Amy dryly – she would probably turn up her nose at the clutter of toys and books and embroidered Ikea cushions, too. After all, it was Nick's idea of hell, and no doubt Anneka's also.

The Faulkner Jones Burnley show homes had used to be so cool and calm when Anneka had been working on them, with 'therapeutic' crystals hanging at the windows and elegant dinner services on display in the dining rooms. But Amy had always remained content being unable to tell the difference between Feng Shui or John Lewis. The ultra-contemporary decor used to merge into a clinical blur when Nick had taken her on 'sneak-preview' tours, pointing out the merits of various mixer taps and thermostatic showers, and how the state-of-the-art loo flushed automatically when you moved away from it (yet didn't wipe your bottom for you, as Amy had pointed out).

5 March Street was a world away from all that, but there were some pleasant neighbours who had dropped by to introduce themselves. And Amy much preferred knowing that there were a few busy young mums like herself to share a brew with now and again, than the fact she had a brand new, stainless-steel, Russell Hobbs kettle – as a moving-in gift from her work colleagues – to make it with.

'This place has really taken shape, hasn't it?' Jonathan looked around appreciatively. 'It's almost unrecognisable from the house we saw back in June . . . Well, not this room, as such, but the others.'

Amy nodded, a familiar beat of pride in her chest. 'It's wonderful. You should have seen the difference it made just having that awful carpet ripped up. And when Paul said we should just varnish the existing floorboards . . .'

'Inspired,' nodded Jonathan.

Amy wouldn't have gone that far. She'd had the same idea herself. 'These kitchen cupboards, for instance, the oak's so much mellower now it's been stripped and waxed – or polished, or whatever it was they did to it.'

'And cheaper than forking out for a whole new kitchen,' Jonathan pointed out.

It was Paul who had suggested revamping the old units, to retain maximum character, and Amy had entirely gone along with it.

She'd agreed with the majority of his suggestions, including knocking an arch between the dining room and lounge to increase the sense of space and make it easier to keep an eye on the children. It wasn't that she'd been hanging on his every word. She wasn't that sad. His ideas had just been one step ahead of hers. He had seemed to have the same vision for the house as she had.

'I'm really happy for you, Amy.' Jonathan stretched across the table and cupped his hand over hers. 'I just wish things could have been different . . .'

She sighed. 'But they're not, so I don't want you worrying about it. You've got enough on your plate.'

The first Amy had known of his return from Ireland last month had been the sight of his car parked in its allotted space at the end of her mum's lane.

Back in August, he had sent her flowers for her birthday, arriving a day late, with a simple, platonic message, but no word of when he would be home.

And then, one day, there he had been.

Amy had taken a deep breath and knocked on his door. She'd been caught off guard when a girl of around nine or ten had answered it, looking up at her blankly.

'Er – I'm going to guess that you're Sally-Ann,' Amy had smiled, recovering. 'Hi. It's really nice to meet you. I'm Amy.'

The girl had still regarded her vacantly.

Then a woman had come out of the kitchen, drying her hands with a tea towel. 'Can I help you?' She was attractive. As short as Amy, but with light red hair and a much slimmer figure.

'Hi . . . I'm Amy. You must be Niamh.'

Still those blank looks. At which point, Jonathan had come catapulting down the stairs.

'Amy, hello!' He'd taken her loosely by the arm. 'This is Niamh Grady, and my daughter Sally-Ann.' He'd turned to them and said, as if introducing a mere acquaintance, 'This is Amy Croft – my neighbour. Well, strictly speaking, her mother Elspeth's my neighbour, but Amy and her children are staying with her for a while.'

Amy could recall a couple of swift, polite nods, and then Jonathan had stepped outside into the lane with her, on the pretext of fetching something from his car.

'Amy, listen' – he'd looked paler and thinner than he had a few weeks previously – 'we can't talk now, but . . .'

She had more or less guessed what he had to say, anyway. 'You didn't tell them about me,' she'd muttered accusingly, even as she'd seen an escape hatch opening.

'I didn't have an opportunity.'

'You've been gone long enough.'

'Amy, I'm sorry. It's been difficult.' He'd glanced towards his house. 'Niamh's taking Sally-Ann shopping tomorrow, for a school uniform. I'll pop into your mum's at lunchtime. I'm not back at work till next week. They had to get cover in and everything. They've been great, really.'

'That's good,' she'd muttered blandly, and watched him walk shiftily over to his car.

And so, the following day, she had come back from Little 'Uns at noon, rustled up a couple of sandwiches and waited for Jonathan to let her off the hook. Which he had, if falteringly.

If she had loved him, what he had done would have broken her heart. And if her mother or Tilly had believed that she cared about him in that way, they would have called him treacherous and recreant. As it was, he took on the status of a champion and martyr, and all three women turned a blind eye to the cowardice he had shown on the one hand, and simply played up the sacrifice he was making on the other.

'Jonathan,' Amy had asked, 'are you trying to tell me you're back together with Niamh?'

'No!' he'd refuted adamantly. 'It isn't like that. Niamh and Sally-Ann . . . they're alone. There's no family, really; just an elderly aunt who can barely take care of herself . . . Who else is Niamh supposed to turn to? She knows I can't stay in Ireland, and her job wasn't working out anyway. It seemed logical that they should come back with me. I can take care of them both here.'

'I know why you feel obligated to your daughter,' Amy had counselled, for his sake, because she could see him heading down a long, difficult path, 'but why Niamh? She left you. She walked out of your life when you thought things were fine, with no warning whatsoever . . .'

'It's not like you and Nick,' Jonathan had insisted. 'There wasn't anyone else involved. And we're not together . . . not that way. It's only for Sally-Ann. Niamh needs treatment. She's ill. No one can expect a little girl to take all that on board by herself. You of all people, Amy . . .'

'I do understand.' Gently, she'd touched his arm, grazing his skin and feeling nothing but relief. No misery, no passion. 'I just want to help.'

Even now, Amy wished she could absolve him of his lingering sense of responsibility towards her. But how could she do that without turning the past few months into a sham? How could she tell him that it had all been a mistake, without hurting him to some degree? She felt hypocritical, but couldn't see how to reverse that.

Niamh's treatment would be continued over here, and for the foreseeable future, Sally-Ann would be attending Harrisfield Primary. The prognosis was good, Jonathan had explained, but Niamh wasn't handling it well. The word cancer on its own had been enough to freak her out.

'So Nick was right,' Paul had commented, one evening when he had been showing Amy the latest stage of work on her house, and she had finally enlightened him on exactly how things stood with Jonathan. 'Nick warned you what the man was like, didn't he? He said Jonathan Simmons was the kind of person who needed to be leaned on, like a pair of crutches. And look at you now – you're strong enough on your own. He's got nothing to give you any more, and he's reconciled himself to that the only way he knows how.'

Amy hadn't replied, although she'd wanted to point out that Jonathan hadn't made Niamh ill; that had happened all by itself. But the threat of tears had loomed too large in her throat, because it was only then that she had realised that she was alone again. Only then, when Paul had put it into words. When Paul – fulfilled and committed in love himself – had alluded to her solitary fate. And because she hadn't answered, he had stopped and studied her more closely, no doubt reaching the conclusion that Jonathan had been her second downfall.

If Paul had been able to read what was really going on in her twisted little mind, she wouldn't have seen him for dust. She had pretended then, just as she was still pretending now.

It wasn't as if she would have to keep it up for ever, after all. Crushes – even the non-adolescent variety – had their lifespan. Brief and bittersweet, they would die down as quickly as they flared up; like an angry pimple, raging then invariably retreating. Occasionally there was a small scar, but it would fade, until at last there was scarcely any memory of how it had felt.

'If you and I had carried on seeing each other . . .' Jonathan startled her suddenly from her introspection, almost making her knock over her tea. His hand pressed tighter on hers across the kitchen table. He looked at her with those slightly hangdog eyes. She realised she was flushed from thinking about Paul, and hoped Jonathan wouldn't misconstrue it.

'I know why we couldn't,' she said quickly, 'I do understand.' She wondered how many times she would have to say it.

Jonathan was shaking his head. 'I told you it was because I couldn't give you one hundred per cent and it wouldn't be fair on you . . .'

'I'm aware of that . . . You don't need to keep justifying it—'

'I do,' said Jonathan firmly, releasing her hand. 'And, besides, it isn't entirely true.' He sighed. 'I want us to be friends, Amy . . .'

'We are – aren't we?' She felt confused.

'I'd like it if you could come to consider Niamh that way, too, whatever happens. She needs all the friends she can get right now.'

'Well,' Amy shrugged weakly, 'I've said you're more than welcome to come over for dinner one night, Sally-Ann included, of course . . .' She wasn't certain what Jonathan wanted her to add.

'I've told her about us.' Jonathan swallowed hard and gazed down at the table, tracing a grain of wood with the tip of his forefinger. 'About the fact we were going out . . . and why we're not now. I should have just been honest with you both from the beginning.'

'Oh . . .' Amy was even more fazed. 'You didn't have to tell her, not on my account . . .'

'On mine, then. Because it needed to be said. I couldn't fake it any more. No one should have to live like that, with so much pretence.'

Amy stared at him in a faint fuzz of panic. She felt as if he could see right through her. As if he were aware of her every thought, even about Paul. All this talk of pretending . . .

'The thing is, Amy, I had to pip you to the post . . . This business with Niamh and Sally-Ann . . . well, while I was away, it gave me time to think. Time and distance. And it didn't take long to realise that this wasn't working out . . .'

'Jonathan—' Her voice was lacklustre, even to her own ears.

He shook his head again. 'I couldn't lose control again. I'd done it once in my life, and if I'm honest, I'm still recovering now. I let Niamh walk all over me,' he held up his hand, as Amy opened her mouth to speak, 'but it was a different Niamh, Amy, a different person. She's changed. And so have I. We're not a *couple*, no . . . I don't know if that will ever happen, but I can't say I'm ruling it out, or that some small part of me doesn't want it. But I kept women at arm's length after she walked out on me. They all seemed the same . . . except you. You were different. Softer, somehow.' He sighed. 'I mean that in a good way, Amy, really. You're not weak, far from it. That's the problem . . . I wanted you to need me, I wanted to make myself indispensable to you. And for a while, we had the right balance – or lack of it, that I was looking for. But only for a short time.'

'Please don't say I deserve something more,' she said, swallowing hard herself.

'You do. And I *will* say it. We both deserve more. We were never going to find it with each other, however long we strung it out. Something had to give, someone had to take the initiative, and even though I knew it was over, I didn't want to have to hear it from *you*.'

Amy blinked at him. He looked her directly in the eyes again.

'It had to be me who ended it,' he added. 'And I'm only sorry I was such a bastard, such a coward, and went about it in such a crap way . . .'

'Well,' Amy tried to shrug it off, even though her shoulders felt much heavier than normal, 'I'd been through it once already this year . . .' That had come out all wrong. It had made her sound almost spiteful.

'Please,' he looked agonised, 'I wish I'd been the strong one, the one who had it dealt out to, not the one doing the dealing . . . I just thought I was doing you a favour. No, that's not right, that sounds too cold, as if it didn't matter.'

'Jonathan' – this time, she was the one who reached out and took his hand – 'it's OK. It was for the best, and in the long run, it doesn't matter who did what, if the outcome would have been the same . . .'

He nodded, but only looked marginally soothed. For a long moment, silence pervaded the kitchen. They both stared at the floor.

'The tiles look good, don't they?' Jonathan muttered, as if out of nowhere.

Distractedly, Amy looked up again. For a crazy, absurd second, she wondered if the conversation they had just shared had been nothing but a figment of her imagination.

'I, er, never imagined they'd look so good with just the minimum of effort,' she muttered back, wondering if she or Jonathan would ever again refer to the demise of their relationship – the romance that had never quite got off the ground – at least with the same frankness and candour.

'Paul must have a real talent for this kind of thing. It's a shame Faulkner Jones Burnley only seem to want to ruin people's view of the countryside, rather than renovate properties that are already there.'

Jonathan, like so many villagers, resented the new development at Cherry Tree Farm.

'That isn't Paul's choice,' Amy felt compelled to clarify. 'And all houses were new once,' she stressed, even though she was hardly a fan of Faulkner Jones Burnley herself.

'Yes, I know, but . . .'

Thank God. The baby monitor had crackled into life, not a moment too soon. Lucas was stirring, as disgruntled as usual if he woke up prematurely, like today.

'Well . . .' Jonathan scraped back his chair. 'I'd better be going. Thanks for the tea. And if you're sure the boys will like their gifts . . .'

She nodded as he returned them to the shopping bag. 'They will.'

'I'll wrap them up then,' he told her, 'and drop them off before the party. Unless you're waiting till their actual birthdays . . .?'

'A bit of both,' she shrugged, seeing him to the door and thanking him again.

'You don't need to thank me, Amy. For anything.'

'I do,' she nodded emphatically, and suddenly found herself lunging forwards and hugging him. 'I'll see you around,' she whispered shakily, releasing him just as abruptly. She waited until he was at the end of the cul-de-sac before closing the door.

By the time she got upstairs, Lucas was already on his feet in the cot, rattling the bars like a prisoner. Amy picked him up and held him close, his fine, slightly curly hair tickling her chin. After a few moments, he stopped grizzling, and Amy wandered to the window to look out over the garden.

In one way, she relished this time of year. The fiery colours, the earthy smells, the nights closing in when you were warm and snug indoors. But in another, it was depressing to realise that summer was over and the commercial pageantry that was so much a part of Christmas these days was already underway. Earlier and earlier every time, it seemed.

As Lucas dribbled on her shirt, and grinned up at her in a winsome way with his four front teeth, and that tiny gap between the upper two, Amy reflected on what she had been doing this time last year.

It was incredible to think that she had still been living at the flat with Nick, expecting 'Lucy' at any moment, and unable to resist buying a few newborn dresses and a small rag doll with a pink tutu. Joseph and Mikey had seemed babies themselves back then. But now, Joseph especially could be considered nothing less than a little boy.

So much had changed and shifted about, that Amy could see few constants. And the one that seemed to stand out among the others would have to be avoided as much as possible, for now, if she was to succeed in getting her act together again.

Because Paul had been a fixture in her world for so long, it was difficult remembering what it had been like before they had met. And if it was bad enough to imagine things without him as the ally he had become, how much harder was it going to be if she let her temporary insanity get the better of her?

29

Dissatisfied with her reflection in Rowena's downstairs cloak-room mirror, Elspeth pinched her cheeks. It was the simplest way of summoning up a bit of strategic colour without actually applying blusher. She'd done it as a girl, when her mother had deemed her too young for make-up, but when Elspeth had obviously felt too old to play with dolls.

She adjusted her crimson scarf, and repinned the oval marcasite brooch with the onyx centre, which was holding it in place. Her dress was taupe, straight and woollen, and Tilly had hooked up her lip at it in disdain. ('Not that old thing. It's *beige*. I thought it went to Save the Children ages ago.') But it was still Elspeth's favourite, and came out of hibernation on special occasions when she didn't want to trawl the shops for something new.

Jewellery, scarves and shoes were Elspeth's weaknesses, and most other things she was resigned to make do with. When you had always been size ten up top, fourteen down below, with a size twelve waist – except when pregnant or breastfeeding – you could consider yourself lucky in some respects, but not when it came to buying clothes. Especially if sewing wasn't your forte, and adding a simple tuck could end in disaster.

Over the years, she had painstakingly built up as classic a wardrobe as possible, paying as little attention to fashion as she dared. Now, in spite of what Tilly thought, Elspeth felt she had plenty to pick and choose from, whatever the occasion.

Rowena's philosophy was clearly the opposite. Needless to

say, her vital statistics amounted to a perfect size ten, with slender hands and feet to match. Not that she dressed in the least bit delicately. And she'd probably never worn the same outfit more than twice.

While Elspeth's hair was longish and curly, with the mousy redness still vying with the grey for supremacy, Rowena's was ash blonde, cut short and razor sharp, with every strand of grey glossed over. Elspeth secured her unruly locks with a hairband and half a dozen pins. Rowena no doubt kept hair gel manufacturers in business.

They were as different as east from west. But as east and west coexist, Elspeth and Rowena were forced to rub along on days such as today for the sake of the three grandchildren they had in common.

Elspeth had got as much antagonism as she could out of her system this morning, inflicting a torrent of emotion on her poor, unsuspecting piano. She had therefore been as calm as she was going to get when she and Tilly had arrived at Rowena's house for the boys' birthday bash. Yet it had all gone awry when Rowena had unveiled her lavish gift, after gathering everyone in the large conservatory where they would have a better view outside.

'It will have to be kept here, of course,' Rowena had preened over the electric-powered jeep, perfect for two children to sit in side by side. 'I've got a double garage which rarely gets used, so there's masses of room. And it's best to have the run of a big garden.'

Elspeth had glanced at Amy, but it was plain that her daughter hadn't known anything about this particular gift. As Joseph and Mikey had launched themselves at it, and Lucas had chewed on Amy's hair, which she'd had to keep tugging out of his grasp, Amy had turned to the woman who had once been the equivalent of a mother-in-law.

'I wish you'd discussed this with me first.' Her voice had

been low and vexed. 'For one thing, if it's meant to be a joint present, then it's not fair on the baby.'

'He'll grow into it, Amy,' Rowena's husband had interjected. 'And Rowena wanted it to be a surprise.'

'I did ask Nicholas for his opinion,' Rowena had shrugged.

'I don't see him anywhere.' Amy's annoyance had sizzled just below the surface. 'And it's not as if flights cost the earth. He could have been here if he'd wanted to.'

'He's very busy, Amy, and he can't just drop everything when it suits him. But, rest assured, he'll be over again at the end of the year. And as Conrad said, I wanted the jeep to be a surprise. Not just for the boys. I'm sure you won't begrudge them a little fun. They deserve it, after everything they've been through.'

Elspeth had itched to belt her one. Instead, of course, she had gripped her Pimm's tighter and allowed Tilly to embark on a discourse about their own presents for the boys.

Amy, although still restrained, hadn't exercised as much diplomacy. 'Next year, Rowena, please run it by me first. In fact, that stands for every gift you're thinking about buying them that costs over fifty quid.' And with that, she'd hurried outside to referee an argument between Joseph and Mikey over who was going to sit behind the steering wheel first.

'I'm afraid that's ingratitude for you.' Isabelle Faulkner Jones had come into the conversation late, but she had been close enough to overhear it. In Elspeth's limited experience, Paul's mother had never been one to withhold her opinion, even if it was uttered in a voice that would give treacle a run for its money.

'Amy doesn't need anyone's charity,' Elspeth had been quick to rejoinder.

'That's not what Nick's bank statement must be saying each month,' Isabelle had returned.

Elspeth had been about to blow, like Vesuvius over Pompeii, when Isabelle's handbag had started to purr.

'Excuse me . . .' Her phone was silver and shiny. She'd flipped it open. 'Oh . . . hello, darling . . . No, no, I'm still here at Rowena's . . . No, of course I told her where you were. She understands . . . I don't think you need to bother . . . Well, all right, we'll see you soon.' She'd flipped it shut again. 'That was Paul. He's caught in traffic.'

'Oh, dear,' Rowena had commiserated. 'Did Francesca catch her plane all right?'

'Apparently. Paul's on his way back. He still hopes to make it.'

Elspeth had frowned. The fact that Paul hadn't been here already had felt odd, because the whole party had seemed like some Faulkner Jones Burnley convention. And there were too many adults, with nowhere near enough children. In fact, there were probably five balloons for every child present. Hand a bunch to Lucas and he might float off.

Rowena and Isabelle were still nattering to each other as Elspeth returned from the toilet, looking for Tilly. Her younger daughter wasn't by the large, potted palm where Elspeth had left her. The two female Faulkner Jones Burnley directors were hovering there now, and as Elspeth had virtually walked right up to them, she swallowed her earlier hostility and endeavoured to be as civil as George would have wanted her to be. At least for ten seconds, while she asked them if they knew where Tilly had gone.

'Of course, Rosewood Grange is picturesque in its own way,' Isabelle was sighing, 'but I told Ken only last week, a marquee on our lawn would be perfect for a June wedding.'

'That's so romantic,' Rowena gushed back. 'I had a marquee for my second marriage. Do you remember? It'll be lovely for you. I feel so sad that I missed out with Nick . . . Oh, Elspeth – hello. We were just discussing Paul and Francesca.'

'Really? You mentioned a wedding . . .'

'Ah, yes.' Rowena tapped her nose. 'Things are getting serious.'

'This is just between us, of course,' Isabelle nodded, smiling at Elspeth. 'Nothing's official, yet. But I have to admit, the idea of being a grandmother is growing on me.'

Elspeth looked at her aghast. 'Francesca's pregnant?'

'No, no.' Isabelle laughed in a genteel, yet brittle fashion. 'At least, I don't think so! I meant, one day. After the wedding, I'm sure it'll only be a matter of time. Francesca has her career, but that never stopped me. She does like children. And Paul's very fond of them, too.'

Elspeth spoke again, without thinking first. 'I'm surprised Amy hasn't said anything to me.'

Rowena and Isabelle exchanged what Elspeth took to be a pitying glance.

'I hope you won't be offended,' began Isabelle, wetting her lips, 'but Amy's hardly likely to know anything on that score. Paul's been wonderful helping her out after everything that's happened, I'm sure even Rowena won't mind me saying it. But it would be a different story if Nick and Amy had split up normally. Mutually, that is. Paul feels responsible to an extent, even though he shouldn't. It's in his nature to care about the underdog, though. When he was a boy, he once brought home a baby thrush with a damaged wing. Wanted to save it from a cat that was prowling around.' Isabelle sighed. 'He's very protective, and he gets too involved. Of course, I'm sure he sees Amy as a friend to some extent, but he's hardly going to be confiding in her about Francesca. He's more inclined to be the secret-bearer.'

Elspeth's brow had puckered the more Isabelle had gabbled on. Paul's mother didn't sound entirely convinced by what she was saying; as if it was something she wanted to believe, rather than anything concrete.

'Well,' said Elspeth, knowing exactly how Amy would react to being called an underdog if she ever found out, 'I'm sure you'll be very proud to have Paul settle down at last. He's been sowing his wild oats for long enough. And having a marquee's a splendid idea. White, I take it? To show off the groom's tan. Lovely, really.' Elspeth gestured across the room, wondering if she'd sounded bitchy, and hoping she had. 'Will you excuse me? I've just seen Tilly . . .'

Her two daughters were shepherding the few children present around a trestle table laden with a 'feast' for the youngsters. Basic finger food, by the look of it. Nuggets, crisps, jam sandwiches, orange squash . . . The caterers had used their imagination, thought Elspeth acidly. And did the parents of these children think Amy and Tilly were running a crèche? There didn't seem to be any other adults orbiting the table keeping order.

'Someone will be asking me next if I can fetch them a drink,' simmered Elspeth, as she joined them. She tweaked Lucas's nose as he clung to Amy like a baby koala in his grey linen dungaree set.

'Huh?' Tilly dipped into the French fries.

'Nothing. I just feel a bit . . . subordinate, that's all.'

'That's what comes of talking to Isabelle and Rowena,' said Amy. 'But you seemed to be quite pally with them just now.'

'Like a witches' coven,' muttered Tilly, then beamed assuagingly at Elspeth. 'Wouldn't it be nice to see them more often, Mum? Maybe you've all got a lot more in common, these days, now that you're getting on in years. You should ask them over for cocktails one evening.'

Elspeth narrowed her eyes at Tilly, then took a tissue to Mikey's nose as he presented it to her for wiping. Something was stalling her from blurting out the gossip she'd just heard. Instead, she said offhandedly, 'Isabelle got a call a while back . . . Paul's stuck in traffic.'

'Oh?' Amy's face took on a mask-like blankness, which was more telling, thought Elspeth, than if she had just continued to look mildly interested. 'Isn't he going to make it, then?'

'He might.' Elspeth hesitated. 'Apparently he went to the airport to drop off Francesca.'

'And there's me thinking he wasn't here because he had better things to do with his time,' sighed Tilly. 'A kiddies' tea party, after all . . .'

Amy jiggled the weight of the baby on to her other hip. Lucas was looking peaky, and refusing to eat. 'Didn't I tell you earlier . . .?' Amy swept back her hair insouciantly. 'Paul rang this morning to say he might be a bit late getting here.'

This was the first Elspeth or Tilly had heard of it.

If forgetting to tell them was supposed to make Amy seem less bothered by it, then why, thought Elspeth grimly, did it have the opposite effect?

'Where's Francesca going then?' Tilly frowned, and reached across the table to grab a mini choc-chip muffin for Joseph.

'Spain, Paul said.' Amy shrugged. 'She's got a friend on the Costa del Sol. Estepona, I think. Apparently this friend's having some personal problems, and asked if Francesca could go over. I don't know all the details. I'm not sure Paul does, either. He said she was lucky to get a flight at short notice, and that he'd offered to drive her to the airport. But he did want to be here.'

'It would have been nicer for the kids than this bunch of strangers,' Tilly grumbled under her breath.

Elspeth glanced around with a sigh. 'We could always make our excuses soon and go. We've been here long enough. The boys are getting tired.' She leaned towards her daughters, lowering her voice. 'And I don't think we'd be missed much.'

Amy immediately shook her head. 'We can't just walk out. It'd seem ungrateful to go while virtually everyone else is still here.'

Elspeth wondered if that was the real reason, or just a cover.

'And I'm pretty sure there's going to be a massive birthday cake coming through those doors any minute,' Amy added. 'Not to mention all those presents stacked up in the dining room – those'll need opening.'

'We'll wait for the cake, but why not just take the presents with us and unwrap them at your place?' Elspeth shuffled from one foot to another, wishing she'd worn low, wedged heels rather than high, skinny ones. 'Otherwise, at this rate, we'll be here all night. There'll probably be a disco soon.'

'Oh, Mum!' Amy pursed her lips, and tried to tempt Lucas with a breadstick.

Paul grimaced at his watch, and decided to slip in through a back door, if he could find one open. It would look less obvious than waltzing in through the front, and broadcasting how late he was. Besides, the drive was lined with cars, and he'd ended up coming round the side anyway and sneaking his Audi TT between Rowena's and Conrad's cars in the pseudo-cobbled courtyard in front of the garage. Cocky of him, but safer for his car when you considered all the reversing and three-point turns that would be going on when everyone started to leave.

Luckily, the kitchen door was unlocked, and he passed through the large utility area first, before entering the main room, with the granite-topped island taking pride of place, just as he would have designed it himself.

Suddenly, he drew up short.

Tilly was leaning against one of the pristine white kitchen cabinets, holding a vol-au-vent in one hand, and by the look of it, sending a text message with the other.

Since their encounter at Hula Palace, they had run into each other on a couple of occasions at the house in March Street. Neither of them had mentioned that night out in Chester, not even in relation to Amy, and Paul was content to leave it at that. However, he had noticed that the teenager was staring at him rather too often for comfort. Yet every time he turned to look at her more closely himself, as if trying to catch her out, she was staring at Amy. It was odd and unnerving.

Tilly looked up from her mobile and spotted him. She held his gaze for a moment, before her face took on a sly, Mona Lisa quality. Nudging her head towards the closed door that led to the hall, she explained conspiratorially, 'I had to get away for a minute. It's like Toys "R" Us in the conservatory. Plus there's the bonus of the leftovers in here.' She gestured to the disposable 'silver' platters balanced on the island. 'I'd tuck in, if I were you.'

Paul picked out a sesame prawn toast. 'Toys "R" Us?' he echoed.

'The boys are opening the last of their presents. Amy's going to go mental when she sees all the stuff they've got. Hope I'm not around to witness it. Talk about not spoiling them.'

'Oh . . . isn't Amy here?'

Tilly glanced at the kitchen clock. 'You've missed her by about fifteen minutes. She took the baby home.'

'Why's that?' asked Paul, maintaining an air of cavalierish detachment. 'What's up?'

'Lucas isn't well. He's been whingy since yesterday, and he threw up all over Amy while she was trying to give him his bottle a little while ago. She reckoned he was hot, but she didn't have any Calpol in the nappy bag. It seemed best to take him home and try to put him to bed.'

'But Joe and Mikey—'

'—are still here. Father Christmas couldn't drag them away at the moment. Probably for the best, anyway. Let Amy get Lucas settled. Mum said we'd take them home later.'

'You came in two cars?'

'Yeah, so we'd have more than enough room for all the

presents.' Tilly snorted. 'By the look of it, we'll be needing a trailer.'

'Ouch.' The cogs in Paul's brain were turning vigorously. 'Well, doesn't look like I'm missing much here, really,' he murmured. 'Thought I'd show my face, but . . .'

Under the curtain of her hair, Tilly seemed to be grinning. She studied her mobile phone again. 'It is pretty late. Hardly seems worth it now.'

'I got held up. There was a contraflow.'

'Well, if no one else has seen you come in, then they'll probably just assume you couldn't make it.'

'Do you reckon?'

'If I were you, I'd cut my losses and run. Trust me, I'm a teenager.'

'OK, then . . .' He devoured the last of his canapé. 'See you around.'

'You bet,' he thought he heard her mutter. Then suddenly, out of nowhere, she exclaimed brightly, 'Oh! Congratulations, by the way.'

Paul glanced back vaguely over his shoulder. 'What for?'

'There's a rumour circulating that you and Francesca are planning on getting hitched next year. June, to be exact. I think the reception started off at Rosewood Grange, but now it's progressed to a marquee on your mum and dad's lawn.'

Paul swung round to face her again. 'You're having me on!'

'As if. Just ask my mum – she's heard it, too. I suppose it was meant to be all hush-hush, but you know what these things are like.'

'It's crazy!'

'So you're saying it's not true?'

'I haven't asked Francesca to marry me, let alone started planning a wedding. We've never even discussed it. Moving in together, maybe. A while back. But *marriage* . . .'

Paul was shell-shocked; and yet, when he considered it, it

wouldn't be the first time his mother had tried to precipitate something by nudging him in the 'right' direction.

'Oh, well. You know what mums are like,' sighed Tilly. 'And if I were you, then I definitely wouldn't go in there now. You'll be discussing morning suits before you know it.'

Paul couldn't make his getaway fast enough.

30

Amy didn't know precisely what made her put on the tape of Joseph as a baby.

In the consoling glow of a small reading lamp, she nestled into a beanbag on the lounge rug, the remote controls on her left as she gazed up at the TV, and a packet of Maltesers with a glass of white Zinfandel on her right.

The rush of emotion that tore at her heartstrings was more intense than she had expected. It was only really now, by replaying what Joseph had been like when he was little, that she could identify another similarity in her children apart from the flaxen fair hair. It was something about their mannerisms and expressions, which wasn't obvious when you looked at photographs or tried to rely solely on memory.

She was so glad that Nick had bought a digital camcorder when she'd been pregnant the first time. And she had made sure that she had looted it from the flat – along with the television, video and DVD – when they had split up.

Huddling into her old Aran cardigan, she watched with tears trickling from her eyes, as Joseph turned one. She would never have that moment again. Never bend over his high chair and help him blow out that single candle as he tried to stretch out to touch it. Life, she realised ruefully, was a series of unique and unrepeatable moments. And it wasn't to be squandered.

The doorbell sounded. It was an almighty, reverberating 'ding-*dong*' if you happened to be in the kitchen. With the bedroom doors shut upstairs, though, it didn't usually disturb anyone's sleep, which was a blessing if the kids were napping. Amy had vowed to do something about it when she had first moved in, until it had struck her that it would have to compete with the clamour of her household anyway.

She sighed raggedly and scrambled to her feet, almost knocking over the wine. It was slightly earlier than she'd expected, but it was probably just her mum bringing Joe and Mikey back and apologising that she'd forgotten her spare key again. Amy didn't bother peeking through the curtains to check.

A few seconds later, she wished she had. If not to pretend that no one was home, then at least to have given herself a chance to shed the out-of-shape old cardigan, and do a better job of smearing away her tears.

There on her doorstep, in one of his 'weekend' suits, with his hair gorgeously spiked and his shirt collar casually undone, stood Paul.

'Hi,' he said cheerfully, then a second later, looked concerned. 'Are you all right?'

'I was just playing back Joe's first birthday.' She sniffed, and held the door open to let him in. 'My idea of a chick flick. But don't mind me, I'm just a soppy old mare.'

'You don't have to apologise for being sentimental,' Paul smiled. 'Sorry I missed the party today, by the way. I feel bad for the boys' sake.'

Amy shrugged and closed the door after him. 'Couldn't be helped. But Joe and Mikey are still at Rowena's. I only came home because Lucas is under the weather.'

And because it wasn't any fun without you there, she added in her head, leading Paul into the lounge.

She'd been playing tug of war with herself all afternoon, in fact.

It would be better if Paul didn't make it to the party, the

voice of Sensible Amy had asserted. You're attempting to avoid him, after all.

But then Crazy Amy had hissed back: Yeah, right. When all's said and done, you're avoiding him like you'd avoid a winning lottery ticket. You don't want to leave yet. He might still turn up.

Eventually – mainly because Lucas wasn't well and because even Crazy Amy didn't want Paul to see her these days with baby sick down her top – Sensible Amy had prevailed.

She had brought Lucas home and, feeling queasy at the smell of regurgitated milk, got changed herself before mopping him down thoroughly, putting him in his pyjamas and giving him the maximum dose of Calpol for his age. Then, cuddling him in her arms, she had settled in the rocking chair her mum had bought her when she was pregnant the first time. It hadn't taken long for Lucas to fall asleep, but she'd sat with him for a while afterwards, just to nuzzle her cheek against his hair and feel him breathing in and out against her chest.

When her arm had started to get cramp, though, she'd put Lucas in the cot. Then she'd trudged downstairs to pour herself a medium-sized glass of wine, satisfied that she deserved it and that it wasn't going to make her any less of a good mother if she stopped at that. The Maltesers had come out a short while later, when Sensible Amy had begun to feel the first niggles of loneliness, and Crazy Amy had started mouthing off again.

'Drinking on your own?' Paul smiled, hooking up an eyebrow at her wine glass, as he sat down in her one and only – borrowed – armchair.

Amy had ordered a brand new three-piece suite, on interest-free credit, which was meant to arrive sometime this side of Christmas, if the salesman was to be believed. It was also supposed to be lavishly Scotchgarded, although she'd had to fork out extra for the reassurance that blackcurrant stains wouldn't become a permanent part of the upholstery.

'Would you like some? I know you're driving, but if you're not in a hurry to get off . . .' Amy picked up her glass and took a sip. 'Although – it might be a bit too much of a "dessert wine" for your taste.'

'I'm not a wine buff. I just like what I like. Where's it from?'

'California.'

'I usually dig those, as Tilly might say. I never know which words are cool and which aren't these days.' Paul settled back, sounding fatigued as he let out a long, heavy sigh. When Amy returned with the wine bottle and another glass, he seemed to realise he was hogging the only comfortable chair, and sprang to his feet again. 'I'm sorry, I didn't—'

'It's fine.' Amy sank as gracefully as she could to the floor, propping herself against the beanbag again. 'I wasn't sitting there anyway.'

'If you're sure . . .' Paul paused a moment, then sat back down. He glanced around, looking gratified. 'There's a really welcoming atmosphere in here now.'

Amy looked round, too, taking in the ornate open fireplace – unlit, as yet, because it wasn't cold enough – and noting that the safety guard she'd bought from Mothercare didn't exactly enhance the original Victorian feature. Still, it wasn't for ever.

Pulling a mortified face, she gestured through the new archway at the play area beyond. 'Yeah, it's got a great atmosphere if you like living in a tip.'

She had been late leaving for Rowena's, so she hadn't had a chance to tidy up before. And she was too worn out and in totally the wrong mood now.

Paul grinned. 'It's not that bad. The lived-in look suits you, and it goes with the territory. By all accounts, though, you're getting loads more stuff to find room for . . .'

'What do you mean?' Amy lowered her eyelids and looked

at him suspiciously, all the while worrying that the lived-in look he'd referred to included her jogging pants and cardie.

'I did actually make it to the party,' he confessed. 'But only for five minutes, so I don't know if that counts. I ran into Tilly and she told me what'd happened.'

Amy frowned, feeling as if she was missing something. 'So you knew about Lucas?'

'That was one of the reasons I came . . . To see if you needed any help. Have you called a doctor?'

Amy indicated her glass of wine. 'Do I look as if I have? Anyway, intuition tells me it's nothing to worry about. He's a bit hot, but it's not a raging fever, and a good night's sleep usually does the trick. If he's still off colour tomorrow, I might call the surgery.'

'Joe and Mikey are OK, though?'

'At the moment, but these things spread like wildfire. Still, if they're distracted by a load of new toys, it might not hit them so hard. Otherwise, they're typical men when they're sick.'

'Oh, ha! Very funny. I'm not that bad.'

'Really. That's not how I remember it.'

'You make it sound as if we're divorced or something.'

Amy almost spilled wine on the rug. She recovered fast. 'I was only referring to the times you used to sprawl on the sofa, moaning that you were dying. Anyway,' she went on quickly, 'talking of the kids, what have you got them yourself then? Is it big, noisy or messy? Or, the nightmare scenario – all three?'

'It isn't a joint present, there's something for each of them. But I think it would be better if the boys all opened them at the same time, seeing as they're connected.'

'Oh?'

'I've gone and left them in the car . . . But I might as well tell you, anyway. They're adoption certificates. For animals at Chester Zoo. I tried to pick out the boys' favourites. And I got

Lucas a soft toy giraffe, to go with it, and those rubbery, lifelike ones, you know the sort, for Joe and Mikey.'

'Oh!' Amy was touched by Paul's sincerity. He'd always been generous with his gifts, though, and clearly put some effort into choosing them rather than just grabbing the first thing he saw on a toy shelf. 'I took them to the zoo in the summer,' she went on. 'They loved it. That's when Joseph first got it into his head that the reptiles were baby dinosaurs.'

'Yeah, I know. He raved on about it to me. It was then I got the idea.'

'Paul, it's brilliant. Thank you! Thank you so much . . .' She drew short of hugging him. Best to leave that to the kids. Once she started, she might not be able to stop.

He flapped a hand dismissively, modestly. 'Maybe—' he hesitated. 'Well, maybe we could take them to the zoo again sometime soon, so they can meet "their" animals.'

'You and Francesca, you mean?' Amy couldn't stop herself. She forced out a small laugh. 'Do you fancy trying out your parenting skills, then, before taking the plunge yourselves?'

Paul frowned, and faltered. 'Well, actually—'

Amy realised she didn't want to hear it at first hand. Not that indirectly was much better, but it would take the edge off a tiny fraction if it wasn't coming from Paul's lips.

'I think you'd make wonderful parents,' she declared, injecting enthusiasm into her voice with the mighty syringe of self-sacrifice.

Just as long as he was happy . . . Her feelings would pass. Eventually. If she kept telling herself they would.

'So . . . you heard the rumour going around today,' said Paul, still frowning, 'about the wedding . . .?'

Amy hadn't heard any such rumour. She'd been so wrapped up in making sure the kids were enjoying themselves and not wreaking havoc, that the majority of adult conversation had just washed over her. So, her prophecy about the engagement ring had been correct. And could Paul actually be hinting that Francesca was pregnant? Amy had mentioned them being parents, then Paul had alluded to a wedding – it would fit. Like the missing piece of a jigsaw.

Her chest felt as if it were caving in, restricting her breathing, but still Amy managed to say – after a large gulp of wine – 'Oh, wow! I'm really happy for you. That's amazing news! At long last – Paul Faulkner Jones finally meets his match.'

Trance-like, Paul was staring down at her from the armchair. Gradually, he seemed to come round, looking away, then blinking down into his wine.

'Yeah,' he muttered. 'At long last.'

'So,' Amy pretended to be momentarily distracted by something on the TV, 'have you set a date yet?'

'Er . . . no . . . not exactly . . .' Paul turned to the TV, too.

Amy had put it on mute when Paul had arrived, but if she were to turn it up now, there would be the din of happy voices and the chink of cutlery and glasses. It was Christmas Day at the flat. Nick had been adamant about squeezing everyone in, although Amy had done the bulk of the work. Fortunately she'd had her mum and Tilly helping. And there was Paul, carrying a stack of dishes to the kitchen and winking at the camera . . . Amy must have been filming. The camera wobbled slightly, and then pointed downwards, as Joseph – barely walking on his own – staggered up to her leg and tugged on her skirt.

'I remember that year . . .' Paul was shaking his head at the recollection. 'My folks buggered off to the States to stay with my uncle and his family, and left me on my own.'

'They didn't leave you. You just didn't want to go with them. And you were never on your own for long, were you?' Amy nodded at the screen, as a leggy brunette in her mid-twenties sashayed into view, snuggling up to Paul like a proprietorial cat.

Paul squinted, and grimaced. 'This is going to sound awful, but I can't actually remember her name . . .'

Amy curled her lip. Why didn't that surprise her? The girl had only been a three-week fling. Some secretarial temp Paul had pulled at the Faulkner Jones Burnley Christmas 'Gala', as the directors pretentiously liked to call it. The girl's parents had been away for Christmas, too, if Amy remembered correctly, so she'd invited herself over to Paul's for the holidays. He had dangled her like a bauble until January, when he'd shed her along with all the other decorations.

'Tabitha,' said Amy grimly.

'Sorry?'

'Her name. Wasn't it Tabitha?'

Paul squinted exaggeratedly at the girl again, then nodded. 'I trust your memory better than mine. After all, you probably kept a catalogue of my disasters to use against me.'

Amy bridled. 'You really think I'm that much of a bitch?'

'No, and don't get all uptight. But let's just say that if I ever became a world-famous, celebrity architect, and the press wanted some dirt on me, then you know full well they'd only need to have a chat with you to get their front-page exclusive.'

'That's *so* not true!'

'It is. But you're not a bitch,' said Paul gently; then added, with vitriol, 'Unlike Tabitha. She started temping for some high-flying executive type, and dumped me the minute she'd slept with him. I think he was married. But, of course, his wife didn't understand him.'

Amy felt herself blush. 'I thought . . .'

'You assumed the worst of me. But that's OK,' he shrugged, 'I expected it.'

'Paul . . . I'm sorry.'

'No, listen. You're right, in part. I haven't been Mr Commitment over the years.'

'But you are now.' Amy tried to pre-empt whatever he was

about to say that would drive a knife into her heart. 'You were just waiting for the right woman to come along. Well, not waiting. Swimming around in circles, I guess. You weren't exactly inactive. And if you were starting to worry that there was some deep-seated psychological problem – you know, to do with your mother or something – then this thing with Francesca's proved you wrong.'

Paul was regarding her with a mystified expression. Amy realised that prattling on the way she had could be as marked as a long, brooding silence. She smiled tensely, and was rooting around in her head for a different subject to switch to, when the sound of a car horn curtailed her.

'That might be Mum . . .' Amy clambered up and lifted the curtain, peering into the street. 'She can't park, there's no room.'

Paul seemed to waver, then stood up himself. 'I'd better be going. She can have my space.'

'No.' The word was out of Amy's mouth before she had a chance to rein it in.

Paul halted in his tracks. It hadn't taken much. Maybe he'd realised he ought to stick around to see the boys.

'It's – um – fine,' Amy explained. 'Tilly's getting Joe and Mikey out, Mum's just waving. She probably wants to head off home.'

Amy let them in. Both boys carried a stash of toys each, and Tilly was hidden behind a load more.

'Didn't anyone give them clothes?' sighed Amy, who would have appreciated some new things for Joseph, considering he had gone through yet another growth spurt.

'Nope,' said her sister. 'A few books, but they're still in the car with the larger stuff.'

'Super. "Larger stuff." Can't wait.'

Amy watched as Joseph and Mikey dumped their toys on the rug and flung themselves at Paul, jabbering about their new 'jeep car'.

Tilly leaned against the doorframe. 'Hello, again, Paul.'

'Oh, er, hi.'

'This is a surprise.'

'Well, um, I thought I'd drop my own presents round, and see if Amy needed a hand.'

'That's thoughtful of you. How is Lucas?'

'As well as can be expected. He's asleep,' said Amy. 'He wasn't much bother. Hopefully he'll be over the worst by tomorrow.'

'Good. Mum says if you want help getting the other two to bed – considering they're a bit hyper – she'll try and park somewhere.'

'I can help Amy,' piped up Paul. 'I've – er – got nothing to rush home for.'

'In that case,' Tilly smiled dazzlingly at him, as if she were a quiz show host and Paul had given her the right answer, 'I'll tell Mum everything's under control. Do you want me to bring in the rest of the stuff from the boot?'

'No,' said Amy quickly. 'It can wait till tomorrow. The boys have got enough here to keep them busy before bed.'

Tilly nodded, grinned again, and let herself out. Amy debated going outside to speak to her mum herself, but decided not to, in case Elspeth launched into another diatribe about Paul or his mother.

'Mummeee!' Joe and Mikey chorused in unison. 'I'm hungry!'

Amy racked her brains, trying to picture what was in the larder or fridge. She would need to get to the supermarket tomorrow. Her reserves were seriously low considering she had a nestful of offspring to sustain.

'Didn't you eat enough at the party?' she grumbled.

'Growing lads.' Paul smiled indulgently, then patted his stomach. 'Actually, I'm getting peckish myself . . .'

Damn. He was probably used to Francesca rustling up a

gourmet snack in no time at all. Amy could barely stretch to cheese on toast or spaghetti hoops. Paul didn't seem keen on either, once she'd listed the options.

'How about a Chinese?' He whispered it so the boys wouldn't hear.

'The new one in the village?'

'I can ask them to deliver.'

'But we'd have to wait until Joe and Mikey went to bed, or we wouldn't have any prawn crackers for ourselves. If you're hungry now . . .'

'I can wait. I've got all night.'

Of course he did, Amy frowned inwardly. He'd said it himself – there was no need to rush home. He would welcome the distraction, considering he'd put his beloved on a plane earlier and was probably already missing her.

While Amy relished the idea of spending the rest of the evening with him, it was also the cruellest form of torture, because if Francesca had been around, then he wouldn't be here at all.

Guiltily, she wondered if this was what a mistress felt like, when the wife was away.

31

In the shop window, the signature small, green topiary trees had been replaced with golden ones – simple and elegant compared to the masses of tinsel elsewhere. They signalled the fact that Halloween and Bonfire Night were over and done with, and it was all downhill now until Christmas and the January sales.

Paul was feeling especially cynical this year as he stared at the rows of diamonds in various sizes and settings. A man would find it hard to pick just one ring out of this selection – if he were thinking of picking a ring, that was.

It was the first time Paul had ever really stood outside a jeweller's of this calibre and absorbed the magnificence of the stones, rather than just whistling at the prices and counting himself lucky he didn't have to fork out for one. And it was the first time, on a personal level, that he'd felt the weight and wealth of emotion that went behind the gesture of asking someone to belong to you exclusively.

He'd stood here once with Nick, possibly in the same spot, while Nick had pointed out the ones he liked, badgering Paul for an opinion.

'Well, what would you go for, mate?'

Paul had shrugged, and prudently, yet with tact, tried to talk his friend out of it. After what had happened, he'd been right to try.

How many stones here went to waste like that?

It was just as well that Francesca had been away when the

rumour of their impending union had sprung up. According to hearsay, they were engaged, yet Paul hadn't been able to laugh it off with her over the phone. Consequently, she still knew nothing about it; and she was coming home this week-end. He would have to tell her before someone else did. But first . . . he would have to reach a decision, one way or the other.

If Amy had been right – if he had been swimming around in circles for most of his adult life – then now, maybe for months, he had been merely treading water. He didn't seem to be going anywhere, in any respect. Yet, if she'd just given him a sign, a glimmer of hope . . .

It was everything she had said, and everything she hadn't, that had brought him here, to this point in time. And it was totally the wrong reason, he realised, catching a shop assistant's eye over the window display. Hunching his shoulders and shoving his fists in his coat pockets, Paul rapidly averted his gaze and strode away.

It was bitingly cold outside the ornately decorated shopping arcade. The northerly wind sliced through his new coat, but Paul still succeeded in losing himself in thought, staring at the cobbles as he walked.

Just as there seemed to be no particular instant he could pinpoint when he'd consciously thought to himself, *I want to be an architect*, there was no singular moment when he'd acknowledged, *I want her*. Like Lucas's wooden building blocks, things had just built up over time. One on top of the other. With that night in August bringing it toppling down around him, making Paul realise that this was something he couldn't ignore.

Except it hadn't stopped him trying.

If he had bought a ring back there for the woman who was actually his girlfriend, it would have counted as the most reckless of all his decisions; which was saying a lot, because the worst resolutions of his life had been rash and impulsive.

The feeling growing inside him was neither of those things.

He had been muddling along for years, never quite rebelling outright, always finding a compromise. But allowing his mother to get her own way with regard to who he spent the rest of his life with – or rather, vowed to spend it with – would have been lethal.

And just as Paul was never going to head up the Faulkner Group, or be involved in it in any way, he wasn't prepared to tread the safe middle ground of his current existence, either.

Not any more.

Francesca usually lit at least half a dozen candles. Today there was only one. Paul found this a promising sign as he stepped into the kitchen-diner of the ground-floor flat in Boughton.

Her flatmate was still there, tucking into a slice of pizza.

'Are you early?' Donna looked like a severe schoolmistress with her dyed blue-black hair and horn-rimmed glasses, especially as she was frowning. 'Or am I running behind?'

'Paul's as punctual as always,' said Francesca, as she stirred something on the hob.

'Then I'm late. Shit. Good to see you, Paul.'

'Likewise . . .'

But she was gone, banging the front door behind her.

In the past, on finding themselves alone, Paul would have crept up behind Francesca and wrapped his arms around her waist, burying his face in her neck and the soft spirals of her hair.

Today, he just offered to open the wine.

This was their first real 'date' since she'd returned from Spain. She'd been busy at work and catching up with her friends, and Paul knew that he'd been resigned to let her carry on avoiding him for as long as she liked, if that was what she'd been doing.

It wasn't that he felt a definite friction between them as

much as a sense that things were strained. He wondered
whether the time away had made her re-evaluate their relationship from her own standpoint. When he'd picked her up from
the airport, he'd finally told her about the 'engagement', and
she had laughed as if it was the funniest thing she'd heard,
before stopping as suddenly as she had started. The oddest
reaction, Paul had thought, not sure what to make of it. But
Francesca had been too tired to pursue anything deeper that
day, claiming she just needed to crash out at her place on her
own.

The meal this evening had been her idea. She'd cooked
paella. 'As authentic as I could get it,' she smiled, when at last
she spooned it out.

As he drank the Rioja and ate the seafood and rice, Paul
studied her across the small, round, glass table. She had a glow
about her that you couldn't get from a sunbed. It was more to
do with a slower-paced lifestyle, with the sea meeting the
mountains, and late nights compensated by lazy afternoons. It
was about being in a different world for a few weeks, instead of
just lying under UV rays for half an hour.

'Spain suits you,' he said, as they ate crème caramel for
dessert.

She was silent a moment. 'You mean I get more freckles?'

'You'd think it, with your hair and that, but you don't seem
to.'

'Paul . . .' She put down her spoon. It tinkled against the
glass table top. 'This is really difficult for me . . .'

'What is?'

He wanted her to be the first to admit aloud that this wasn't
working. The coward's way out. Instead of having to broach it
himself, he could go along with whatever she said. And if she
simply suggested a 'break' from the relationship – although
maybe she had found her time away in Spain sufficient to
make up her mind definitively – then at least it was the first

step. She was smart after all, something he'd been attracted to in the beginning. Although he hadn't seen much evidence of that side of her lately.

'When we first started dating' – she looked at her half-finished dessert rather than into his eyes – 'it wasn't supposed to get serious . . .'

Now he categorically knew where this was heading. He'd broken up with women enough times. He'd been on the giving end mostly and sometimes the receiving, and he felt as if he knew the script off by heart. Even though this was the longest he had been out with anyone, without counting Fiona Smollett from uni, he doubted it would be all that different.

'I wasn't looking for anything long-term,' she confessed, pulling a corkscrew of hair back behind her ear. 'And you had the perfect reputation.' Fleetingly, she met his gaze, and smiled wanly. 'I was just after a bit of fun – in the interim – nothing that would leave any scars, or mean I'd be carting around baggage for the rest of my life.'

Paul hesitated. He could sense a 'but' hanging in the air. 'I didn't get that impression myself,' he said finally.

'I didn't think I'd need to spell it out. I thought things would just begin and end. You were exactly what I was looking for. Someone who shied away from commitment.'

'Francesca—'

'No.' She held up her hand. 'I'm sorry. I got you all wrong. I started to realise that when you asked me to move in with you. Yes, everything was fabulous between us. Yes, I even contemplated changing my plans—'

Paul frowned in confusion. 'What plans?'

'Maybe I should have told you sooner. But suddenly . . . suddenly it seemed too late. I was never supposed to get *involved*. And then – how was I going to tell you? Things haven't been easy between us for a while now, but that's been my fault. I tried pushing you away, gave you every opportunity to get bored. The more I felt for you, the harder I tried to walk away. But it was like being on a length of elastic. I kept springing back. And now . . .'

Paul stared at her, feeling sick. This particular scenario hadn't been rehearsed before. Yes, there'd been clingy girls, who didn't want to let go even after a couple of dates. The ones who filled you with dread if you'd seen *Fatal Attraction*. But Paul had always handled it like a gentleman, never knowingly leading anyone on. Sometimes he'd felt misled himself, because women had said one thing while evidently thinking something else. Even so, there were rituals to the dating game; and obstacles, hitherto negotiable. He'd been able to deal with them. But this . . .

'When I moved up to Chester,' Francesca was still trying to explain, 'I moved up because my father knows Ken MacIntyre.'

'Your boss?'

She nodded. 'He owed Dad a favour, and he said he'd take me on. I needed more experience, you see. I needed the sort I could get at MacIntyre and Bright. But Ken always knew I'd only be there a year, tops. He's been great, the best mentor, because he's always known where my ambitions really lay. He was the only one apart from Jules – and my family – who did.'

Paul regarded her dimly. She was looking back at him now as if she was making perfect sense, and he was the one being obtuse. 'What's Jules got to do with it?' he asked.

Francesca hesitated, then came straight out with it. No more preamble.

'I'm going to work with her, Paul. I was always going. She had more experience than me, though, and she was just setting up – she didn't need an "apprentice" at the beginning. But there's more than enough for two of us to deal with now.'

Paul blinked. The penny dropped. 'You're moving to Spain?' His voice seemed to have got stuck somewhere in his throat. The words sounded raspy and incredulous, as if he'd been dealt a huge blow. But it was surprise that had made him react like that, not dismay.

'And it's perfect timing, don't you see?' She reached across the table and clutched his hand. 'This last time I went over . . . I was just paving the way, finding an apartment to rent—'

'There was no big emergency?'

'I'd had it booked for weeks. But I couldn't tell you, Paul. You weren't ready.'

He drew his hand back, like a tortoise retreating into its shell. 'And I am now?'

'I couldn't believe it when I came back and you told me you wanted to quit Faulkner Jones Burnley.' Francesca's frenzied enthusiasm was almost dizzying. 'And I agree – you need to. But it was more than I could have hoped for. We both need a fresh start, Paul. And it's waiting for us. It's out there.'

He shook his head, dazed. 'What exactly are you saying . . .?'

'I'm asking you to come to Spain with me.' Her voice was firm and fervent as she added, with more audacity than he had ever credited her with, 'I'm in love with you, Paul. And we could be happy together. I know we could.'

The invitation was on cream embossed card, with frayed gold edging.

'*Faulkner Jones Burnley requests the pleasure of the company of Miss Amy Croft & Guest . . .*'

The Christmas Gala. Amy stared at the card, where she'd perched it on her dressing table a few days ago. She hadn't expected to be invited this year, even though she had attended most of the previous ones.

Why hadn't she just chucked it in the bin the minute she'd opened it?

Amy mulled this over, while blowing her nose and then

tugging on the woolly socks she wore to bed. It wasn't as if she was planning on accepting. Even if she'd still been seeing Jonathan, she doubted she would want to go, and take him with her.

'I don't know why they bothered asking me,' she'd griped to her mother.

'Rowena needs to keep you sweet, doesn't she? She has to make it public that she's being nice to you.' Elspeth had provided the insight Amy seemed to be lacking these days. 'She knows very well that you could still make things difficult for her with regard to the boys.'

'But the "Gala" . . . I thought Rowena knew I wasn't keen on them. And don't you think it's a bit spiteful, considering I was always there with Nick . . .?'

'I hate to say it, but I don't think even Rowena's that devious.'

'You could take me as your guest,' Tilly had chirped. 'It sounds like a laugh.'

It had always had the potential to be a wonderful night, Amy acknowledged, if only it wasn't so bogged down by the sense of occasion. For a Christmas party, it was more a case of putting your hair up than letting it down.

'I'm not taking anyone,' Amy had informed her sister, 'because I'm not going.'

But if that was the case, shouldn't she have RSVP-ed by now, declining the invitation with as good a grace as she could muster? Rowena and Isabelle probably hadn't expected her to attend, anyway. After all, how would Amy have the balls to show her face without her children to hide behind?

And even though it was a chance to be near Paul, could she endure seeing him with Francesca on his arm sparkling like a Hollywood starlet at the Oscars? Maybe even with the dreaded engagement ring on her finger . . .

The answer, on both counts, was simple. It was high time she faced up to it.

With a defiant scowl, Amy plucked the invitation from her dressing table and tossed it into the wicker wastebasket by the door.

The coffee Francesca had insisted on making had gone cold. After the bombshell about Spain, Paul had never wanted it anyway.

They had migrated to the lounge, where a modern electric fire flickered around large, smooth, white pebbles and a background of brushed stainless steel.

'I don't understand.' Perched on the sofa, Francesca turned towards him, her hands twisting and untwisting in her lap in a nervous manner he'd never seen about her before. '*Why* can't you come with me, Paul? Moving abroad – it's the opportunity of a lifetime! Do you know how many people would *kill* for a chance like this?'

Paul shrugged. 'I can't . . . I won't . . .' He felt exhausted, in body, mind and spirit. 'There doesn't seem to be a difference, in this case. You claim you're asking me to go, but it feels more as if you're ordering me.'

Francesca opened and closed her mouth, struggling to grasp the concept that she was being turned down. It was written all over her – sheer disbelief. Now she was looking at him as if he was the criminal, the one in the wrong. Her effrontery was expanding by the second, at the same time as her loveliness and her allure seemed to be diminishing.

'But,' she stammered, 'I've already told you . . . I love you, Paul . . . What more is there to say?'

'I'm not sure what you're feeling, but from where I'm sitting, it isn't love,' Paul diagnosed glumly. 'That's probably where you've got the most nerve, claiming that it is.' He shook his head. 'You don't even know me. You've never taken the time to get to know me, not properly.' She was still no closer to understanding the person he was than the day they had first met.

'Paul,' she seemed truly stunned, 'I don't know how you can say that.'

Sighing and rubbing a hand through his hair, Paul wondered how to impart his message without sounding like a total bastard. 'Because it was all so *superficial*.' He hesitated. 'I'm having trouble trying to even remember a moment when it was real.'

'At the beginning!' Francesca protested. 'And when you asked me to live with you . . .'

But even those instances when he'd been mesmerised by her looks and her gazelle-like, physical grace, her lust for life and her ambition and intelligence . . . even those times were being sucked into a huge vacuum. He felt so empty. There was nothing there.

Yet, somehow, he was as guilty as she was. He must have used her. To ease the loss of a best friend, perhaps . . .

At first, though, Francesca had seemed to be all he had ever wanted from a soulmate and partner. But even her 'wisdom' and wit seemed measured now, and calculated; designed only for her own ends. It was so obvious to Paul that while she had once been everything he had ever imagined for himself, she was also the very last thing he needed.

'I'm sorry.' He threw up his hands despairingly. 'I am. *Truly* sorry. And this isn't about Spain, or the fact that you were lying all that time . . . It's about me, for once, and what *I* want.'

Francesca leaned across and clutched his arm. 'Paul, I can be anything you want. Anything. Just tell me . . .'

'If I asked you to stay here in Chester . . .?'

But she was silent; failing the test, even though it meant nothing to him.

'As I thought.' He had been spineless long enough. 'It

doesn't matter, anyway,' he murmured, realising there was only one way to get his point across so that she accepted it, once and for all – by being completely, totally frank with her. 'You see, you fall at the first hurdle.'

Like an animal springing back from a trap, she snatched her hand away. 'Why?' she challenged, her voice quivering. 'What is it, Paul? What is it you want?'

He paused, and frowned at an old ring mark on the coffee table. 'To be brutally honest – somebody else.'

32

Elspeth leaned her elbows on Amy's kitchen table, and cupped her chin in her hands. The holiday brochure lay open enticingly before her, the sea cyan and the sky azure.

'So, what do you think I should do?' she sighed. 'Your father would have hated the idea . . .'

Amy set down two mugs of tea. 'What do *you* want to do?'

'That's what Tilly asked, and it's no help. She more or less implied I was still living in your father's shadow.'

Amy looked at her over her glasses, and didn't reply. She'd had a bad cold recently, and hadn't been able to wear her contact lenses. Her nose and eyes were still red and puffy, and her cheeks a pasty white. If she'd been eating properly, she would have recovered by now, but she was still only picking at her food, like a little bird.

And that was another thing, thought Elspeth. Another reason why she couldn't just drop everything next spring and go on this cruise with Carol. How would Tilly and Amy cope without her for a whole fortnight?

'If it's Tilly you're worried about,' said Amy, 'she can come and stay here. I'll keep an eye on her.'

'I know she'll be seventeen in January, but that doesn't stop me worrying . . .

'Don't I know it,' Amy muttered fondly under her breath. 'I suppose there's the money side of things,' she said louder, with a shrug. 'Cruises don't come cheap.'

Elspeth bit the inside of her mouth. She decided to take the bull by the horns. With a little glossing over, of course. You couldn't just act as if you'd been lying about your financial status for years, even if you had.

'Actually, money isn't the issue,' she said, wetting her lips. 'Your father had more stashed away than I thought . . . there was an endowment policy . . . I can cash it in in the new year, or whatever the term is . . .'

Amy paused with her mug of tea in mid-air. 'Really? Well, in that case, you *should* take a holiday with the money. Lord knows you deserve it. When was the last time you were abroad?'

Elspeth was pleased at her older daughter's reaction. When she'd told Tilly about the supposed endowment, the pound signs had lit up in the teenager's eyes.

She'd put it down to Tilly's age, because the girl had cheekily asked, 'You wouldn't be able to stretch to that school holiday in Greece, too, would you, Mum?'

And Elspeth had just said that she would see, knowing full well that she had always meant for Tilly to go; apparently it was highly educational.

Now, Elspeth admitted to Amy, as if she were in a confessional, 'The last time I was abroad was France, 1967. With my parents.'

Amy regarded her pityingly. 'If Dad hadn't been so xenophobic . . .'

'He wasn't!' countered Elspeth swiftly. 'He didn't *hate* foreigners, he wasn't afraid of them . . . he just didn't fancy that sun and sangria lark. He got a jippy tummy with a spaghetti bolognese.' She sighed. 'Now and again, I would have liked to go somewhere a little further afield than Cornwall or Devon, but your father was very . . .'

'British? In an old-fashioned sense.'

'He just liked the simple things in life, but the things he was *used* to. Ice cream and sandcastles at Newquay. A plate of fish and chips, and a pint of real ale to wash it down with. I'm not criticising him for it—'

'But you don't need to continue the tradition, either. You've never expected it of Tilly and me.'

'No, but that's different.'

'Why?' challenged Amy. 'No one's asking you to forget Dad or go off with someone else. This isn't some bloke asking you out. It's not about that. It's just you doing something for yourself, for a change. I know you feel you've done that with this music thing at the nursery, and trying to branch out to children's parties and stuff, but it's almost as if you've gone too far. You've never been busier.'

'Hmm, maybe. And I'd be doing Carol a favour – you could look at it that way.'

Amy nibbled on a custard cream, as if someone was invisibly forcing her to eat it. 'I suppose there's that. Why did she ask you, though? Presumably she could go with her husband, or is he Velcroed to the sofa now that he's retired?'

'Well,' sighed Elspeth. 'She's always fancied a cruise, and he gets seasick on the ferry to the Isle of Man. That's his excuse, anyway. She just thought I might be more amenable to the idea now that Tilly's older and easier to leave to her own devices.'

Elspeth didn't like the way Amy looked momentarily scep-tical about that, but at least she'd offered to keep an eye on her sister. Elspeth could rely on Amy to be the responsible one when it came to other people, if not to herself.

As the phone rang, and Amy rose with a groan to answer it, Elspeth flicked through the brochure again. It did look lovely. Yet . . .

Her attention was diverted by Amy suddenly sounding as if she'd sucked helium out of a balloon.

'The Christmas Gala?' It seemed to be an echo of whatever the other person had just said.

Elspeth tried not to listen, but it wasn't as simple as closing one's eyes; her ears didn't have lids to act as shutters.

'I hadn't been intending to go . . .' Amy went on. 'What do you mean it's your last one . . .? Well, can't you just tell me now? What's going on, why are you being so cagey? I'm really not sure . . . the invitation said "*and guest*", and who am I meant to bring?' There was a long pause. 'Oh – she isn't? Well, at least let me think about it. Can I call you back . . .?'

Amy hung up the phone and sank back down at the table.

'Who was that?' said Elspeth nonchalantly, pretending she was still engrossed in the brochure.

'Paul.'

'Oh? What did he want?'

'He was trying to persuade me to go to the Faulkner Jones Burnley party.'

'The Gala?' Elspeth couldn't help sneering as she looked up. 'I thought you'd already decided you weren't.'

'I had. But Paul's being mysterious about something.' Amy hesitated. 'To be honest, I think it's just a ploy. He's always hated going to these things on his own.'

'On his own? What about Francesca?'

'Apparently she's not going.'

'Why not? I would've thought it would be right up her street.'

'Paul didn't say exactly, and I didn't want to pry . . .'

Elspeth narrowed her eyes, as if it would make it easier to determine the truth if she looked unconvinced. Was Amy fibbing, or did she honestly not know?

'That isn't very fair on you,' she began, but Amy interrupted, as if she didn't want to see the downside.

'Why not? He's not asking me on a date, after all.' She snorted as if the notion was ludicrous. 'I've got my own invitation, so I wouldn't be his guest. He was just ringing to check if I was planning to go, so he'd have someone to—'

'Hang from his arm?' Elspeth couldn't help scoffing.

'To *sit with* at dinner. These things are boring enough as it is, without having to talk shop all the time.'

'So you've changed your mind and you're going now?'

'I didn't say that.' Amy took off her glasses and rubbed her eyes. 'Just look at the state of me. I'm a wreck! I'd hardly shape up in four days.'

'Four days? I suppose you expect me to babysit?'

'It's too short notice, and these things always drag on . . .'

'I could have the boys over at mine. Then Tilly could help, and you wouldn't disturb them coming in late.'

Elspeth found it hard to believe she was offering. It was odd. As if she and George were having an argument in her head. He would have disliked Paul. Yet deep down, under several layers, and against everything she stood for, Elspeth knew that she didn't.

Amy slipped on her glasses again and frowned at her mother. 'Are you sure? I still don't know if I feel up to it . . .'

'Well, you'd better start eating properly then. I'll make you some chicken soup for tomorrow, you've always liked that.'

'But *four* days!' Amy moaned. 'I've got nothing to wear!'

'It doesn't have to be brand new, does it? What about something you've worn before?'

'The gowns were always hired, Mum. Although for the price, I might as well have bought them. Nick said I'd never wear the same one twice, though.'

'Amy, look, if it's the money you're worried about . . .' Now Elspeth knew she was going barmy. She was offering to pay for her daughter to buy or hire an evening gown, to go to a party where Rowena and Isabelle would be flaunting their own designer apparel, and in the company of a man whose girl-friend, fiancée, whatever she was, would be notably absent.

'I haven't said I'm going yet,' Amy sighed.

'But if you do,' said Elspeth, 'I'd like to think you could hold your own against that lot, and that means looking the part.'

'It's the worst month of the year to get an appointment at the salon. You've got to book weeks in advance, and I just let it slip . . .'

Amy groaned again and peered at her murky reflection in the oven door. Even the loving eye of a mother could see that a simple, basic makeover wouldn't be sufficient; but Elspeth also realised that that wouldn't deter Amy if she made up her mind to go.

Four days wasn't long . . . But, aside from the question of finding a suitable dress, it might be long enough if your mother's best friend's daughter was a hairdresser, and you had a teenage sister with a drawerful of make-up to raid.

33

'Just pull over here . . . Great! We're in luck. There's a space.' Paul indicated to the cab driver to park, and then hopped out. 'Hopefully I won't be long, but you know what women can be like.'

With a grin, the driver shrugged. 'It's your money, mate.'

Adjusting his tie, Paul walked up to the green front door and knocked. A few seconds later, it swung open.

'Hang on a sec,' said the vision who'd answered it, 'I've lost an earring. Can you see it? It's long and dangly and – well,' she twittered nervously, 'it's just like this one.' And she tilted her head and pointed at her ear.

Paul stood rooted to the coir doormat.

Out of the depths of memory, he could dimly hear the lyrics from a musical his mother loved. A man prancing around Paris, warbling about a girl whose potential he had overlooked up till then. Something about standing up too close to her, or too far back.

His mother had been watching it only the other week, her head resting on Paul's father's shoulder while he caught forty winks on the sofa beside her. Paul had been round to collect some plans, and had unwittingly ruminated on how his daily routine as a child had never seemed to coincide with theirs much. Segregated mealtimes, segregated leisure time, including a separate TV from the age of three, which hadn't been as commonplace back then as it unfortunately seemed now. A segregated life, when all was said and done. But how much more warped would he be, Paul had wondered, if his parents' relationship hadn't been as strong and as stable as it evidently still was.

'Oh!' exclaimed the vision in front of him now. 'There it is!' She bent down to retrieve the earring, and Paul was inadvertently treated to a glimpse of her bosom, tightly packed into the fitted bodice. The dress was made from satin, or some similar fabric, and deep greenish-blue in colour. ('Teal', according to an ex-girlfriend who'd worn something like that as a bridesmaid.) It was strapless and straight with deep slits.

Paul knew that most men would just appreciate the overall effect, but he'd always been the sort to notice each element that went into it, too. And it wasn't as if he didn't have the practice.

'Amy, you look . . .' But he tailed off, because he didn't have the nerve to be at his most charming just yet, when everything hung in the balance.

'I scrub up OK, then?' Her reflection smiled at him in the hall mirror as she reclasped the earring. 'And is that your idea of black tie?'

'I never wear a DJ. You know I don't. I can't take myself seriously. I feel like James Bond – as if I'm about to lapse into a Scottish accent and take off Sean Connery.'

Amy giggled, and turned round from the mirror. She reached for a silver-grey, faux fur coat draped over the bottom post of the stairs. He could vaguely remember her wearing it before on special occasions. 'And you don't feel like some sort of gangster in that?' she commented archly.

Paul looked down. He was all in black. Even the shirt. 'A bit funereal, maybe?'

'But it's all in the cut.'

'Well,' he bristled, 'it is.'

'And the label?'

He feigned impatience. 'Are you ready, woman? And where are the kids?'

'I said when I rang you, they're staying at my mum's.' She locked the front door and slipped the keys into a small beaded handbag. 'Is that our taxi?'

'What does it look like?'

'A Ford Mondeo.'

'I'll let that pass.'

He held open the car door for her, but refrained from helping her in. Pulling her leg was one thing, actual physical contact was another. He would need at least two glasses of champagne tonight before attempting it.

'All set?' The driver glanced at them in the rear-view mirror.

Paul nodded. 'As we'll ever be.'

'Thanks for saying we should share a taxi,' Amy murmured a short while later, as they drove out of Harrisfield, past the Cherry Tree Farm site.

'No point drawing straws to see who was going to drive.'

Amy fidgeted in the seat beside him. 'To be honest, I'm surprised Francesca didn't want to go . . .'

Paul frowned out of the window. He didn't know how to tell Amy about Francesca's proposition to him without making it obvious that he wanted her to be aware of his reply.

'She had other commitments,' he said instead.

'Oh.' Amy seemed to hesitate. 'Paul – as friends – you'd tell me, wouldn't you, if anything was wrong . . .?'

As friends . . . Paul was starting to hate that phrase. It implied that Amy was doing him a favour by coming to this party tonight, motivated only out of the goodness of her heart.

If he wasn't honest with her to some degree, though, how could he expect to pull this thing off? However he said it, however it sounded, he needed her to know.

Paul took a deep breath. 'Francesca's moving to Spain . . .'

'*What?*' Amy's head instantly swivelled round to face him.

'. . . and she's asked me to go with her.'

*   *   *

Amy pressed a hand to the side of her face, blinking into the mirror over the vast expanse of pearlescent-veined marble. The taps gleamed, like pirate's gold. The lights embedded in the ceiling winked down at her like stars. Rosewood Grange, she was beginning to appreciate, with the zeal of a born-again connoisseur, really was the most beautiful place.

A girl came out of the far cubicle. She'd been sitting at their table earlier. 'Hiya . . .' Her merry smile rapidly collapsed. 'Are you OK?'

'Oh, um . . .' Amy plundered her brain for something to say.

'You look flushed.'

'A bit too much to drink, probably.'

'Know what you mean – but, hey, it's free!' The girl washed her hands, retouched her lipstick and then glanced at Amy again. 'Are you sure you're all right?'

No, not really, thought Amy. But where to begin?

On the plus side, she felt more glamorous tonight than she ever had in her life. Her hair was exactly how she had imagined wearing it on her wedding day, minus the tiara and veil, of course. It was a sort of Roman style with a modern twist, the gleaming coils invisibly held in place. Carol had confided that her daughter Cherry owed her no end of favours, and it was time to call them in. So she'd managed to drag her back from Manchester for a few hours – all painfully thin, trendily tattooed, five-foot-ten of her, not forgetting the pink-streaked hair – kicking and screaming, Amy had surmised.

The make-up was Tilly's doing. She had begged and bribed Amy to let her, and it had taken some getting used to. But it had suited the glitzy look, even if it was starting to fade a bit now.

The gown had been down to Mum, after hours trawling through Chester, seemingly in vain. Elspeth had spotted it through the window of a nondescript boutique they had missed on their first trek round. It was intended to be worn shorter, around mid-calf, but Amy preferred it to her ankles anyway. As destined as Cinderella's glass slipper, it had been the only one that had fitted around her middle without any need for alterations.

In fact, when Amy had got ready this afternoon, she had felt as if she had not just one, but three fairy godmothers, magically preparing her for the ball. But that was where the happily ever after had ended, because Prince Charming had turned out to be Prince Putting-A-Brave-Face-On-Things. Amy couldn't blame him, considering his most serious relationship ever had just hit a huge, rocky patch. She knew she'd been deluding herself these last four days, but that hadn't stopped her dreaming.

Paul had confided that he wasn't going to Spain with Francesca, but was intending to leave Faulkner Jones Burnley regardless. If not for ever, then for long enough to work out precisely what he wanted from his career. He had explained to Amy that his parents had come to terms with it, accepting his right as an adult to make his own decisions. Amy hadn't seen much evidence of that tonight, however. There was obviously an atmosphere. She was surprised if Paul hadn't noticed, and concerned if he was just pretending to ignore it.

He seemed on a professional high about his plan to go into business on his own, or at least have a crack at it. He wanted to follow his heart for once and devote himself to restoration. Amy had pointed out that there had to be masses of old buildings in Spain, but Paul had pulled a face like a grumpy old man and told her no one could expect him to just up sticks like that. This had only led Amy to question whether he was employing one of those reverse psychology tactics, trying to make Francesca change her own mind by acting as if he didn't give a damn.

All in all this evening, Paul had been his most charismatic, evasive, moody, enigmatic, witty, attentive, confusing self. And Amy wished she wasn't around to witness it, almost as much as she longed for the night never to end.

Everyone required at least one loo-break, though, and it had given her some much-needed breathing space.

Sighing resignedly, she turned away from the mirror and headed for the door. If she hung around here too long, there was more chance of bumping into Rowena or Isabelle. Both women had been cordial bordering on cool with her tonight. She hadn't expected otherwise; as if the children had to be around to remind Rowena who Amy actually was. And Isabelle had never hidden the fact that she adored Francesca, so this hiccup in her mission to make her her daughter-in-law was clearly frustrating her. Amy's presence was only exacerbating matters.

'I think we're raising a few eyebrows tonight,' said Paul, accosting her just outside the Ladies.

Amy gave a start, her hand fluttering to her chest. 'Bugger, you made me jump!'

Paul grinned. His eyes possessed that slightly glazed effect that went with imbibing too much alcohol, but there wasn't any hint of a slur in his voice, so he couldn't be that drunk. 'I've had at least two people asking me – confidentially, of course – if you and I are an item.'

'Really.' Amy sniffed, and made to flick back her hair, forgetting that there was none of it hanging down to flick. 'Well, I suppose it might look as if we came here together . . . But do they really think you'd be so – so cool, after everything that's just happened with Francesca? It's not as if it's even officially over . . . People change their minds all the time, they change their plans . . .' It was agonising to say it, but it was true.

Paul stared at the floor, and leaned languidly against the wall, while Amy frowned up and down the corridor that led off from the reception area, wondering why they were just dawdling there.

'Anyway,' he shoved his hands in his trouser pockets, 'the point is, you and I – we *did* come together. We shared a car, we walked in together, we sat down to dinner together . . . It doesn't take much to trigger a rumour. Believe me.'

Amy wasn't enjoying this conversation. Being tipsy didn't prevent her blushing; in fact, it aggravated it. There was one topic she knew of that was guaranteed to make Paul stop winding her up.

'Was Nick invited tonight, d'you know?' she asked nonchalantly, as if the notion had just entered her head.

Paul hesitated, then nodded. 'He was, even though he's got nothing to do with Faulkner Jones Burnley any more. Except on a personal level, I guess. But, from what Mum says, he's pretty tied up over in the States. I don't envy him.' He frowned, a little thrown. 'Didn't you speak to him recently yourself, though?'

'Mmm,' said Amy non-committally, because she'd known the answer to her last question before she had even asked it.

Paul was right. She'd spoken to Nick about the fact that he was coming back for New Year, discussing how and when he was planning on seeing the kids. She had wanted it all clear before he arrived.

'He does seem busy,' Amy agreed. 'And Anneka seems to have perked up.'

Paul regarded her for a long moment with an expression she couldn't fathom. 'Amy, can I ask you something? Hand on heart . . . are you completely over him?'

Amy could feel the words surge into her mouth. The desire to blurt out the whole, impossible truth. But all she could manage was a nod, a shrug and, 'I'm over *him* – if not exactly over what happened.'

'I don't know if you ever get over something like that, do

you?' Paul stared broodingly again at the short-pile, salmon-pink carpet.

'But you knew I was over Nick,' she frowned. 'When we saw him, last summer . . .'

'Maybe I just needed to hear it again. And Jonathan . . .?'

'What about him?' Amy shrugged again. 'Niamh's responding to treatment, and he loves having his daughter around – and Niamh too, I think, although it's still early days on that front. There'd be so much to sort out, considering their history . . .'

'You don't miss him?'

'Paul, I've told you before—'

He looked up. Something in his eyes made her stop dead.

'Come on.' He took her hand. His fingers were warm and firm. 'D'you realise we haven't danced yet? Plus, we've got a rumour to spread. If we can't laugh with them, we'll laugh at them.'

And faced with her confounded silence, he laughed himself, albeit edgily.

34

In her susceptible state, Paul could have led her to the ends of the earth, however weirdly he was acting. Amy found herself being steered back to the main banqueting suite. Some jazzy number was flowing silkily over the parquet. A disco would have been too tacky; at least for Isabelle, who always seemed a different woman on the dance floor if there was an Ella Fitzgerald soundalike crooning a few classics. Maybe there was a millilitre of romance in her soul, after all.

'I'm not very good at this,' Amy warned, as Paul took her in his arms. He was perilously close to having his foot impaled by her heel.

'Dancing's about feeling, not thinking,' Paul murmured, his breath washing over her and ruffling the fine wisps of hair that had progressively broken free of their constraints. Amy had been poking nervously at her coiffure all night; Carol's daughter would have had kittens.

'That's not my quote, by the way,' Paul went on. 'I think I read it somewhere. Personally, I'm a crap dancer, too. But if you never give it a go . . .'

Amy smiled, and relaxed. If it was all about feeling, then there was nothing wrong in being held this close.

His chin rested against her brow. She closed her eyes dozily, wondering if people ever snatched a quick snooze like this – it felt as if Paul could effortlessly prop her up. It would be so easy to let her mind get carried away, allowing herself to believe precisely what other people might be thinking on seeing them like this.

'Amy . . .'

'Mmm?' She lifted her head automatically in response, but instead of words, she found his lips. As soft and warm and fleeting a kiss as the last one they had shared on his roof terrace. Just as she'd been powerless then, she was a wimp about resisting now. Too weak and dazed to do anything other than blink up into his searching eyes, wondering what was going on. Was he taking the mickey again, or just out to make fools of everyone else?

Amy didn't care. As long as he was still holding her, nothing else seemed to matter much. His mouth brushed against her forehead, and slowly he pulled her closer against his chest. Amy melted into him, like ice cream on a hot day. Resting her head on his shoulder felt so right, so natural. It was one of those moments she wished she could bottle and keep in perpetuity; like first setting eyes on her newborn babies, or watching them take their first solo steps, without their tiny hands wrapped for security around her finger.

'Amy . . .' That voice again, irresistibly Paul.

As she looked up into his eyes, the most amazing shade of chocolate ever created – a thousand times more delicious than anything Willy Wonka could have made in his chocolate factory – she felt her stomach lurch and her heart race.

He stopped dancing, and still holding her hand, started leading the way through the other couples on the dance floor. The faces around them blurred as they wove a path towards the door . . . And then finally they were alone, in a corridor she had never seen before. Paul came to a stop, gave a cursory glance around and then turned to face her.

This time, his kiss meant business. It seemed to involve not just his mouth, but his arms and hands and every part of him she came in contact with, surpassing all Amy's memories of past embraces, both recent and distant. It enveloped her and swallowed her up; sent her spinning and caught her again. His tongue was both ardent and hesitant, his hands gentle but fierce. It was a paradox, yet perfect. Exquisite. Mind-blowing. Whatever invention he was using on her, it ought to be patented.

They drew back at last. His hands gently cupped her face, his fingers tapering up into her hair. His chest rose and fell like a wave beneath the shirt and jacket she was straining not to rip off.

'Amy,' he murmured, 'if you want – I've got a room here . . .'

Ever the pragmatist, she heard herself ask, 'What about the taxi home?'

'I'll cancel it.' As he took out his mobile, he hesitated. 'Amy, you don't have to—'

She silenced him with another kiss, this time perpetrating it herself.

Without asking her again, he made the call, then took her hand and led her towards the stairs.

What happened next was a kind of dance in itself. It didn't seem to involve much thought, but feelings were paramount.

First there were the kisses. The fast, hungry ones as Amy and Paul kicked the door shut behind them, followed by a slow, fumbling, behind-the-bikesheds-style smooch while they both struggled ineptly to free her hair from its constraints.

Giggling feverishly, they staggered towards the enormous, high bed. Paul hit it first, and sat down, wrestling off his jacket. He pulled Amy, still standing, against him. She felt his fingers grapple blindly with the hook and eye fastening at the back of the dress, before tackling the long zip that imitated the curve of her spine.

His clumsiness made her giggle all the more, prompting

Paul to grumble, 'Keep still, woman. How's a bloke supposed to do this with you jiggling about like you're on a spring?'

She traced the line of his jaw with her fingernail. 'And I thought you were so accomplished at this sort of thing.'

'Just for that . . .' He pushed his mouth up against hers again, and in one swift flick of the wrist, had removed her strapless bra and flung it across the room. She wriggled in surprise. The dress crumpled stiffly to her ankles, like a reluctant concertina.

There was only a fraction of a moment in which self-consciousness shivered through her, before passion overtook it with an even greater energy. Paul's mouth worked its way like a small fire down her neck. One arm held her firm against him, while the other cupped her breast, caressing and fondling before slowly tracing the shape of her tummy, which she abruptly sucked in.

As a finger came to rest tantalisingly on the lacy band of her knickers, she jerked and pulled away. They were the prettiest pair she owned, and the ones with the least visible panty line, but she didn't want them to come under close scrutiny. They clearly weren't a size ten, or a thong.

'My turn now,' she murmured.

She knew enough about undoing a tie to manage it – even with her trembling fingers – and dealing with the shirt was a piece of pie. Once bared, Paul's torso was arousingly masculine, without being too hairy or looking as if he spent every waking moment at the gym. Amy ran her hands over it as if it was her life's ambition, but paused as she reached his waist. Even in her heightened state of lust, there were some things that were still taboo. She had never undone a man's trousers. Nick had been put off by any over-assertiveness on her part in bed.

Paul spared her blushes. He pulled something out of his trouser pocket and put it on the bedside table, then stripped off quickly, whipping off the bedcovers and drawing her up beside him before covering them with a sheet again. They lay facing each other, their heads on the pillows, their bodies barely touching, their eyes fused in the longest of gazes. Amy wondered dizzily if anything more was actually going to happen, which allowed common sense to enter her head long enough for her to whisper, 'What about . . .'

He seemed to read her mind. 'It's OK, I've got some,' he muttered back, reaching towards the bedside table.

And then passion took over again. At some point, her knickers and hold-ups came off; she wasn't sure when. Suddenly she was completely naked, but without inhibition or fear. Her body, every part of it, including the wobbly bits, seemed to delight him. And his own keen sense of exploration made her reciprocate. Her hands and tongue roamed and adored, until at last his breathing quickened and he straddled her, primed.

By now, she was desperate herself, and guided him in, moaning as she wrapped her legs around him and drew him in deeper. Her fingers pressed into his back with a mounting need she recognised but which Nick had seldom taken his time to satisfy.

Paul's tongue dipped into her mouth, thrusting hotly and expertly as he mimicked the rhythm of his body. Amy's urgency grew: intensely sweet and yet almost a sort of torment, turning like a coil inside her until eventually – as he started to shudder – the coil was released . . . and she shuddered uncontrollably, too, the seismic explosion of pleasure overwhelming her entirely.

Amy heard herself cry out as if she was so far away she would never be able to find her way back. Yet moments later, she was opening her eyes and blinking in a rosy, dreamlike manner around the hotel room, absorbing details she had been oblivious to before. The framed print of a traditional English garden hanging opposite the bed . . . the china cups on a tray on the dressing table . . . the trouser press . . . the chintz . . . the dark wood . . . Paul's jacket tossed irreverently on the floor.

She felt his head sink on to her shoulder, and his hair, springy with wax or gel – not sticky like Nick's, as she'd expected – lay soft against her cheek. With an elementary sense of fulfilment, Amy was aware of him kissing her neck one last time before his eyes closed and his breathing slowed and settled. Her own arms were still draped around him, but he didn't seem able or willing to peel himself away.

The pillow was like a magnet, dragging her down. She struggled against it, trying to cling to happiness while it was still in her grasp. But she was too exhausted, too sated and too drugged by alcohol and emotion to sustain the effort.

Thinking about what had just taken place was an impossible feat right now, but for the few seconds between consciousness and sleep, she couldn't shake off a niggling portent that when the thoughts finally came, they wouldn't be ones she would welcome.

35

Amy opened her eyes, struggling with the weight of her eyelids. For a few seconds, she blinked grittily at her partially blurred surroundings. Gradually, as her vision cleared, the fragments of memory floated back and aligned themselves to form a still slightly nebulous whole.

Sitting up slowly, with a muted groan, she pulled the sheet over her chest, feeling vulnerable and exposed even though the man beside her was still fast asleep.

She weighed up her options, and finally slid quietly off the bed and made a dash for the bathroom, scooping up her scattered clothing as she went. It would be a luxury to have a bath or shower here, but although her body ached for one, there wasn't time.

Her reflection was ashen in the glaringly lit mirror over the basin. Her eyes glinted strangely, with the first sparks of insurrection, and her lips looked crumpled and red, as if made sore by all those kisses. The numerous layers of her hair were matted. After all that friction against the pillow, it wasn't surprising. Blushing at the recollection, she dragged her fingers through the tangles, trying to ease them out while her brain attempted to make sense of how she could feel so many disparate emotions at the same time.

She dressed quickly, contorting herself as she struggled with the zip, dreading the sound of movement from the outer room. It was only just gone seven. Something had woken her early, like a warning alarm. Adrenalin was coursing through her now, though, rousing her further like the buzz from a strong espresso.

She slipped out of the bathroom and hesitated, gazing down at the man lying on his front, half under the covers. Unwittingly, her eyes traced the curves of his calf, his thigh, his back . . . finally resting on his face, calm and unravaged. So at peace, as if he'd died and found heaven. Damn him.

Even as Amy wondered what would happen if she woke him – longing stirring again, with a mind of its own, in her loins – the intelligent part of her swiftly assessed that she didn't have the strength to explain away the events of last night as if they didn't matter to her, or to accept out loud that it was just a one-night stand. 'We got carried away,' would sound puny, a cop-out.

And besides, this hadn't been just a spur of the moment thing.

Anger writhed in her stomach and flashed in her eyes. Paul had planned this, although for how long was debatable. He had lured her here to Rosewood Grange, plied her with Moët, lulled her into a false sense of security – and then *wham*. He'd had a bed on standby and some Durex to hand.

Perhaps he had been trying to exact a callous revenge on Francesca. Was it all supposed to filter back to her, to stir her into a jealousy frenzy? Maybe, from his vast experience, Paul had sensed Amy's secret attraction to him and had opportunistically played on it. Or perhaps he had just decided that it was about time he satisfied his curiosity and slept with her, like reaching a last outpost known to man? Either way, she'd been stupid and weak, which to some degree made her as culpable as he was.

Amy didn't want to see herself as a victim. She had been as consenting an adult as you were likely to come across. It was her own fault that she was now flitting guiltily like a thief down this empty hotel corridor, making it obvious by her attire that she hadn't planned to stay the night. As far as she was concerned, carrying a torch for Paul was not a mitigating circumstance. And if she was being hard on herself, it was for her own good.

The reception didn't appear to be manned, Amy realised, swearing under her breath as she entered the foyer. She didn't have time to mess around trying to find the name of a reputable taxi firm. She seldom had a need for them, and couldn't remember the one Paul had used last night.

Bitterness rising inside her, Amy scanned the large mahogany counter, then imperiously jabbed her hand down on a brass bell. A door opened to the left behind the reception desk, and a young man slid out. He would have looked slimy and unctuous even if his hair wasn't scraped back over his head like an oil slick. He glanced at her evening dress, and his lips acquired a hint of a sneer. She wondered if she was being paranoid, then realised it didn't matter if she was. Whether or not he was being visibly judgemental, he was thinking it.

'Yes, madam? Can I help you?'

'I need a taxi, please.' Amy kept it short and to the point. The fewer words, the less chance of sounding as fraught as she felt.

'You'd like me to call one for you? No trouble at all.' He sounded so condescending, she could have punched him. 'When would you like it for?'

'Um, as soon as they can come, really . . .' It was only propriety that kept her from leaning across, grabbing him by his maroon silk tie and yelling, 'FIVE MINUTES AGO, you creep!' All men over eighteen were fast becoming the scum of the earth.

This one in front of her now reached for the phone. 'And where would you like a taxi *to*?' he enquired calmly, as she drummed her fingernails on the desk.

'Harrisfield. And could you ask them to hurry please?'

He did as she asked, and replaced the receiver. 'A car will be here in fifteen minutes.'

Amy's insides burst into a mad panic. *Fifteen minutes!* Paul was going to wake up at any moment. He was going to wake up, find her gone and . . . And what? She felt panic dissipate, overtaken ironically by desolation and despair.

He was going to do nothing; or nothing that would involve coming after her, anyway. He would probably frown in bemusement, shrug matter-of-factly, make himself a coffee, take a shower and perhaps ring room service for some breakfast. Not necessarily in that order. And if he felt one ounce of remorse or regret for what he had done, then he would be even more inclined to sit it out.

'Fifteen minutes,' Amy repeated, and swallowed hard to retain her composure. 'Thank you. And, er, one more thing. I left my coat in the cloakroom last night. I can't seem to find my ticket. But it was grey fur with—'

'Don't worry, madam, I'll go and look for it now. Please,' the receptionist gestured to an armchair, 'take a seat. I won't be long.'

Amy couldn't sit, though. Arms folded stiffly over her chest, she paced a faded Persian rug instead. There wasn't a soul about. More than a few people must have stayed over at Rosewood Grange last night. There would be some inescapably sore heads to nurse this morning.

Within five minutes, the young man returned with her coat. Amy instantly shrugged it on, as if up until now she had been wearing nothing but her underwear.

If it had been summer, and sunny, she would have waited outside, seeking solace in the gardens. As it was, she loitered in the porch, frowning out into the dank grey gloom of a rain-washed, wintry morning, wishing she had a thermal vest on instead of a strapless, underwired bra that cut into her ribcage like a medieval implement of torture.

It was only when the taxi came that Amy realised she would have to raid the emergency cash tin in the kitchen when she got home. She only had loose change in her purse.

The driver looked as if he hated early morning starts. For safety's sake, she hoped he hadn't been working all night. He didn't seem in the mood to make small talk, but Amy was glad of the detachment.

She was glad, too, that she'd remembered to put the last of her tissues in her evening bag yesterday. She dabbed furtively at her eyes. If she did possess a stiff upper lip – although there was very little evidence of that – then it was working flat out right now.

Her head was starting to pound. At this moment in time, she wanted only to get home and make a steaming hot cup of tea with a mountain of sugar and take it upstairs to a steaming hot bath. Beyond that – and for the first time since Nick had walked out on her – Amy would have been the first to admit . . . she didn't have a clue.

'Nana, why is it a toothbrush and not a *teeth*brush?' asked Joseph, examining the green one in his hand with a pensive frown.

'I'm not sure. But go on brushing,' Elspeth urged him. 'You've got to keep going till it stops flashing.'

'Mine's stopped!' Mikey triumphantly waved it in the air.

'Good boy. Spit into the basin, then.'

'Nothing to spit. I ate it.' Mikey dropped the brush on the floor and ran off down the landing, his grubby blankie trailing along the carpet behind him.

Elspeth cast her sternest look after him, then transferred it to Lucas, who was sitting on the bath mat intently sucking the bristles of his own brush. He gazed up at her with his mother's eyes, and Elspeth instantly relented.

'So,' said Joseph, after spitting out blue froth, 'why is it called a toothbrush, Nana? Even Lucas hasn't just got one tooth any more.'

'I, um . . . I don't know.' Elspeth sighed. 'Maybe for the same reason a hairbrush isn't a hairsbrush.'

'Which is what?' continued Joseph, cocking his head to the side.

Elspeth shrugged. 'Nanas don't know everything, Joe.'

'Well, people brush their *teeth*, but they only brush their *hair*.'

Grief. At this rate, he'd have a doctorate by the time he was six.

'Why don't you ask your teacher at school on Monday?' Elspeth suggested helpfully.

'O-*K*. It's Christmas soon. It'll be a holiday. That means I don't go to school and Mummy doesn't go to work.'

'Yes, I know, poppet.' Thank the Lord for small mercies. The child had changed the subject.

'Nana, why did we have to brush our teeth after *lunch*? Mummy makes us do it after breakfast and at bedtime only.'

Oh, damn. 'Because you had orange juice and ice cream,' Elspeth explained, muttering under her breath, 'and your mummy will kill me for it.'

'Why will Mummy kill you?'

Joseph obviously had superior hearing.

'Er – because all that sugar's bad for your teeth.' Not to mention everyone else's sanity once the sucrose kicked in.

'Nana, is Mummy coming here soon, or are you taking us to our house in your car?'

Mulling this over, Elspeth nibbled on a thumbnail. Amy was supposed to have rung by now. It was after half one.

'I'm not sure. I'll have to speak to her, Joe.'

He seemed satisfied with that, and ran off to play with Mikey. Elspeth scooped up Lucas, wrestled the stubby tooth-brush out of his grasp and carried him downstairs, snuffling and squirming like a small wild animal against her chest. He'd caught another cold, poor mite.

Tilly and Keira were both poring over the computer in the lounge.

'You're not on the internet, are you, Tilly, love? Amy might be trying to get through . . .'

'No, Mum. It's just a new game. A sort of blind date thing.'

Very girly, thought Elspeth. Although whether it was better than zapping villains with ray guns or ghetto blasters, or whatever they were called, would be worth looking into later, considering the content of teen magazines these days. Or, worse still, those not-so-teen glossies Tilly had started buying. George would have had a fit. And Elspeth didn't even understand what half the articles were going on about, which no doubt meant that Tilly did.

'You really should consider broadband,' suggested Keira. 'My dad's had it ages.'

Longer than his current girlfriend? Elspeth wanted to retort, but bit her tongue. Keira was getting on her nerves these days, ever since she'd hit seventeen and had had her naval pierced as a birthday present. Tilly now wanted hers pierced, too, but Elspeth was digging her heels in.

'You let me have my ears pierced when I was ten!' Tilly had pointed out bolshily one day.

'That's different.'

'Why?'

'Because it is. And I only let you wear small, gold studs.'

'Well, all I want to wear in my belly button is a little, silver stud. Amy doesn't think there's anything wrong with it, do you, Amy?'

'Er, if you've got a nice taut tummy, I suppose not,' Amy had muttered diplomatically over her Lemsip. 'You'd never catch me drawing attention to my spare tyre, though.'

Tilly, Elspeth had conceded, had the figure for it. But if you had a piercing like that, she'd reasoned to herself, then you'd want to show it off. And that would mean even lower hipster trousers and shorter crop tops.

Tilly was either a late bloomer, or Elspeth just hadn't been paying enough attention, because she was looking more like a young woman by the day, and an attractive one at that. Soon, there would be a boy loitering about, with intent. Elspeth was surprised that there hadn't been one already.

'I think I'm going to ring Amy,' she announced decisively, plonking Lucas on the floor with some wooden blocks to amuse him. He just stared at them, groggy from his cold.

'Oh, Mum,' sighed Tilly, 'Amy probably had a really late night. I think you should leave her to it. She'll call when she's recovered.'

But something – a mother's intuition, maybe – was telling Elspeth not to. She rang the house first, but there was no answer. So she tried Amy's mobile. It was switched off.

'That's it.' Elspeth reached for her coat and rummaged in her bag for her car keys. 'I'm going round there. Something's not right.'

'*Mum—*'

'No, this is all my fault. I should never have encouraged her to go to that bloody party.'

Tilly and Keira stared at Elspeth with wide, round eyes. She realised she had sworn, but didn't care.

'Well, I encouraged her, too,' shrugged Tilly.

'But I'm old enough to have known better.' Elspeth patted her hair, which felt windswept even though she hadn't set foot outdoors yet today. 'Lucas will want his bottle around three. It's in the fridge.'

Keira's eyes grew even rounder. 'But we're going out.'

'If I'm back soon, then by all means you still can, Keira.'

There was the sound of banging from upstairs, followed by wailing. 'Mikey broke my Power Ranger!' howled Joseph.

Keira's eyes now seemed charged with panic. Tilly, on the other hand, looked wearily resigned. Unless a girl was broody beyond hope, taking care of other people's children was sometimes the best contraceptive available. Elspeth felt reassured that Tilly would cope with her nephews as responsibly as always, but couldn't help smirking at the image of Keira wiping a pooey bottom.

Her smugness soon receded, however, as she slammed the front door behind her and hurried to her car. She couldn't shake off the heavy, ominous feeling that something had happened, and she was bagging a parking space in March Street a few minutes later.

There was no answer when she knocked and rang the bell, so she exercised her prerogative as a concerned mother and used her spare key.

'Hello?' she called softly . . .

There was no one downstairs, and it was only as she went back into the hall again that Elspeth hesitated and felt her cheeks glow like hot coals. What if Amy wasn't upstairs on her own . . .?

But then the thought struck her: what if Amy wasn't up there at all? Where could she be?

Elspeth called out another hesitant greeting, and thought she heard rustling. She ascended slowly, and reached halfway when a figure suddenly appeared at the top of the stairs, making her freeze.

'Mum?' Amy was scratching her head, her face scrunched up in confusion. 'What time is it?'

'Nearly two . . . I tried calling you a while ago.' Elspeth took in the old mottled dressing gown, followed by the dishevelled hair, like Kate Bush on one of her wilder days. Which made it highly unlikely that there was anyone up there with Amy to witness it. 'Are you ill?'

'If a hangover counts. I lost track of time, Mum, I'm sorry. I had a really bad headache before and took some of my stronger painkillers.' Amy winced as she said it. 'They must have knocked me out.'

'Not a very good idea if you've been drinking.' Elspeth frowned. 'You look terrible. What time did you get home last night?'

Her daughter looked away, chewing on her lip.

'Amy . . .?'

'I didn't,' she replied tonelessly. 'I didn't get home till about eight this morning.'

Elspeth blinked. 'Oh . . . But the party couldn't have gone on—'

'It didn't. I stayed over at Rosewood Grange.'

'Oh,' said Elspeth again, marvelling at how she could feel so calm. 'Right.'

'It wasn't, though.' The pitch of Amy's voice was rising. Elspeth recognised the threat of hysteria, and immediately hastened up the last few stairs. 'It wasn't right at all,' Amy thrashed on, 'it was the biggest mistake of my life . . .' And with that, the floodgates opened, letting a torrent of emotion through so that Elspeth had to act fast.

She had a quick scout around, then returned to her daughter's side, putting a consoling arm around Amy's trembling, heaving shoulders.

'I'm afraid you'll have to make do with toilet roll, love.' She'd torn off a long strip, hoping its cushiony softness would be adequate enough to soak up the tears. 'I can't seem to find any tissues . . .'

36

Elspeth felt as if she were twenty again. A snivelling wretch, hunched up on her bed, her face buried in a handkerchief embroidered by her mother with her initials, ELC . . . Elspeth Laurel Cullen. A mouthful, she'd always thought. Too many 'l's. It had been a pleasant change to become a Croft, keeping the same initials yet with a nicer ring to her name. Of course, all ELC had predominantly come to mean to her was Early Learning Centre, but she'd long ago ceased being peeved about it.

And all that mattered right this minute, anyway, was her daughter; because this time it was Amy who was the snivelling wretch sitting hunched on a bed.

The circumstances surrounding it were similar, Elspeth acknowledged. At any rate, it was to do with a man. Beyond that, it was still hazy. Elspeth couldn't quite get a grasp on it. Maybe because Amy had babbled the story between sobs.

She was growing calmer now, although indignation was still glittering in her eyes. She sat clutching a pillow to her stomach, her chin resting on it with a bruised but defiant air.

'So,' ventured Elspeth, sighing, 'let me get this straight. You're telling me that Paul and Francesca have split up?'

'Sort of split.' Amy sniffed, and leaned back against the pine headboard, still clutching the pillow, like a shield. 'She's going to Spain – I'm not exactly sure when, it could be tomorrow for all I know – and Paul says he isn't.'

'The wedding's definitely off, though?'

'I'm not convinced there was a wedding in the first place. While we were having dinner at the Gala, Paul said something about a misunderstanding. He even seemed to imply that Tilly knew about it. But he was being so bloody obscure, and I didn't want to act as if it mattered that much to me.' Amy snorted sardonically.

Elspeth frowned. 'And Francesca will be working in Spain for this friend of hers?'

'Apparently she's been planning it for ages, but conveniently forgot to mention it to her boyfriend.'

'And you're trying to say that Paul . . . "orchestrated" last night with you on the rebound?'

Elspeth hadn't wanted to know the finer details – this was her daughter, after all – and thankfully, Amy had been too embarrassed or ashamed to elucidate.

Amy picked at a long thread on the pillow cover. 'On the rebound. Maybe to get back at Francesca.' She shrugged. 'Or because he likes a challenge.'

Elspeth wet her lips, realising that it was about time she stopped skirting around the issue of Paul Faulkner Jones, or dropping sly insinuations instead of asking Amy outright. It was also no good being prudish about something that was too late to undo. Paul and Amy had more than just danced last night. Elspeth had to grant that she'd played a part in the lead-up to it. And what was the point in trying to close the stable door once the horse had bolted? Much better to stop whinge-ing about it and go searching for the horse instead.

'Are you sure it would have been a challenge?' she said, wishing Amy would lift her head so she could look her in the eye.

Amy did look up, in an obstinate, flinty manner. 'What do you mean?'

'I mean . . .' Elspeth sighed, distractedly smoothing the rumpled bedcovers, 'that you haven't been as distant with Paul lately as you used to be.'

Amy stared at her for a long moment, then groaned. 'Is it that obvious?'

Elspeth chose her words painstakingly. 'That you care about him?'

'"Care"?' Amy snorted again. 'Had a massive, schoolgirl crush on him, more like! And I've acted like a schoolgirl – letting him seduce me like that.'

Even to Elspeth, this sounded a rather old-fashioned way of putting it, but it was the fact that Amy was calling it a crush that stood out more. To a 55-year-old mother of two and grandmother of three – even if she had led a slightly cloistered existence – it somehow didn't strike the right chord.

'Is that all it is?' she insisted. 'A crush?'

'You can call it an infatuation, if you want,' scowled Amy, 'considering you've got a degree. A stupid, mad *infatuation*. For Pete's sake, this is Paul we're talking about, Mum! Straight out of some Gypsy Rose Lee crystal ball. Tall, dark and handsome. Every woman's fantasy – and my curse. He always has been. There's probably some psychological term for it. These last few months, I've been depraved. Mooning over some other woman's boyfriend. Someone I used to wish would just drop off the face of the earth. Oh, don't look at me like that, Mum. It doesn't matter whether or not Paul and Francesca are together any more. They were definitely going out back then. That's what counts.'

'Surely,' floundered Elspeth, 'Paul's own feelings ought to come into it somewhere, too?'

'His feelings?'

'He must have some, you know. His heart's not a brick. But you're making out he's some sort of pathological Machiavellian type. All these months he's been helping you and the boys . . . are you trying to say it was all part of some elaborate scheme?'

Amy looked sheepish. 'No . . . I haven't got a big enough head to imagine he'd been planning this for months.'

'Well, then.'

'But he *had* planned it. The room was booked, he had . . . thingies on him.' Amy picked at the loose thread again, her face so red it was almost luminous. 'All it took was a few glasses of champagne and . . .' She squeezed her eyes shut, as if to block out the memory. 'I'm not saying I was trolleyed. But I wasn't sober, either. He'd probably worked out ages ago that I fancied him. He knew it wouldn't take much . . . Shit.' She shook her head. 'Sorry. But I can't work out how all this happened. He used to do nothing for me. Nothing. And I went from that to . . . to *this*.'

Elspeth rubbed a hand tiredly over her brow. 'I fell in love with your dad in five minutes flat. Five minutes – that was all. And I thought I was so heartbroken over Nigel . . .'

Amy jerked her head up. '*Nigel?*'

'My "first love". My first boyfriend. My first everything, basically.'

'Your . . .? But – Mum! I always thought . . .'

'That's what I wanted you to think, you and Tilly. How would it have looked, otherwise? Your perfectly moral mother, not being a virgin on her wedding night. But it was just the once, and I wasn't exactly sober, either. It was at university . . . I wasn't one of the in-crowd, never very cool or popular. People said I was pretty, but that I didn't make the most of myself. I suppose that was simply the way I was brought up. I was into books. Just like Tilly. Or at least, like she used to be. I loved the classics. Jane Austen, the Brontës . . . On a personal level, love and romance were much easier – and safer – between the pages of a novel.'

She sighed raggedly. 'But then Nigel came along. Well, I suppose he'd always been there. One of the popular set. But I can't say I really noticed him until he actually deigned to notice me. We went out a few times, and on one particular occasion, his car ran out of petrol . . .'

Amy's eyes were on stalks. 'You fell for that one?'

'One of the oldest in the book. Well, since cars were invented. But I did. And not long later, I realised I was pregnant.'

Amy was now sitting cross-legged in front of her, mouth gaping open, the sanctuary of her pillow long since discarded. Elspeth reached out assuagingly and stroked her daughter's hair.

'It wasn't you, love. I lost it long before I was even showing, but not before Nigel had broken up with me. I thought I'd never get over it. I was convinced all men were like him, and the only kind I could trust was the fictional sort, provided they were the heroes of course and not the villains.'

'But Dad . . .?'

'Well, you know how we met. I ploughed into him on my bicycle. And he acted as if it was all his fault. I mean nowadays, he probably would have sued me or something.' Elspeth laughed introspectively. 'But back then . . . He was so concerned about whether *I* was all right, he never seemed to notice the great gash on his arm.'

Amy reached for the toilet roll that was lying on the bed between them. She tore some off, and then divided that into two and passed a piece to Elspeth. She sighed, and trumpeted her nose loudly. 'You and Dad were perfect for each other.'

'But he's gone. And no one's a hundred per cent perfect for someone else. It would be dull if they were.' Elspeth blew her nose, too, and dabbed at her eyes. 'Sometimes, I think I remember him in totally the wrong way.'

'Not how he really was, you mean?'

'No . . . By trying to *be* him. Act like him, think like him. I've been doing it for fourteen years. It would be nice just to be me.'

Amy nodded slowly. 'And you're recalling Dad as he was.

He would have changed as he got older. In small increments maybe, but no one stays exactly the same.'

'I like to think he might have mellowed . . . He was a good man, but he expected everyone else to be just as good. It would be nice if the world worked that way – the way he saw it. If everyone had the same loving childhood, and the same capacity to pass that on in life.'

'Mum, you're getting maudlin.'

'I'm counting my blessings, love. And I'm trying to say that I wouldn't swap the time I had with your dad, even if I'd known then that it wasn't going to last as long as we were planning.'

Amy squeezed her mum's hand. 'You were lucky you found him.'

Elspeth began to nod, then realised that it wasn't quite the truth. 'No,' she said carefully, 'I was lucky that I *recognised* I was lucky. Some people never do.'

Amy looked away, out of the window. The afternoon light was dwindling fast. 'Did Dad know about you and Nigel? Did he know about . . . the baby?'

Elspeth could still see George's face even now. He had been five years older than her. Protective and idealistic, he had lifted her on to a pedestal where she was sweet, innocent and unblemished; academically clever, yet naïve in the ways of the world. Honesty and exasperation had forced her to confess to him that this image of her was tarnished.

It was love, she supposed, that had turned things around when they could have gone so wrong. Love that had let him see past her mistakes. That was the day he had stopped calling her his Little Ellie, and had asked her to marry him. The day he had started treating her as his equal, and appreciating that she was just as capable of looking after him as he was of her.

'Yes, he knew about Nigel,' Elspeth nodded. 'And he knew I'd had a miscarriage. But he also knew that what mattered most was how we felt about each other.'

'It wasn't as if you'd cheated on him. He didn't have anything to forgive.'

'No. No, he didn't.'

'I wish you'd told me all this before.'

'Why? And why do you think I'm telling you now?'

'Um . . .' Amy shrugged, the ancient dressing gown almost slipping off her shoulders, revealing the strap of her oldest, comfiest, ugliest nightie. She had clearly opted to regress, to make herself feel better, Elspeth noted. Like a child sucking their thumb again when they'd long since stopped. 'So I don't feel so bad about what happened last night?' Amy continued. 'Because it happened to you once, with this Nigel?'

Elspeth pursed her lips in frustration. She couldn't work out how to get her point across without drawing a diagram. And yet, how could she, when she wasn't completely certain herself? She couldn't read Paul's mind; she wasn't privy to his thoughts. It was just a hunch.

How Amy felt was another matter entirely, though, and maybe it would be enough for now merely to get her to see that.

'Paul's nothing like Nigel,' Elspeth said firmly. 'He's more like George, really.'

'Like Dad?' Amy's naturally slender eyebrows shot upwards. 'But he's everything Dad hated.'

'He's everything good that your dad was,' smiled Elspeth. 'Of course, with a few extra bits that George, admittedly, wouldn't have approved of. But if you scratch the veneer long enough . . . and Lord knows, I've been doing it as long as you have . . . he's a decent man.'

'With another notch on his bedpost today,' argued Amy stonily.

'I don't believe he'll see it that way. Whatever happened, you're his friend.'

Amy grunted. '*Was*. Past tense. How can I just go back to

how we were before? I know people do it, but I can't face it myself. Something has to change. And in this case—'

'Well, if it wasn't all that platonic in the first place . . .'

'Rub it in. As if I don't feel crap enough already. Sorry, Mum, but I do.'

'Perhaps another one of your mistakes was not sticking around this morning to hear what he had to say.'

'Right.' In another defensive stance, Amy folded her arms over her chest. 'If it was that important, wouldn't he have come round here by now to say it?'

'Why should he? You ran off earlier without giving him the chance. What's he supposed to think? In the end, who rejected who?'

Amy was truly glaring at her now, but as long as all this was making her think, Elspeth wasn't deterred.

'It's not about rejection, Mum.'

'What's it about, then? If he had woken up while you were there this morning, what would you have wanted him to say? Amy, what do you want to hear most?'

Her daughter was staring past her now, at the wall dotted with photos of the boys as babies. Amy loved photos everywhere around the house, making it so much her own space, it was an estate agent's nightmare.

She didn't reply, so Elspeth went on softly, 'I think you need to speak to him, love. You can't leave it hanging like this. And he won't be horrible to you. Not Paul. Whatever he has to say, it won't be half as bad as everything cluttering up your head right now. You're only being cruel to yourself by letting this stew.'

Amy gulped, nodded, and slid off the bed. 'Maybe . . . I need to think about it.'

Elspeth rolled her eyes despairingly, *à la* Tilly.

'Don't look at me like that, Mum. Time's getting on. The boys'll be wondering what's happened, and I don't want them messed around any more than they already have been.'

Amy was right on one score, Elspeth acquiesced. Joseph, Mikey and Lucas mattered most. And in the short term, goodness knew what horrors Keira and the three children were mutually inflicting on one another.

Elspeth sighed, and stood up herself, her joints aching from having sat in such an awkward position for so long. 'Do you want me to go and fetch them, then?' she asked.

'If that's OK?' Amy was peering in the mirror, dragging down her eyes to scrutinise them better. 'Oh, hell. I look like death warmed over.'

So that was that, thought Elspeth wearily. Definitely no facing Paul today. Not when the whites of Amy's eyeballs would be better renamed the pinks.

Elspeth remembered the day she'd bared her soul to George . . . No mascara (in case of tears – and there'd been plenty, mainly of joy, thank God) but a soft smudge of peachy lipstick, so natural it was barely there. And as for her hair – she'd never taken so much time over sweeping up her gleaming chestnut curls into the style he'd liked best.

Catching a glimpse of her reflection now as Amy moved away from the mirror, Elspeth stopped dead. Still the same style, just not so much time and attention lavished on it. And as for 'gleaming' – that was a joke. How many of those brittle, wiry hairs were grey, and how many were merely split ends?

Perhaps it was about time she cut herself loose, Elspeth frowned, tweaking determinedly at a curl straggling over her ear.

In more ways than one.

37

That was it, thought Amy, tossing the phone down on the bed. This was what the world was coming to. You sent a perfectly straightforward text message to your little sister's mobile and got a reply in a language only teenagers and twenty-some-things understood.

She slid down under her duvet, appreciating the silence that descended on the house when the children were all in bed, but knowing she wasn't going to get much sleep herself.

The bottom line was, she was ancient. Backward. And the knowledge had all come about because Tilly was out, and her mobile was either off or had no coverage. Amy had left a message, but had then decided to text her, too. 'Need to speak to you – asap.' And eventually, around half tennish, a reply had beeped back: 'will b l8 in 2nite, c u 2morrow, r u ok??'

Amy had deciphered the code, of course. Just as she'd deciphered that Tilly was with Keira and the rest of the blonde brigade, and possibly up to no good. But as she could hardly talk, considering what had happened at Rosewood Grange the night before, Amy decided not to press her mother on it.

According to Elspeth, Keira's mum would be driving Tilly back to Harrisfield because she was dropping Keira off at her dad's anyway. How girls got home when they were out late, thought Amy, always seemed more of an issue than what they were actually up to while they were out.

Tilly looked remarkably spry for someone who had prob-ably been gadding about past midnight, noted Amy enviously, when her sister arrived just after breakfast the following morning. Hands tucked into the pockets of her voluminous pants, she ambled into the living room as if all was well with the world, straight into an argument where *Thomas the Tank Engine*, the movie, was vying with *Bob the Builder*, the long-length Christmas special.

'Uh-oh,' Tilly pulled a face, 'bad time?'

Amy wrestled the DVDs out of her elder boys' clutches, and slid in an old Teletubbies video. Lucas immediately stopped playing with some Mega Bloks and turned to stare at the TV screen, sucking his thumb, enthralled. Sulkily, Joe and Mikey flopped on to the sofa and after a few moments of huffing and puffing, settled down to watch Tinky Winky prancing about in a tutu.

'Welcome to my world,' sighed Amy, dragging her slippers into the kitchen. Tilly followed, looking so perky Amy wanted to boff her. 'Tea?' She lifted the gingham cosy she'd bought at a craft fair in the summer.

'Christ, Amy, are you making it by the bucketload now?' Tilly blinked at the huge teapot.

'Let's face it, I'm turning into Mum. And don't say "Christ" like that. I'm trying to get Joe to stop saying "Oh, *God*," like he's some great theatrical actor, and that's bad enough.'

'Sorry. He can't hear us from here, can he?'

'He can hear through walls. Then again, so can I. At least, I can hear the kids.' Amy slumped at the table. 'So, do you want tea, or not?'

'Not. Thanks. Just some water. I'm detoxifying myself before Christmas.'

'So you were teetotal last night, were you?' Amy watched as Tilly helped herself to water out of the fridge and then sat down at the table.

'Actually, I was on the Evian. We went to see a film.'

'Oh . . . I thought . . .'

'Well,' grinned Tilly, 'I'm not quite as debauched as you.'

Amy chewed on her lip. There was no witty comeback to that. 'Er, did Mum . . . did she say anything to you about . . .?'

'You and Paul? Hope you were careful, by the way, if you know what I mean. And she didn't have to say anything – even though she did – I could work it out for myself. Anyway, it was all a bit rushed when she got back from here yesterday, but I've had an earbashing this morning. She wanted to know what I knew – about Paul and Francesca. And *how* I knew. And why I hadn't said anything.' Tilly paused, pushing the glass of water around the table. 'I s'pose that's why you want to talk to me, too.'

'I'm confused . . .'

'You don't say.'

'Tilly, Paul hinted something about his engagement to Francesca being a rumour that went too far. He insinuated that you knew about it, but he didn't seem overly surprised that you hadn't mentioned it to me . . .'

'Chinese whispers, or what,' snorted Tilly. 'What was I supposed to do? Paul had plenty of opportunity to tell you himself, but he didn't. So I figured that maybe he was trying to make you jealous, and it wasn't my place to interfere.'

'Not your place? You're always interfering! And why would he be trying to make me jealous?'

'*Because*,' sighed Tilly. 'Do I have to spell it out? Anyway, there was obviously some grown-up game playing going on, and I didn't want to muck it up, me being a child and all that.'

'Tilly,' said Amy exasperatedly, finding herself no nearer to unravelling this mess than when her sister had turned up, 'these are people's feelings you're talking about. I can't help thinking you've been playing games yourself for months.'

'Hey, don't accuse me of being anything other than a concerned sister. And according to Mum, you're the one making out Paul hasn't got any. *Feelings*, that is.' Tilly loftily adjusted the toggle of her sweatshirt. 'I hate to sound clichéd, Amy, but if I'd just been able to bang your heads together, believe me, I would have.'

Amy wondered how much of that would stand up to a lie-detector test. Tilly had a mischievous sense of humour that delighted in playing games. She would have fitted in perfectly in *A Midsummer Night's Dream*. Plus, she loved trying to get into other people's heads. Which might actually mean that she was the best person of all to have seen this debacle from both points of view. And if she genuinely wanted to help . . .

'Tilly—' Amy began, more serious than ever, but she was interrupted by Mikey trotting into the kitchen and hoisting himself on to her lap, demanding a 'huggle'.

Amy frowned and cuddled her son, but ploughed on regardless, 'Tilly, what do you – um – think I should do . . .?'

'Go and see him,' said the teenager, without hesitation. 'You skipped out on him, after all. Paul might not want to lay himself on the line again . . .'

'Mummy,' said Mikey, latching on to this, 'what line doesn't Paul want to lie on again?' But before she could rack her brains for a reply, he rambled on in his characteristic, desultory way, 'He hasn't seen my Action Man trainers. They're new. He likes Action Man. He told me he had one once upon a time, and its eyes went like this.' Mikey wiggled his baby-blue eyes from side to side.

Tilly smothered a laugh. Even Amy had to concede a smile.

'So,' said Tilly, 'it's sorted then. That's what you should do.'

'What?' said Mikey.

'Your mummy will have to go and see him.' Tilly emphasised her words carefully. 'As soon as possible. Before it's too late.'

'Today?' enthused Mikey.

Amy shook her head. 'Not today . . . I can't. We're going to eat at Jonathan's, remember? It's been planned for ages . . .'

'Yay! I like Sally-Ann. She lets me play with her 'puter games. And her mummy's nice, too – she tickles me and does "Round and Round the Garden like a Teddy Bear" lots and lots!'

Tilly was still staring fixedly at Amy. 'Tomorrow, then. You can go and see Paul tomorrow, can't you? It's your day off.'

'Yes.' Amy nodded. 'Yes, it is.'

'I want to go.' Mikey prodded at the tea cosy.

'You'll be at nursery,' said Amy. 'But don't worry, I'll tell Paul about the trainers.'

'And he can come to our house, and I can show him? When can he come, Mummy? Wendy's Day? Fur's Day?'

'We'll have to see,' said Amy, wondering when she'd be able to laugh again. 'I can't promise anything . . .'

'But she's going to try,' said Tilly pointedly. 'With all her *heart*.'

Most of the way on the A55 towards Chester, Amy wanted to turn the car one hundred and eighty degrees and flee back home. Aside from the fact that she was on a dual carriageway and would have crashed if she'd tried to do it literally, she knew she couldn't go on being a coward any more.

She had called her feelings a lot of things lately – except the one heading they all came under; but relabelling it, or cringing from it as if it might sting her, or simply pretending that it didn't matter . . . none of that made how she felt go away.

And since the Christmas Gala, things had only got worse; like a superbug virus that had taken hold and wouldn't respond to simple antibiotics. The only way to get better seemed to be the hardest medicine of all to take. Because how was she going to tell him? How was she even going to form the words? And how would they sound in the confines of his flat and the cold light of day?

She eventually found a parking space in the road adjacent to his, and forced her feet along the pavement towards his front door. It was shut fast. The intercom system must be working – for once. With a shaking hand, she pressed the button for Flat B. There was no answer, so she tried again. Still no answer. And she couldn't see his car parked anywhere . . .

Amy huddled deeper into her anorak, and stared miserably at her black ankle boots, splattered with mud. She hadn't seemed to register how dirty they were before. She had been so single-minded in her purpose this morning, she'd probably sent the kids to nursery in mismatched socks.

Paul wasn't in. That was a risk she'd taken, because she couldn't reconcile this as the kind of confrontation that you made an appointment for. It was launch-right-in-blindly-and-hope-you-make-sense sort of stuff. If she'd called and said she was coming over to speak to him, what if he'd said no? What if he'd just hung up? Her mind was in overdrive, zig-zagging around the various possibilities. Choosing a time of day when he might be at home working had seemed the best plan. Obviously, it had backfired. But Amy didn't want to go back to Harrisfield yet to face her mother.

The centre of Chester would be heaving with Christmas shoppers, too stressed and one-track minded for her to endure. She could go to the river, though, and walk along there for a while. It wasn't so cold that she would freeze. In fact, the crisp air might clear her head and energise her, enough to bring her back here later to try again.

Just as Amy was turning away, though, she heard a clicking sound. Swinging back round, she saw the door opening. Her heart leapt with the anticipation of seeing him again. In the dizziness of the moment, it overrode all her fears.

But it wasn't Paul standing on the threshold.

The elderly lady was shorter than Amy, with frizzy white hair that stuck out around her head as if she'd been recently electrocuted. Her eyes looked full of sparks, too, yet the skin of her jowls hung down like soggy crêpe paper. It was impossible to guess accurately how old she was. She seemed to be somewhere between eighty and a hundred and ten.

'I was on lavatory,' she announced crossly, her voice crackly and loud, with an accent that Amy found hard to pinpoint as anything other than European. 'I could not come to door sooner.'

Amy apologised, then added confusedly, 'Are you a relative of Paul's?' Both his grandmothers were dead, and his Great Aunt Bronwen was Welsh, not Italian or Lithuanian or whatever this lady in the Seventies' flowery housecoat was.

'Of Mr Paul upstairs?' She jabbed her long, bony finger upwards and curled her lip in distaste.

Amy nodded, and the penny dropped. 'You live in the flat below, don't you?'

The old lady nodded briskly. 'And buzzer is not working properly again. Always bloody cocked-up. The idiot who fixed it last time mix up wires, and when my button is pressed it ring in Mr Paul's apartment, and when you press his button it ring in mine. You are looking for him, yes? I recognise you.'

Amy nodded breathlessly, her heart leaping like a wild deer again. 'So Mr Paul – I mean, Paul – is in? If I press the button for Flat *A*, then—'

The elderly little woman was shaking her head. 'No, no. Gone. He is gone. I was cleaning in hall. No one else would clean, not even cleaner he has who come once a month. She is lazy. Old. So, I am cleaning, and Mr Paul come down the stairs with suitcase—'

'A suitcase?' Anchored down with a sudden dread, Amy's heart stopped skipping about. 'When . . .?'

'This morning.'

'Did he say where he was going . . .?' Her voice had now been reduced to a croak.

Paul's neighbour shrugged and shook her head. 'He not say much. Just goodbye and how he is in hurry to get to airport. He look ill, but I not ask questions. It will be quiet while he is gone. Good, I say. He walk on floor upstairs, and it sound like bloody herd of bullocks. And when he play music like rock and roll!' She threw her hands up in the air. 'Maybe he go away now for all of Christmas. I can pray to God, yes?'

Amy felt as if this batty-looking old woman had torn her to shreds with one single slash. Unwittingly, of course, but it had killed her nonetheless. It was clear where Paul had gone. So glaringly obvious it might as well have been written in a neon sign above the door.

Paul had gone to Spain.

He had gone to Spain to be with Francesca.

PART THREE

'Heap on more wood! – the wind is chill;
But let it whistle as it will,
We'll keep our Christmas merry still.'
                    Sir Walter Scott, *Marmion*

38

'Why are you wearing a pillowcase?' asked Tilly, cocking her head to one side.

'It's an old one,' muttered Amy, determined not to rise to the bait. 'Has Mum got Mikey and Lucas?'

'Nope, I brought them. Mikey wanted to walk here – past the sweet shop, of course – and Lucas was asleep in the buggy.'

'So where are they now?'

'Well, Mikey's with Joe's lot – I think he wants to join in, be a shepherd or something – and Lucas is in the baby room, but he's still flat out.' Tilly glanced around the Little 'Uns kitchen, then put down the Tupperware container crammed with cupcakes on the nearest available space on the worktop. She stood back to survey Amy further. 'You know, I don't care if it's old or not,' she said, back on the subject Amy had wanted to divert her from, 'it's still a pillowcase.'

'Stop looking at her like that,' frowned Maria. 'I think she looks fine.'

Tilly switched her attention to Amy's boss. 'I didn't know elves wore pillowcases and had woolly pom-poms on the ends of their hats.'

'If you don't have anything positive to say, why don't you just go home?' sighed Amy, glancing at her watch. 'Where's Mum, anyway? She was supposed to be here by now.'

'She had to go shopping, apparently.' Tilly shrugged. 'Don't ask me. I walked all the way here to bring you those cakes, and it's bloody well starting to snow.'

'Is it? Mikey must have liked that . . .'

'Your help's always appreciated, Tilly,' said Maria, 'but you don't have to hang around if you don't want to, and if you do, can you just curb the "bloodies" a bit? There are delicate ears around, and I don't want an irate mother coming in here in the new year accusing me of corrupting her child.'

'As if parents don't do that themselves,' Tilly mumbled, then looked back at Amy again. '*Please* can you tell me why you're wearing a pillowcase, though. I'm not having a go at you, I'm just curious.'

In exasperation, and tired from blowing up balloons, even with a handpump, Amy glanced down at her attire. 'We had to improvise. We left it too late to get any costumes. It seems that the world and his wife want to be elves this year. It's an old pillowcase, anyway. Some continental size I can't get new pillows for. It doesn't matter.' Maria had dyed it green for her and cut out holes for her arms and head, and Amy was now wearing it over the top of a tight, red, polo-necked sweater.

'You added an extra bit at the bottom, I see,' noted Tilly, 'to make it semi-decent.'

'It's not that bad, is it?'

'Well . . .' Tilly twisted her mouth. 'I like the tights. Can I have them when you're through with them?'

'They're red,' said Amy sceptically. 'You only wear black ones.'

'But they're nice and thick. Just for sitting around at home watching TV . . .'

'OK, OK.' Amy didn't have much fight in her these days, and why waste her breath over a pair of tights she was never going to wear again herself, anyway?

'Please tell me you got a Santa outfit without any problems?' Tilly continued with her bombardment. 'You didn't have to improvise with that, did you?'

'We've got an old one, from other years.' Maria jostled her out of the way. ''Scuse. I need to find the napkins.'

'So who's Santa then?'

'Sean,' said Amy. 'Maria's husband.'

'He won't need any padding this year, either,' scowled Maria, 'he's got plenty of his own. Shit, dammit, sorry.' She put a hand to her mouth and looked worriedly over her shoulder. 'Has anyone seen the napkins?'

'Try in that carrier bag.' Amy frowned at her watch again. 'Where's Mum?'

'Don't worry,' soothed Tilly, 'she's not going to let the kids down. And she's been rehearsing the Nativity bit for the last fortnight with Joe's class.'

'It's going to be great,' enthused Maria.

'But in front of all those parents, too . . .' Amy felt her stomach contract with panic. 'What if she's got stage fright?'

'She hasn't! She's brilliant at it,' boomed a familiar voice. 'It's in her blood!'

They all looked round to see Carol in the doorway, taking up most of the space.

Maria grinned. 'Hi, Auntie. Have you got the Santa sack? Did you manage to wrap the rest of the presents?'

'Your father's dropping everything off in a bit. I walked here, petal.'

Maria's grin faded. 'Dad's bringing them?'

'Now, don't look like that! My brother's scatty, not senile.'

'Scatty's not good, either.'

'Can't you be loyal to your own father?' Carol harrumphed, sighed, scanned the hive of activity in the kitchen, and finally rested her gaze on Amy.

'Hello, petal . . . how are you doing?'

Automatically, jerkily, Amy turned away, returning her attention to the balloons.

It would be easier to act normal, if everyone would just let her get on with it. It was bad enough that the whole of Harrisfield seemed to know what had happened.

Heartbroken . . . hopes dashed . . . twice in one year . . . In her paranoid state, Amy could hear the whispers even now. Except that she hadn't really had any hopes with Paul, not really. With Nick, her expectations *had* been crushed. All her naïve, pretty plans for the future. It had been painful in an entirely different way. In spite of what she'd thought at the time, she couldn't honestly be sure now if her heart had come into it at all. The most difficult part had been staring people in the face; she had been so complacent up until then. And after so many years with someone, to be left like that . . .

When all was said and done now, though, she wasn't ill, she wasn't dying, she wasn't a charity case. She had her health, her own home, a job she loved and three wonderful children. She was lucky to be alive. And she was determined to get over It – Him – The Mistake – as soon as possible, because, after all, it was just a feeling. It could be remedied with reason, if you had enough to distract you. It had been madness to go potty over someone like Paul, and she was a sane, rational, grown-up woman.

'I'm fine,' she said now, looking at Carol again with the most convincing smile she could fake. 'Why wouldn't I be?'

The woman appeared to be buried beneath a giant fir tree.

Paul could see the fracas as he peered into the living room through the window of 5 March Street. He tried the front door, on the off chance that it was unlocked. Fortunately, it was, and he hurried inside. Heaving up the tree, he heard gasps and oaths, and finally the woman emerged, looking as if her pride had been more at stake than anything else.

'Elspeth!' Paul felt thrown. 'I thought . . .' He remembered his manners enough to help her up. 'Are you all right?'

'Bloody tree,' she hissed, looking frazzled and battered as

she straightened her long skirt. 'Get it this far, take off the net, and it decides to attack me!' Slowly she seemed to recover her poise, and swept back her hair, which Paul couldn't stop gawking at.

The chaos of her former style – there could be no other way to describe it – had been replaced by a soft, chin-length bob. The browny-red, steel-wool curls were now full, sleek waves, and there wasn't a hint of grey in sight. It shone like a copper kettle. She looked younger, and somehow more like Amy. It was something to do with the eyes, thought Paul. The fact that you could see them properly now, without a cloud of hair hampering the view, probably helped.

'Where would you like the tree?' asked Paul, reminding himself it was rude to stare. He spotted the large pot. 'In here, I'm guessing.' And without waiting to be told, he grappled with the spiny monstrosity and eventually slotted it into place. The branches flopped outwards into a spreading, green mass. It listed slightly, then settled.

'Thank you.' Elspeth's voice behind him sounded distant and awkward.

He turned round. 'Sorry – I, er, just let myself in . . . I saw you were having trouble, and the door wasn't locked . . .'

'No. I've still got to go back to the car to fetch the decorations.'

'Are you sure you're OK?'

'A bit scratched, but aside from that . . . Thank you,' she said again, her tone more off-putting by the second.

'No problem. Big tree, though.'

'Yes, well, it didn't seem so big in the garden centre, or when they strapped it to the top of the car,' she said stiffly. 'I should have realised there was a problem with it, though, considering there weren't that many left. Hopefully, Amy will appreciate it, at least for the sake of the kids.'

Paul nodded, even as he questioned to himself whether Amy

really would welcome the coniferous version of the Incredible Hulk in her living room. 'I, er, would have thought she'd have a tree by now.'

'She kept saying she was going to get around to it . . . Considering it's nearly Christmas, I decided to take matters into my own hands.'

'Has she, um, been busy then?' Paul wondered how much Elspeth knew about the Gala night at Rosewood Grange. By reverting to her former touchy self around him, probably all of it. Yet it wasn't the whole story. How could it be? She'd only heard one side of it.

'Busy?' Elspeth's eyelids fluttered and widened. 'You could say that. Ever since you scarpered off to Spain, she's been running herself into the ground. It's amazing how much damage you can do to yourself in little under a week.'

'Spain?' frowned Paul.

'So, what happened to bring you back so soon? Francesca had enough of you, too?'

Paul was starting to feel as if he were on a particularly bad ferry crossing. 'Francesca?'

'Do you know,' grimaced Elspeth, 'I even phoned Rowena, on the pretext of wanting some architectural advice. I didn't ask *outright* on Amy's behalf, I wasn't going to make her seem desperate. But Rowena claimed she didn't know where you were.' Elspeth snorted. 'Right! As if I believed that for one second.'

'Actually,' ventured Paul – it was about time he intervened, before this got any bloodier – 'Rowena didn't know, I didn't want her to. Not many people did. I thought it would be best to—'

'Skulk off for a while? Allow the dust to settle? No point in letting Amy get the wrong idea.'

It struck Paul that Elspeth's behaviour might be a good sign. 'So, er, you know then? About Amy and me . . .?' There was no way he could have faced up to Amy's dad like this. Her mother was bad enough.

'You could say that.' She stood with her hands on her hips and her head slightly thrown back. Her most dominant stance, Paul supposed, feeling small by comparison. For someone like Elspeth, who was fairly dainty, it was a laudable feat. 'I know all I need to know, at any rate.'

Paul gave his nose a quick scratch. 'Actually, you don't. I'm not sure where this idea came from that I was in Spain with Francesca . . .'

'Amy told me.'

'And she heard it from . . .?' He had an agonising moment wondering if his mother had meddled in his life again.

'Your neighbour, apparently. The lady in the flat below yours.'

'*She* said I was going to Spain?'

'Er – no – not exactly.' Elspeth seemed to be faltering, as if her argument wasn't standing up too well in court. 'Your neighbour said you were going to the airport, and you had a suitcase with you. Well, that meant you were going away. And where was the most obvious place for you to go?' Elspeth managed to end on a challenging note, as if daring him.

'How about Boston?' said Paul. 'To see Nick.'

Elspeth wove her way through the Little 'Uns building with polite 'excuse me's, and 'so sorry's – only one goal in mind. To find Amy. She was lugging her canvas bag with her, full of her music paraphernalia, but the fact that within minutes she would be performing in front of this crowd, didn't seem to be registering the way it ought to.

She wasn't nervous about it, and she didn't have cold feet; yet her nerves *were* fizzing away inside her, and the butterflies in her stomach were a hundredfold.

It wasn't to do with singing 'Away in a Manger' or 'Twinkle

Twinkle Little Star', though, at her first major gig, as Tilly had referred to it. It was more a sense of urgency, of being on a mission, of playing a role that was vital, crucial, elementary to a story, and of being so close to the culmination of it that you could almost see it and touch it and hear it.

She had to find Amy. This couldn't wait. Why should it? Every second lost was a second wasted. Another moment feeling sad and lonely while pretending that you weren't. What was the point of a brave face when everyone knew what was really going on behind it? Life was short enough, for pity's sake.

And it was all so *unnecessary*. A few simple words, honestly spoken, should fix it. Elspeth had listened and had believed that young man, because God knew, she had once stood like that, baring her soul and hoping she wasn't going to get told to sling her hook. In this case, it was only what she had suspected anyway; but recent events had blown her off course, so that she hadn't been sure what to think.

'Mum!'

Elspeth swung round. It was only Tilly, with Mikey clutching her leg and Lucas fidgeting in her arms. They were framed in an open doorway, with Elspeth's brood of Nativity players gathered behind . . . angels, a twinkling star, shepherds, lambs, donkey, Mary, Joseph . . .

'Nana!'

'Hello, Joe, you look brilliant, poppet! . . . Listen, Tilly, have you seen Amy?'

'Only on the rampage looking for you! What kept you? I've been phoning home and your mobile and—'

'I was at Amy's. Just organising a little surprise . . .' Well, a big surprise, all six-foot-whatever of it, plus tinsel and baubles, but that was beside the point. 'I really need to find her—'

'Nana, do you like my costume? I'm Baby Jesus's daddy. And we're having a party afterwards, with cakes and crisps and balloons. And Father Christmas!'

'Yes, Joe,' Elspeth tried to give him the attention he was due. 'You look wonderful. Do you remember your lines?'

'"*Is there any room at the inn for us? Any room at the inn . . .*"' He sang the little ditty Elspeth had composed for him. He obviously got his sense of drama from his father.

'Mum!'

Elspeth swung round again. 'Amy!'

'Where've you been, Mum? We've been frantic!'

'Have you? I'm sorry, darling . . .' Elspeth looked her elder daughter up and down, feeling a little fazed. But what on earth had she been expecting? Blue taffeta and a crinoline? This was the twenty-first century, Harrisfield, Flintshire. Not *Gone with the Wind*. If a happy ending involved a home-made elf's outfit, complete with false pointy ears and an overstretched, red bobble hat, then so be it. Amy would probably fare better than poor Scarlett, anyway.

'Where's your coat, darling?' Elspeth asked her now.

'My coat?' Amy looked equally fazed. 'What are you on about?'

'Never mind, borrow mine.' Elspeth shrugged off her old, grey, military-style coat, and thrust it at her daughter. 'You'll freeze without it.'

'Elspeth . . .?' Maria, who was right behind Amy, was also looking at her oddly. 'Are you OK?'

Elspeth nodded. 'But there's someone outside to see Amy.'

'Me? Who . . .? Mum, what's going on?'

'It's too busy in here, love, and this can't wait. Is that a side door? Perfect. Save you trying to get out past that crush back there. He should be round the front. He gave me a lift, but of course, parking's a nightmare today. He dropped me off and then went to find a space.'

'*Mum—*'

'Go on then,' interrupted Tilly, finally cottoning on as she turned to her sister too, 'what are you waiting for?'

Amy looked peculiar, as if she was going to be sick. She was suddenly very quiet. She didn't move.

It was Maria – also cottoning on – who finally grabbed the grey coat and bundled Amy into it. Clearly, she'd had practice with the kids. In one swift manoeuvre, it was on.

Elspeth propelled Amy towards the door. 'Go on, love,' she urged. 'Please. For me. For *yourself* . . .'

'But the show—' Amy muttered.

'It's being videoed,' said Maria. 'And Joe doesn't come on till halfway through, during the Nativity bit. You can be back in time.'

As Elspeth hurried Amy through the door, and watched her stumble slightly in the side-alley where all the rubbish and recycling bins were lined up, she felt as if it were Amy's first day at school again. Watching that small, if not slight, figure, trudging away from her . . . It had been an inevitable fact of life, yet that hadn't eased the sudden maternal onset of wistfulness and nostalgia. Independence always came at a price.

But now, it was all up to her daughter. There was only so much Elspeth could do. Although, thinking about it, perhaps she could have made Amy take off those ears . . . Anyway, too late. She shrugged to herself, crossed her fingers and said a quick prayer in her head. After all, you could lead a horse to water, yet even though it was obviously parched, you couldn't always get the damn thing to drink.

39

The first snowfall of this winter in Harrisfield had stopped for now, but the grey and lemon-tinted clouds were still threatening more. Amy watched her footing in her slightly-too-large, olive-green wellies. They'd been the best foot-wear she could lay her hands on to complement her costume.

She knew who she was searching for as she rounded the side of the old schoolhouse and came out into the lane lined with parked cars. The way her mother had been going on, she couldn't imagine that it was anyone else.

The last of the parents of the four- to five-year-olds who were putting on the show were now filing into the building, making their way to the extension on the left-hand side where the removable partition 'wall' had been tucked away at the sides to make it into a spacious hall. Amy glanced up and down the lane, zealously scouring it for the one face she longed to see above any other.

And then she did.

He was standing a little way away, on his own beside a cluster of ancient, gnarled trees on the fringes of the church-yard. He looked cold and pale, huddled in a long overcoat with his shoulders pulled in, his arms straight and his hands thrust deep in his pockets. He didn't smile, nor make any move to cross the road.

As Amy slowly trudged over to him, she became aware of his gaze skimming over her. Bugger. In her breathless anticipation, she'd forgotten how much of a ninny she looked. It was just as well the pillowcase was well hidden.

'I'm supposed to be an elf,' was the first thing she said, frowning as she shuddered to a halt a few feet away.

'Right.' Paul acknowledged this with a nod, the corners of his mouth hooking upwards, but only slightly. 'I'll try and overlook that – unless Santa's going to come hunting for you at any moment. I don't want him to think I'm monopolising his little helper.'

'That's not funny.' Her frown became a scowl. 'None of this is funny.' She wanted to hit him and run away, just as much as she longed to fall into his arms and squeeze him senseless. Above all, she wanted this moment to be over and for what she had to say to have been said, to be out in the open, not clogging up her emotions any longer.

Overall, he'd managed to keep a straight face. Now, his mouth straightened out, too. 'Amy, I've let things drift for too long . . . If I'd actually _spoken_ to you, about the important stuff. If I'd . . .'

'Where were you this last week, Paul? Where did you go?'

'Not to Spain, to Francesca. That was never going to happen. I should have made that clearer. She's in Cheltenham, anyway, saying goodbye to her family . . .'

Amy felt relief rush upon her like a sudden downpour, but she was still too confused to dance about with joy. 'Then where . . .?'

'The where's easy enough. It's the why that's harder to explain . . .' He sighed heavily. 'I went to Boston – to see Nick. You could say it was an overnight decision. It felt as if . . . As if there were ghosts I needed to lay to rest. You'd had the chance to do that, the last time you saw him. You'd let go, once and for all. But for me . . .' He shook his head.

Amy's practical side always seemed to rear itself at inconvenient moments. 'You managed to get flights, at this time of year?'

'My mother has connections. How do you think she gets some of those last-minute flights herself when there's a problem at the Faulkner Group? She hasn't got a personal jet, anyhow. I used my name to get my own way – hopefully for the last time. It only took a couple of calls. It wasn't cheap, but I had to see Nick. It couldn't wait.'

'He'll be over here himself in about a week, though . . .' Amy couldn't understand the urgency.

'I couldn't put it off. At the risk of being gung-ho again, I needed it all sorted out before he came back . . . I realised that when I woke up on my own at Rosewood Grange. There was too much baggage. Too much history. I needed to sort things out with him before I could sort them out with you. And I didn't want to have to wait another minute.'

Amy felt her stomach tighten. She didn't reply.

'Why did you leave that morning without saying goodbye, without saying *anything*?' Paul shook his head. He looked ashen, as if reliving it. 'I woke up, and all that was left of you were some smudges of make-up on the pillow and a handful of hairpins. Not what I'd had in mind,' he admitted dourly.

There was no point pretending any more, Amy realised. Wearing Mr Spock ears under a red bobble hat, pride was already a distant memory.

'I couldn't let myself believe in what had happened,' she said slowly. 'I couldn't let myself imagine it might mean more than it really was. This was you and me, Paul. You and *me*. Do you understand?'

'So what did you think it was all in aid of, then? Did you imagine I was *faking* it? Do you really think I'm capable of that?'

'No. Sex is sex.' She exhaled sharply. 'And I just wrote it off as a one-night stand. The beginning and the end, rolled into one.'

Paul rocked backwards and forwards on the spot, his hands still in his pockets. He seemed stunned into silence.

Amy struggled for the right words to explain. Her mother's coat felt as if it weighed a ton on her shoulders. 'You know what you've been like in the past, Paul, with other women. And because of Francesca . . . I just thought—'

'That I was on the rebound? Looking for a consolation prize?' His voice carried a trace of bitterness.

Lace-like snowflakes were beginning to fall again, fluttering to the cracked pavement. Amy started to shiver. Paul took a step closer, close enough for her to see the snowflakes rest for a moment on his hair and lashes, before melting.

'I wasn't pining for Francesca.' He shook his head adamantly. 'I was going to end it anyway, even if all this Spain business hadn't happened. Her wanting to leave like that just made it easier. And that night – at Rosewood Grange, I thought you would understand it meant something . . . No, that's not right. It meant *everything*. I didn't know how you were feeling, though, and I didn't want to come across as desperate . . .'

He paused to grunt self-deprecatingly. 'With hindsight, of course, I could have handled it better. I thought I knew women, but obviously . . . Going about it the way I did – it was familiar territory for me, I knew where I stood, what I was doing, it felt safer. But it wasn't just going through the motions. I thought you could see that. I thought you'd understand.'

'You set me up?'

'No! Yes . . . but not like that. It wasn't how it sounds. I admit, I staged it. I had the room booked, just in case. But I never pushed you. Did you feel I pushed you? Amy, tell me, because I'm cacking my pants here. I just wanted to make you *see*—'

She stretched out, and put a finger to his lips. He was

shivering, too. 'It's OK. I should have stayed, we needed to talk. I shouldn't have just run off. It was hardly the act of a mature adult. But I was so angry, and so . . . scared . . .'

Without warning, Paul whipped his hands out of his pockets and pulled her towards him.

He enveloped her in a giant hug – coat, false ears and all. 'Amy,' he whispered, so gently, the sound of it seemed to caress her cheek. Then suddenly he was kissing her, in exactly the same way as the night of the Gala. And when it was over, she eventually came to and noticed that the bobble hat and the ears had been pushed off her head. Her hair was loose from its ponytail, too, swirling around her shoulders like a cape to keep her warm. His hands were losing themselves in it as they stroked the sides of her face. Miraculously, she *had* warmed up. About thirty or so degrees. The tropics – in North Wales.

'Do you know what it was like,' Paul was beaming now, 'telling your mother how I felt, before I even told you? Bizarre. Like asking for her blessing or her permission.'

'Why did you go to her first?' In spite of the feverish happiness rushing through her entire being, Amy still had a dozen questions demanding answers.

'I didn't. Not on purpose. I went to see you, I thought you'd be at home, considering it's the weekend, but she was at your house.'

'My house? Doing what?'

'Er – I don't know. Dropping off some, um . . . some shopping, I think. The thing is—'

'So what did you tell her, Paul? How *do* you feel?'

'Well, I could hardly show her : . . I had to find the words . . .'

He leaned down and kissed her again, so tenderly and reverently, Amy's knees almost buckled.

'I'd like the words, too, please,' she asked daringly, her voice raspy. 'I don't see why my mother should get all the hard work out of you.'

Paul stared down at her. 'I love you,' he said solemnly. 'I love everything about you. Your smile, your nose, your job, your kids . . . I love the whole package like I've never loved anything or anyone. But don't ask me when, or how. I just *do*, and I've never been more thankful of something in my entire life. And it wasn't just your mother I had to explain it to. Nick knew first. I had to come clean to him. He was too much a part of it.'

'You had to ask for the thumbs up, you mean?' Amy felt herself tense involuntarily. The mention of Nick's name would probably always have that effect on her. 'If he said it was OK, that he could handle it, then—'

'Amy, he was shocked. I mean, *really* shocked. He couldn't believe it, kept saying it was some huge, stupid joke. But of course, he knew it wasn't, I was hardly going to go all the way over there for that. He took a lot of convincing, though, before he accepted how serious I was.' Paul brushed away a tear from her cheek with the pad of his thumb. 'We can hardly blame him, really . . . can we? You and I . . . we were on opposite sides for thirteen years. Nick kept us like that, and he kept us together. If it wasn't for him, we wouldn't be standing here now.'

She nodded. 'In part . . . But I think you also kept Nick and me together as a couple. If you hadn't been there for me to blame for everything that ever went wrong between us, it might have been over a lot sooner . . .'

Paul shook his head, his brow lined. 'I don't know whether I'm happy about that or not. Destiny, fate, kismet, whatever you want to call it – you just don't mess with it. I honestly don't think it would have worked between us if I'd asked you out before Nick did. I was different back then.'

'So was I. But we were younger, that's all. You wanted something else out of life. I wasn't your type.' Amy stared up at him as doubt stole into her mind. What if he was only deluding himself now? 'Are you sure about this, Paul?' she muttered hoarsely, as her blood seemed to run cold again. 'Really sure? I couldn't take it if—'

'Hey, if you're crying because you're happy, I don't mind, but if all these tears mean you're miserable, then . . .'

'No.' She swept them aside as they rolled down her cheeks. 'It's just a long way to fall again. I couldn't bear it a second time, not with you. But you said it yourself, about there being too much baggage. And most of it's mine. I've got so much I couldn't even fit it on a roof rack. You're fond of the kids, you get on great with them, but their father isn't just anyone, a faceless stranger – he's Nick. And besides, you've never had to put up with them twenty-four-seven.'

Smiling again, he wrapped his arms around the small of her back and drew her against him. 'Is that a proposal, of sorts?'

'No!' she blushed, and spluttered, 'I'm not asking you to move in or anything. I just meant—'

'Good, because I don't want to live with you.'

Even though that wasn't what she'd meant, her heart felt as if he'd crushed it with a pestle and mortar. 'Fine,' she gulped. 'I—'

'You've done the whole cohabiting thing. You've been there, you've got the T-shirt. You've even done the long engagement. How many years was it? Four? Five?'

'Something like that. Paul, what are you saying?'

'I'm saying that, whenever you feel you're ready, we should just go the whole way. The question of the best man's going to be tricky, of course. And as for my mother – well . . . deep down, I think she might understand better than anyone. But she's going to go mental over an instant set of grandkids. Although she'll have even more in common with Rowena, so neither of them can complain. Plus the marquee idea, well, I don't think that's us.'

Paul took a breath. 'Anyhow, after we've done the hard part,

I reckon we should just pool our assets. Buy an old farmhouse or barn, convert it, renovate it, make sure we've got more than enough bedrooms for everyone, although bunk beds are the best invention ever. I always wanted a kid brother just so I could nab the top bunk and pull faces at him. And if the next two are girls—'

'Whoa!' Amy gawped at him. She could barely take it all in, he was talking so fast. 'What are you on about?'

Paul's countenance froze in a stoical grimace. 'I was assuming . . . Oh, I see . . . Well, it's not me who has to go through the entire nine months, of course. If you feel three's your limit . . .'

She reached up, and gently cupped his face in her hands. 'I didn't say that,' she murmured against his lips.

They kissed again, even more heatedly, as entwined as the limbs of the old trees growing around them. 'Besides, practice makes perfect,' she whispered, laughing softly as she drew back.

'Here? Next to an old graveyard?' Paul ran a finger around the inside of his collar. 'You've got some really weird ideas about me.'

'Well, Nick told me once that you'd—'

'Shut up, woman.' Paul swept her up in another giant bear hug. 'He embellished everything.'

'Except me.'

'Forget that. You don't need embellishments, you're perfect as you are.' He smoothed back her hair. 'Anyway, you haven't told me how you feel about me yet,' he added archly. 'You made me come clean, but what about you? A lot of fancy words and gestures, but . . .'

Amy hesitated.

Paul wet his lips. 'Your mother said you'd been referring to it as a "crush", but that I wasn't to be fobbed off if you tried that one on with me.'

'Really? Mothers, eh.'

'So . . .?'

'So what?'

'Are you going to say it?'

She opened her mouth, but they were interrupted by a loud yell. 'Oi! You two!'

Amy and Paul both jumped and glanced round. Tilly was standing outside Little 'Uns, flapping her arms at them.

'Joe's on in two minutes,' she cried.

'Oh, damn.' Amy squeezed Paul's hand. 'I can't miss this.'

She snatched up the false ears and bobble hat, and Paul at her side, hurried across the lane.

'Plus we've got a *major* crisis on our hands,' Tilly went on, still waving her hands about expressively. 'Maria's husband just rang to say one of the twins chucked up in the buggy on the way here, and because she's obviously not well, he took her home again. Maria's livid. Says he always has to leave things till the last minute, and something usually goes wrong.'

'But he's supposed to be Father Christmas!' Amy felt a spasm of panic. She had a vision of all those eager little faces waiting for him to appear at the end of the show, her own children included. 'What about Maria's dad? Did he bring the sack with the gifts? Couldn't he do it?'

'Yeah, he brought the sack, but he buggered off again before all this happened. He's flaky anyway.'

'And Carol's husband? Couldn't we call him?'

'He wouldn't get up off his arse to do it in a million years, she says. Even if you paid him. Why do you think Carol had to persuade Mum to go on this cruise with her? Carol volunteered to be Santa, but the costume's too small for her. She would have had the right belly laugh, anyway. It's a shame.' Tilly eyed Paul. '*You'd* be the right size,' she said calculatingly. 'With some extra padding . . .'

'Er' – he held up his hands – 'not really me, I'm afraid.'

'Well, no,' sneered Tilly. 'Granted, it's not the height of sartorial elegance, but I'd say red could be your colour.'

Amy turned to him. He still owed her for that mock kiss on his roof terrace. Even though she'd insinuated she wouldn't bear a grudge, she hadn't exactly meant it at the time. 'You basically just have to say, "Ho, ho, ho!"' she coached. 'The deeper the better. There's nothing to it.'

Paul glowered back at her. 'Not unless you say you love me.'

Lurking in the background, Tilly pretended to be sick while smiling broadly.

Amy narrowed her eyes. 'That's blackmail.'

'Say it, and I'll dress up as bloody King Kong if necessary.'

'Bastard.' She flashed him a scowl. 'I love you . . . You know I do. I love you, *I love you*, I LOVE YOU! Is that enough? Are you happy now?'

Paul grinned, like the cat who'd got the cream, and a whole pudding besides.